JANE AUSTEN LIVES Again

JANE ODIWE

JANE AUSTEN LIVES AGAIN

Copyright © 2015 Jane Odiwe

First published 2015 by Paintbox Publishing

The right of Jane Odiwe to be identified as the Author of this Work has been asserted by her in accordance with the Copyright, Designs and Patents Act 1988

All characters and events in this publication, other than those clearly in the public domain, are fictitious and any resemblance to actual persons, living or dead, is purely coincidental.

All rights reserved. No part of this publication may be reproduced, stored in a retrieval system, or transmitted in any form by any means, electronic, mechanical, photocopying, recording or otherwise, without the prior permission of the publisher or a licence permitting restricted copying. In the UK, such licences are issued by the Copyright Licensing Agency, 90 Tottenham Court Road, London, W1P9HE

For Jade and Zee Zee, with all my love

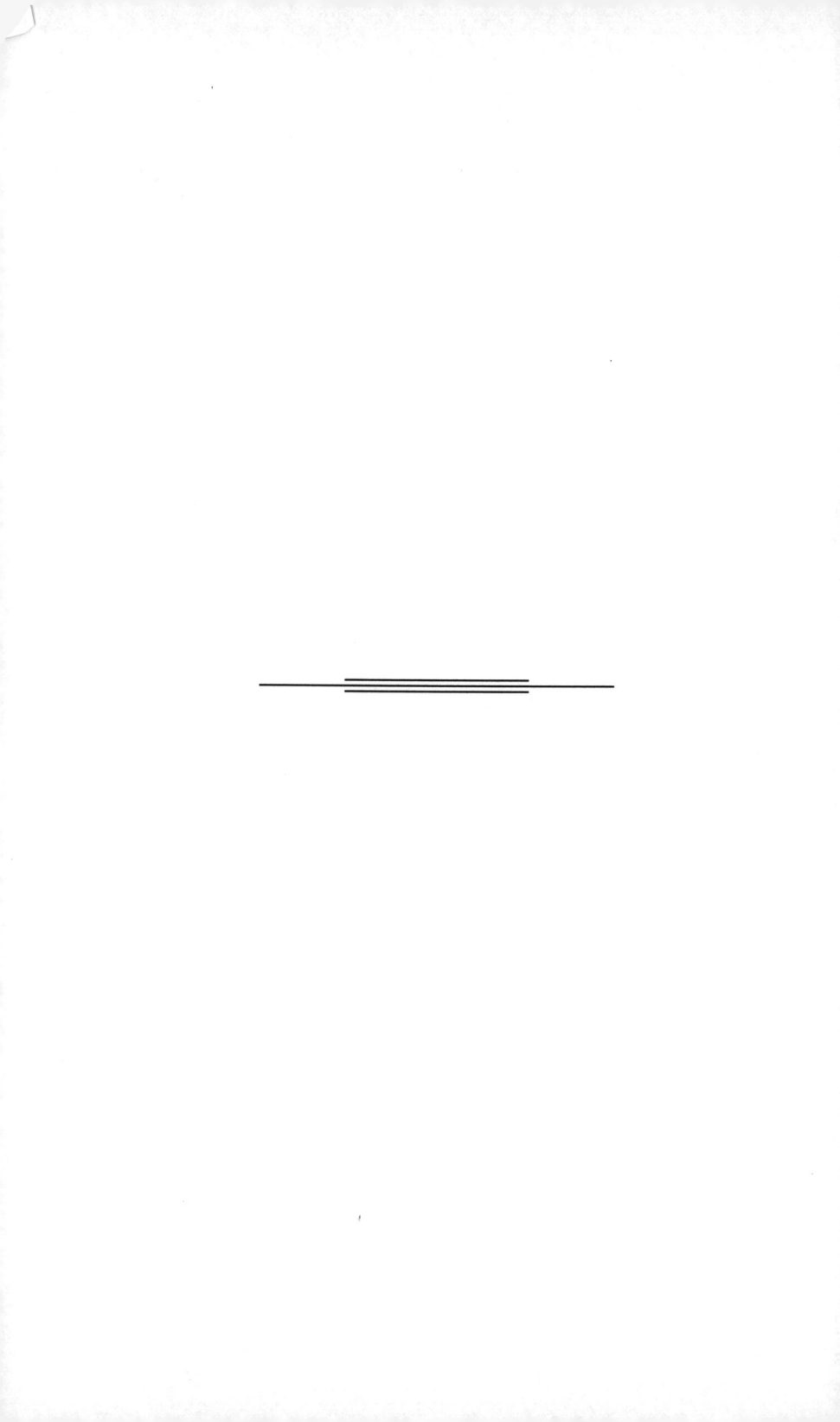

Prologue

When once we are buried you
think we are dead But behold me Immortal.
Jane Austen

Miss Austen's eyes flickered open. She was aware of soft pillows under her head, the fragrance of fresh linen tucked about her, the sputter of a crackling fire and the ticking of a clock. It was a moment before her eyes could focus and other senses quickened into life. The iron taste of blood in her mouth and a bitter tang of something she could not recognise made her long for water. All these sensations, scents and sounds were unfamiliar. Where was she?

'She's awake, Doctor Lyford!'

Jane turned her head to see a young man rushing to her side. He had a look of Doctor Lyford but this was not the physician she knew. This man was younger, slimmer and had a shock of thick, dark hair, which lay in damp, greasy curls on his forehead. He wore only a shirt tucked into outlandishly long breeches and with his sleeves rolled up like a working man, Jane was not altogether sure what she thought about him. He looked wild, his eyes flashing with a topaz light in their depths.

'Miss Austen, can you hear me?' The agitation in his voice was plain to hear.

'I am not deaf you know, there is no need to raise your voice.' Jane struggled to sit up.

'You must not move. Here, drink this.' The doctor placed a teapot with a long spout to her lips.

For a second Jane felt frightened and although dying to quench her thirst she felt so ill at ease in these strange surroundings. The taste in her mouth was disgusting. Was he poisoning her?

Aware that her lips, which were compressed firmly together, were not about to part, Doctor Lyford tried again. 'Please drink, Miss Austen, it will do you good.'

Looking up at the young man, Jane's expression softened. There was real anxiety in his eyes and she saw something else. In those brown eyes flecked with sage green and amber, she saw that he cared deeply. Jane did as she was told whilst taking the opportunity to look around her at the room that seemed filled with a plethora of furniture and furnishings. The walls were profuse with intricate patterns on a dark russet ground – roses spilled from elongated vases that dripped with swags of pearls. Carpets on the wooden floors swirled with sensuous curves of acanthus and exotic flora whilst floating in this sea of overblown elegance were tables, sofas and chairs be-decked with frills and furbelows. It was a strange land and Jane had never seen anything like it.

Chapter One

I am not at all afraid of being long unemployed. There are places in town, offices, where inquiry would soon produce something – offices for the sale, not quite of human flesh, but of human intellect.

Jane smiled wryly at the recollection of penning those words. Published in 1815, her darling *Emma* (of whom she wrote that no one would like but herself) had been written in another time, another place. A hundred and ten years later, and having sold herself into the governess-trade, the irony was not lost on her.

Looking out of the window, she gripped the arm of her chair with both hands as if doing so would help slow down all sensations. The metal monster roared ahead belching thick clouds of hot, black smoke. Like a dragon consumed with fire, she thought, as its sleek body snaked through the countryside at an alarming speed.

She knew her companion, Dr Lyford was studying her face, and determined to look unconcerned by the sight of trees, fields and houses flying past her window, she released the grip on the arms of the chair, folded them in her lap and assumed an expression of nonchalance.

'I know this is all terrifyingly new to you,' he said, 'but there is no quicker way to travel than by train.'

Having always found great amusement in watching people, she observed him searching for the right words, as he paused, and then saw him smile nervously instead. Jane knew she was expected to answer, to assure him that she was fine, but she was in a mischievous mood. Ever playful, she wanted to see what would happen if she remained silent, she wanted to imagine how the scene would play out. The pleasure of waiting for him to continue was coupled with the knowledge that she'd already guessed exactly what he would say.

'It was the best I could do in the circumstances, and it will, at least, resolve the problems of employment on the one hand, and time for your writing on the other. Your sister left no other instructions ... the money she'd put aside was never going to be enough, even taking into account the royalties and the interest you'd earned.'

'Dr Lyford, I do not blame you, nor do I blame myself, or Cassandra. My sister knew my wishes plainly enough and carried them out to the best of her ability. I can never express my gratitude enough to you for the services you have rendered me. It was no small feat to make me healthy once more or bring me back from the dead, and I will ever be grateful.'

'But, it can never have been your plan to become a governess to five girls on a country estate. Nor to have found yourself in a time that is completely unknown to you. A hundred years is a long time, Miss Austen, and a lot has changed. I fear that a month's recovery and a few hastily read newspaper articles may not be enough to prepare you fully for life, let alone for the new role you will assume.'

'Dr Lyford, if I can survive embalming, the subsequent resurrection and the effects of transdifferentiation, I will live to tell the tale, if you will forgive a little punning. I am quite the Turritopsis dohrnii, and if not for your great work on that immortal jellyfish, I would not be here today.'

In many ways, it had been a relief to discover that some things were not changed. She was not essentially altered. Her mind, her habits, and her delight in the absurdities of life, were exactly the same. In the four short weeks she'd been returned to life, this realisation was a source of comfort.

'I wish there had been a greater opportunity to make some more notes, Miss Austen, a further study of the effects of the process. This is pioneering work, and I must be sure that there are no ill effects of which we may not yet be aware.'

'I understand your concerns, doctor, but I am perfectly happy with myself and feel twenty years younger! What forty-one year old female would not be delighted to have the hand of time turned backward? You see, I am vain enough to tell you that I am enjoying the fact that I look quite twenty-one again.'

'Every cell in your body is that of a young woman half your real age. And that is what I am concerned about and longing to research further. What will happen as you age? How lasting are the effects? There could be complications.'

'Doctor Lyford, do not concern yourself. I've never felt better. I feel as if I am about to start a new adventure, even if the thought of five little girls is a disquieting one. More than anything, I will have the time to write all the novels I thought were to be denied to me, and I will endure anything to that end.'

The doctor knew it was useless to argue. He'd only known Miss Jane Austen a short time but that he had quickly learned. It simply was not possible to get the better of her.

'But you must promise me that you will write or telephone if there is anything at all that does not seem right.'

Jane nodded in agreement knowing she had no intention of taking up any more of the young doctor's time if she could help it and she certainly had no plans for ever picking up a telephone. Perhaps she would get used to it in time, but the infernal instrument seemed such an intrusion on one's privacy, though she admitted that she and her sister Cassandra might have preferred conversing through such machinery, compared to the interminable letter writing on the occasions when they'd been separated. That was one thing she could not get used to, and thought she never would. Cassy had always been such a huge part of her life, and the idea that she would never see or hear her again was too much to bear. She caught her own reflection in the glass and started. Sometimes it felt almost as if Cassy were there, a part of her. Occasionally she caught a look of hers in her own image, in the expression of her eyes or in the turn of her head. But Cassy was gone. That was how she'd wanted it. Her practical, pragmatic sister had lived her life to a grand age and was happy at the last to leave in the usual way. Jane was slowly coming to terms with the fact, but life without her beloved Cassy would never be the same.

When Doctor John Lyford had initially hinted that he was experimenting with some success on his work in transdifferentiation at the beginning of her last awful bout of illness, she had not dreamed that it would take several generations to perfect the process. And once she'd first discussed the unthinkable with Cassy, the idea that she might one day cheat death to write again, she'd not considered the possibility of how she would feel at leaving so many beloved people behind. After the sisters removed to Winchester for her final illness, she had every hope that Dr Lyford might cure her, or at the very least keep her alive for a few more years.

Knotting her scarf around her neck and smoothing her skirt in a bid to distract her mind, she wondered when she would get used to her new clothes. Jane was shocked when she saw that young women in 1925 were not only exposing their ankles but their knees as well, and though her dress and simple belted coat were mid-calf, just as short as she found comfortable, after a few days she'd begun to appreciate the freedom that the clothes gave her. Of course, becoming a governess precluded any attempt at being fashionable for which she was thankful. Others might sport the new bobbed hairstyles, but Jane was glad she could still wear her chestnut curls in a simple bun pinned into place on top of her head and hidden under a wide-brimmed hat trimmed with a feather.

Her borrowed valise was stowed in the luggage rack containing all her worldly goods: a copy of *Sir Charles Grandison* - her favourite book, two extra day frocks plus one for evenings, a bottle of Luce's eau de cologne, and a present from the doctor's sister of a box of scented talcum powder, as well as a fountain pen, ink and notebook from the doctor himself. This last present was a most treasured gift, and Jane wondered if she'd ever get used to the miracle of having ink flowing endlessly from a nib that didn't blot.

'Are you absolutely certain you are ready to take on such a challenge?' said Dr Lyford, watching her closely. In the short time he'd known her he'd decided she was a hard nut to crack, but every now and then he'd glimpsed a certain vulnerability, the merest hint of fragility to the woman behind the mask of strength and assurance she wore.

'Quite sure.' Jane continued to stare out at the fields flying by. 'To do anything else would be unthinkable. I have been given the greatest gift, and to squander it would be sinful. Besides, I am looking forward to seeing Devon again and I love the sea. I am used to small children, Dr Lyford, having supervised my own nephews and nieces on many occasions. Dear little Neddy, precocious Anna, and darling Fanny were the delight of my days, to name just three of them. They used to love my fairy stories ... strange to think that they are all dead.'

Dr Lyford wondered what she might think if she knew that some of her brothers' descendants had taken it upon themselves to write her biography and publish her personal letters. Fanny, whom Jane had once described as quite after one's own heart, had taken to criticising her aunt in later life saying she was "*very much below par as to good society and its ways*", and that Fanny's father's influence and superior connections had rescued Aunt Jane from "*commonness and a lack of refinement*". Dr Lyford had shied away from telling her very much about her large family of descendants. He'd concentrated instead on telling her that her work was loved, and how her books were still being published, bringing comforts of home to the troops in the war still so fresh in all their minds. Though pleased to be so well regarded, one hundred years after publication, she remarked on the fact that she'd missed out on a fortune, which would have been more than useful in her present predicament.

'Your memories are very clear, Miss Austen.'

'Yes, I remember everything. Being twenty-one again, Dr Lyford, and seeing my face in the glass as that young girl brings back many bittersweet recollections. I recall the sense of heartbreak and loss when we left Steventon for Bath as if it just happened. And then later on, the memories of finding our beloved home at Chawton, revising my books and sending them out into the world, quite as my own darling children, are still fresh in my mind. I could not forget such dancing spirits when my dearest of them all appeared in print. I am gratified to know Elizabeth is still a heroine my readers admire.'

For a few minutes she was quiet as the train sheared through the scenery like scissors through fine muslin. She didn't want to think about the past, she must look to the present and the future if she were to survive. Looking out through the window she noted the sky clouding up above. The landscape was changed beyond recognition in the towns, she thought, and tried to imagine the lives of those weary looking individuals waiting at grim stations who were so tightly housed together in back-to-back houses, blackened by soot and smoke. The countryside offered a glimpse of a landscape she recognised, and though the people she saw were dressed in the fashions of the day, Jane was sure they were still the same in essentials. Human nature didn't alter, even if their clothes, their hairstyles and their use of slang changed. People still loved and hated, won and lost, struggled, succeeded or sank.

The train came to a halt in a village station, and she saw three children. Dressed in country clothes, white pinafores on the little girls with large black bonnets on their heads, long shorts and a tweed cap on the little boy, she watched them swinging on a gate, back and forth, until the guard shooed them away with a wave of his flag. It was like watching herself with Cassandra and one of her brothers. Henry was the most likely to have been found swinging on a gate with her, she decided. He was always her favourite brother, always eager for fun and games. The children disappeared, running off before the train lurched once more enveloping the platform and the bright pots of marigolds, lovingly displayed, in plumes of white smoke.

'Manberley Castle sounds like a title for one of my books,' Jane said at last, pushing all memories of the past from her mind. 'The Miltons of Manberley has a lovely ring to it, perfect for a novel.'

Dr Lyford smiled. 'I believe it dates back to the twelfth century, though I'm assured there are more modern additions. The last building took place in about 1815 so you should feel quite at home.'

'And how did the Miltons come by their money?'

'Well, they're sugar millionaires, so I'm guessing their family history and wealth was built on the misery of others.'

'Ill-gotten gains, how perfectly dreadful, and at the expense of so much human suffering, though in my day those who profited from the trade of their fellow men had no qualms in doing so. It is a fine thing to learn that such abhorrent practices are completely stopped. I hope the Milton forbears had a conscience, and helped to put right the wrongs of previous generations.'

'I couldn't say, Miss Austen. I am certain Sir Albert Milton is like most men of his class since the war; still trying to hang on to the life he's always known and enjoyed, that of squire and landowner. But times are changing, and their way of life, though seemingly luxurious to many, is not quite as lavish or extravagant as it was once upon a time. I believe Sir Albert is still very much the gentleman of leisure, though his heir seems to have a lot more about him. He runs the estate, providing much employment for local farmers and workers. By all accounts William Milton is very much a modern man, not afraid to get his hands dirty.'

'Quite right, too. I'm not certain I could be in the employ of a feckless family content only to laze away their days. You mentioned there is a lady of the house ... is she an idle creature or am I to expect hidden depths? Is Lady Milton a useful sort of person or one inclined to lie out on a sofa?'

'With five girls I expect she has her hands full, but I'm afraid I don't know anything much about her ladyship or her children.'

'Though you say she is a second wife, and I suppose William must be the son of his first.'

'William is in his late twenties, I believe, and though I'm not certain, I think the succession of younger girls are the offspring of the latest Lady Milton.'

'But you do have a list of their names? I must try and familiarise myself with them.'

Dr Lyford took out his wallet from his jacket pocket, pulling a piece of paper from inside. 'Yes, here we are. I've written them out and made some brief notes. I was able to talk to the housekeeper on the telephone. Her name is Mrs Naseby; rather an abrupt and evasive woman, but seemed able to distil the essential personalities of the children in one or two words. I thought it might help ... give you an idea before you meet them.'

Jane grasped the paper and read. 'Alice ... kind and considerate, Mae ... needs a tight rein, Beth ... headstrong, Emily ... has rather too much her own way, and Cora ... reads excessively. Goodness, if I'd read this before, I'm not sure I would have agreed to your plans, though Alice sounds promising and Cora is clearly a little girl I could get along with.'

'Which is precisely why I haven't shown you this previously. I did wonder if it was a good idea, but I do think Mrs Naseby has probably not painted the Milton girls in the best light.'

'I should say not. Heavens, whatever shall I do?'

'Think of this job as a temporary measure. I couldn't find you any other employment with your limited experience, and at least if you can stick to it, you'll gain some valuable skills along with a reference at the end of a year or two.'

'A whole year ... or two.' Jane found it hard to keep the dismay from her voice. She couldn't help thinking about her dear friend Anne Sharp who'd been a governess to her niece Fanny. Sweet Anne who'd always been a constant source of pleasure, a clever, witty woman, cheerful and capable, the most uncomplaining person she'd ever known, and always determined to get the best out of life. If Anne had managed it, then so could she.

The train was pulling into the station. Dark, sullen clouds up above were brimming with raindrops like the tears she felt welling inside, and before she'd gathered her belongings, the heavens opened. Water fell in torrents, pattering on the roof of the Victorian waiting room, gurgling down the drainpipes and running in streams along the platform, dribbling down the name painted on the station sign. Jane rubbed at the misty glass with a gloved hand, and peered out anxiously. Stoke Pomeroy looked grey and unwelcoming, cold and dark, despite the fact that it was the beginning of June.

'This is where we part company, Miss Austen,' said Dr Lyford. 'Now, you have my address and telephone number in Dawlish if you need me. I shall be there for six weeks before heading back to London.' He looked at his companion of whom he'd grown very fond in the last few weeks. 'Do call or write if you need anything.'

Jane took a deep breath. 'I shall be perfectly fine, Dr Lyford, do not worry.'

'Sir Albert said there'd be someone to meet you.' The doctor opened the door, stepped onto the platform briefly and called the porter to take her suitcase.

'Thank you, Dr Lyford, thank you for everything.' Jane knew the words were vacuous, but it was impossible to express just how she felt. If only she'd written him a letter, she thought, the written word always came so much more easily. She watched him step back inside the train, shutting the door with a finality that left her shuddering with fear at the thought of being alone. Jane told herself to stop being so silly and extended her hand through the window, shaking his vigorously.

The guard appeared, doors slammed, a flag waved and the great beast ignited once more shunting off in loud roars leaving a trail of dragon's breath behind it. Jane watched her doctor being taken away, and suddenly felt rather alone. No one else had got on or off the train apart from herself and she wasn't quite sure what to do, as she waited. Struggling with her umbrella to prevent getting any wetter, she got it up at last and walked up and down the platform. There didn't seem to be anyone waiting for her and then she wondered if perhaps there'd be a pony and trap with a trusted servant waiting outside beyond the gate. Handing her ticket to the man at the exit she stepped out of the safety of the station to discover there was nobody waiting for her there either, but there was a bench under a shelter so she took a seat and watched the rain gurgling in the gutters and bouncing off the road like large pennies.

Nothing could have surprised her more than the sight of a sleek black motor drawing up a few minutes later, and a liveried chauffeur stepping out to address her. Dressed in navy with a smart peaked hat and leather gauntlets, he took her case and opened the rear door with a flourish. 'Miss Austen, please take a seat.'

Jane had never been in a car before, though she'd taken a trip into Winchester with Dr Lyford's housekeeper on the omnibus. She was relieved to be sitting in the back of the vehicle and glad to see a glass partition dividing her from the driver in front. Forced conversation with a stranger was never a very useful activity to her mind, and she didn't want to chat to the chauffeur. He didn't look like the talking sort, and for that matter, wasn't quite what she'd expected at all. He had a very cock-sure way about him, and an arrogant air, which made her feel most unsure of herself. Jane needn't have worried; he didn't speak though once or twice she caught him watching her through the rear view mirror which was unnerving, to say the least. She noted his dark hair underneath the cap, and the way he drove with his head on one side, his elbow resting on the window and one hand casually holding the wheel. He was speeding down the narrow lanes, which made Jane shut her eyes and hold onto the strap as she swayed from side to side. It wouldn't do to be ill, she thought, as she opened one eye to see the world flashing past in a blur of green hedges and cow parsley.

They were ascending out of the valley when she saw her first glimpse of the sea, a slice of lavender ribbon under an oppressive sky, and as they wreathed along the cliff top road she saw the greater expanse below, white horses crashing down on the beach, and a strip of sand stretching along an endless coastline.

The car finally slowed and she saw the chauffeur's hand reaching for the partition to slide it open.

'I'm sorry if my driving is a little fast,' he said.

Jane met his gaze in the mirror. He was staring intently again and she didn't know where to look. It made her feel very uncomfortable and she had the feeling he was enjoying her discomfort.

'I must admit I prefer a slower pace,' she answered, 'I am not used to being driven about.'

'I'll try my best to drive as you wish,' he said, his eyes still on her face. Jane wished he'd watch the road, and although there hadn't been another vehicle anywhere since they'd left the station, she was sure they'd meet with an accident sooner or later if he persisted on staring into her eyes.

There was silence for a while for which she was glad, and then the car turned off the road into a drive between tall rusted gates with ornate gateposts topped by crumbling stone urns. A gatehouse looked neglected, ivy climbed over the windows, which were fogged with green moss and mould. There was no keeper to welcome them or wave them through;

there'd clearly been no occupants for a while.

'Have you been a governess long?' he said at last.

'Not very long, no.'

Jane thought his questioning impertinent and pursing her mouth stared determinedly through the window at the overgrown tangle of laurels and rhododendrons on every side, bursting into flower and dripping in the rain. Her first impressions of the place were not exactly reassuring, but she hoped things might improve as they reached the house.

'The Miltons are an undemanding bunch,' the driver went on, 'though what some folk might call slightly odd or eccentric, I suppose.'

Jane regarded the back of the young man's head steadily. 'I prefer to make up my own mind about people, I thank you, but in any case, I do not think this is a subject for conversation. I dislike gossip and I would appreciate you refraining from further discussion on my new employers.'

'Just as you please, Miss Austen.'

He appeared to find her amusing, she noted, as he made no attempt to disguise the laughter in his voice. He kept his eyes on the road after that and as they drove up the long drive the house made an appearance at last in open ground, a gloomy Palladian façade that time seemed to have forgotten with rows of windows on either side of a central pediment. Crouched on a cliff top, the house would enjoy astonishing sea views, Jane thought, and with the stunning scenery of hanging woods on the other side where the village of Stoke Pomeroy could be seen happily nestled in the valley, she decided she'd never seen such a splendid situation. A tower, the only remains of the oldest part of the 'castle' formed an extension on the west side with crenellations, and gothic windows clearly added at a later date. But for the peeling stucco and an air of abandonment, the house should have been the jewel in the crown. Lashing rain and skies as green as gunpowder added to the general sense of despondency and Jane felt her spirits sink. The chauffeur swung the car round to the left and to the side of the building.

'You'll find the servant's door at the bottom of the steps,' he said, and without another word handed her out of the car and deposited her suitcase at her feet before getting back into the vehicle to roar away over the gravel drive.

Jane stared after him hoping she wouldn't have much occasion to see him again. He thought far too much of himself, she decided, and with his brooding good looks she was sure he must create havoc amongst the maidservants. Overhead she heard the mournful mewing of wheeling gulls, and tasted the brine of the sea on her lips. Taking a deep breath, she picked up her case, and opening the cast iron gate at the top of the stairwell made her way down the steps until she reached the small door at the bottom.

Chapter Two

The housekeeper opened the door. Mrs Naseby beckoned her in to a dismal corridor, lit by a single gas lamp that sputtered and hissed, providing a totally inadequate light.

'Take a seat, Miss Austen, I'll take you to her ladyship in a moment. They've just finished luncheon and she's expecting you in precisely ten minutes. I'm glad to see you're punctual, I can't abide tardiness in any form, though I'm somewhat surprised to see you at the servant's door.'

Mrs Naseby looked just as Jane's imagination had pictured her. She was a spare, thin woman dressed in a long black gown of Edwardian tailoring, a harridan from a former age with a set of keys dangling from a belt round her waist. Small, piercing eyes looked shrewdly down a long nose, examining every aspect of Miss Austen's appearance. Her complexion was pale, as a result of spending a lifetime inside this prison-like fortress, Jane thought, and couldn't help thinking about one of the housekeepers of her own creation, Mrs Reynolds, with her warm personality and devotion to her master Mr Darcy. What a contrast, but then she decided Mrs Naseby might have far more in common with another character of her making, the domineering and opinionated Mrs Norris of Mansfield Park. Scolding herself for jumping to first impressions too soon, she sat down on a bentwood chair and heard the housekeeper mutter something to do with seeing to the maids about clearing the dining room before striding away down the dimly lit corridor. Jane noted the row of bells on the opposite wall, labelled for the upstairs rooms all jangling at once, and a succession of pantries, sculleries and kitchen rooms where a flurry of maids beetled from one to the other or up and down the steps at the end with trays of half-eaten food, empty wine bottles, and towers of porcelain plates.

Was it too late to run away, Jane wondered? This was a world that felt so strange. She'd always helped out at home with daily chores, but she'd been used to being looked after by their own maids, and they'd always had someone to help with the cooking. Besides, Cassandra had always made sure she had time for her writing, and as much as she hoped there'd be time to devote to writing still, the fact was that she would now be part of this new world, almost a servant, unable to have the freedoms she'd always enjoyed.

But before her mind had a chance to even think how she might slip back up the stairs to run away down the drive, the housekeeper returned, and with a single nod of her head, and a long finger wagging in her direction, beckoned her to follow.

'I will take you to see her ladyship, and presuming the interview is successful we will proceed to your new quarters. You will be required to serve the family every day from nine o'clock in the morning until five o'clock in the afternoon, unless you are needed in the evening, which is a distinct possibility. I have been advised to tell you that you may dine with the family at every mealtime, which to my way of thinking is a great honour. I hope you've brought something suitable to wear in the evenings.'

'I have one dress I could wear for such an occasion, Mrs Naseby, but really, it would be no hardship for me to have something in the kitchen with the other servants, or even in my room. I am happy with my own company, and I do not wish to be a bother to the family or anyone else, for that matter.'

'If Lady Milton wishes it, you *will* dine with the family.'

Jane realised that the old housekeeper meant her to know she no longer had any choice about anything she might want to do, and all she could hope was that her new employer would be more flexible than she was being painted. Her idea of spending the evenings writing in solitude seemed to be a dream that was fading fast.

'You will have one day off every third Thursday of the month, unless her ladyship requires you for duty,' Mrs Naseby continued. 'I am sure I do not need to tell you there is to be no fraternising with any male servants, and as an employee discretion and loyalty to the family is paramount at all times.'

At the top of the servant's staircase they entered a short corridor and

Mrs Naseby opened the green baize door at the end, which separated the rest of the house from the domestic quarters. They crossed the large hall where a grandfather clock ticked the hours away, and an empty fireplace looked cheerless with two sagging armchairs on either side. Faded damask on the walls from a previous age was fraying and worn away to reveal pink plaster in places, and in the middle of the room a circular table held a bowl of scented pot-pourri, the faint fragrance of lavender and roses making up for the lack of any fresh flowers. Jane could see the lobby where the coats were hung next to a brass stand filled with umbrellas and walking sticks, and the front door beyond which was open to the elements. The rain was falling harder than ever, pinging loudly into strategically placed zinc buckets, as puddles of water were forming on the flagstones. Following Mrs Naseby up the wide staircase Jane tried not to be judgemental, remembering what Dr Lyford had said about the difficulties that families of great houses were facing after the war. Still, she couldn't help feeling that the general atmosphere of the place exuded more than the neglect from a lack of money. Cobwebs as thick as a man's arm trembled between the balustrades on the staircase and piles of dust rolled in fluffy balls along the stone steps, and where windows easily reached could have been cleaned with a pail of soapy water, they were misted with green mould like watered silk and traced over with spider's webs.

At last they entered the drawing room with its peacock blue walls glowing in the dim space. A slice of light from curtains barely parted glimmered on silver frames, on photographs and portraits, highlighting white muslin and a gash of tan leather glove, the staring eye of a bloodhound and the flash of a sword at a soldier's side. There was a smell of dank flower water and dusty cinders in the grate, offset by sweet peas wilting in a crystal vase and faded peonies dropping their petals from a Chinese jug to stain the linen cloth below.

Jane didn't see Lady Milton immediately. Lying full-length upon the sofa in a scarlet kimono embroidered with a design of blossom trees and cranes in coloured silks, she was camouflaged by the red of the satin couch that enfolded her like a hothouse tomato. It was her mouth Jane noticed first, like an impish red bow curving into a smile which made dimples in the soft pale face that brought to mind the pictures of Hollywood film stars she'd seen outside the cinema just a few weeks ago in Winchester.

'Miss Austen, how much we have been looking forward to meeting you,' Lady Milton drawled with a little shake of her head, her perfectly bobbed hair gleaming as black as the lacquered table beside her. She paused to tap her cigarette on a long holder into an ashtray.

'Thank you, Lady Milton, I'm very pleased to be here,' Jane answered as politely as she could.

The housekeeper rushed over to the windows, pulling at the heavy curtains until light flooded the room.

'That's better, we can't have you sitting in the dark, your ladyship.'

'Thank you, Mrs Naseby, you may leave us now. I trust you've informed Miss Austen of all she needs to know.'

'All but the particulars of the children, ma'am. I thought it best for you to do that.'

Lady Milton visibly sighed. Now that the room was lighter Jane saw her employer was not as young as she'd first thought. Though her hair and make-up suggested a young woman in her late twenties, it was obvious from the lines etched on the plump features that Lady Milton was probably nearer forty if not older.

'Take a seat, Miss Austen,' she said.

Sitting down on a wing chair Jane watched Mrs Naseby walk from the room without a backward glance, closing the door firmly behind her. Lady Milton dragged on her cigarette holder and blew rings of smoke into the air. Her ankles were crossed, and as the scarlet Louis heeled slippers with pom-poms of swansdown tapped against the other in agitation, the kimono fell away from her knees to reveal pale shapely legs. Jane thought she must have been very beautiful once, and stared with fascination at her heavily made up face, powdered and rouged, with kohl-black eyes lined with paint. She wondered if Lady Milton had forgotten she was there for a moment until her ladyship swung her legs round in one perfect move to sit up and face her.

'Now, Miss Austen, where shall we begin?'

'I am very much looking forward to meeting the children,' said Jane thinking it was a prompt for her to speak. 'I was educated both at school, and at home by my excellent father, and can offer a thorough grounding in most subjects suitable for young girls, your ladyship.'

'I'm sure you can, Miss Austen. Dr Lyford wrote very highly of your accomplishments. But I have a confession to make, and I must do it now as Mrs Naseby has chosen not to do it for me.'

Jane waited as Lady Milton puffed once more on the holder and watched her raise a glass tinkling with ice to her lips.

'Would you care to join me in a White Lady, Miss Austen?' she said agitating the glass and swirling the creamy liquid. 'I find it's such a pick-me-up in the afternoon, and revives wonderful memories of dancing at Ciro's.'

'No, thank you, Lady Milton. I think I'd better keep my wits about me for dealing with small children. I hope I shall be able to spend some time getting to know them this afternoon.'

'Yes, indeed, if we can find them.'

'Goodness, are the children lost, Lady Milton?'

'Not exactly. The fact is, Miss Austen, I have you here on quite false pretences. My children do not really need a governess.'

'Oh, I see,' said Jane who didn't understand one bit. All she could think about was how she would have to break the news to Dr Lyford and the inconvenience she'd put him to when she threw herself once more on his mercy.

'My children are not the young creatures you imagine them to be. The truth is they are quite grown-up, and indeed, some are past the age where one might consider them even to be marriageable, let alone in need of a governess. Lord Milton's first wife was the mother of the eldest three - William who is the heir to Manberley, Alice now nearing the age of twenty-seven and quite left on the shelf, and Mae who is twenty-five and absolutely unmanageable. I should not say it, but they were given far too much freedom in their youth, and think themselves beyond reproach. Of my own children, sadly I lost my eldest and dearest Teddy to the perils of the Great War.'

Lady Milton paused to dab at her eyes with a silk handkerchief.

'I'm very sorry to hear of your loss,' said Jane, filling in an awkward pause in the conversation. 'I think there is scarcely a family in the land who has not suffered in some way.'

'I thought my own children would be a comfort to me,' Lady Milton continued, 'but Beth is turning out to be quite as headstrong as her father, Emily declares she will never marry, and Cora never has her head out of a book. Their father quite spoils and indulges them all, you see, Miss Austen, and I am at my wit's end. My nerves simply cannot cope, and that is why I am asking for your help.'

'I'm not sure what I can do, Lady Milton.'

'I need someone to manage them, to help steer my children back on the right track. A girl like you, the daughter of a clergyman from a respectable background, is just the sort of person I think will do the job admirably. Please say you'll help me, Miss Austen.'

Lady Milton looked very young at that moment, and though Jane was sure she was probably inclined to silliness there was something about her desperation that struck a chord. Hadn't she always been an adviser to family and relations? Hadn't they all confided in her, and she rather prided herself at helping many of her younger nieces, particularly in regards to young men. And surely, given the age of the children, she wouldn't be expected to be a nursemaid to them, which might free up some more time for her writing? It was something to be needed, and without doubt, Lady Milton, and it seemed Manberley Castle itself, was in need of much assistance.

'Yes, I will,' she found herself saying, and was pleased to see Lady Milton smile for the second time. It was easy to see how she must have captured Lord Milton's heart, Jane thought, as she glimpsed a much younger girl in the sparkling eyes that watched her own.

Lady Milton rose from her couch, instantly animated with jangling bracelets and sheer relief. Crossing the turkey carpet in two strides she flung her arms round Jane who was taken aback at such a demonstration of affection, and rose awkwardly to receive it. She couldn't remember the last time she'd been hugged in such a way and whilst she felt slightly overwhelmed, not least by the fug of scent that enveloped her, she had to admit it wasn't unpleasant.

Lady Milton let her go at last. 'I cannot thank you enough for your generosity, and I do hope you'll forgive my little deception. I could hardly advertise their ages, could I? People would have thought me completely mad! Now, I shall call Naseby to show you to your room. Heaven knows where the young people are now but they generally make an appearance at dinner. You will be dining with us, I hope.'

'I will be present at dinner if you wish me to be there, Lady Milton, but I would like to ask if I might occasionally have an evening to myself.'

'Shall we see how we go along, my dear? I'm afraid your presence will be required when there are social events, and though we've not entertained lately, I have plans to alter that. The girls need to have husbands found and in that process I will want you to act as chaperone to them, you must understand. You needn't worry about William, of course. In any case, he is a law unto himself. However, I should like to accommodate you and your wishes ... I'm sure we might find you an evening occasionally.'

Jane did not feel comforted by the idea of having little time to herself, and after her initial elation at feeling flattered she was needed so much, was now feeling rather nervous. How did she think she was going to be able to tell young women her own age or even older than herself what to do? She'd temporarily forgotten that she wasn't forty-one any more, and had all the appearance of a much younger person. The idea of taking on what might prove to be an impossible task weighed heavily, and she doubted she was up to the job. But there was nothing to be done. She must face facts and realise she had no choice. Without money or a home of her own, she had to earn a living somehow, and for the time being she had no option but to accept the job and do the best she could.

Mrs Naseby was summoned and led Jane up the back stairs to her room. There were several poky staircases giving glimpses of a gallery and bedrooms leading off endless passages, and landings to be crossed on the way, until they found themselves in the oldest part of the building where the corridors were built of stone.

'You'll be in the tower room,' said Mrs Naseby, 'where the old nursery used to be. Of course, you'll know by now there aren't any children up there any more.'

'No, I hear they're all quite grown-up.'

'Well, that's a matter for you to judge yourself, Miss Austen. I find them to be quite juvenile in many respects, though Beth has a little more about her, and Alice is the kindest girl that ever walked the earth. But then, she takes after her sweet mother who was just the same. What a sad day that was for the Miltons when she passed away.'

'And Mae is Alice's sister, is that right?'

'Yes, poor Lady Milton died shortly after her birth. It's not her fault she's turned out to be so wild, Miss Austen, she's never known the love of a mother, though William and Alice have been the best kind of brother and sister any girl could ask for. After her ladyship's death the children were sent away to stay with their aunt, Lady Celia Broughton. Their father couldn't stand to see any of them, not even William his heir. He said he was reminded too much of their dear mother, but it broke Alice's heart, and Mae never knew what it was to have a mother or father. His lordship married again within the year, and the new Lady Milton had her own children very swiftly after that. After Teddy was killed, Lord Milton came to his senses and the children were invited back to their rightful home. But, it's not been easy, I can tell you. Well, I daresay I've already spoken out of turn. Here we are … the last set of steps are the steepest and the narrowest, but I think you'll enjoy the views when you get to the top.'

Jane was surprised the old housekeeper had confided in her so much, but perhaps she was now one of them, she'd decided to unbend a little. She followed her up the dark and twisting staircase until they reached the top where a gothic door stood open to reveal the stone tower. Jane's imagination had conjured up a gloomy room rather like a cold prison so she was pleasantly surprised to find a comparatively light and airy space despite the awful dark weather which had set in for the day. It was a large room, simply decorated in white distemper, with a fireplace on one side displaying an empty mantle above and a basket of logs below shrouded in a grey film of cobwebs. There was a single bed, a chest of drawers that held an ornate Victorian dressing mirror along with a plain jug and basin for washing, and a small oak wardrobe in the corner. A bookshelf on the opposite side held a few dusty books, obviously left over from the previous governess and a glimpse of the nursery adjoining showed a sad looking room with a few discarded and forgotten toys. There was an abandoned dolls' house with a few sticks of broken furniture looking quite as uncared for as Manberley itself, and a rocking horse with just a few wisps left to its tail.

But despite the general lack of luxury there were two features of the turreted room, which made Jane's heart beat with gladness. The splendid gothic window was made up of five long glass panels set in sinuous tracery like piping on an iced white cake, giving different views from each one towards the sea on one side and the valley on the other. Set before it was a mahogany desk with a leather chair, a most magnificent sight to behold.

'Sally will bring you hot water in the morning. There is a bathroom with hot and cold running water on this floor, but his lordship only has water heated once a week on a Sunday, and you may find by the time the water gets up here it's not so hot. Breakfast is at half-past eight, except on Sundays when it's served at nine, and lunch is at one in the afternoon. The dressing bell rings at five, and dinner is served at seven. Do you have any questions?'

'I can't think of any at present,' said Jane feeling overwhelmed, 'I expect I'll get used to everything in time.'

'Well, you'll be the first at Manberley to do that!' said Mrs Naseby, 'Don't be late for dinner, Lord Milton gets in an awful rage if people don't know how to be punctual.'

Mrs Naseby turned on her heel and left. Jane picked up her case and deposited it on the bed. She took out the bottle of perfume and the tin of talcum powder and placed them on the chest of drawers, hung up her clothes in the wardrobe, and set her book on the little table next to her bed in an attempt to make the room look more cheerful. There was a small electric lamp with a mica shade on the desk, another miracle of the modern age, which would be invaluable in the evenings if she managed to escape and do some writing. Fetching out her pen, ink and notebook, she arranged them with pride before she sat on the chair to take in her new domain. It wasn't much, she thought, and it didn't feel exactly homely, but she was sure she could make a few improvements in time. It was to be a paid post, after all, and perhaps she could cheer the place up with a few more books, or buy some fabric to make a colourful coverlet for the bed. She'd made a beautiful patchwork quilt once with her mother and sister, sitting at leisure in the evenings perfecting her fine stitches, and matching the diamond patterns, but she pushed that thought out of her mind very quickly. It was too painful to think about memories of home, she decided. She must concentrate on facing new challenges and doing what she could to embrace her new life as positively as possible.

The desk more than made up for the lack of homely touches, and she felt very inspired sitting there and thinking of all that she might write of next. She was just admiring the view and thinking how beautiful it might look if the sun was shining when there came a knock at the door.

'Come in,' she said, wondering whom it might be, and stood up immediately, feeling a little guilty for enjoying such pleasant selfish thoughts of her writing.

The door opened and a young woman looked in rather timidly. 'Miss Austen? Welcome to Manberley. I'm Alice, by the way.'

Alice stood on the threshold with a nervous expression. Jane saw a kind smile forming on the girl's lips, and liked what she saw. Dressed rather plainly in an old-fashioned gown Alice's long hair was piled high on her head, which lent itself more to a late Edwardian style than the present fashion. Jane recognised someone for whom time had stopped after the Great War. She'd seen other young women like her, scarred forever from the losses of an entire generation of men, and wondered if Alice had lost a sweetheart like so many others, in what she'd heard was the most terrible of all wars.

'Alice, how lovely to meet you. Do come in, it's so kind of you to come all the way up here to meet me.'

Gesturing to her chair Jane watched Alice take the seat whilst she perched on the end of the bed.

'I just wanted to make sure you had everything you need,' said Alice looking round the room. 'Goodness, it's a few years since I've been up here, and nor has anyone else by the looks of things. It's rather lacking in creature comforts ... I shall see what I can do straight away. And you really need a fire lit on this cold day. Heavens, look at the cobwebs. I am sorry, but we're all muddling along as best we can and sometimes the obvious things get overlooked. I was sure someone had been up to get everything ready for you.'

'Please don't apologise, I have everything I need.'

'Except a cosy fire, a warm counterpane on your bed, fresh towels, and a jug of flowers, at the very least. It is no excuse ... it has been hard since we lost so many staff, but this is no welcome. I shall go this minute and make improvements.'

'Please do not worry,' Jane insisted, 'I should prefer you stay and talk to me, if you have time.'

Alice looked up and smiled. 'I should enjoy that, if you're sure I cannot help. I was so excited to hear that you were coming as a companion to us all. Since we left London I have not enjoyed the same discussions on books, literature and art that I used to share with my mother's old friend, Lady Rivers. My sisters do not share my love of classic works, and though William loves to read too, he is always so busy about the estate to spend as much time with me as he once did. Cora is a great reader, but unfortunately only likes to scare herself with horror stories and gothic tales.'

'It is her age, I imagine. I daresay she'll grow out of it and widen her interests in time. What about you? Do you have a favourite book, one that you read over and again?' asked Jane. 'Mine is Richardson's *Sir Charles Grandison*, though I'm also very fond of Frances Burney's books. I believe Camilla is the most delightful heroine in creation.'

'I confess I've never read Richardson or Burney, but I'd love to try them. Like you, I enjoy the writers of the past more than modern novelists. My favourite book is *Persuasion* by another Miss Austen, your namesake. Are you related, by any chance?'

Jane could feel the warmth of a sudden blush making her normally pink cheeks even redder. 'I do not think so, Miss Milton, it is a common enough name ... I know of the book you mention, it happens to be one I am fond of myself, though of all that author's works I feel sure it would have benefitted from a little editing.'

'*Persuasion* is quite perfect to my mind, though I read once that it was Miss Austen's last book and her brother published it posthumously. Perhaps she did not have time to work on it as much as she would have liked.'

'I daresay there is some truth in that,' said Jane thinking of Henry who she missed with all her heart. 'And I'm sure she had an idea that time was running out. She had a story to tell, and was determined to reach the end.'

'It's such a poignant tale, that has me asking many questions. I've often wondered if Miss Austen ever experienced the kind of love that Anne Elliot and Captain Wentworth found. There is such truth in her writing, as if she must have known the kind of longing that Miss Elliot suffered through the years when she and the captain were separated.'

'I am sure most authors write about what they know and have experienced to some extent, even if their imaginations are also used to great advantage. If a writer truly experiences life and love, it will inevitably reveal itself in the written word.'

'And in *Persuasion* those experiences are so movingly described that I feel in my heart she must have suffered.'

'Only someone who has loved and lost would say such a thing, but forgive me, I am being presumptuous.'

'Not at all. I was in love once, Miss Austen, but there the comparison with Miss Elliot must end. My story has no happy ending.'

There was silence for a moment. Jane wished she'd not spoken out of turn. 'Real life cannot always mirror the happy endings we find in a book, Miss Milton, but I'm sure you would agree that to have experienced such love even with the associated pain is better than to never have known it at all.'

There was another pause during which Jane was sure their thoughts ran on similar lines. She wondered if she'd said too much, but her companion looked up and smiled.

'Miss Austen, I'm so very glad you're here. I look forward to many more discussions, but I must go and see to one or two tasks before dinner. And, if you ever need me, you'll find me on the gallery floor in the room next to the niche where the statue of Athena resides.'

Alice Milton started to walk towards the door, but turned at the last minute. 'I do hope you won't mind too much if my sister Mae seems out of spirits. She doesn't mean to be rude, but she has a habit of saying exactly what comes into her head, and no amount of correcting her from Will or myself seems to do any good.'

'I expect she thinks she's too old to have a governess, and quite rightly so,' said Jane. 'I hope Mae will realise that I have no wish to treat you all like children. I came here expecting to be a governess to five little girls so I'm rather getting used to the idea of my new position in the household.'

'On the contrary, Miss Austen, whether you're a governess or a lady's companion, I think we all know the Miltons need someone to help glue the family back together. I have a feeling you may be the very person to do just that.'

Jane watched her walk away feeling more unsure than ever about what she was being required to do. She was feeling very nervous about meeting them all at dinner, but Alice had turned out to be so lovely she decided the evening really couldn't turn out to be as bad as all that.

Chapter Three

Time was racing along at a pace, which Jane thought was typical considering how much she wished it could slow down and delay the dinner hour. She pulled on her evening dress over her head and examined her reflection feeling quite pleased with the result. Dr Lyford's sister had bought the dress in Gorringes' winter sale a few years ago in London, and whilst it was not quite in the first fashion now, Elsie Lyford said she thought it would not look too shabby to be worn at the dinner table or at a dance, black being most suitable and practical. It could always be livened up with a bright scarf, a string of pearls or one of the new long necklaces, and turned into at least three different outfits, not that Jane had any jewellery to try that out. It might even be possible to alter it and lower the waist though Elsie added it might not be the done thing for a governess to attempt to out-do her employers in the fashion stakes. The satin dress felt smooth as silk, it was embellished with a few tiny jet beads and black fringe just below the bodice line, which was still quite high, and had a cape of sheer Georgette sleeves. Looped at the sides the dress felt very elegant and Jane decided she didn't look too bad after all. A check on her hair scraped up into a bun on her head, followed by a spritz of cologne, and she was ready to face the family.

She almost got lost in the rabbit warren of staircases and passages on the way down, but catching sight of the gallery with its glimpse down into the quadrangle of the spacious hall below, Jane felt she was on the right path at last. With little idea of the time she ended up running down the last set of stairs anxious that she would be late. With minutes to spare Alice was there to meet her. Jane felt relief flood through her when she saw her waving across the hallway; she'd feel so much better not walking into a room on her own.

We're having drinks in the drawing room first,' Alice said. 'Come on through and I'll introduce you. It's just the family tonight ... Lady Milton thought that would be ordeal enough for you, and she's keen for you to get to know everyone.'

Jane detected no animosity in Alice's voice towards her stepmother, but she wasn't surprised. Though it must have been very difficult feeling like a stranger in her own home when they'd first come back to Manberley, Jane thought that if anyone could have coped with little fuss it would have been Alice.

As if she could read Jane's mind, Alice spoke. 'My stepmother means well enough, Miss Austen. She has always been kind to my siblings and me, and naturally she is disposed to favour her own children. Lady Milton would like us all to be off her hands, I think, well married and in our own homes, which I suppose is the natural desire of most mothers.'

'And are any wedding bells to be heard soon?' Jane asked as they entered the room. They were the first arrived after all, so she need not have worried.

'I'm afraid not. William is oblivious to any of the girls that are presented to him, Mae has such high ideals that any suitor is snubbed on his appearance alone, and the younger girls have only just come out. My stepmother's anxiety levels in that regard are reaching fever pitch. She'd like them to be presented at court, but my father says, as Mae and I never had that privilege it will have to be forfeited. They have horrible discussions about it sometimes, but he seems to think there are enough suitable gentlemen in the local area that would make good husbands.'

'Is he right?'

'Of course there are not so many young men left, but rather older men, one or two widowers who lost their sons in the war, keen to take new wives and carry on the line. And then there are local landowners like Jonathan Keeling at Buckland Priors, and Captain Bartlett of Sherford Park lives just a mile away; I'm sure you will meet him sooner or later. He's a friend of my father's though he is a younger man, about thirty-five. There are soldiers staying in the village too, part of the army stationed here.'

'And which one will steal your heart, Miss Milton?'

Jane saw Alice's expression grow sombre. 'The one that stole my heart has gone forever, Miss Austen.'

'I'm sorry, I should not have asked.'

Alice smiled. 'I think I would like to tell you about him sometime if you'd care to listen.'

'I would like that very much.'

The room, which had been a haven of peace, was suddenly alive with people and chatter. Lady Milton burst through the door with two girls hanging on her arms, all talking at once, with another trailing behind, her nose in a book. A man who could be no one else but Lord Milton came in next with another young woman whom Jane guessed must be Mae from the cold stare she received. A beautiful girl, and clearly a very spirited one, her features were temporarily spoiled by her sulky expression though she seemed to smile at her father and patted the seat next to her on the sofa for him to sit down.

'Ten minutes, and then dinner!' boomed his lordship ignoring his daughter and moving to a small table where a silver tray of drinks was set out. 'Can't abide cold food. Now, what's your poison?'

'Albert darling,' called Lady Milton, 'come and meet Miss Austen. She's here to help me look after the girls.'

'Not that we need a nursemaid,' said Mae glaring at Jane. 'It's too bad someone of my age has to have someone trailing after them watching everything I do. Anyhow, I'm not having someone younger than me telling me what to do. Daddy, tell Flora I won't have it.'

Nobody seemed shocked or embarrassed at this outburst, except Alice whose pleading expression as she looked anxiously at Jane begged forgiveness for Mae's rudeness.

Lord Milton ignored his daughter again and crossed the room with his hand outstretched. Jane noticed the lapels on his dinner jacket were rather shiny from age and too much careless pressing of an iron. 'Miss Austen, I am delighted, Flora's been telling me you're a miracle worker, and Lord knows we need one at Manberley Castle.'

'Oh, Albert, things aren't that bad, don't exaggerate,' said Flora Milton with a pretty, affected laugh. She perched on the arm of a sofa and crossed her long legs. 'Miss Austen is here as another pair of hands, as a companion to us all, and as a sort of lady factotum. She's a wonderful listener, you know, and it will be so nice to have someone to hear all our troubles.'

'Where's Will?' Lord Milton paid no attention to his wife, and picked up a bottle of gin from the tray.

'He's gone out,' said Mae.

'Gone out and missed his dinner? I never heard such a thing. Drat the boy, and the damned butler who announced after he'd finished dressing me that he had urgent business in the village. I daresay he's slipped out with Will to one of their usual haunts. You can't get the staff these days, Miss Austen. Never mind, I'll make 'em myself. Is it Atty's all round then?'

Jane was beginning to think she'd landed in the middle of a novel in the making, and though it was quite interesting to watch the family dynamics she'd begun to realise that she wasn't an outsider merely looking on, but was expected to become part of the scenario, which was a very frightening idea. And as she watched his lordship sloshing gin and vermouth in large quantities into every glass she felt quite alarmed. Though she wasn't averse to a glass of wine or two, a cocktail was quite another matter. It would only go to her head and she might let anything she wasn't meant to mention slip out.

'Not too heavy on the absinthe or crème de violette if you please, Albert,' said Flora selecting a cigarette from a silver box and fixing it into a long scarlet holder to match her dress. 'I do not wish to see green fairies dancing at the end of my bed tonight.'

Lord Milton was getting flustered as he topped up the cocktails and handed out the drinks. 'He's never here when you need him. I daresay he's gone on pleasure bent '

'Well, you're only young once,' said Lady Milton, 'isn't that so, Miss Austen?'

Jane smiled, and nodded a little, feeling that to answer truthfully she'd have to reply in the negative. She'd had to lie about so much lately, but she felt a certain justification. The truth would certainly horrify them all, especially Cora who would, no doubt, imagine her in the direst sense as a walking corpse or worse. She sipped at her cocktail which she thought hideously perfumed, and ignored Lord Milton's urgent pleas to 'drink up quickly, we must hasten to the dining room!'

She was listening to Lady Milton loudly bemoaning the expense of new silk stockings and their scarcity in Devon when Jane noticed she was being scrutinised by Cora. A tall slim girl who looked about eighteen, she was sitting on a leather pouffe with her legs outstretched, her girlish organza dress billowing over the sides, a book folded in her lap, but with one finger keeping its place on the page. The one touch to modernity was a low-slung sash round her hips in apricot silk, but Jane was pleased to see her appearance befitted her age. Her hair was short but curled into her neck, and a pair of forget-me-not blue eyes gazed wide-eyed between two rows of dark lashes. A pretty girl, but clearly an intelligent one, and when their eyes met Cora quickly looked away, as if she knew she'd stared too much for politeness.

'May I ask what you're reading?' asked Jane.

Cora looked up. 'It's a novel by Walter de la Mare, about a very small girl who at twenty could be taken for a child of ten. At times awfully strange, but terribly good and it's simply enchanting. I've read it before … the images created get stuck in your head, Miss Austen. There's a particularly vivid one near the start where the tiny heroine, Miss M, is sitting in a tartan frock on her father's pomatum pot on his dressing table.'

'So she's very tiny, like an elf or fairy.'

'Yes, in a way though size isn't really the point of the book, I don't think. It's more about how we view the world, and how overwhelming it can be, and all wrapped up in the most beautiful sentences.'

'I should like to borrow it when you've finished, if you wouldn't mind. And if you'd like to discuss it further when I've read it, I should enjoy that very much.'

'I'd like that,' said Cora putting the book down and drawing up her legs to hug her knees. 'It's always fun to get another opinion on a book; hardly anyone at Manberley reads, Miss Austen.'

Jane smiled. 'Can you recommend a good bookshop nearby? I have only one book with me and I should love to start a new collection.'

'There's a most delightful bookshop in the village, Miss Austen. I should love to show you, I think you'll like it very much. It's such an old-fashioned place with a brass bell that tinkles above the door, shelves upon shelves of books lining every wall, and tottering piles covering what's left of the floor. There are so many books that it's hard to find the proprietor sometimes, though he's generally to be found at the back of the shop in a cosy chair oblivious to the world. I shouldn't wonder if he doesn't get lost one day amongst the mountains of books.'

'I can't wait to see it. Are you free tomorrow? I'd love to walk down to the village.'

'We could all come,' said Beth who'd been listening to their conversation. 'Alice told me you need one or two things for your room, Miss Austen. Mother said we should buy whatever is required, and I'd love to show you the village and help you pick something out.'

'Oh, how kind of you,' said Jane noticing Beth for the first time. A younger, more attractive version of her mother unadorned by heavy make-up, she was a striking looking girl, perhaps a couple of years older than Cora. Dressed in a modern gown in vibrant yellow, which suited her glossy brown hair, her very dark velvet eyes and the fine arching brows above them, Jane warmed to her instantly.

'And we're bound to meet some of the officers,' said Emily, nudging her sister. 'I think Lieutenant Dauncey is rather sweet on Beth, and she on him. I am dying to get them together.'

'Emily, I am not interested in Lieutenant Dauncey or anyone else, whatever you think,' Beth said quite crossly. 'I'd rather you didn't meddle. One of these days your match making schemes will land you in trouble.'

'But I'm so good at it,' Emily insisted, tossing her mane of blonde curls over her shoulders. She was the only one of the girls to be so fair, and with her long, unrestrained hair and green eyes flecked with hazel she had an otherworldly quality. 'You must admit, if not for me Mr Stephens wouldn't have even noticed Daisy Stocks, and now they're married. Mr

Stephens is the local vicar in the village, Miss Austen. And as for the vicar at Moorford, Mr Wallis, I've got someone lined up for him too!'

Jane saw Alice rise to her feet. She looked a bit flushed, and her hands trembled as she spoke.

'We really should go into dinner, cook hates it if the food is left to go cold.'

'Let's not discuss the Wallis's, Emily,' said Flora Milton in a low warning voice, rising to her feet. 'You know how much it upsets your sister.'

Everyone stood up then, and Alice led the way out to the dining room. She was noticeably upset, and it clearly had something to do with the mention of the Moorford vicar. Jane couldn't help feeling sorry for her, and wondered if he'd been the young man to break her heart though she dismissed that idea when she remembered she'd been given the impression that her sweetheart was no longer living. Perhaps she'd learn more in time if Alice chose to confide in her, but what she'd be able to do to help she couldn't think. Being in love with someone who could never be yours was a wearing business, Jane knew from past experience, and as she followed the others into the dining room, she suppressed her own memories and the associated emotions rising from the past.

Jane noticed the details of white linen, gleaming silver set for several courses, white candles guttering in the breeze from an open window, and the dying evening light slanting through French windows onto flocked walls, green as the velvet interior of a jewel box. It was a picture of a dining room from an age of opulence, though on closer inspection she could see that the crystal glasses were rimed with dust, there were stains on the cloth and tarnish on the cutlery. It did not bode well.

'Miss Austen, come and sit next to me,' said Alice, and Jane tried very hard not to show her sense of relief. Beth sat on her other side, and she felt pleased she'd have a chance to speak to her again.

Jane looked round the table. Lady Milton was trying to engage Mae in conversation but she was being completely ignored. At every attempt Mae turned her head as if she hadn't heard her stepmother, and was soon talking loudly to Emily on her other side. Lord Milton was chatting away to Alice, looking rather fondly on his daughter, as his wife attempted to interrupt them, shouting across the table that she couldn't hear what was being said.

'I ought to warn you,' Beth began in a low voice inclining her dark head toward Jane's ear, 'that besides the fact that we're a disparate bunch, dinner is a bit of a hit and miss affair, and between you and me, rather lacking in content and variety. It's not cook's fault, in the old days when money was plentiful meals were absolutely splendid, but like everywhere else in the castle cutbacks have been made.'

'Please don't worry, Miss Beth. I have been used to frugality most of my life,' Jane answered truthfully, 'and of course, we are living in very difficult times.'

'Though not everyone in Stoke Pomeroy seems to suffer as we do,' said Beth. 'Mr Keeling at the Priors has the most splendid dinner parties to which we are occasionally invited. We stuff ourselves when we go there because the food is so marvellous. There was lobster to start last time we went, and roast lamb, followed by rhubarb crumble with jugs of custard. I have dreams at night of dining there when we've had a particularly poor dinner. Mr Keeling is from one of the old families and he seems to have pots of money left.'

'Is he a young man?' Jane asked.

'Well, he's of marriageable age, I suppose, if that's why you're asking, though no one here would consider him like that, however much my mother would wish it. We've known him since we were babies, Miss Austen, and he's like a doting big brother. I'm sure you'll meet him soon; he's always here. The castle is like a second home to him, he says. He's very generous and often sends us a gift of venison, beef, or fish when in season, and his gardens produce the most wonderful fruit. Then it feels like a holiday, and everyone is happy because we go to bed with full stomachs.'

Jane was just wondering if she dared ask what had happened to the Milton sugar fortune when the first course arrived, a huge tureen of soup, carried in ceremoniously by a footman who proceeded to dole out ladlefuls of watery consommé into the dishes before them. There was a faint taste of something meaty, which surely came from the bones that had been boiled to produce it, though Jane could not decide exactly what. It was lukewarm, and the accompaniment of a slightly stale bread roll did nothing to improve it. Jane was still getting used to the fact that not all the courses arrived on the table at once, and though trying to embrace every facet of her new life, she thought there was a lot to be said for being able to miss out certain dishes if they were not to your liking.

'Civility costs nothing, Mae,' Lady Milton was saying in an exasperated tone. 'I just asked you a perfectly reasonable question.'

Jane saw Mae roll her eyes, but she sat tight-lipped, behaving as if a response wasn't expected.

'Albert, talk to your rude daughter, please. I will not be ignored in my own home.'

Jane saw Lord Milton pick up his wine glass and drain it. The room, which had been lively with chatter, was suddenly silent.

'Come on, ladies, let's not squabble,' he said without looking either of them in the eye. He dabbed at his moist forehead with a large cotton handkerchief.

'I am not squabbling, Albert. I am trying to have a conversation with your daughter and I am having no luck. I think you need to be firmer, and tell her that she is behaving like a spoiled child. I cannot do anything about the fact that her mother is dead, and that you chose to marry me, but I do not see why we shouldn't be able to sit at the dinner table and be polite, even if we hate the very sight of one another.'

'Flora, for goodness' sake, let's not have a quarrel now,' said his lordship, beckoning to the footman to fill his glass. 'I'm too tired for all this nonsense. It's got to stop.'

As the dishes were cleared in preparation for the second course Jane couldn't help feeling sorry for Lady Milton. Whilst the dinner table wasn't the place to start an argument, she could see the lady was at the end of her tether, and Mae, who clearly had her father wrapped round her little finger, was enjoying the fact that he and her stepmother were at odds. It was obvious that Mae was playing a little game, one she thought she'd easily win every time. But, despite the fact that Jane thought her behaviour was uncalled for, she suspected Mae was not coping well with life and lashing out at anyone who tried to show they cared. Whilst Alice had accepted her mother's death and the idea of her father being happy with someone else, her younger sister was railing against the world, and anyone she thought might divert her father's attention from herself. Lord Milton wasn't helping. He didn't seem to be engaged with any of the women in his family, particularly, though Jane detected a slight preference for Alice and Beth.

The dollops of macaroni cheese doled out with a serving of cabbage did nothing to lighten the atmosphere, and though Alice and Beth started up a conversation on some new music they'd heard about, the dinner limped along to its inevitable dismal conclusion along with some stewed apple and lumpy custard for pudding, watered down to a runny consistency.

Jane excused herself as soon as she could leaving the disgruntled company in the drawing room, who were now pretending that nothing untoward had happened. Lord and Lady Milton were knocking back more cocktails, and sitting next to one another on the sofa, she laughing girlishly at everything he said.

It was rather eerie finding her way up to her room in the dimly lit passages, but when she entered her room she was struck by the beauty of silver moonlight shining through the windows and the sight of the sky studded with stars, twinkling like diamonds. She felt suddenly revived and thought how she would make the best of the moment by using the time before bed for some writing. Jane sat down at the desk and switched on the lamp, which flashed too brightly then promptly popped with a loud crack. A new bulb would have to be added to the shopping list, she thought, and wished she had a candle to write by. These new fangled lights were all very well, she thought, but a candle was always reliable. The moon chose that moment to hide behind a bank of cloud, darkening the room to black velvet and feeling quite deflated, she decided it was time to give in and go to bed. Tomorrow was another day, and her new book could wait until then.

Chapter Four

When Jane woke the next morning she was delighted to see a remarkable change in the weather. Sunlight poured through the long windows leaving golden lozenges in bright bars across the carpet and over her bed. She stretched, arms overhead, feeling quite deliciously happy for a moment as she luxuriated in the warmth and sense of wellbeing, having slept well despite the lumpy mattress. Leaping out of bed she went to stand at the window, and fiddling with the catch on the last pane at the end where the glass had been divided to make it into a casement, she flung it wide open. The smell of the sea and the sound of gulls mewing up above could do nothing but fill her with a sense of pleasure, making her instantly remember holidays spent in Lyme and Sidmouth in another place and time.

Leaning on the sill she could see the blue expanse of sea and sky, across to the valley and the village on the other side, glittering after the rain, and down to the steaming garden below. Breathing in lungfuls of air, she'd never felt so alive. The memories of her last illness were so fresh that every morning since she'd been brought back she was filled with such a sense of hope and elation as she felt the blood coursing through her veins by a beating heart that felt stronger than she'd ever known.

Down in the garden she could see a twisting path following the line of a stretch of water at the bottom of the tower, and she watched a white swan fly in to land, spraying foam in an arc upon the moat, thick with water lily pads. She was watching the bird preening with a golden beak when along the path she caught sight of Alice and Mae emerging between the rose bushes whose blooms drooped like crushed tissue after the rain. Dressed for the day, Jane noticed the absolute contrast in their styles, Alice in a gown of white lawn flowing down to her ankles, Mae in a pair of trousers with a loose blouse tucked into the waistline. Though still an unusual sight, Jane had seen women occasionally wearing trousers, and thought how comfortable they looked. Mae's were wide-legged, looking very masculine, and she wondered if they'd been altered from a pair of her brother's. Jane could just imagine the sort of rows that would ensue when Lady Milton clapped eyes on Mae's outfit, and she'd bet money on the fact that her stepmother would find fault with her appearance.

Alice and Mae were deep in conversation, their heads bowed, and though she couldn't hear all that they were saying, odd words, and snatches of conversation drifted up to her on the summer breeze.

'Will thought you should know … you mustn't be upset … with luck you may avoid him,' Mae said.

'I do not know why Will should say … I've long given over thinking of … I would happily see him, what have I to fear?' Alice answered.

'I think Will might be relieved to hear that … they were always such friends.'

'And if I make it easy for everyone, you'll still be able to meet … I've no wish for awkward scenes, Mae … you coming down to the village later?'

'No … not be told what to do.'

'I wish you would … not Miss Austen's fault …'

They rounded the curve of the path and Jane could hear no more. There was a little mystery about someone Mae thought Alice might not want to see, and it looked as if there'd be another day of scenes between Mae and Lady Milton. Jane felt a little uncomfortable at having eavesdropped, but really it was very difficult not to hear those intriguing snatches of conversation. Wondering whether she'd come to learn what it was all about, she left the window on the latch to allow the warm air to circulate, and hearing the clock striking eight, decided she'd better hurry and get herself dressed for breakfast, though after last night's meal she wasn't expecting much culinary excitement. There didn't seem to be any sign of hot water left outside her room so she filled the jug with cold from the basin in the bathroom for a wash, and set about getting ready for the day.

Jane hurried along the corridors and passages, down one staircase after another. She saw one or two maids bearing breakfast trays groaning with teapots, silver food domes and racks of toast, which made her wonder whether many of Manberley's residents would be joining her in the dining room. It was empty when she walked in, but there were several covered serving dishes on the side, which rather surprisingly held a vast variety of breakfast treats, until Jane reasoned that the Miltons probably farmed the land, and would keep pigs and hens. Jane helped herself to sausage and bacon, scrambled egg and fried bread, thinking that it might be an idea to stock up on food if dinner was to be another poor affair.

She was just enjoying her solitude when the door opened, which made her start a little, especially when she saw who was walking in. It was the driver who'd picked her up from the station, looking as if breakfasting in the dining room at this hour was a regular habit. He mumbled something, which Jane thought might have been "good morning", before coolly helping himself from the side. With his plate heaped high, he sat down on the chair opposite her, and spent the next ten minutes without another word, eating his way through a mountain of food in silence. Jane couldn't help thinking his presence was most unusual, even taking into account how times had changed. In her day servants ate in the kitchen, and though she'd been surprised to discover that she was invited to eat with the family, she decided the Miltons must be most unconventional to allow the chauffeur the same honour.

It felt very uncomfortable sitting there without any attempt at conversation. Jane observed her companion who was now unfurling a newspaper from his pocket, and spreading it open on the table, with hardly a pause from the movement of his fork from food to mouth. He was very well dressed in a suit of country tweed, no uniform today, and she couldn't help noticing how well the greenish flecks in the tawny cloth complimented his tanned skin. He was broad-shouldered, yet she detected a slim torso beneath the waistcoat he wore, and with long limbs and strong, capable-looking hands he could be described as a very good-looking young man. Dark, unruly curls had been fixed as well as they could into place with a neat parting and brilliantine, but those at the nape of his neck where they met the collar of his shirt refused to be tamed.

He must have been aware she was staring because he suddenly looked up which made her jump a little out of her seat. She saw a wide mouth curving into a generous smile at her obvious discomfort, and a flash of white even teeth.

'Not run away yet, Miss Austen?'

His accent had a faint trace of something she couldn't make out, but it was a friendly voice, and she couldn't help smiling too.

'No, not yet, Mr … I'm sorry, I didn't catch your name.'

'It's Will Milton.' There was a pause during which his eyes connected with hers. 'Just call me Will … everybody does.'

Jane felt the blood pound in her temples, and knew her face was flooding with crimson. Will Milton? A hundred thoughts flashed through her mind, as she wondered if she could have done or said anything yesterday that she should now regret. He was no ordinary chauffeur she realised in that moment, but the son and heir to Manberley castle. Of course she had been a little snooty, telling him off for discussing her employers, but he'd been obviously playing a trick on her and that was hardly her fault. Besides, he'd had the nerve to drop her at the servant's door when she knew he should have treated her as a lady and escorted her through the front entrance. Jane thought she detected amused arrogance in the curling of his mouth as he continued to read. She went from embarrassment and shame to downright livid indignation in the time it took for Will to close his paper.

'Do you always dress up as the chauffeur and pretend to be someone you're not?' she said crossly, unable to stop the thoughts coming out of her mouth.

Will seemed to find this funny, and threw back his head to laugh out loud. 'I don't have to do it very often, pick people up from the station, I mean, but I thought it might put you at your ease, and I hoped to learn a bit more about you and what you were thinking about coming to work here. We don't have a driver any more, and on the few occasions I've taken on the job, I must admit it's always fun to listen to the conversations of incoming guests. I've learned a lot, and then the moment of realisation is always worth the wait … and such a hoot.'

'I'm glad you think it's so funny,' said Jane, already deciding that she'd never met anyone more unprincipled. Above all things she disliked this sort of trickery, having fun at others' expense. These Miltons were an odd lot, and she'd best keep her wits if she were to keep her sanity.

'I didn't mean to upset you,' he said and she caught that drawl in his voice again. His eyes were pleading with her but she would not be drawn into the depths of those dark brown eyes. 'Please forgive me, Miss Austen, I would hate to disappoint my new governess.'

He was making fun of her again. 'I am not your governess. Your stepmother has made it quite clear to me that you're a law unto yourself. I am here merely to advise Lady Milton and help with the girls.'

'I expect she's told you I'm a wicked stepson,' he said, his eyes twinkling with amusement, 'with no morals and a string of women in the village.'

'Lady Milton has said no such thing, and even if she had I would not repeat it.'

That made him laugh again, and Jane couldn't help wondering, as she stared at him, whether there was some truth in what he'd said. She saw that arrogance again, and imagined the confident heir to Manberley leaving a trail of broken hearts behind him amongst all the young women of Stoke Pomeroy. Well, he wouldn't be charming her with his good looks and fine eyes, she decided, not that he'd be interested in anything about her except as a vehicle for his jokes and what he imagined was wit. Jane thought it wouldn't take her long to put him in his place now she knew what he was like, and looked forward to having the opportunity again sometime.

'I wonder if I could ask something of you, Miss Austen.'

'Well, you could try,' she answered rather stiffly, knowing she wasn't being very friendly.

'Could you keep an especial eye on my sisters? Alice is a sweet girl, and she's been through so much, always taking it upon herself to try and fill the place of the mother we lost. I don't want to go into detail, but something imminent might just throw her off course a little. She's been bruised in the past, and though I shall do all to protect her against further hurt, it would be so nice to know someone else was looking out for her. And Mae is lovely too, when you get to know her. Alice told me her behaviour last night left a lot to be desired, and that she's been rude within your hearing. We talk to her all the time, but we're at a loss to know what to do for the best.'

'Of course, I shall do all I can to help,' said Jane in a warmer tone, slightly revising her thoughts about him. At least he seemed to care about his sisters. 'Please don't worry too much, Alice is such a kind young woman, and I'm sure Mae just needs time, Mr Milton.'

'I knew the moment I set eyes on you that you'd be good for Manberley, Miss Austen, thank you for taking us all on. I'm glad you're not about to run away, but if you ever consider it, will you discuss it with me first?'

Now it was Jane's turn to laugh. 'Mr Milton, I hope that will not be the case just yet, but I'd also hate you to think I will have a solution for every problem. I am ill qualified as a counsellor though I've had a little experience with young people in my own family. It will be as much trial and error for me too.'

'No, I won't have that. You've made a difference already ... even Mrs Naseby has a good word for you, which is saying a lot. You may be young and inexperienced, but you're a breath of fresh air, and that's what we all need.'

Jane didn't say a word; she could hardly contradict him. But she felt young, even if her mind still held onto the past of an aging woman. She watched Will dab at his mouth with a napkin before he stood up, pushing the chair behind him.

'I hope I'll see you later, at dinner.'

'Yes, Mr Milton.'

'Will,' he said with a knowing wink. 'Please call me Will, everybody does.'

Mae didn't want to hang around being told what she could or couldn't do on such a glorious day. She'd already decided to go out on her bicycle, and take a little picnic down to the beach. Mrs Wickens, the cook had made her a packed lunch and even though she knew it was fish paste sandwiches and a flask of tea, it would be better than enduring an insufferable afternoon at the tea shop in the village with her sisters and that new governess who was so prim and proper.

She went down to the old stables where the stalls had once been full of horses. Now there were only two left, her brother Will's chestnut thoroughbred, Achilles, and a pony, Valentino, which all the girls were meant to share. Valentino whinnied when he saw her, and reaching inside her trouser pocket she fetched out a sugar lump for him. Leaning her head against his noble one as he munched, his velvet nose sniffing for more, she felt the warmth of him melt her heart.

'No one understands me like you do,' she said, draping her arms round his neck. 'But I'm sorry, my darling, I can't take you with me today, I shall be gone for too long, though I promise we'll ride along the sands tomorrow.'

Mae kissed his neck, and stroked his mane, as he nuzzled her fingers in hopes of another sugar lump. She fed him one more, and went in search of her bicycle. Propped up in the last stall, she put her packet of sandwiches and thermos flask into the basket at the front, and backed it out. Will's motorcycle gleamed in the next stall. It was a beautiful object, an Indian scout he'd bought in America a few years ago when he'd been to stay with their Uncle Harry who'd treated him to the exotic machine and even shipped it home for him. Uncle Harry, their mother's brother was a very wealthy man who divided his time between his brownstone in New York City and his summer mansion at Newport, Rhode Island. He had sons of his own, but the hope was that Will might still come into some of Uncle Harry's money. Mae knew that her mother had come from a prestigious family, but she'd never met any of them though she was intrigued by the idea of her exotic American relations. They hadn't wanted Edith to marry her father who they'd considered a pauper compared to the families with whom they associated, and when she eloped with him to England, they'd cut off all ties. It was only after her mother's death that Uncle Harry had expressed a wish to meet Will, and though the visit had been a success, lasting two years, in all that time he'd never asked to meet the girls.

Mae wished she could try out the motorcycle. When it was running, it was like a beast. Will had let her try it once and she'd loved the purr of the engine and the feeling of power. Resting the bicycle against a post she wandered over to admire the sleek lines and the scarlet paint. She'd watched Will start it up many times, and wondered if she could do it herself. Leaning over, she turned on the gas, as Will called it, pulled on the choke, adjusted the advance and the throttle, and then leaning her full weight on the handlebars tried to kick-start the cycle. It took three attempts before it sputtered into life, and then, as the engine ticked over, Mae thought it would do no harm just to try it out for size. Remembering to kick her leg high she eased into the saddle, and the moment that was done, the most daring thought entered her head.

Chapter Five

After Will had gone, Jane sat alone for a while wondering what she should do next, and though she longed to explore the house and grounds or even take a stroll by herself down to the sea she thought she must be patient and wait for instructions. It would be good to have an idea of her timetable for the day to see if there was any possibility of spending some time writing, and hoped Lady Milton would call in soon to tell her of the most recent plans. There was no sign of their mother, but she didn't have to wait long before Beth, Emily and Cora walked in with a hail of friendly greetings.

Beth helped herself to some bacon and eggs, but Emily and Cora contented themselves with a cup of tea from a pretty Spode pot, saying they'd had breakfast in bed.

'Though why I bother, my boiled egg was congealed by the time Elsie managed the stairs, and the toast stone cold.'

'Emily,' Beth scolded, 'Elsie's not as young as she was, I'm not surprised it takes her so long.'

'Then mother should replace her if she can't do the job properly,' Emily answered petulantly, flicking back her golden hair. 'What we need is some young blood, another girl from the village, willing to please.'

'Elsie's been with us for years,' said Beth. 'She's been a loyal servant who has spent the last few years happy to work for reduced pay, and if you don't like a cold breakfast then I suggest you get up and come downstairs. The maids have enough to do just trying to keep this house clean without waiting on spoiled girls, hand and foot.'

Jane couldn't have put it better herself. 'How many maids do you have?' she asked.

'There are only four left now, along with Mrs Naseby, of course,' said Beth, 'and two of them are rather young and inexperienced. I try and help out where I can, but what with cleaning, changing beds, laundry and lighting fires, not to mention preparing and washing up after meals there's not enough time to do it all. We try and keep the main rooms clean, but something really needs to be done about the hallways, windows and passages. Mr Naseby used to see to all the big jobs, but he's long passed on, and of course Mr Bell, the butler has only two footmen under him now.'

'And I think he'd prefer it if the *maids* were under him,' said Emily with a wink. 'Only the young ones, of course!'

Jane bit her lip, and studied a stain on the tablecloth to stop herself from smirking. Emily was proving to be a completely spoiled brat, but there was something about her precocious behaviour that amused her, none the less. She was lively and intelligent, even if she engaged her mouth far too quickly before her brain had a chance to think about what she was saying.

Beth grinned. 'Emily, you're too wicked for words.'

Jane noticed that Beth said no more on the matter, and she detected there might be more than a hint of truth in what she'd said. Mr Bell must be the young man his lordship had referred to last night, and she remembered that he'd also mentioned the likelihood of him being out and about with Will Milton. Well, that wouldn't surprise her, she thought, as she remembered her dashing breakfast companion, and wondered if Mr Bell was as handsome.

Alice walked in just as Cora was saying they were all going to the teashop for lunch after their shopping. Jane noticed she looked very out of sorts; her eyes were red-rimmed, and she looked as if she'd been crying. No one else seemed to notice, and if Jane hadn't said hello, she doubted any of them would really have bothered to say anything to Alice at all. One thing was clear. Besides the obvious disparity in their ages, the two sets of sisters seemed at odds, though at least Beth was civil, being the only one of the younger set to even smile at her stepsister.

'I have a list compiled,' said Alice. 'Will said he'd give us a lift down into the village and pick us up later if we telephone from the post office.'

'What about Lady Milton?' asked Jane. 'Is she coming shopping too?'

'Oh no,' said Emily instantly, with a laugh. 'Mother never gets out of bed before two in the afternoon. Besides, she has her friend King Zoot coming to visit, so it's likely we won't see her until dinnertime.'

'King Zoot? Goodness, is she entertaining royalty?'

Emily laughed so much, Beth had to nudge her to stop.

'He's a jazz musician, Miss Austen,' said Alice quietly, as she rapidly turned beetroot red.

'And he's very famous in London where she met him at the Kit Cat club,' Emily continued. 'Zoot's an old friend, and they spend hours together whenever he's down in Devon. She met father at the nightclub too, when she was performing.'

'That's enough, Emily,' said Beth in a warning tone. 'I'm sure mother will tell Miss Austen her own life story if she wants to tell it.'

Jane hated to admit it but she was intrigued. She knew it was very wrong to jump to conclusions, but she couldn't help wondering if Lady Milton had been a nightclub singer or dancer, like those she'd read about in the newspaper. With those film star looks, and her shapely figure she wouldn't be at all surprised from what had been hinted. Nightclubs were completely unknown to Jane, though she'd read enough in the papers to hear they were 'dens of iniquity', whatever that might mean. As for jazz, she'd heard quite a lot played on Dr Lyford's gramophone during her stay in the little terraced house on the outskirts of Winchester, and after a while had quite enjoyed it. The machine was Dr Lyford's pride and joy, he told her, having saved for a whole year to buy it. And it was a small miracle to hear music coming from a moving disc and trumpet.

Jane couldn't put her finger on why she'd warmed to Lady Milton. But there was something in her independent spirit she admired, and Jane always loved to hear stories about poor women having the chance to better their lot. She felt quite shocked that she wasn't at all horrified by anything she'd learnt that morning and began to feel her morals must be already corrupted. Putting it down to the fact that she'd always led such a sheltered, narrow existence, she felt as if she were being given a second chance to take life by the hands and live adventurously, or at least watch those brave enough to be fearless about it. Having lived cautiously, and under strict rules and regulations for so long, Miss Austen felt the winds of change blowing across the Devon landscape.

Mae was trying to justify her reasons for why she was now roaring at great speed down the narrow country lanes at full tilt. She'd decided to take the motorcycle out for a quick spin, donning Will's leather helmet and goggles, heading out the back way where no one would see her. Circumnavigating the village boundaries, she could be back before anyone realised she was gone, least of all Will who she knew was visiting one of the estate farms. Accelerating down the lane, her jauntily tied scarf flying back in the wind, she doubted she'd ever felt freedom like it. Mae loved her bicycle for the independence it gave her, but this was something else. The engine throbbed beneath her legs as the landscape flew by in a blur of burgeoning greenery, the tops of frothing cow parsley tickling her elbow as she rounded a curve in the road.

She didn't see the car coming full pelt in the opposite direction. Blinded by the tall hedges, and careering too fast down the left-hand side of the road, when she heard the loud tooting and the screeching of brakes it was too late. Swerving to miss the elegant motor Mae almost crashed into the bank, but managed at the last to bring the cycle round, just catching the trunk of a tree and scraping her elbow and knee back to the bone on the bark. Skidding to a halt, and wincing with the pain, she realised with a sinking heart that the wheel on her brother's cycle was horribly buckled, and that blood was pouring from her limbs.

'What the hell, you blithering idiot, you could have killed us both,' called an outraged voice.

Mae saw the stranger jump out of his car as she climbed off the bike, pulling off her goggles and attempting to undo the helmet. He was very angry, and she felt quite frightened.

'Good God, you're a woman,' he said, stopping abruptly when he reached her, as Mae threw the goggles onto the floor in frustration. She was having no luck with the strap on her headgear, and tears were smarting at the corners of her eyes she was in so much pain with her arm. When she tried to put her weight on her leg, it buckled; she was sure her knee was twisted too.

'Hey, just a minute, let me help,' said the young man, in a calmer tone. 'Take a seat in my car, let's have a look.'

Mae took a step and winced, as the pain shot up her leg.

'Put your arm round my neck,' he insisted. Mae saw the anger leave his face, as he smiled. 'I won't bite, I promise.'

Mae put her arm round his neck, but wasn't prepared for him lifting her into his arms like a hero from a romantic novel. He was dressed for a game of tennis in white shirt, trousers and shoes, and she realised that apart from her father, she'd never been so close to a man before, let alone felt a strong masculine heart beating through his thin cotton shirt or muscular arms gripping her legs. But, she rather liked it, especially when his blue eyes met hers, and the smell of his cologne made her want to snuggle her head down on the smooth pillow of flesh below his collar bone. His hair was very dark, almost black so his eyes were a startling feature in a tanned face. It was only a few short steps, but she was sorry when he put her down, fetching a towel from his tennis bag to dab at her grazes. Again, she fiddled with the strap until his hand firmly cupped her chin, and she felt his fingers reaching for the buckle. As they brushed hers, she dropped them into her lap as if she'd just been scalded. He released the strap at last, and she allowed him to ease off the helmet, freeing her hair, which blew back in the wind to show off her beautiful features.

Jane followed the girls across the gravel drive to the garage, their shadows etched in shades of violet in the strong sunlight. She saw the roof was down on Will's car in tribute to the sunshine as he backed it out, and as Jane climbed into the seat with the other girls, she couldn't help remembering the awful weather of the previous day or how Will had fooled her into thinking he was the chauffeur. She sat in the middle of the back seat, with Alice on one side and Beth on the other. Alice, she noticed, was subdued, and Beth lost in thoughts of her own. In contrast, Cora and Emily shared the seat next to Will, the latter keeping up a constant stream of chatter, grabbing the steering wheel now and then to try it out. It was lovely to motor along in the fresh air, and watch the sea sparkling in shades of azure blue and turquoise down below them. Once or twice her eyes strayed to view the back of Will's head above those broad shoulders, his hair neatly combed into place, with the exception of a few rogue curls that danced in the breeze.

Jane wasn't sure if it was her imagination, but she was determined not to check on the fact that she'd seen Will staring at her every once in a while through the rear view mirror. His eyes were so penetrating, which she put down to the fact that they were so dark, like black velvet. He made her feel uncomfortable, as if he were constantly trying to weigh her up. It was a long time since she'd felt under such peculiar scrutiny, and though she was sure he didn't stare because he was dazzled by her beauty, Jane reflected on the fact that in her former life, she'd grown used to being ignored by the opposite sex, content with becoming invisible as the years passed and her bloom faded. Since her first days venturing out with Dr Lyford and his sister, she'd been surprised at the attention she'd got from passing gentlemen. It wasn't entirely unpleasant, just strange, and she was unused to it. But, she couldn't and didn't want to look up again, and kept her eyes on the panoramic views, as they snaked their way along the twisting lanes down to the village.

They turned onto the high street and were met with an extraordinary sight. Both sides of the road were lined with people, mostly women, and there was a policeman directing traffic, and another, looking rather red-faced doing his best to keep the girls and ladies of all ages from spilling into the road and blocking the path of those trying to use it. There wasn't ever much traffic in Stoke Pomeroy, and few cars were seen passing through the main road, but it looked as if the milkman with his horse and cart, and a miller with a wagon loaded with sacks of flour were giving up trying to get past the throng which surged around the entrance to the teashop. They shook their heads at Will, and suggested he find another way through.

'It's mayhem, you're taking your life in your hands if you're going down the high street, Mr Milton,' said Mr Endicott, the milkman, stopping to doff his cap. 'It's some famous film star got out at Mrs Foxworthy's, and the women are going wild. Begging your pardon, ladies.'

'Good Lord,' said Will, 'I think I know what's happened here. I'd better get out and help. Well, that didn't take long for word to get round.'

All the girls craned their heads, as Will got out of the car, and Emily stood up in her seat to get a better view. Jane was as fascinated as the others, but it was impossible to see anything for the crowds.

'Who can it be?' shrieked Emily excitedly standing on tiptoes, and Cora, now sitting on top of the seat blocking the view of the others shouted gleefully, 'Douglas Fairbanks junior?'

Jane had seen his photograph at the cinema in Winchester along with Louise Brooks on whom Lady Milton clearly styled herself. She turned to see Alice who was pointedly staring in the opposite direction, apparently not interested in seeing or knowing about who was causing such a commotion. And then quite uncharacteristically, she turned and said snappily, 'It's Frankie Wallis.'

'Frankie!' shouted Emily and Cora together, turning round excitedly, 'Has he come back?'

Alice was looking very pale. 'I believe he's here on holiday.'

Beth stretched her arm over Jane in a spontaneous gesture, taking Alice's hand. 'I'm so sorry, how awful for you. Will he be here long?'

Alice attempted a smile. 'Don't worry, Beth, I'll be fine.'

It didn't take a great detective to work out that Frankie Wallis was the man who'd left the huge hole in Alice's heart. After thinking her young man must be dead, it was clear he was very much alive, and breaking the hearts of dozens of young ladies, by the look of things. Jane watched Alice withdraw further. There might not be anything she could do to help but listen, so she hoped Alice might confide in her later and she'd discover the full story behind her sadness.

Will was coming back to the car, and directed his first words to his sister. 'Are you all right, Alice?'

Jane saw Alice take a deep breath. 'Yes, don't worry, Will, he's perfectly entitled to come home. Let's face it, I've had an easy seven years without having to bump into him every day. And if he's back for a while, I'll just have to get used to it. It's not as if we'll see much of him anyway, he'll be invited everywhere else by very glamorous people, I've no doubt. I'm sure he won't want to be spending any time at Manberley.'

'That's just it,' said Will. 'He's asked if we'll join him for lunch. Yesterday, when I met him at the pub he said he'd stayed away too long, and that he'd like to come and say hello to Pa and Flora.'

Alice bit the corner of her mouth. 'I've got to meet him sometime, it might as well be now.'

'Are you sure? I can make an excuse if you'd rather. Look, it's a lot to expect, you've only just found out he's in the area. I'll tell him no.'

Will was being so kind and considerate that for a moment Jane forgot that she wasn't very sure about him. He reminded her of Henry, the brother who'd always protected and loved her as much as Will clearly loved his sister.

'No, he's your friend,' Alice answered, 'and I hope I can meet him on friendly terms. I don't want there to be any awkwardness between you … best friends are meant for life.'

'Well, only if you're sure; I couldn't bear to see you unhappy.'

'I'm absolutely fine, Will. Come on, let's go.'

Will looked doubtful, but opened the car door to let her out. 'The policemen have assured me that we'll be allowed through. Beth, Emily, Cora, are you ready? Miss Austen, please allow me to help you out.'

Chapter Six

The teashop was closed in their honour, Mrs Foxworthy insisted, especially as some of the young girls outside waving autograph books still pressed their noses up against the bow windows trying to see into the dim light of the wood-panelled shop. Alice saw him straight away, but she couldn't look longer than the two seconds it took to establish where he was in the room, and then Will was pushing forward, hugging Frankie like a long lost brother and there was a lot of noise and exclamation over meeting old friends, as the introductions took place, that she was grateful it gave her a bit of time to catch her breath. When Alice and Frankie came face to face and shook hands there was a moment of awkwardness, as she observed a look from him that she recognised as pity in his grey-green eyes. Apart from the fact that it felt so horribly formal, Alice imagined that he hardly recognised her, the striking girl he'd once known was now replaced by a frump in dowdy clothes of a style long gone by. There were no words, and she was thankful that everyone was still talking at once. The worst was over, thought Alice, and it was all so surreal.

Mrs Foxworthy showed them all to a large round table at the rear of the shop, and they sat down to pore over the menus as the initial small talk dwindled into self-conscious observations on the state of the weather. Emily and Cora took over the conversation wanting to hear all about Frankie's life in Hollywood as a star of the silver screen, and Alice tried to look as if she attended to the conversation instead of dwelling on the past. Staring absently at a glass vase filled with sweet peas on the crisp, damask cloth, her mind wandered back to another time and a different landscape where the man who now held his audience captive was tenderly holding her hand and saying how much he loved her.

'And you know Laurette Taylor personally?' Emily was asking. 'We loved her in *One Night in Rome*, didn't we, Cora? Mrs Wickens said she saw you both together in *Lovers' Dream* at the Torbay cinema when she went to visit her sister in Paignton. She said you were on the newsreel before the film started, dancing a foxtrot and looking so very happy together.'

Frankie shook his head. 'Oh, we do all sorts for a bit of publicity. You wouldn't believe the number of stars I've been linked with, and coincidentally, have fallen passionately in love with just before the film was released. The studios insist on it, they say it encourages the fans to buy cinema seats.'

'So, none of it's true then,' asked Cora, looking most put out.

'Not a word,' he said, shaking his head and smiling.

He was more handsome than Alice remembered him, his hair more golden, and now with an American accent, stronger than the one her brother had acquired in the states, he was even more impossibly glamorous than her memory and imagination could have pictured him. Frankie's clothes were impeccably tailored, and the gold watch he wore on his tanned wrist was clearly expensive, yet typically understated.

'What about 'Young Doug', Mr Fairbanks junior? How well do you know him?' said Emily who kept abreast of all the film stars.

Alice remembered seeing a picture of Frankie and Douglas Fairbanks junior pictured together in Mrs Wickens's film magazine. They'd had their arms round one another, and she thought Frankie had never appeared so good-looking.

'I know most of the stars,' Frankie answered, 'but we all live in the same place, so it's a bit difficult not to spend all our time together. It's probably boring for everyone else, all our 'talking shop', but acting is our life.'

'Are you joking?' said Emily, sitting as close to him as possible. 'I wouldn't be bored, it would be a dream to be an actress in Hollywood, and attend all those parties. I know I could certainly get used to the money. Oh, what shopping I would do!'

Frankie looked amused. 'You've never seen stores like the ones they have over there. In New York you can't see the tops of buildings from the ground, they're so high they call them skyscrapers, and the stores are filled from floor to roof with everything you could ever want.'

'Oh, I wish I could see it,' Emily enthused. 'How did you break into films, Frankie, was it easy?'

'Not at first, I can't say it was a piece of cake. I had to work hard, do a lot of jobs I hated whilst I was trying to get noticed, but I kept going, and in the end it paid off. I spent a miserable time in repertory here for a few years after the war, living in dingy bed-sits, and taking bit parts, but once I arrived in America my luck changed, almost overnight. Anyway, enough of me, I want to know what you've all been doing ... a lot of growing up by the looks of things. I wouldn't have known you, Emily ... and Cora, you were still in pigtails the last time I saw you.'

Alice remembered that fateful afternoon too well. She'd known her father hadn't really approved of Frankie, as a friend of Will's, least of all as someone qualified to court or, heaven forfend, marry her.

'Cora's coming out this year,' Emily announced on her sister's behalf, 'to join Beth and me at all the dances, not that there have been many in sleepy Pomeroy. Alice and Mae come with us sometimes, though it's hard to drag them away from the castle. I'm so glad you've come, Frankie, we need more men to come dancing, but I suppose it might be a bit difficult if you stop the traffic every time you go out.'

Frankie laughed. 'But, I'm sure *you'll* be the one doing that from now on, Emily Milton. With such stunning sisters, Will, you must have your work cut out.'

Emily flicked her hair over one shoulder and beamed, staring adoringly into Frankie's eyes. 'Say you'll come to the next dance, Mr Wallis.'

Beth stepped in, aware that her sister needed her flirtatious behaviour curbed. 'Are you staying here long, Mr Wallis?'

'Please everyone, we're old friends, just call me Frankie. I've got a couple of months off before we start shooting in the fall,' he said, and as he said the words Alice felt his gaze. Even the way he said "the fall", instead of "the autumn", sounded so thrilling. She looked up for a moment and wondered if the perceived look of sorrow in his eyes was just in her imagination.

He'd been sent home injured from the front at the beginning of spring in 1918, and Alice had nursed him alongside a ballroom of soldiers at the castle through April showers and on through a gloriously hot summer, but by autumn the falling leaves and the onset of winter saw him anxious to get away, especially when it was made clear to him that he was not good enough to marry Alice Milton. She could never smell damp leaves underfoot without feeling the pain of such sadness when they parted. Looking back, she knew he'd been determined to prove himself both to her and her father.

Mrs Foxworthy appeared with plates piled high with food. Alice looked nervously at her slice of ham and salad of lettuce leaves and sliced tomato, feeling that she wouldn't be able to eat a morsel. They were quiet for a moment whilst Frankie charged their glasses with the wine he'd ordered, and raised his glass to them all.

Will was just getting up to make a speech when a loud knocking on the glass pane of the door alerted them to the sight of one of the policemen hammering at the door. Mrs Foxworthy rushed to open the door and in the next second, they saw another young man waltzing through with Mae in his arms. Her clothes were stained with blood and her trouser leg ripped to the knee, which was bandaged. He set her down on the chair, pulling another forward to rest her injured leg on. Despite her dishevelled appearance Mae still looked devastatingly beautiful even with her cheeks smudged with dirt and greasy smears of oil. Though they could see she was hurt, she didn't appear to be in much pain, and was grinning with pleasure at all the attention.

'Mae, what on earth has happened - are you injured?' said Alice in a concerned voice, rising to her feet and dashing over to her side.

'What on earth's been going on?' said their brother calmly taking in the situation, and coming forward with a hand outstretched. 'I'm Will Milton.'

'Julius Weatherfield, Mr Milton ... how do you do. I'm so sorry, your sister's been in an accident,' he said taking Will's hand and shaking it firmly. 'I've done what I can, and there don't appear to be any breakages ... we had a bit of a collision on the Cockington Road.'

'It was my fault,' Mae insisted, as she was instantly surrounded. 'I'm perfectly well; there's no need for alarm. A lady in a nearby cottage helped dress my arm and bandage my knee.'

'Oh no, you poor thing,' said Alice, 'and I don't expect your poor bicycle came off too lightly, either.'

Mae's hand flew to her mouth and her eyes clouded with tears. 'Please don't be too cross with me Will, I have a dreadful confession to make. ... I was riding your motorcycle when it happened.'

Will looked thunderous for a second or two, but Mr Weatherfield stepped in again.

'I took the liberty of sending it along to my mechanic, and it seems the little damage will be easily rectified at no cost to anyone. He owes me a few favours, and was glad to do it. I hope you don't mind, but I couldn't leave it on the road, and we were just yards from his garage. It seemed the sensible thing to do.'

'That's jolly sporting of you,' said Will. 'Are you sure there will be no costs involved? I couldn't have you putting yourself out.'

'No, I'm happy to help. What an incredible machine ... American, isn't it?'

'Yes, I was lucky enough to buy it over there a few summers ago just after the war.'

'How wonderful ... it's a dream of mine to travel to the states.'

Mae breathed a sigh of relief as she watched them chatting away sharing a common passion for speed and motoring in all its guises. Julius was so charming and kind, however cross Will might feel inside, his own good manners wouldn't betray him.

After all the excitement and drama of the afternoon, there wasn't much time left for shopping. It was three o'clock before they'd finished Mrs Foxworthy's rhubarb crumble and custard, and then Will insisted on taking Mae home immediately, for despite her protests to the contrary, he said she should really be resting after such a shock. Frankie excused himself saying he needed to go to the post office because he was expecting a telegram, and he'd promised to be back by late afternoon to help his brother plant out some seedlings in the garden.

Alice couldn't imagine the glamorous film star getting his hands dirty, but she remembered he'd always loved pottering about in the rectory garden he'd shared with his brother before he moved away. He seemed to have a special way with plants and animals, she thought, they always responded well to the love he lavished on them. Come to think of it, he was just the same with people, and recalled how he'd made her feel cherished like never before. But that was then, and now he'd hardly acknowledged her, all those old confidential glances and secret looks exchanged, long gone.

'Look, I know it's a bit late notice,' Frankie said, standing to his feet and throwing his jacket round his shoulders, 'but we're having a bit of an impromptu party up at the rectory tonight. I don't suppose you'd be able to come, but I'd love it if you could. It'll just be people from the village, the old friends I've bumped into, and some of those army chaps who seem quite spiffingly up for anything. Oh, do say you'll come, and Julius, you must come too.'

Will glanced over at Alice whose quiet nod gave him the go-ahead. 'We'd love to, that's awfully kind, old sport.'

'That's settled then, and if your Ma and Pa wish to come, ask them too. Shall we say eight o'clock, and bring your dancing shoes ... we'll dance the night away.'

Emily and Cora clapped their hands together in unison. 'A party, how exciting!'

Alice was surprised he'd invited Flora and her father, but such was his confidence that he probably knew he wouldn't be rejected again by them, and wouldn't care if they did. She didn't think she'd be able to cope with the idea of a party, and besides, she hadn't a thing to wear. She could feel one of her migraines coming on, and that would suit her just fine. When Frankie left, Alice said she'd return to the castle with Will and Mae, and handed Jane the shopping list, with instructions to Beth to help where she could.

'I've a little headache, I hope you'll excuse me, but I should like to take Mae home, and make sure she's comfortable,' Alice explained.

'I quite understand,' said Jane taking the list and folding it in two, 'take care of yourself. Perhaps you would benefit from having a lie-down, and then you'll be fit for the party.'

Alice smiled rather weakly, Jane thought, and couldn't help wondering if her headache had been a direct result of seeing Frankie Wallis.

In the end, it was Beth, Emily and Cora who accompanied Jane round the shops but she couldn't remember the last time she'd had such an enjoyable time. They stopped in the newsagent's first where the girls chose the latest film magazines, and Jane selected a fashion paper for Mae in the hope that it would cheer her up, and go some way towards offering a hand in friendship, though she had little hope that anything much would be accomplished by one small token.

They carried on to the linendraper's and haberdasher's where Jane felt very spoiled as she chose new sheets, a soft cream blanket, matching pillow cases, a satin eiderdown with a paisley pattern in pastel greens and shell pinks, and after she'd picked them out the proprietor promised to send them up to the castle that very afternoon. A new light bulb was purchased from the ironmonger's along with a small alarm clock, and a few candles, which Jane requested, saying she was used to candlelight at home. Beth insisted she should choose a rug to put next to her bed from the selection of rolled up carpets in a corner of the shop, and Jane managed to find a pretty rose-covered one on a pale ground, with loops of blue forget-me-nots round the edge. Alice had also included a new bookshelf on the list, and having put their order in from the carpenter further along the high street, Jane looked forward to visiting the bookshop to find some volumes to fill it.

'Isn't Frankie the most handsome man you've ever seen?' said Emily with a sigh. 'I hope I get a dance with him later ... and though I would die to dance the Charleston with him, a slow tango might be more thrilling.'

Cora laughed and Beth scolded. 'Emily, you must not be such an outrageous flirt, you'll get a reputation.'

'I bet he's used to more than a mild coquettish teasing,' Emily retorted, 'and at least I wasn't behaving like some of the girls with their noses pressed up against the window ... I was positively restrained.'

'Well, just behave yourself this evening, and don't try and hog all his attention. You never know, he and Alice may want to spend some time together, it's been years since they saw one another.'

'I doubt that,' answered Emily, 'they hardly spoke to one another, if at all, and I didn't see him looking at her, not once.'

Jane didn't quite agree with that assumption. She'd seen the moment their eyes had met confirming her suspicions that once upon a time they had meant a great deal to one another.

The bell tinkled above the door of the bookshop when they walked in, just as Cora said it would, and Jane was delighted to see the shop was exactly as she'd described. It was like an Aladdin's cave, shelves of books lined the walls, and further piles lay in random stacks in front so there was barely room to put one foot in front of the other.

Mr Quance, the bookseller came out from the back of the shop to greet them. Although a fairly young man, he was short, and pale in complexion, having the pallor of one who didn't sit outdoors very often. He wore a maroon velvet frock coat belonging to another age, rather worn on the cuffs and lapels, with slim trousers, and a velvet smoking cap on his head with a long gold tassel.

'Good afternoon, ladies,' he said peering over the top of a pair of pince-nez, 'I hope the Miss Miltons are well?'

'Yes, we're very well, thank you, Mr Quance,' Beth answered politely. 'We'd like to introduce you to Miss Austen who is staying up at the castle. She is a great reader, and we knew she'd love to come and visit your shop.'

'That is most kind, Miss Milton,' said Mr Quance scrutinising Jane from head to foot. 'How do you do, Miss Austen ... is this your first time in Devon?'

'On no, sir, I spent one or two holidays in the near vicinity when I was a child, though I know Dorset slightly better.'

'I am very partial to Lyme Regis and Sidmouth myself.' He took off his spectacles but continued to stare. 'And a very strange stranger it must be, who does not see charms in the immediate environs of Lyme, to make him wish to know it better.'

Jane started in surprise for she remembered penning those very words when writing about the seaside resort in *Persuasion*. But, it was not such a profound statement, and surely many people must have heaped similar praise, and uttered the same words about a place that was so beloved.

'Do you know your namesake's work, Miss Austen?'

'A little,' said Jane, knowing she was not telling the whole truth. She felt it imperative to change the course of the conversation as soon as possible.

'You have a look of her,' he said, almost as if he'd known her, though Jane knew that couldn't be at all possible. 'It's quite uncanny.'

He shuffled through the narrow space between the piles of books to the back of the shop, and appeared again moments later with a book. He opened it up at the frontispiece, carefully peeling back the tissue paper that protected it. Jane recognised it at once as a copy of the little portrait her sister had once painted. Cassandra had wanted to paint her so badly, on several occasions, but Jane disliked sitting still for long, and didn't like seeing her painted image, not wanting to be reminded that her face was too round and her cheeks always so red. To think this hideous picture was actually printed in a book. Even Cassy had acknowledged that it wasn't her best work, and now here was someone who seemed to recognise a likeness from it.

'May I?' she said.

Mr Quance handed over the book for Jane's inspection. It was a biographical work she noted, and feeling very intrigued longed to peruse the pages properly. Though Dr Lyford had told her about some of the success as an author she'd had since she died, she'd not been shown any work of this nature. Had they been kind about her, she wondered?

Beth leaned over to see the picture. 'Oh no,' she said, 'I can't see any resemblance. Do you know of any past relationship to the author, Miss Austen?'

Jane felt her cheeks glowing brighter as she denied it. 'No, though I suppose there is always the possibility of a distant connection.'

'Besides, this portrait of Miss Jane Austen makes her look more than a little bit cross,' Beth continued, 'and that cap is most unbecoming. There is a likeness in the eyes to an extent, and in the curl of her hair on her forehead, but her lids are rather puffy, not at all like our Miss Austen.'

'Quite,' added Jane in complete agreement, 'and I'm sure if Miss Austen were alive today she would not recognise herself from that dreadful daub.'

'Perhaps I was too hasty,' said Mr Quance closing the book, 'though I cannot help thinking what an exquisite possession a good picture of her would be! I would give any money for it. I almost long to attempt her likeness myself.'

Jane regarded the little man with suspicion. There he was again, quoting *Emma* at her. What did he mean by it?

'Well, I will allow you ladies some time to look around ... I shall not be far away should you need me.'

He disappeared once more to the back of the shop. Jane couldn't decide whether to purchase the book or not, then decided against it. After all, it was highly likely she'd read something she didn't like or find out an error or a collection of mistakes, and she didn't need to read a book someone else had written about her life to tell her what had happened. What she really needed was a little book on Devon and its resorts. At the end of her life she'd been writing a book set in a seaside town, and she had an idea to update it in a contemporary setting. A novel or two for some light reading would also be good, though her funds were limited. In the end, unable to decide on a novel, she chose a book on *Devon and its Environs* by a local author, and carrying her newfound treasure she took it along to Mr Quance seated in a chair at the rear of the shop, almost drowning in books. He wrote down the title in a ledger, and noted the price.

'I wonder whether you should like to read a couple of articles about Miss Austen I found in a paper published last year,' he said, removing his cushion and producing the newspaper beneath it. 'E M Forster is a self-confessed admirer of her work, and a noted novelist ... I am sure you know. Have you read *A Room with a View*?'

Jane shook her head. 'I have not, Mr Quance.'

'I'm sure it would be to your taste, Miss Austen, indeed, he learned all he knows from your pen.'

At that precise moment a black kitten sprang onto the desk and looked up at Jane with green eyes. Reaching out she fondled the top of his head and he began to purr loudly.

'Quince is very particular about whom he befriends, Miss Austen, but he's an enormous fan of your books. He loves nothing more than to hear them read out loud.'

She must have misheard him, Jane decided, but now Mr Quance was scrambling round on the floor, searching through pile after pile to find the right book. Perhaps he's not quite right in the head, she mused, because it just wasn't possible that he should know anything about her.

'Ah, here it is,' he said at last, popping up from behind his desk. 'I think you'll find the characters and the plot development very interesting, and whilst he is a great imitator, I've no doubt it was done from love. Take the paper too, and be not afraid to read it, he is exceedingly complimentary.'

Oh, thank you, most kind of you.'

'And, I have just one more book I think you'll find interesting, though I will admit, I have some hesitation in showing you.'

He gave her what Jane could only describe as a meaningful look before he opened a drawer of his desk, and pulled out a volume with the title, *Sanditon*, by Jane Austen, encased in blue-grey boards.

Jane gasped and plumped down on the little chair just in front of the desk. She couldn't help it, for there, in his hands, was the novel she'd started just before her last illness took hold.

'It was published at the beginning of the year.'

'But it's not finished, and besides that, it was to be entitled, *The Brothers*.

'Yes, indeed. Please do not upset yourself, Miss Austen, but you must understand that the six completed novels you wrote, whilst works of genius in themselves, were not enough to satisfy the appetites of your adoring public. They are always wishing there were more.'

Jane was now fully on her guard, and looked around her to make sure Beth, Emily and Cora were still out of earshot. 'Who are you, Mr Quance, and what exactly do you think you are saying?'

'I do apologise most profusely, but I had to be absolutely certain I was addressing the real you, and no one else. We have a mutual friend, Miss Austen who has your best interests at heart.'

As the little kitten sprang onto her lap and settled down, purring louder than ever, the light suddenly dawned and Jane knew in an instant he could only be referring to one person. 'Dr Lyford ... yes, I see.'

Mr Quance nodded. 'We were at the same university, and I moved in some of the literary circles where your work was much admired. Do not blame him for not telling you all you should know. He thought it best for you to learn a little at a time.'

Jane nodded, and took the proffered book to stroke its cover. Her eyes filled with tears. 'Thank you for showing it to me, I never thought I'd see it in print.'

'It's yours, my dear, perhaps you will be inspired to finish it.'

'But, I must pay for it. Please, how much do I owe you?'

Mr Quance covered her hand in his, and gave it a gentle pat. 'Not a penny, my dear, and if I can serve you again in any way, please do not hesitate to call upon me.'

Jane started to protest, but the shopkeeper raised an index finger to his lips. 'Please, Miss Austen, for all the pleasure you have given me and so many others I beg you will accept my small gift. We'll keep this to ourselves ... I should not like the Miss Miltons to get wind of it. I wish you to know I am here if you ever need me, as is my dear friend at Dawlish who hopes you are settling in well.'

Beth, Emily and Cora walked up just then, with a book each. Feeling terribly guilty that she'd not paid a penny for her books, she watched the sisters pay for theirs as Quince stretched and yawned before dropping off to sleep.

Chapter Seven

By the time they'd walked back to the castle along winding lanes with the smell of the sea on the soft summer air, it was time for the dressing bell. Jane almost ran up the stairs to her room knowing she had two whole hours to indulge in a little writing. Seeing her last manuscript in published form had been most inspiring, and she couldn't wait to read it and start writing again. It wouldn't take her long to get ready, she only had one dress to choose from, and she could hardly mount the stairs for her growing excitement. Even if she could only manage two hours a day, it would be enough to write several pages, and at least she'd make a start.

Throwing back the bedroom door she was not prepared for such a change of scene, and her mouth formed a little 'Oh' in surprise. Someone had been into her room and arranged all the purchases from the afternoon. The bed looked sumptuous with its starched pillows and colourful eiderdown, and the pretty rug before it was placed just where her feet would find it. The little clock sat on her bedside table, and there were candelabra studded with fresh candles scattered round the room, on the mantelpiece, on the bookshelf, and on her desk. Above the mantelpiece a beautiful painting of a seascape had been hung, and below it on the shelf was a fragrant arrangement of roses in a cloisonné vase. A fire flickered in the grate, an indulgent luxury, for though the day was cooler as the sun lowered in the sky Jane knew she'd not be there for long to enjoy it. There was only one person who could be responsible for this heavenly space, and her name was Alice, Jane thought.

Remembering the little she'd learned that afternoon she wondered how Alice was faring. That she'd accomplished all this whilst not feeling well and after what must have been a distressing experience, Jane thought showed just another aspect of her extraordinary character, and she was determined to thank her. Putting aside her own selfish desire to indulge in some time on her own for her writing she decided she'd go and find Miss Milton and thank her in person, and on the way downstairs she could leave the magazine she'd bought for Mae with one of the maids. Jane had written a little note to say she was sorry about her accident and hoped she'd soon feel much better. She wasn't sure it would do any good, but she hoped Mae would see it as a gesture of friendship.

The fashion paper dispatched, it was easy to find Alice's room, next to the statue she'd mentioned, but when she got there Jane hesitated. Was she being presumptuous? It was only a moment before she decided to take the risk, and knocked on the door, but when she heard Alice's friendly voice telling her to go in she was sure she'd done the right thing.

'I just wanted to come and say how wonderful my room looks and to thank you for all your kindnesses to me,' said Jane standing just inside the door.

Alice was sitting in a pretty chintz covered chair by the window in a room where time stood still. Pale pink satin and ruffled lace were draped over the bed and at the windows in ruches and flounces, with a profusion of over-blown flowers in paintings and in vases that filled the room. Sunlight filtered through ornate lace panels dotting the Aubusson rug, highlighting the swags of tea roses and sage green garlands.

'Come and sit down, Miss Austen. I am so glad you like your room, but I'm also sorry it did not give you the same welcome when you arrived. It's a work in progress, and we can make it finer yet.'

Jane took the opposite seat. 'Oh no, Miss Milton, please don't trouble yourself further, it is utterly delightful. I don't think I ever had such a pretty room in all my life. I do hope you're feeling better, headaches are so tiresome.'

'I only seem to suffer from them when I cannot face life. It's as if I allow myself to become ill when I could just as easily run away given the chance.'

'I think we all do that to a greater or lesser degree. Sore throats are my weakness, and nobody ever suffered as much or had such bad ones.'

Alice laughed. 'It is easier to be ill than to deal with one's emotions, I find, and if I tell the world to go away and lie in bed for a day or two it passes for a while.'

There was a silence and Jane could see Alice was deep in thought. She didn't want to press her to talk, thinking that she when she did, she'd be ready to confide in her.

'We were engaged briefly,' she said at last. 'Frankie came home horribly injured in the last year of the war. Manberley Castle became a hospital and I helped nurse him back to life. We fell in love during the spring, and in the summer when he was almost fully recovered we spent whatever time we could together. He'd always had ambitions to become an actor, I knew that from the start, and wished him well. When he asked me to marry him I didn't hesitate, though I knew the news might not be received with enthusiasm from my father.'

'Did your father consider his profession unworthy of you?'

'Yes, you might say that,' Alice said. 'Frankie and his brother, who is the vicar at Moorford, were genteel enough but poor, and though my father welcomed the brothers to Manberley at Christmas and on special occasions, they were never mentioned in the same breath when prospective husbands were discussed. Frankie had no money then, of course, but I knew he'd be successful, whatever he chose to do with his life. He was ambitious, and hardworking, and determined to be the best actor that ever lived. I admired his drive and purpose, but my father couldn't see it. I suppose in hindsight I understand he was worried for me. He thought I'd live a life of poverty, but I was very young, and I couldn't understand. Suddenly, it seemed to me that my father was sitting in judgement on the Wallis brothers. They were two young men who'd sacrificed so much, willing to give their lives so that we might live our useless existence. But still the old snobbery survived, and Lord Milton wasn't going to allow a daughter of his to marry a bohemian.'

'I understand how hard that must have been. You could see qualities in Mr Wallis that your father failed to acknowledge.'

'Quite ... and I felt his objections misplaced. Who were we to set ourselves above our neighbours, a dear clergyman and his brother? The Miltons were frittering away a dwindling fortune squandered by my father and his new wife, contributing nothing except providing a building for the wounded whilst we carried on our idle lives.'

'But, yours was evidently a very useful one if you were caring for the wounded. Nursing is hard work, I have had a little experience of it myself.'

'Did you nurse in the war, Miss Austen?'

'No, Miss Milton, but once my brother Henry was dangerously ill, and I stayed with him in London until he was right again. But, that was nothing to the suffering you must have seen.'

'I hope never to see the like again. Frankie was injured but he made a remarkable recovery, and though we were surrounded by death and pain every day, just being with him and talking to him was wonderful. We were so close at one time, I knew his every thought, and he mine.'

'What happened then?'

My father refused permission for us to marry, and Frankie wanted me to leave with him ... elope together, but I couldn't leave Mae, and I realise now I was too much of a coward to go and face an uncertain future. How I have regretted it since, but it felt the right thing to do at the time, and I dread to think what might have happened if I'd gone. Mae is a complicated character at the best of times, even with all the love we try to lavish on her.'

'I think you did the right thing,' said Jane. 'You acted as your conscience dictated, and put your sister first. If you'd run away your father and Mae would have both been distraught. You did what you thought was best and no one could blame you for that.'

'But, if I'd followed my heart and married Frankie, we might have been able to persuade my father to change his mind.'

'You might have, but Frankie might never have been so resolved on proving himself. You let him go, gave him the freedom to pursue his dreams, which was a great gift. If you'd married, life may have been difficult especially if children had come along.'

'I suppose so, though there will always be a part of me that will wonder how it might have turned out.'

'In any case,' said Jane, 'he is not married, and he has come back.'

'And all hope is lost,' said Alice before Jane could say any more.

'There is no longer any spark between us, or any feeling ... our meeting confirmed that. He might as well be married, and I think if my sister Emily has her way that might be a possibility before the end of the summer.'

'Have you no feelings left for him?'

'I don't think I will ever recover from the love I had for Frankie, Miss Austen. But, neither of us are the same, and we are as changed as if our love affair never happened. Besides, I do not think I could marry anyone now. Like so many of the women of my generation, I fear it is too late.'

Jane reached out and placed her warm fingers over those of her companion. 'It's never too late, Miss Milton, please don't give up hope so easily. Believe me, though it has its compensations the life of a spinster is a dreary one.'

'You are young, Miss Austen, I should not put myself on the shelf if I were you. I am twenty-seven next birthday, and cannot fool myself any longer that I am of marriageable age. I have plans to leave, perhaps get some employment in London and lead an independent life. If I could just see Mae settled. All she needs is someone to love her.'

'Promise me you won't do anything hastily,' said Jane feeling comfortable enough to offer advice. 'London is not a place where many survive, and it can be the loneliest place in the world. Forgive me for speaking out, but I spent quite some time in the capital and nothing would ever induce me to live there for all its fine attractions.'

Alice smiled. 'I don't think I could ever be happy being too far away from home ... at least, from Will and Mae. The truth is if I wanted to be independent I would have to move away. No one would treat me seriously here if I declared my intentions. I have a fantasy of working in an office and learning how to use a typewriter, though it is just a dream.'

'There is nothing like staying at home for real comfort,' said Jane, 'though if being completely independent would mean moving away, it must be seriously considered. I have seen the advertisements for typewriters, but I have never seen one used. I must admit I would love to own one.'

'Do you have ambitions to be an author like your namesake?' asked

Alice. 'I've written a little poetry myself, but couldn't possibly attempt to write a novel.'

'I confess I do, though it is a great secret and must not be shared. I have written one or two things in the past, and it is my dream to write something new and see it published. But, I am not sure your stepmother would be pleased to learn of my spending time scribbling away when I should be supervising your sisters.'

'Oh, I'm sure Flora would not mind what you do in your spare time, Jane. I hope you don't mind the informality, but I feel we are becoming such friends.'

'Not at all, Alice, we are friends, indeed. I've always said friendship is certainly the finest balm for the pangs of disappointed love. How wonderful to discover you are a poet, I should love to read some of your poems.'

'And my confession is that I too have nurtured an idea to see them published. What fun it is to find someone with such similar tastes.'

'I shall enjoy having you to discuss writing and books,' added Jane. 'We seem to have so much in common. Tell me, do you enjoy dancing?'

'I used to love it, Jane, but I have not danced for some years now.'

'That seems such a pity. Dancing always seems to take me out of myself. I enjoy it so much, though like you, I have not had the opportunity to dance in recent years or learn the new dances I heard Emily talking about today.'

'But, you will have the chance to do just that this evening,' said Alice. 'The Wallis parties are usually very good, and there is always music and dancing.'

'And you'll be able to dance too,' said Jane watching Alice's face. 'You are coming, aren't you?'

'I do not think I can face it. There are too many memories, too many emotions that might come spilling out, and I do wish everybody else to have a wonderful time.'

'I understand perfectly,' said her new friend, 'though you will be sorely missed.'

'If I could just persuade Mae to rest her injuries I should have an excellent excuse, but I have a feeling that seeing Julius Weatherfield again will be high on her list of priorities.'

'Even if she can't dance.'

'I am certain my sister will be more than happy to sit out every one for a chance to get to know Mr Weatherfield better, though I feel sure Captain Bartlett will get his nose put out of joint.'

'Is Captain Bartlett in love with your sister?'

'He has not declared himself, but it is very obvious that he likes her. He is in his thirties, and a very sweet man though Mae thinks he's as old as the hills.'

'Oh dear, I pity the poor captain. At least if she cannot dance then she won't be able to disappoint either of them.'

'Oh, Miss Austen, if only that were true.'

Alice didn't make an appearance at dinner as Jane suspected might happen, but all the other Miltons were in attendance along with Lady Milton's friend King Zoot. Despite the mutton stew, which was tough and thin in equal parts, everyone was already in a party mood, except for Lord Milton who complained that he had better things to do than frolic at functions.

'I see quite enough of the local village vicars on Sundays,' he said, 'without having to socialise with them.'

'Albert, you are such a spoilsport,' said Lady Milton. 'I am longing to meet Eddie's brother again, he's quite a celebrity in Hollywood now, and filthy rich, I've heard.'

'I don't hold with the stage, as well you know.'

'Well, it didn't stop you from courting me, did it, dear? You weren't so fussy when you used to come calling at the Gaiety in the old days, or at the Kit Cat club.'

'Ha, hardly the same thing, and everyone loves a bit of harmless hoofing. You were a wonderful Gaiety girl, my dear, and I was the envy of every aristo in the land. No, my objection to the theatre and those ridiculous silent films is that they are crammed with so-called actors, and aesthetes from objectionable backgrounds who set themselves up as stars and such-like. And then they expect their audiences to fawn on them as if they were royalty ... well, I'll not be a party to it, if you'll forgive the pun.'

'Just as you please,' said Lady Milton. 'Zoot will be happy to take me and dance all night if he doesn't thrill the crowd with a performance. The boys are coming, aren't they?'

King Zoot's brown eyes twinkled as he let out a baritone laugh which seemed to bubble up from the depths of his very being and shake his large frame like one of Mrs Wickens's jellied confections.

'They haven't let me down yet, and with the added attractions of a few free nights at the Tolleywicks Inn in the village I'm assured if charabancs and high spirits combine to play their part, we'll see them yet.'

Zoot's news was rewarded with loud cheers from Emily and Cora who couldn't have been more pleased and excited. From across the table Jane discovered Will was staring at her once again, and from the way he winked at her and gave a little laugh, she was sure he'd been able to read her every thought.

Chapter Eight

Jane followed the others out to the waiting cars, and hung back, unsure in which car she'd be invited to take a seat. Lady Milton stepped out first, arm-in-arm with Zoot, and Jane watched as he opened the door of his splendid automobile and Flora's long legs slid sensuously into the place next to the driver's seat. Emily, Beth and Cora clambered excitedly into the back seat, which left Mae standing on her own, pulling a sulky face. She looked for a moment as if she'd turn and get into Will's car at his suggestion, but Jane noticed the look of disdain from Mae as their eyes met in a moment of realisation. Mae was soon heard complaining that she wasn't travelling on her own with the paid help, and shouted at the others to budge up. No amount of Lady Milton's insistence that she travel in Will's car had any effect, whilst Jane stood by, feeling completely mortified by the episode, the sound of grumbling voices exclaiming over crushed dresses and squashed limbs as the engine purred into action and drove away.

'I'm so sorry about that, it looks like it's just you and me, baby doll,' said Will.

'I'm no baby, and far from being doll-like,' said Jane crossly, thinking that she might just turn round and walk back to the house. 'I never heard such a ridiculous phrase. I suppose it's this new slang I've heard much about; whatever does it mean?'

'It's a term of endearment, but one I shall never use again within your hearing, Miss Austen,' Will answered in a cool and detached manner. 'Forgive me, but I imagined you would find it amusing or at the very least, that you had a sense of humour.'

Jane noticed the impish light in his eyes had gone and felt sorry she'd been so waspish. She felt suitably chastened, and couldn't think why she'd snapped at him so quickly even if it was the silliest expression she'd ever heard. She didn't want to admit that she'd suffered so many assorted feelings of unease and helplessness, coupled with a mixture of indignation and furious pride at Mae's uncalled for reaction, or that she felt extremely nervous being around him. And what was worse, she knew she must look hugely flustered.

'Your carriage awaits,' said Will in a formal tone, his expression closed and serious as he opened the back door with a flourish.

'Would you mind terribly if I sat in the front seat?' Jane asked. The thought of catching those eyes of his in the mirror was too disconcerting. At least if she sat next to him she could look straight ahead at the road.

'Not at all, Miss, allow me.'

He held the door for her and took her hand as she stepped forward. It was a gentlemanly gesture, but totally unnecessary, and though she allowed his fingers to grip hers as he handed her in, she pulled her hand away as soon as she could. Smoothing her dress down with her fingers she could not rub away the warmth of his touch or his fragrance, a spicy scent of sandalwood and ginger, which lingered on the air. Worse still, the hood of the car was closed, and when he climbed in and sat beside her, she realised the space was more confined than she'd imagined. He was tall, and though slim, he was a well-built man with a large frame and broad shoulders. He seemed to fill the car and there was the smallest gap between them. As he adjusted the wheel she watched his long fingers flex then tense on the stitched leather and felt the merest touch of his long leg brush against hers. Jane flinched and edged as closely to the door as possible, feeling overwhelmingly claustrophobic, reaching for the window handle even though she didn't know exactly how it operated. Will immediately leaned across her to help, and though apologetic, she was so close to his cheek she thought she could have kissed it. It was all over in a moment, and with cheeks to match the scarlet leather seats, Jane looked purposefully out through the window, gulping in breaths of the sea air as Will started the engine and pulled away.

'Thank you for trying to persuade Alice to come,' he said at last, breaking the awkward silence. 'I tried too, but she insisted she was feeling unwell.'

Jane was glad the conversation was taking a turn. 'I think the afternoon took its toll, understandably.'

'Yes, I should have known it would be too much. I shouldn't have expected so much or put her in that position in the first place. I feel awfully selfish.'

'Alice wants you to be able to keep up your friendship with Mr Wallis,' Jane said warmly, 'and above all, she wished everyone to enjoy the party. Anyway, perhaps it will do some good. Mr Wallis might realise what he's missing.'

'I'd love you to be right, Miss Austen, but there are no feelings left on either side now. It was all over a long time ago, I'm afraid.'

Jane said nothing. As far as she could see the two people in question were still very much aware of each other, pointedly ignoring one another the entire time, possibly with feelings decidedly unchanged. If that didn't tell her something about their true feelings then she decided she'd lost her touch. Human nature, its follies and inconsistencies did not alter, and she'd made a study of many personalities in her short life. From what she'd seen Alice and Frankie couldn't even look one another in the eye for more than a few seconds. If there'd been no feelings left at all she was convinced they'd have spent all afternoon happily chatting over old times and looking the other squarely in the eyes.

'What did you think of Julius Weatherfield?' asked Will. 'Seems a good sort to me. He plainly likes Mae, and she him.'

'I think it's a little early to say, but if charm and good looks are anything to go by I would say, on first impression, that he has all the requisites to captivate the heart of any young girl, and especially one who seems quite a vulnerable personality.'

'You don't sound too sure about him.'

'I'd rather take my time to form an opinion about anyone, Mr Milton. During my lifetime I have discovered it's wise to be cautious in these matters.'

Will chuckled. 'For one so young I'm not sure you can have had that much experience, surely. You sound like Flora who is twice your age. Perhaps you've had your heart broken once or twice ... is that it?'

Jane looked down at the hands nervously clasped in her lap. She must sound quite ludicrous, she realised. 'I'd just rather spend a little time getting to know someone.'

'And have you formed an opinion on me yet, Miss Austen, or is it too early to tell?'

'I haven't exactly a clear picture of your character, but then, I hardly know you. We have shared but three short conversations on trivial matters, and I am no wiser about your opinions on the important subjects of life than on the very first day I met you. So far I have learned you are capable of lying and duping the innocent, though in other respects you appear to be a loyal friend and a caring sibling.'

'So my charm and good looks have not yet lured you into captivation on an entirely different level?'

'Mr Milton, it may be your ambition in life to enthral as many ladies as you can, but not all women are enchanted by handsome looks and a few good manners alone. Most require something else, intellectual stimulation, brilliant conversation, or an interest in shared pursuits. It is not enough to fall in love with someone based simply on their physical attributes. And to return to our earlier discussion on your sister I would say it is clear there is an attraction between her and Mr Weatherfield, but if Mae were my sister I'd just keep an eye on things for a while.'

'Yes, you're right, and I will. It's easy to see how attracted Mae is to him. Poor George Bartlett, he's going to find he has a little competition this evening. He's head over heels in love with Mae, and while she tolerates his attentions it's always been clear there's no spark on her side. It's a great pity, George is a good man and he's also wealthy. His estate at Sherford Park is well worth marrying for, though I've heard Mr Weatherfield has his own place at Salcombe Magna.'

'Well, Mae has youth, beauty, and is keen to be loved. I'm sure they won't be the only gentlemen vying for her affections. Older brothers have their work cut out when it comes to looking after their sisters.'

'You speak as if from experience. And now I am sure I have guessed correctly. Did you give your brothers much trouble at home? You've left a string of broken hearts behind you, I am sure.'

Jane didn't answer. She knew he was teasing her, and suspected he was enjoying having a little fun at her expense. But she didn't mind. He could not possibly have guessed, but the truth was she had broken a few hearts in her time, and had known what it was to fall in love several times, flirtatiously, fleetingly, but also with a long and lasting passion.

They were soon arrived at Moorford, an idyllic village with the church and Georgian rectory at its heart, a triangular green before it and a scattering of thatched cottages around the edge. Jane was reminded of her former home at Steventon as she walked up to the central front door with windows blazing with light on either side. Apart from the sound of jazz music drifting across the lawns she could have imagined herself running inside to greet her beloved father. The door was open and on entering the hall, Jane still felt the space seemed familiar with its pair of demi-lune tables adorned with blue and white porcelain, a central lantern strung up on a long chain, gilt candelabra, and a grandfather clock ticking loudly in the corner. A maid appeared to usher them into the drawing room on the left, and when they walked in a loud cheer went up.

The room was noisy with chatter and music. King Zoot's band was in full swing on one side of the room enthralling their audience with a quick-paced set. Everyone else looked as if they'd already been made very comfortable, and they were all sipping cocktails as they lounged on comfy sofas and wing chairs from a bygone age.

Frankie Wallis and a man who could be no one else but his brother, sauntered over with a tray of champagne glasses filled with golden bubbles.

'Will and Miss Austen, so pleased you could come,' said Frankie. 'Let me introduce Eddie who is my big brother, and a dab hand at mixing dangerous drinks. We have a champagne cocktail tonight which is guaranteed to get you in the party mood.'

'Eddie was always a dab hand,' said Will with a smirk. 'He learned everything he knows at theological college, Miss Austen.'

Eddie grinned, and handed Jane a glass. 'Of course I did. What else was there worth studying after bible class?'

The resemblance between him and Frankie was striking though he was not so fashionably dressed. He had a kind face, and whilst his hair was not quite as fair as Frankie's, his eyes were the same intensity of green.

Will leaned over to whisper in Jane's ear as the brothers moved on to replenish glasses elsewhere. 'He's probably more your type, Miss Austen. Good looks and intelligence combined, and what's more, he has a wealthy brother who would keep the wolf from the door, or at least supplement a clergyman's poor stipend.'

'Mr Milton, I am not here to find a husband, nor am I interested in marriage. Eddie Wallis seems a very pleasant young man, but he is neither my type nor to my taste, and I would be grateful if you'd cease trying to engage my heart in any way, shape or form.'

'Miss Austen, I shall endeavour to do as you say, though I fear you protest too much. It is clear there is a strong attraction.'

'I have known my fair share of clergymen in my time ... indeed, my father was one, and two of my brothers took orders. But, having said that, I would never be inclined to marry one. I am here to fulfil my obligations to your family, and to earn my living. An independent life is the one I seek. I like my own company, and do not need a man.'

'And your mother was a suffragette, I suppose.'

Jane had lately read about women's suffrage and admired the work of the movement. Will was being truly insufferable.

'Mr Milton, I wholly endorse the work of women who are putting their lives at risk to achieve what is only fair and right. Do you not believe women should be entitled to the vote?'

'Of course, I didn't mean to sound flippant, I ...'

Jane cut him off in mid-sentence. 'Thank you kindly for escorting me here, Mr Milton, but I will pay my respects to your family now, if you please.'

Will watched her walk away with some amusement. He couldn't put his finger on why he enjoyed teasing her so much, but he supposed it was because she was such an open person, and not too clever at hiding her feelings. He had her well and truly rattled, he was sure.

Jane was glad that she'd finally put Will in his place. There was a lot to be said for having the experience and wit that comes with age, but coupled with the energy of a much younger person. Having met the type before, she couldn't help thinking about a former love, Tom Lefroy, the first scoundrel who'd broken her heart. He'd been very pleased with himself too, and had flirted outrageously with her. Her sister had warned her, but she'd chosen not to listen, and when he broke all his promises to her she was left feeling hurt. Of course she'd written much of the bitterness away and thrown herself into writing novels where she alleviated her feelings, but she'd been wary of men for a long time after that.

Lady Milton was sitting next to a smartly dressed young man in his mid-thirties with a kind face. Jane guessed immediately he must be Captain Bartlett from the way his gaze was fixed on Mae's lovely face at every opportunity, even though he tried to look attentive to his companion's conversation. Mae, in turn, had her attention set in rapt wonder upon Mr Weatherfield's face, evidently enthralled with his effusive chat. Jane watched the way they couldn't take their eyes from the other as they sat closely together on a chintz-covered sofa. Mae was running her fingers through her golden-brown curls and he was leaning into her, as if he needed to get closer to hear her responses. There was a great attraction between them, Jane could plainly see. Behind them Emily stood talking to another man, of a similar age to the captain. She was laughing at something he was saying, and holding on to his arm in an affectionate way. They seemed to be sharing a joke, and with him mocking her in a brotherly way, she was tapping him playfully on the arm.

'That's Jonathan Keeling,' said Beth, coming to stand next to Jane and following her direct gaze. 'I'll introduce you when he comes over. He and Emily have always been close. I think he sees her like the little sister he lost. It's a tragic tale, Eleanor died of tuberculosis when she was just twelve years old. He has a married brother who lives in Exeter, but we've always been like a family to him, and Emily is his protégée.'

Jane saw Jonathan smile indulgently at Emily, just a second before Frankie joined the pair with fresh drinks. Emily eased her arm out of Jonathan's and practically turned her back on him, chattering with a fresh animation and flicking back her hair in the habitual way she had. Jonathan looked unconcerned and turned his attention to another young lady Jane hadn't noticed before who was standing with an older, rather sensibly dressed lady who looked completely out of place.

'That's Miss Beales, and her niece Jessie,' added Beth. 'They run the milliner's in the village, and live above the shop. Mr Keeling is always so kind to them. They don't have much in the way of treats, but he makes sure they have everything they need and a few luxuries into the bargain.'

'I am beginning to like Mr Keeling very much,' said Jane. 'It's a pity Emily doesn't like him as much as he obviously likes her.'

'Oh, I don't think he's fond of her like that,' said Beth, 'and in any case, I think we can see just where she's setting her sights.'

Emily was brushing something off Frankie's sleeve, and Jane observed a look of concern flash across Beth's face. She was just wondering what to say, when yet another gentleman, coming into the room, gained their attention. When he saw Beth his face lit up, and she seemed equally happy to see him.

'Miss Austen, please allow me to introduce Lieutenant Dauncey,' Beth said as soon as he joined them. 'He's new to the area, but is doing his best with the captain to protect our shores.'

'How do you do, Miss Austen,' said the lieutenant, smiling into her eyes. 'I'm sure you'll agree that to be a newcomer in such a friendly place as Stoke Pomeroy has its compensations. I've never met with such delightful neighbours here at Moorford or in our own village.'

'I've been made to feel very welcome, Lieutenant Dauncey,' Jane agreed, 'but am yet to really find my bearings. I'm looking forward to exploring the area.'

'Have you been down to the beach yet? We're thinking of having a picnic there tomorrow if you'd care to join us.'

'Well, I'm not really sure of our plans, and what Lady Milton might have in mind.'

'Do say you'll come, Miss Austen,' urged Beth. 'We'll all be going, even Mae, and I know Flora won't mind one bit. She'll expect you to chaperone us, I'm sure.'

Jane was a little shocked to hear Beth address her mother by her Christian name, but then it wasn't the first time she'd heard it used by the Milton offspring, and she wondered if it was Flora Milton's preference. She had an idea Lady Milton wouldn't be too keen for people to realise she was old enough to have grown-up children, and it would be typical of someone so keen to give the impression of youthfulness to have them address her by name.

'In that case, I'd be delighted,' Jane said. 'It's a long time since I spent a day by the seaside. I always enjoy watching the sea.'

'I was fortunate to grow up by the coast,' said Lieutenant Dauncey, 'between St Just and Sennen in Cornwall.'

'I love Cornwall, don't you, Miss Austen?' said Beth. 'It always seems to be a place redolent with drama. Devon has its undulating valleys, but the rugged Cornish coastline is something else.'

'I have never travelled so far west,' answered Jane truthfully, 'though I've heard the scenery is unlike any other. I believe the area you speak of is famous for tin mining, Lieutenant Dauncey.'

'Yes, indeed, Miss Austen. I was brought up in a house built entirely on the profits from that industry, a vast estate. You may have heard of Rosamorna, it is well documented as the inspiration for many a dark romance novel.'

'Sadly not, though I'm sure with such a delightful name, it must be a beautiful place. Do you manage to go home often?'

'I wish I could say so, but I've not been back for many years, Miss Austen.'

'Lieutenant Dauncey's life history is a sorry saga, his awful story could be in a novel of its own,' added Beth.

'It is a bit of a tale,' he continued and stopped to take a slug of his drink. 'I was lucky enough to be adopted by the Dauncey family who'd mined the area for two hundred years. My adored mother, unable to have any more children, chose me after a visit to the local orphanage to be a young brother and companion for the heir of Rosamorna.'

'Goodness, that does sound like the beginning of a promising plot for a fairy tale,' said Jane.

'One might think so, but you don't know the whole story, Miss Austen,' said Beth. 'The lieutenant's beloved father and mother tragically died in a motoring accident in the south of France.'

'I'm sure lots of people know what it is to lose a beloved parent,' said Lieutenant Dauncey.

'Yes, but you were unfortunate enough to lose both at once, and with the most awful after effects,' Beth went on passionately. 'May I tell Miss Austen the particulars?'

Lieutenant Dauncey looked hesitant for a moment, as if he might say no to Beth's request, but she was determined to say her piece.

'Not only did he lose his parents which was quite dreadful enough, but his step-brother, the very one he'd been a companion to all his life, found fault with the wishes included in the will. As a result, he found himself homeless and penniless shortly after the funeral.'

'How perfectly dreadful, Lieutenant Dauncey, but did you not attempt to contest the will?' asked Jane, knowing how such matters easily ruptured family relationships.

He twisted the glass in his hands and looked down at the floor. 'It was made very clear to me that I was no longer welcome in my own home, and not yet having come into my money I was powerless against the lawyers who were immediately placed against me. The will that was presented was an old one, and with no mention of my existence there was nothing I could do.'

'And did your brother do nothing to help you?' asked Jane.

The young man shook his head. 'Not a thing, I'm afraid. I always knew I wasn't to inherit property, but I did think there might be a little money to see me on my way in life.'

'Fergus Dauncey sounds like a ghastly beast, and if I ever met him I'd give him a piece of my mind,' declared Beth. 'No one could have suffered and borne it all as you have.'

'Well, dearest Beth, I came into this world with nothing, and at least I have found my own way, which is perhaps for the best.' Lieutenant Dauncey shifted slightly, looking rather uncomfortable for a moment. 'Still, let us not dwell on such gloomy thoughts. With such a night as this, could life be any better? I hope you'll excuse us, Miss Austen, but I've been dying to ask Beth for a dance.'

Beth looked pleased and excited as Jane watched them walk hand-in-hand over to the end of the room where the carpet had been rolled up and removed to make a dance floor. There was a romance in the making she thought, and Lieutenant Dauncey seemed like a nice enough fellow even if his relations sounded perfectly horrid. He was very good-looking and charming, which was always helpful, but she wondered if Lady Milton considered him as a suitable marriage partner. She was sure her ambitions for her daughters were set much higher, involving copious amounts of money, which could be ciphered into Manberley's coffers.

Beth and her handsome soldier were first on the dance floor. Jane knew it wouldn't be long before some of the others would be up and dancing, though she was quite unprepared for the strange sight of waving arms and legs, and the frenetic movement in all directions when it started. Jane stood and stared; she'd never seen anything like it. This must be the Charleston they'd all been talking about. Deciding at that precise moment that to hide in a corner or another room would be an excellent idea, she'd never wished so much that she could just vanish and disappear in a puff of smoke. Emily and Frankie were the most enthusiastic of all the couples, certainly the most adept, and for all the oddity of the dancing, Jane liked watching them for their obvious joy and verve. They were enjoying themselves so much, competing with the other to make the most outrageous moves.

As she observed them all Jane saw Jonathan kindly ask Jessie, who'd been sitting on her own, up to dance. Clearly timid and shy, she hesitantly smiled and took his hand. Eddie partnered Lady Milton, whilst Captain

Bartlett danced rather awkwardly with Miss Beales who seemed completely out of her depth, but was eager to please.

'Captain Bartlett, I'm very honoured to dance with you,' Nora Beales began, her hands twisting awkwardly on her knees, 'it's so very kind of you to take pity on me. Isn't it a lovely party? I feel quite as if I've been transported to Scheherezade's magic garden! Everywhere looks so pretty and sparkling with the candles lit, and have you seen the paper lanterns up on the terrace? It brings to mind that lovely painting by John Singer Sargent. Oh, what's it called? You know, it's in the Tate gallery … it mentions all the flowers … something like Lily Rose, and Carnations. Well, I don't think that's quite the right title, I've forgotten now, but it looks just like that now the sun is setting. All that's missing is two little girls in white dresses.'

Captain Bartlett tried hard to pay his full attention. He was used to Miss Beales wittering away with endless questions whilst not requiring an answer to any of them. Every now and then he smiled at her, which seemed reward enough, and he turned to look once more upon Mae's beautiful face. He couldn't help sighing. Though he'd always suspected he only had a slim chance to gain her heart, he decided he really must look about to fall in love elsewhere. He was sure Mae was falling in love with Julius Weatherfield, and though it might only be an infatuation disguised, he knew when he was beaten. George looked around with an eye to see if anyone else would strike him as a suitable partner in the dance as well as in life. But as much as he tried, he could not help his eyes returning to the face he loved best.

The only other person who seemed to be sitting the dance out was Cora. Jane felt rather sorry for her; it was easy to see how she longed to dance. The room was filling up now with people she didn't recognise, all streaming in through the doors to pack themselves onto the dance floor. Cora hugged her knees, and her chin drooped, but as Jane watched, she suddenly saw her face light up. Will was there to take her hand, and lead her off to whirl her round. It was lovely to watch them both, Cora followed every movement as well as she could, and when she was unsure of the steps Jane could see Will patiently showing her what to do. He was a very good dancer Jane had to admit, though she would never have told him so.

On the far side, there was a glimpse of another room through open folding doors where an overspill of people were chattering and laughing. When she was sure no one was watching she moved through the crushing crowds into what seemed to be another sitting room with book-lined shelves. Beyond were French doors leading out onto a terrace, with wonderful views over the valley and steps leading down to a sunken garden. Roses bloomed over an arbour fixed at points along the terrace, and the scent on the evening air made Jane feel she'd been transported to some foreign clime she'd once read about. There was no one else in sight and leaning on the balustrade she watched the sun lowering in the sky sending blue shadows over the black and white tiles, setting the pots of white lilies aflame. A few Chinese lanterns bobbed in the warm breeze above her head, blushing pink as if lit by glow-worms. It was incredible to think she'd found such a peaceful haven, and though she knew she couldn't stay there all night, at least it gave her a little respite from all the frenzied activity inside. The music floated out on the scented air, and she could imagine them all kicking up their heels, until there was a pause and tumultuous applause broke out, and a loud voice announced a foxtrot to slow down the pace so they could get their breath back. Jane couldn't imagine what that dance could be, and couldn't help picture a sly fox with a waving bushy tail trotting his way down a henhouse full of plump birds. She laughed out loud for it really was a ridiculous picture.

'Is it a good joke?' said a voice behind her.

Spinning round she came face to face with Will, the last person she expected to see.

Chapter Nine

'I've never heard of a foxtrot and I've got a wild imagination.'

As soon as the words were out she thought how gauche she must sound.

'Goodness, you've led a more sheltered existence than I thought,' Will exclaimed. 'I was just coming to ask you to dance.'

'I'm not sure that would be possible or appropriate, Mr Milton,' Jane answered, searching for the right words. 'I cannot dance, nor do I have any wish to make an exhibition of myself.'

It was an attempt to put him off, and even though she knew the reverse was true, that she loved nothing better than to dance, she'd already decided that to start again by having to learn modern dances to the music that was starting to jangle noisily and persistently in her head, would be impossible. She liked to be the best at everything, to excel at all she endeavoured to try. Failure was not a word she liked or allowed in her vocabulary, and besides all that, the memories of the past were crowding in on her.

She saw a line of eager young bucks, all waiting to take her hand in the dance. As if seeing from a distance, a familiar room glowed with candlelight and exquisite chandeliers, as Tom Lefroy took her arm, squeezed her hand, and led her through the intricate patterns, whirling her round in a country dance. The room throbbed with passions unspoken, of bodies meeting, fingers touching, hearts and minds open to tacit thoughts and caresses. And later, stolen kisses and a sweet promise beyond the confines of the house, now blazed across her memory and the gulf of time, as swift and searing as if it had happened yesterday.

'I don't believe you,' Will was saying as Jane jerked back to reality when she heard his insistent voice. 'You have the definite look of a dancer to me. Come on, let me teach you.'

He came to stand next to her leaning his weight with crossed arms on the balustrade as she did, and Jane hoped he wouldn't see the tears that sprang to her eyes blurring her vision and thoughts. It was silly to be so stirred up and emotional at thoughts of the past, but she was overwhelmed by a sudden desire for all that she had ever known, and for all those she had loved. She longed to share a conversation with someone who spoke the same language in the cadences and timbre of her youth, and to feel a kinship and connection with every living creature in her own time, sharing an appreciation of what was expected, whilst operating within a familiar system. And although she'd often railed against such conventions, she almost craved such customary restrictions now. Knowing she couldn't go back made her feel worse, and she had to focus her mind to bring herself back from sudden despair. Blinking back the tears she turned to see Will looking into the distance, and for the first time she thought she saw a look of vulnerability. There was an expression of sadness in his eyes as if he might be far away in his thoughts too.

'I'll be a poor pupil, I'm certain,' she said, finally giving in to his pleading expression. 'And I'm supposed to be chaperoning your sisters, not trotting about.'

She nearly added, 'like a fox', but the uncharitable thought crossed her mind that if anyone were like a fox it was Will with his chestnut brown hair, and she cast herself as a plump hen with ruffled feathers waiting to be snaffled up after one easy pounce.

'Are you changing your mind?' he said, turning to face her with a smile that spread to his velvet eyes, sloe black and glittering in the dying light. 'Have I convinced you to dance with me?'

'I hardly know,' she muttered before he caught hold of her, pulling her arm gently towards him until she released her tight grip on the stone rail, and took her hands in his own.

'Let me help,' he said, easing his right arm round her waist and coming to stand so closely before her that she felt the blush spread like madder rose paint on a sheet of moist watercolour paper. Jane felt his fingers pressing into the small of her back, and he held her other hand aloft. Part of the trouble was that the music kept stopping, and being so close in the twilight calm felt so intimate. She was sure any onlooker would think she was allowing herself to be insulted at his will, and then laughed inside at the idea of being "willed by Will" to such bad behaviour.

'First, take a step onto your right foot towards me,' he instructed as the music struck up once more, 'and then just a small one back again. Follow me after that, and you won't go wrong.'

She was not prepared for what happened next as she obeyed his instructions to the letter. As she stepped back, so he pulled her against him, following quickly through on the advance with three rapid steps, until there was no space left between them. Jane allowed him to guide her, though she could feel the shirt buttons of his dinner shirt pressing into the silk of her dress, and his leg moving against her knee, brushing her thigh. His head was next to hers, she felt his skin, and his breath warm and fragrant on her hair. Suddenly, it was too much, too soon, and the coiling spiral of desire curling in delicious sensations from the pit of her being, struck her forcibly. Jane stopped, and pulled back. He saw the fear in her eyes, and her face flushed with crimson. Will knew he'd gone too far, and felt sorry that he had. It really hadn't been his intention to frighten her or take advantage of her innocence.

As if she could read his mind, she was determined not to stay a moment longer. Perhaps she had made an utter fool of herself by over-reacting, but she knew she didn't want to allow herself to experience feelings like those ever again. It was a lifetime since she'd felt such physical longing for another human being or been so close to a man.

'I'm sorry, Will, I don't feel like dancing any more,' she said, and averting her eyes from those dark ones that were studying hers intently, she dashed away.

Will watched her light figure skipping over the black and white tiles to escape back through the French doors as quickly as she could. At least she'd called him 'Will', he thought, though he was certain it was quite by accident, but surely that meant they were making some progress, even if it wasn't quite correct to think of her in terms like that. Good lord, what was he doing, thinking that way? He wasn't even attracted to her, he thought, least of all by her dimples in that too round face or by those hazel eyes that resembled amber jewels lit in sunshine. Why had she reacted so badly? He'd only asked her to dance, and now he really couldn't understand why he'd bothered. If she wanted to play being a stuck-up governess, that was fine. He was only trying to be kind, after all, and make her feel more at home. Miss Austen was such a prissy young thing, and too full of her own self-importance. What gave her the right to be so puffed up, and superior? He'd never known anyone like her, and he couldn't fathom just what it was that he found so fascinating on the one hand and disenchanting on the other. He decided to ignore her from now on, and let her get on with doing what she clearly loved best, feeling herself to be high and mighty above them all.

Mae and Julius were still glued to the other's side when Jane walked back in to the room. Mae thought she didn't care how much that disapproving governess stared, to say she was enjoying herself was an understatement, and she was going to stay exactly where she was, right by Julius's side. Generally aware that she had a devastating effect on men, Mae was confident that Julius was attracted to her as much as she was to him. Besides the fact that her slight form was ravishingly swathed in turquoise blue chiffon and pink roses, a panniered *robe de style* gown designed by Lanvin a couple of years ago and sent from Paris by her aunt, Lady Celia Broughton, Mae knew that Julius hadn't been able to take his eyes off her all evening. The conversation between them was effortlessly flowing, and they'd discussed mutual subjects of admiration. She knew he liked playing tennis as much as she did, and couldn't wait until she was fit enough to play against him. They'd talked about their love of art, the bohemian lifestyles of the Newlyn painters, and the Cornish artists like Laura and Harold Knight whose paintings were filled with light. They shared the same romantic ideals when it came to literature too, admiring the writers and artists of the Bloomsbury set with their unconventional lifestyle.

'How I should love to be set free, and live the life of a truly liberated spirit,' said Mae earnestly. 'I have never cared much about conforming to society's constraints … all I ask is an independent allowance and a string of admirers to call on me in my very own London flat every day. Of course, I would not like to idle my life away entirely. I'd be happy to spend time dabbling in watercolours, perhaps, or doing charitable works.'

'And spend your evenings in jazz clubs dancing the night away, I suppose. It sounds like fun ... but I don't suppose you'd have a spare room for a friend, would you? I love nothing more than expressing myself in oils.'

'For you, darling Julius, anything might be possible,' Mae answered knowing she was being completely outrageous.

'So, you're not a country girl at heart? You wouldn't miss Devon and its glorious coastline if you were cooped up in smoky London?'

'Well, of course I would prefer to divide my time between the two if I could. There is nowhere like the sea for inspiration. I love to paint *en plein air* ... there is nothing better than to be out in the elements for capturing the light.'

'I quite agree. I wish you could see my place at Salcombe Magna, which I'm sure would be just to your taste. It's utter perfection for painting sweeping landscapes. The house is set in a valley very close to the sea against a backdrop of lush green ... you must come and see it sometime.'

Mae could not contain her excitement. 'It sounds perfect, Julius, when can we go?'

'We'll take a drive there as soon as you're mended and you're fit enough to walk all over it. Some of the walks down to the sea are only accessible by foot, and I'd hate you to miss seeing the private beach or the summerhouse I've had built there.'

'Do you live all alone?'

'I have been on my own for some years now, but I'm used to it. I usually spend the winters in London and the house is left empty until the first of May when I come home. It's at its best in summer ... Salcombe Magna can be rather gloomy in the depths of winter. There were catastrophic shipwrecks in the area in the past, and when the wind is high and the stormy sea bashes the rugged rocks of the coastline on a grim

February night, one can almost imagine you can hear the cries of the dead and wounded calling for help.'

'How dreadful for you. I believe in ghosts, or at least feel that there are vibrations left behind in ancient places and buildings, especially where there might have been tragedy or suffering of any kind. I can just imagine how that might be the case by the sea. I often feel an overwhelming sense of sadness when I look out over a vast ocean. It's as if the disappointed hopes of all the people who have stood there have been trapped in the water to rise out of its depths when a like-minded someone pauses to contemplate time and space.'

'How wonderfully poetic,' said Julius, 'I just know you will love the house ... there isn't a more romantic place, or one so in harmony with its surroundings. Promise me you'll be healed very soon.'

'It's only a twisted ankle and a swollen knee. My elbow is healed already, and I'm sure I'll be completely better by next week. In any case, I'm certain everything will be cured all the quicker if you promise to visit me until I can visit you.'

Julius took up her tiny hand and kissed it. 'That's a deal, Mae, you have my word, I promise.'

Lady Milton introduced Jane to Captain Bartlett just as they were coming off the dance floor. As soon as she'd done it, Flora was off, making a quick excuse that she had to make sure King Zoot and the band were being looked after. It was obvious the captain wasn't a great talker, and Jane felt at a loss to know how to steer the conversation. There was an awkward moment or two whilst she thought about whether she should be the first to speak, but she could see he was struggling, searching for the right words.

'Do you live far from here, Captain Bartlett?' she started to say, and then wished she'd thought of something more interesting or original to say.

'I have a house at Sherford,' he answered, 'just a couple of villages away. It's on the estuary with some fine views towards Exeter in the distance. But you, Miss Austen, are not a native of these shores, I believe.'

'No, I daresay my Hampshire accent gives me away though I have lived in many places as well as in that beloved county. I spent some time in Bath, Southampton, and Winchester, as well as in Steventon and Chawton. Yet, I am sure that does not impress a soldier. I suppose you have travelled in your job, captain, and probably to places I have never been.'

'I spent a lot of time travelling, it is true, and particularly in India, Miss Austen.'

'India is a fascinating continent. I had an aunt who lived there for some years and my cousin was born there although they left for England a few years later. I used to bombard Eliza with questions about her time spent in such different surroundings to mine. India to me was a land of exquisite spices, textures and fragrances - they often sent us exquisite parcels of flowered chintz, fine muslin and brocades - the very paper they were wrapped in seemed infused with the scents of jasmine and attar of roses.

'Yes, there is no place quite like it, but I sadly had to leave when my wife became ill. We came back to England and I was stationed nearer home.'

Jane was surprised to hear him talk of a wife; she had not thought he was married. The captain paused, and she wondered if the conversation was over. He looked very sad, she noted, and she waited to see if he'd say any more.

'We moved back to Sherford, but sadly, we were not timely enough, and the sickness that had taken hold of her abroad claimed her short life at home.'

'Oh, Captain Bartlett, how very remiss of me. I am so sorry to have reminded you of such distressing times, please forgive me.'

'Not at all, I like to think of Mary, and to talk about her sometimes. People who know me around here are reluctant to speak of her for fear of upsetting me, I think. They do not know what to say, and so it's easier not to say anything at all. But, it's over eight years ago since she passed away, and I think it's time I was able to talk about the past.'

'It is not possible to dictate to one's heart how long grieving should last,' Jane said observing the sorrow in his blue eyes, 'but time is a great healer.'

'Yes, that's true, though I sometimes wonder whether I will ever recover from the memories of her and the life we shared. Occasionally I think I could marry again, and feel almost ready to take a step to that end, and at others I know the time is not right.'

'I am sure you will find someone to share your life just when you should,' said Jane looking up into George Bartlett's kind eyes.

'Ah, yes ... though that's proving to be more difficult than I expected.'

Jane saw his gaze shift to Mae's face, and a look of defeat and resignation showed in his expression.

'Mae Milton is a beautiful young lady who needs someone to look after her,' he said. 'I rather hoped I might be the one to persuade her in time, but I think that idea is beyond all hope now.'

'Only time will tell, captain. Mae and Mr Weatherfield have just met, and are merely in the first throes of getting to know one another.'

'But there is something in their behaviour together, and in their admiration of the other that I recognise. Mary and I used to be that way, and were drawn like magnets from the very first time we met. No, I have come to realise there is something rather bleak about a one-sided love, and if I'm honest I wonder if part of the attraction for me is that she reminds me so very much of my darling wife.'

'To love without any hope of being loved in return is a comfortless state,' said Jane. 'Perhaps it would be wise to look around for someone else, a lady who would return your feelings and love you with all her heart.'

'You offer sound advice, and I'm sorry to have burdened you with my troubles,' the captain said, 'but it has been so easy to speak to you on many subjects I've avoided lately. I haven't had a chance to talk to anyone like this for such a long time ... thank you for listening.'

'It's my pleasure, Captain Bartlett. It is easier to talk to strangers sometimes, I've found that true myself.'

'Don't be a stranger, Miss Austen. I hope I will get to know you better in the coming weeks. I shall certainly heed your suggestions.'

'One thing I've learned in my life is that sometimes the most unexpected events can turn one's life in a moment to new and exciting times. You may find something happens when you least expect it ... I hope you will not have to wait too long.'

'I hope so too, Miss Austen.'

The captain moved away then and Jane later saw him leading Jessie Beales to the dance floor. The party was in full swing, and almost everyone was up and dancing. Emily and Jonathan Keeling were laughing their way through an overly dramatic tango, King Zoot had left his band to dance cheek to cheek with Lady Milton, and Eddie Wallis was gently teaching Cora the art of the Latin American dance. Will was dancing with one of the girls who'd arrived in a large party from the village, and Lieutenant Dauncey was partnering Beth, yet again.

Jane watched from a corner of the room hidden in the shadows, intrigued and curious, but glad to have escaped anyone's notice, or so she thought. Frankie Wallis was circulating with a bottle of champagne, topping up empty glasses, and he stopped when he reached Jane.

'You're not dancing, Miss Austen,' he said putting the bottle down on the sideboard behind her. 'Can I tempt you out onto the dance floor?'

'I'm afraid I don't tango, Mr Wallis, and I'm just as happy standing here watching everyone else.'

'That's a great pity, I'm sure you'd enjoy a tango if you tried. There's not much to it, I hope you'll allow me to give you a lesson sometime.'

He looked as if he might pick up the bottle again and move on, but he hesitated. 'Will you tell Alice I'm sorry she's feeling unwell. It's a shame she couldn't come, I know how much she used to love dancing.'

'I will pass on your message, Mr Wallis, but you should come and tell her yourself.'

'I'm not sure she'd want to hear it from me,' he said. 'Anyway, I hope you've enjoyed yourself this evening even if you haven't had a dance.'

'I've enjoyed myself very much,' said Jane thinking of all she'd learned, and of the unsuccessful attempt to dance with Will. 'I hope we'll meet again soon.'

Frankie reached for the bottle of champagne and Jane was left alone once more. It wasn't quite like any party she had ever been to, but it had given her an opportunity for more observation, and she felt she knew one or two of the guests rather better than she had before she'd arrived. She decided she must be more vigilant when it came to Will, and make more of an effort to avoid him. On the whole she'd enjoyed it, and couldn't wait to see Alice. She was sure Frankie had missed her not being there, and it gave her the slightest glimmer of hope that not all was completely lost between them.

Chapter Ten

Alice received Jane's news the next morning with her usual stoicism, privately deciding that Frankie was simply being polite, and that she would not read anything else into it. It would have appeared rude if he'd made no enquiry, and he'd obviously done so at the last minute. Mae had found an opportunity to tell her that Emily had thrown herself at Frankie all night and that they'd hardly been separated, and whilst Alice didn't want to dwell on those facts, at least she knew he wasn't interested in making any overtures to her. She'd already decided he was completely indifferent, reasoning that in all the years they were separated he could at any point have written to her or picked up the telephone. The truth was that he didn't love her any more, and had not loved her enough to pursue her again. Their meeting in the village had been like that of two strangers, but worse than that, because Alice knew there was no possibility of ever getting back together. The thought of the picnic arranged for the afternoon filled her with dread, and she knew she wouldn't be able to make another excuse.

The day started with fine weather as on the previous morning, but by lunchtime gunmetal clouds were sweeping across the sky with the resulting tumultuous rain set in for the afternoon. The only person who felt any pleasure in seeing the stair rods of water was Alice, and she thought herself left off the hook. Any plans for a picnic on the beach were quickly abandoned, and as a result, an indolent torpor seemed to settle on the house and all its inhabitants.

The weather didn't improve for a whole fortnight, and whilst Jane was hopeful that it might give her more time to write, she found she had to be available to sit and chaperone the girls at all hours of the day and in the evenings too. One thing she was grateful for was that she didn't see much of Will. He seemed to be busy about the estate, she'd caught a glimpse of him more than once through the front door, battling against the elements, suitably attired in working clothes, gum boots, and a sou'wester. He rarely made an appearance, only occasionally showing up for dinner where he appeared to ignore her as much as she was trying to avoid him. Occasionally their eyes met across the table, and sometimes she felt his gaze intent upon her features, but whenever she stared right back, he looked away.

Julius Weatherfield, true to his word, arrived every day to see Mae. Jane was grateful for the fact that Alice came to sit in the drawing room too, and they passed their time reading or playing card games with Emily and Cora who seemed restless unless they had plenty to do. On the Thursday of the following week Lieutenant Dauncey called, and by Friday afternoon they had a house full of visitors with Jonathan Keeling and the Wallis brothers joining the other two gentlemen.

Lady Milton was in her element, enjoying the fact that her drawing room was filled with some of the most eligible men in the county. She drew the line at inviting them to dine, but welcomed them enough to spend as much time as they liked in daylight hours.

Jonathan was talking about his disappointment that the picnic hadn't taken place, and was suggesting that until the weather turned again, they must have a gathering at his house.

'I've some news that I think you'll enjoy,' he said. 'An old university friend of mine is coming to stay tomorrow. Kit lives down in deepest Cornwall, but when I heard he was thinking of coming up to Devon for a few weeks I made sure he was going to spend some time with me. Kit's got his sister Camilla and a friend coming too, and I can't wait for you all to meet him. It's short notice, but do you think you could all come for dinner tomorrow night. It'll be all of us here, of course, and the usual suspects ... Jessie and Nora Beales, as well as Captain Bartlett.'

'Oh no, not the captain,' said Mae, 'he just mopes about all the time and is such dull company.'

'If I've heard the best way to make an Indian curry, I've heard it a thousand times,' said Julius, 'and I've only just met him. One would think he was in his dotage, not in his early thirties.'

'I think he's feeling a bit under par at the moment,' said Jonathan trying not to show his frustration at Mae and Julius's comments, 'he gets very lonely out at Sherford all by himself, and I'm sure he's always glad of a bit of company. I noticed he and Jessie were dancing on more than one occasion at Frankie's party, and I'd like to encourage that.'

'Well, that's some relief to hear ... at least he'll leave me alone if he's after Jessie,' said Mae, none too quietly, turning to bestow a winning smile on Julius.

There was an awkward silence. Mae didn't seem in the least perturbed by what she'd said, but Jane saw Alice was colouring up, and looking downcast into the hands clasped nervously in her lap.

Emily, who realised the time was ripe for diversion and longing to show her excitement for the invitation, instantly turned to Frankie who was sitting next to her on the sofa, with a huge grin. 'Oh, what fun, I think it's a case of the more, the merrier! You'll come, won't you, Frankie? Though I wish this wretched weather would stop. All our plans for picnics and excursions out are completely put on hold.'

'I couldn't agree more,' said Mae, adding mysteriously, 'I've a few plans of my own I'd like to put into place.'

'Yes, I'd love to come,' said Frankie turning slightly away from Emily and addressing the whole room. 'I'm sure I echo the thoughts of all in this room.'

Jane had been observing the pair all afternoon. She thought there was an obvious attraction from Emily towards Frankie, but she couldn't make up her mind about him. He seemed quite engaged by her on occasion, but Jane also noticed he was more enthusiastic towards Emily if he thought Alice was watching them. And though Alice tried very hard not to look, Jane knew that she'd seen all that was going on. Frankie had not exchanged one word with Alice at all, and seemed distracted. No, more than that, thought Jane, he was not his usual effusive and happy self.

Frankie was mildly irritated by the company, and he was feeling particularly needled by Alice. He thought how much she'd changed, he'd even said to Emily he would not have recognised her if he'd passed her unknowing in the street. She was so quiet and timid, and couldn't even be bothered to acknowledge him. The least she could do was be pleasant and ask him how he was doing, and he began to think she'd grown just like her father. Clearly, the old family snobbishness was still evident. He would never forgive her or Lord Milton, though Lady Milton seemed worth encouraging.

'Yes, Frankie, I'm sure we're all in agreement,' said Lady Milton. 'Indeed, we'd love to come for dinner, the invitation is so very generous of you, Jonathan darling, and it's always a pleasure getting to know some new young men. I cannot speak for Albert, but I know Zoot will love to be there and I shall tell him later when he comes up from the village. Whereabouts in Cornwall does young Kit reside?'

'His family were in tin mining until fairly recently, but have moved to St Ives to establish an estate.'

'New money,' said Lady Milton, pursing her scarlet lips in approval, 'but, there's no shame in that these days with the majority. Is he very rich?'

'I believe he is extremely well off,' said Jonathan, who was finding it hard not to laugh, 'but I'll leave that for you to find out.'

'And I shall enjoy doing so enormously,' Flora answered with a deep-throated giggle. 'I think he sounds quite perfect for one of my girls.'

'Lieutenant Dauncey, have you heard of the family?' interrupted Beth, anxious to move her mother's outspoken thoughts on. 'What's his other name, Jonathan?' asked Beth.

'It's Branwell, Kit Branwell.'

'No, I don't know the name,' Gilbert Dauncey replied after a moment's hesitation, 'but Cornwall is a big place, and I only know of the old mining families in the area. I don't have many connections there now.'

'Cornwall is not far away,' Lady Milton announced, 'it will be splendid to have such a short distance to visit my grandchildren. And he's bringing a friend, you say.'

'Yes, I think he's from the same area near St Just ... he didn't say too much ... only mentioned him as his great friend Fergus.'

'Oh, what a splendid name, he sounds like a hero from a Scottish legend,' Lady Milton enthused. 'I cannot wait to meet them. Cora, your head is always full of romance, Fergus sounds most suitable.'

Jane couldn't help feeling sorry for Cora whose embarrassment at her mother's faux pas showed in her crimson cheeks. The other person she was most concerned about was Alice who'd hardly spoken a word all day. Jane knew Alice was in an impossible situation, but it seemed she was fading faster into the background, and becoming ever more reluctant to speak in company. It just wasn't right, and she decided she must do something about it.

The next day brought slightly finer weather. Although it was hardly flaming June, at least the rain had stopped, and the odd patch of blue could be seen up above the white clouds.

Beth was up bright and early, and feeling excited about the evening. She hoped she would be able to sit next to Gilbert Dauncey at dinner, and she thought about the afternoon they'd spent together the day before with pleasure. He was handsome, charming, and best of all, he made her laugh, and when she thought about what a rum deal he'd been handed in life Beth decided he must be an extraordinary character to have survived so well, with such a joyous outlook and his sense of humour intact.

Crossing the hall, she noticed the pile of morning post on the table, and rifling through the letters found one for herself. It must have been hand-delivered, she thought, because there was no stamp, but she couldn't think who might be writing to her, as she didn't recognise the handwriting. Quickly tearing open the envelope she scanned the page, and saw Gilbert's name at the bottom, but if there were any first hopes that it might be a love letter they were dashed when she read its contents.

Dear Beth,

I thought it best to send you a note, as I have no hopes of seeing you today. I am so sorry, but I find I am unable to fulfil this evening's engagement after all. I've been contacted by my solicitor and am going to London on his instruction for he has some pressing news for me, and several items of importance to discuss. It is impossible for me to say how long I shall be gone, but I hope to be returned in a week or so.

I wanted to explain my absence, and hope it will not be too long before I shall see you again. Please send my best to your parents.

Kindest regards,
Gilbert Dauncey
PS Rest assured, I have also written a letter of apology to Jonathan Keeling.

Beth read the letter through twice. It was rather formal, and far from being romantic, though it did mention that he hoped it wouldn't be too long before he saw her again. Not exactly the stuff to set her heart racing, and she couldn't help feeling disappointed. She wondered what could possibly be so important that it would take him off to London. He'd sounded rather guarded, but she hoped it had something to do with sorting out what was rightfully due to him in his inheritance. Pocketing the letter, she set off for the dining room to have some breakfast, though suddenly she didn't feel she had the appetite she'd had before Gilbert's news.

Alice was getting ready for breakfast, and despairing at the state of her wardrobe when she heard the knock at the door. She was surprised to see Emily who didn't usually make a habit of coming to see Alice in her room, but it wasn't very long before she found out why she'd been so eager to visit.

'We've been having such a lovely time since Frankie arrived, don't you think?' Emily asked directly, almost as soon as she was through the door. Collapsing into a chair she picked up a cushion and proceeded to squash and pummel it round its edge, pulling at the bobble tassels. Alice couldn't answer truthfully, and say she'd never felt so miserable in her life before so she decided on a half-truth to satisfy her sister. 'Yes, it's been lovely seeing him again.'

'And do you like him as much as you ever did, Alice?'

'I don't know quite what you mean, Emily,' Alice faltered, not wishing to share her intimate thoughts.

'It's just that you hardly seem to speak a word to each other,' Emily continued, twirling a tassel round her finger, 'which in the circumstances, is understandable.'

'Well, I suppose we have nothing really left to say to one another.'

'You don't want to talk to him?'

'Not exactly, but … it's too complicated, Emily, and I don't want to talk about it.'

'Do you know what Frankie said to me yesterday?'

Alice tried not to let her irritation show. She wished she'd hurry up and say whatever it was she'd come to say. 'No, I don't, Emily.'

'He said he thought you were completely altered, and that he wouldn't have recognised you if he'd bumped into you in the High Street.'

Alice was completely taken aback. She knew the passing years and her disappointment at life not turning out quite how she'd wanted had taken its toll, but if this was the case she could hardly bear it.

'I think that's probably true,' Alice said bravely at last, 'I have changed. You probably don't remember how I looked all that time ago, but he's probably right. Time has not been so kind to me, as it has to him.'

'I just wanted you to know that I really like him, and if you don't have those same feelings any more, well …'

'If you're asking me for permission to see Frankie, you don't need it. There's no love lost between us, Emily, I know that.'

'Then I have your blessing?'

Emily already had her hand on the door, as she took Alice's wan smile to be exactly that.

Alice's tears flowed freely after that, and when she'd exhausted all her emotions, all the pent-up feelings, she dabbed her face dry. She really had to make some changes and a few decisions, she thought. The first one resolved on putting Frankie out of her head for good, and the second was one involving her stepmother, and a change she'd been considering for a long time.

Chapter Eleven

Jane was feeling very nervous. When she'd walked in to have breakfast at the usual time, she'd been very shocked to see Lady Milton sitting in her chair at the head of the table, looking for all the world as if she was up at such an early hour every day. Alice was seated next to her, and it appeared as if she'd interrupted an earnest conversation when she first walked in.

'Ah, Miss Austen,' said Lady Milton, 'Alice said you wouldn't be long … do take a seat. We've been cooking up a plan, which I hope will meet with your approval. There is no time to waste, and I shall not beat around the bush, as they say. I have always been a direct person, and therefore forthright in my opinions. What I am about to say I hope will not hurt your feelings, but it has to be said.'

Jane sat down wondering if she was in trouble by the tone of Flora Milton's voice, and racked her brain for some thought of any misdemeanour she might have made. Her mouth felt dry, and she bit her lower lip anxiously. Perhaps it had been remarked upon that she'd not been doing a very good job of chaperoning the girls, and instantly thought she should have discouraged Julius Weatherfield from coming to see Mae so often.

'Don't worry, Jane, everything is fine, truly,' added Alice reassuringly, after noting the distress in Jane's face.

'Stand up please, Miss Austen,' said Lady Milton firmly, 'I want to look at you.'

Jane was apprehensive, but did as she was told, and ran her hands over the cheap cotton frock she was wearing in an attempt to look as smart as possible. Lady Milton was always so perfectly turned out and it was impossible to feel anything but shabby under her scrutiny.

'What do you think, Alice?' said Lady Milton. 'I have to say I feel sure she is a similar build. The same height and long, slim legs … she could make an excellent dancer.'

Jane was not prepared to stand meekly any longer. 'May I ask what all this is about,' she said. 'I'm sorry, but I feel as if I'm on exhibit in the cattle market. I've told everybody here I don't dance, and I promise you, I do not need lessons.'

Lady Milton laughed. 'Dear Miss Austen, this has nothing to do with your dancing abilities, I assure you. The point is I've been attempting for some time to bring Alice into the 1920s without much success, but having finally persuaded her to have a new dress to wear in the evenings, she has brought to my attention that you are very short of evening attire yourself.'

'Oh,' said Jane both shocked and surprised, 'but I am quite happy with my black dress, I assure you.'

'You might be, Miss Austen, but I have had quite enough of its drab appearance at every mealtime and soirée.'

'Lady Milton has a couple of dresses she no longer has any use for,' said Alice. 'We think you are about the same size.'

'And I'm sure they would fit.'

'No, I couldn't possibly put you to so much trouble,' said Jane, 'I do not think I have the figure or …'

For once she couldn't think what to say. The idea of wearing anything so modern or short as the dresses Lady Milton wore was enough to make her feel faint.

'The dresses are beautifully tailored,' said Alice. 'They've been in storage, only worn once or twice a couple of years ago, and I know will be perfect for you. Please say you will have a look at them.'

'It would be very churlish if I didn't,' said Jane remembering her manners and knowing that she could trust Alice's judgement in such matters.

'Good, that's the first thing,' said Lady Milton. 'And now we'll broach the second.'

'I'm having my hair cut today,' Alice interjected, 'and Lady Milton wondered if you'd like to have yours done too. I'd feel so much better if someone shared the experience with me. I'm feeling very anxious about it as I haven't had a lock cut off since I was a little girl, except the ends, of course.'

'Alice, why are you having your beautiful hair cut off?' Jane demanded, speaking her thoughts out loud. 'You should stay true to yourself, and be who you want to be ... not some slave to fashion!'

'Please be assured I've been thinking about it for a long time. Since the war ended I've been living in a time warp, and I've decided I shall do so no longer. Please don't feel *you* have to do anything, but you've been such a dear friend to me since you arrived, I thought you might like a haircut too.'

Jane gazed at Alice and thought she saw a brave new spirit emerging from the girl who'd seemed content to hide in the background. She could identify with that so easily. And what was it that she was so afraid of, she asked herself? It was only a haircut, and after all, even if it were disastrous it would grow again. Alice's eyes beseeched her, and she found she couldn't say no. And she had to admit that a small part of her was quite excited at the idea of emerging as someone new and unrecognisable.

'I'll do it,' she said in the next breath before she could stop herself, 'Alice, let's cut our hair together.'

'There'll be no need for doing it oneself,' Lady Milton exclaimed. 'Marcel will be here in half an hour, which will give you just time to have a bite to eat. Alice, bring Miss Austen up to my boudoir after breakfast, and we shall see what can be done.'

Eddie Wallis was worried about his brother. Frankie had been at the rectory for nearly a month now, and after the initial excitement of his arrival, seeing him again, spending long hours sharing his wonderful company, talking together and hearing all the stories about his glamorous lifestyle, he'd become increasingly concerned. Eddie admitted to himself that initially he'd felt rather envious of his brother's good fortune, and couldn't help comparing where he found himself in life in relation to Frankie's incredible journey. But, as time was passing he knew something was troubling Frankie, and he began to think that not all was rosy in his brother's world. There were times when he was silent and dour, withdrawing from any conversation, preferring to stay in his room, quite unrecognisable from the Frankie he'd once known who always seemed so happy and carefree. Privately, he wondered if Frankie had ever really recovered from his love for Alice, but getting him to talk about it was like attempting to open a tin can with a spoon. He might make a few dents, but could not break through the impervious outer layer.

On this particular morning Frankie was in a horrible mood. He'd already snapped at Eddie because he couldn't find his gold cufflinks, and his brother had heard him being short with the girl who came in to do the cleaning and make the breakfast. Dora was sobbing in the kitchen when Eddie walked in to see what was delaying the meal, and he had to work very hard to get her to stop.

'They don't know 'im like I do, those girls in the village,' she said, banging the frying pan down on the stove. 'Oh, they think he's so gorgeous, but I've a mind to put 'em straight! I've only got one pair of 'ands, and I can't go any quicker! If I told 'em what he was really like...'

'Come now, Dora, you know Frankie isn't a morning person. I'm sure he didn't mean it.'

'Maybe not, but he needn't think he can go round acting like the Lord Almighty because he's treated like royalty elsewhere. I always heard such good things about Frankie from my Mum, but I think he's changed. Got a big 'ead now, my sister thinks, and I don't like to agree, but I think she's right!'

Eddie marched back into the breakfast room to face his glum brother who was hiding behind a newspaper. 'Frankie, Dora is crying into the best tea towels in the kitchen, and unless you want to face a mutiny in Stoke Pomeroy with every female member against you forever, I suggest you get in there and make amends. Why are you in such a bad mood?'

Frankie peered from behind the paper, took a deep breath, and put it down. 'I'm sorry, Eddie, truly I am. I promise I'll sort it out.'

Five minutes later he was back, and when Dora came in seconds later bearing hot plates of bacon, egg, and extra slices of fried bread, she was beaming, and her cheeks rather pink. It really was infuriating, Eddie thought. If that had been him, Dora wouldn't have spoken for a week, let alone be all over him with eyelashes fluttering. When she'd gone, he waited a few minutes until Frankie had consumed most of his breakfast.

'Just what's upsetting you? I wish you'd talk about it, and don't tell me you're fine because I've been watching you get steadily worse all week.'

Frankie paused, before he put down his knife and fork to gaze out across the rectory garden. The roses were in bloom, and seeing the little bench covered by the arch where they tumbled didn't improve matters. It had been a favourite spot for him and Alice to talk of their plans all those years ago. 'I suppose I'm just not easy to live with any more.'

'Oh, come on, Frankie, that's nonsense and you know it. I recognise this behaviour of old. If you want my opinion, and I know you probably don't, I think it's a woman, or at least, one in particular.'

'Who do you mean?'

'You've been stirred up ever since you saw Alice Milton for the first time. You might think you're fooling everyone by flirting with her sister, but I'm not convinced.'

'Well, you're wrong, Eddie. Yes, it's been unsettling seeing Alice again, not least because I can't believe what's happened to her. Where has the girl gone that stole my heart with her dazzling personality and stunning beauty? Where is that sweet, kind and lovely person I fell in love with?'

'Alice is still there, Frankie, but it's been hard for her, I'm sure. You know what Lord Milton is like, and life hasn't been easy since the war.'

'Hard for *her*? She made her choice, Eddie. Not only did she throw our engagement away, but made it quite clear that I wasn't good enough. I tell you now, whatever you think, I have no feelings left for her, and I know you will not want to hear this as my brother and spiritual guide, but I cannot forgive her either.'

Eddie didn't speak for a moment. He'd probably said too much he thought, and hadn't been as sensitive as he ought. Where he was normally patient and understanding with his parishioners, his brother always managed to rile and bring out the worst in him. He hated to see the two people who anyone could see belonged together unable to even have a conversation, let alone ever be as they once were, and now it seemed it was too late.

'Why can't you forgive her?' Eddie managed to say in a measured tone.

'Because she should have stood up to them, she should have told her father that she was leaving, and that she couldn't live without me. I thought she was strong, but I've come to learn Alice was just weak, and I've no room for anyone in my life like that.'

'So, it really is all over between you?'

Frankie nodded. 'I will admit, I loved her like no other, and I've never met anyone to match her equal, but I've no desire to rekindle any kind of relationship with Alice.'

Knowing how deeply Frankie was clearly affected, Eddie felt he couldn't offer any advice. He just felt really sorry and sad that there was nothing to be done. All he could hope was that in time Frankie would realise how stubborn he was being.

'And before you say anything else, Eddie, I've made up my mind. I'm quite ready to fall in love again, and either one of those Milton girls will do. Cora is sweet, and Emily is very eager to please. Besides, she has a strong character, as well as being an absolute darling, and something tells me that this time her father won't put any obstacles in our way.'

When Jane stepped into Lady Milton's bedroom she nearly gasped out loud. Dove grey walls were contrasted with swathes of glossy pink silk swagged across the windows, and draped over the bed, whilst underfoot a soft cream carpet completed the picture of opulence. It was a very modern room filled with the latest furniture, of highly polished pieces with sinuous legs, and curving sunbursts in a variety of woods. Two wonderful examples were displayed at the ends of Lady Milton's huge bed that was magnificently crowned by a *ciel de lit*, from which were suspended more swags of the same shimmering silk to form a canopy. Unlike the rest of the house there'd been no expense spared in this room.

Invited to take a seat on one of the satin covered slipper chairs, Jane sat down whilst Lady Milton fussed about one of the maids who was arranging armfuls of dresses over the bed. Alice had been right, Jane saw a collection of evening wear selected on its suitability for a governess, nothing too short or outlandish in colour, but nonetheless the dresses were made of the finest silks, satins and chiffons. It was a long time since Jane had felt girlish excitement on seeing such confections, but she couldn't help feeling rather pleased.

A knock at the door heralded Marcel, and after the inevitable exchange of kisses on each cheek, Lady Milton introduced his clients. He stood at a distance and regarded them, his head first on one side and then on the other. There was a lot of clucking and twirling of his waxed moustache, and several times when he came closer to ruffle Jane's hair she thought he might catch her ear with his twirling scissors.

'There's nothing else to be done,' he said in broken English, 'it must all come off! Luckily, Miss Alice has the perfect shaped head for a close bob, and Miss Austen's curls will frame her face quite delightfully.'

'Then there's no time to lose,' said Lady Milton and instructed the maid. 'Daisy, let's take Miss Milton and Miss Austen to the bathroom and you can help by washing their hair to start.'

Large mirrors hung above two console basins on porcelain legs, and a capacious curved bath was arranged against a backdrop of pale grey tiles, and soft pink walls in the vast room. Again, nothing had been skimped on, and an additional dressing table, complete with built-in shell lights was littered over with exotic looking phials and bottles filled with scent, powder bowls, and enormous swansdown puffs on long handles.

Marcel flourished his scissors and the girls sat down to take turns having their hair washed before nervously taking a seat at the dressing table for their haircut. Alice went first, and Jane watched her long thick hair fall to the floor in a few short snips. Marcel circulated and considered, tweaked and trimmed until he was happy, and when Alice turned round there were genuine sighs of admiration.

'Oh, Alice, my dear,' cried Lady Milton, 'you do look a picture.'

Alice beamed, and Jane thought how very much the short hair suited her elfin face. Her friend couldn't stop smiling, and patted the bare nape of her neck.

'I feel so very modern,' Alice giggled, 'and quite girlish.'

'It's taken years off you,' said Lady Milton in her inimitable way. 'You'll have a queue of suitors just waiting to escort you now, you'll see!'

When it was Jane's turn she was too nervous to watch in the mirror as Marcel set to work. She saw her chestnut curls lying on the bathroom floor as Daisy bustled round to sweep them up in a dust pan, before they were gone forever. Marcel twisted and twirled, fluffed and finger-waved, until he stood back at last and declared he was finished.

Jane's eyes had been screwed tight shut, but now she was forced to open them and take a long look in the mirror.

'You look beautiful,' said Alice, coming to stand next to her chair, 'and though you were before, I have to say short hair looks wonderful on you.'

It was astonishing to see the difference the haircut made. Jane loved the short bob on sight, not just because she admitted to herself that she looked quite pretty, but also because it felt so liberating. It was dry already, and the curls forming round her face swept round to her neck where she felt a breeze from the open window kiss her nape. She felt a little giddy with pleasure, and decided she liked the boyish look.

'Now, Marcel, we need a finishing touch,' said Lady Milton. 'Have you brought your cosmetics?'

'Oh no, I don't like anything on my face, I …' Jane began.

'I will simply enhance what is already there, my dear,' insisted Marcel, as he unlocked a large silver box filled with bottles, assorted potions, and glass jars filled with cream. 'Do not fear, I am not here to make you look like a clown.'

Alice and Jane gave in to his commands while Daisy acted as assistant. Their faces were steamed with hot water, cleansed with creams, refreshed with astringent lotions, and patted dry with crisp white cloths. They were massaged and stroked, dabbed at and daubed, until their complexions were smooth as marble.

Jane had to admit her tingling skin felt soft to the touch, and silkier than it had ever done before. When Marcel insisted on a light touch of ivory powder she allowed herself to close her eyes and surrender to the whisper touch of the swansdown puff.

'One moment,' he said, as he instructed her to lean back in the chair and close her eyes again. 'Now you will see how make-up need not be a man-made mask, Miss Austen. I will merely add to your natural beauty.'

Alice looked equally beautiful. 'I feel rejuvenated,' she said, 'and I'm so glad I had you to hold my hand through the whole experience, Jane.'

'I wouldn't have missed it for the world,' said Jane with genuine appreciation. She couldn't take her eyes off the stranger who looked back in the mirror.

'Now for your dress, Miss Austen,' said Lady Milton. 'Daisy has arranged a selection on the bed, and you must take your pick. Don't be afraid to take at least three, I have no use for them any more, and I'd rather someone had the benefit. Besides, it'll free up some space for some more.'

Jane wanted to laugh at that, and did her best to stop the smile forming on her lips. They all trooped back into the bedroom, but the sight of the dresses was overwhelming. She'd never seen so many and couldn't imagine how many Flora Milton must own if these were just the cast-offs.

'There's a screen over in the corner. Take a few at a time, and try them on. That's the best way to do it, I find. Sometimes a dress can look nothing on the hanger, but a body can make a transformation.'

Lady Milton was being very kind, Jane thought. With Alice's help she picked out a pale blue silk dress in tiers trimmed with coffee coloured lace, a dress of Nile green chiffon with a dropped waist, and a coral velvet, topped with a net bodice. Lightly embellished with bugle beads or pearls, the dresses were examples of understated taste, which suited Jane perfectly. When she emerged from behind the screen there were gasps of approval.

As if that wasn't enough two pairs of evening shoes were found, and a box of necklaces were brought out of a cupboard to be spilled out onto the pink silk counterpane. Lady Milton insisted on picking out some long beads; Venetian glass to go with the blue dress, Jade to go with the green, and a string of long pearls to contrast with the coral velvet.

'I couldn't possibly accept them,' Jane insisted, but Lady Milton wouldn't budge.

'Nonsense, my dear, if you are to represent the family when out with my daughters, we cannot have you looking anything but suitably dressed and adorned. Besides, they are all faux, of a refined style, and most fitting.'

Alice quickly agreed that Jane must have some jewellery, to cover Lady Milton's gaffe, emphasising the fact that no one wore real jewels out any more.

Jane felt relieved, and glad she wasn't going to be the guardian of a set of precious jewels. It was decided she should wear the pale blue silk for the evening's dinner, and when she had it on again Alice stood behind her to clasp the Venetian beads round her neck.

'Now, take a look in the glass,' Lady Milton instructed.

Jane stared in shock. She couldn't recognise herself in the long glass mirror or the transformation that had taken place.

'I hardly know myself,' she gasped.

'But it is you, and you look simply divine,' Alice enthused.

Jane felt caught up in Alice's excitement at her transformation, and even felt a thrilling sense of decadence, a sensation of being both wicked and wild, and a little sinful to be taking such pleasure in being young and feeling so ecstatically alive again. The young woman in the mirror had a peaches and cream complexion. Jane's red cheeks had always been a cause for concern, glowing pinker than ever when she was nervous or embarrassed, but Marcel had managed to tone down the effect to one which had her turning her head first one way and then another in amazement at her reflection. She was still blushing, but now her ivory skin was tinted with a hint of pale rose. Her eyelashes were not exactly darker, but looked thicker, gleaming with a silky sheen, as moist as her lips, artfully painted an enticing rouge, just a shade brighter than her natural colour. The effect was lovely, and she had to agree that it was not too much, and no one would know she had anything of artifice about her at all.

The calf-length dress caressed curves she didn't know she had, and her heeled shoes showed her pretty ankles at their best. Something about the magical combination of the glacé blue silk and coffee lace made her hazel eyes glow as if stippled with lustrous sapphires in their depths. Being both restrained with its lace trim, and daring in its cut, the dress gave off an aura of elegant finesse, and twinned with her new hair made her look like a woman of fashion.

Jane no longer saw a governess too afraid of life to be herself. Her reflection showed a goddess of poise and refinement, an intriguing lady of sophisticated splendour who looked as if she was ready to take on the world. It was simply wonderful to feel such blissful pleasure in being so vain, a luxury she hadn't allowed herself in an age. All she could think about was what Will would think of her new look, and though he was bound to tease her, she couldn't help hoping that he might like it.

Chapter Twelve

Mae, Beth, Emily and Cora shrieked out loud when they saw Alice and Jane poised on the landing, and everyone, including Mae, said how much they loved their hair.

'Will won't know you,' Mae exclaimed hugging her sister with a generous squeeze, 'I can't wait to hear what he has to say. Alice, you look truly beautiful.'

Alice glowed and seemed to be enjoying the attention. She looked wonderful in her new oyster-pink silk dress, embellished with tiny beads in a fish scale pattern. For once she met the gaze of the others who stared in admiration.

Their new look had given them both a confidence boost, but as Jane descended the staircase behind Alice and the other girls she felt a moment's trepidation when she saw Will standing in the hall waiting for them, though she was glad to see he was occupied with arranging an evening scarf round his neck and didn't look up. The other girls were first down and to some extent shielded them from view. Will gave them all a cursory glance, and started to head for the door, but as if something suddenly registered in his mind, he flipped round, and did a double take.

His jaw literally dropped open when he saw Alice, and rushing over he picked her up in his arms and twirled her round.

'Oh my, Alice, what a stunner you are ... may I say how much I love that new dress, and as for the rest, you must be the most beautiful girl on planet Earth. But, you always were, you know.'

'Will, I fear you exaggerate, but thank you,' Alice said. 'It's just me, when all is said and done.'

'It isn't *just you*, Alice, you don't know how very special you are both inside and out ... to me, and to all of us. It's lovely to see you looking so happy.'

'Thank you, Will, it's taken a while, but I do feel myself again. I have decided to look to the future and put the past in its proper place.'

'And I couldn't be happier for you.'

Jane stood at the back of the group, delighted to see Will's reaction to his sister. Alice's transformation was so much more than putting on a new dress and having a haircut, and Will had known just what to say. The other girls joined in, and Beth remarked how lovely she thought Jane looked too. When Lord and Lady Milton appeared, the praise didn't stop, though as might be expected, was tempered with the usual backhanded compliments from Flora.

Will held the door open for them all and the others trooped off to the waiting cars. Jane was the last out, and though he didn't utter a word as she passed him by she felt his eyes watching her closely. She couldn't help feeling a little disappointed that he had nothing to say to her, but then remembered how she'd behaved at the party when she wouldn't dance with him. Jane knew she'd given the impression of being proud and perhaps a little too aloof, but then he'd also made an excellent job of ignoring her completely ever since. She reprimanded herself for caring so much what he thought of her, and decided that from now on she'd use one of Mae's expressions, and wouldn't give a hoot.

King Zoot was waiting for them outside, and half the party went off with him, leaving Will, Alice, Jane and Cora to get in the other car. Mr Bell, the butler was sitting in the driver's seat, and Cora begged to be allowed to sit in the front, which left Jane and Alice sitting either side of Will in the back. There was plenty of room, but Jane's nearness to Will reminded her so much of the last time she'd driven in the front with him to the party, that she felt restless. It was sheer stupidity to linger on such recollections, and she put them out of her head as quickly as possible. Alice, fortunately, struck up a conversation and Jane turned to her, though Will turned his face towards hers, as if interested in her answer. Easily flustered because Will's face was an inch from her own, everything she said came out all wrong. She was sure he was staring at her on purpose, that he knew just how embarrassed she felt by his behaviour, and grew more determined than ever not to be cowed by him.

At last they were travelling down the driveway of Buckland Priors, a large house built onto the old Cistercian abbey, which Henry the eighth had sold to Jonathan Keeling's ancestors after the dissolution. It was an imposing building, of a kind that exuded the air of a wealthy bachelor about it, and Jane couldn't help thinking that it could do with a feminine hand to soften the rigid design of the gardens, which were set out in formal lines with little vegetation.

There were many familiar faces waiting when they were shown into the drawing room, which similarly had a masculine feel. Several tapestry cushions with a heraldic pattern, frosted glass lamps and a vase of cut flowers considerably cheered up the dark wood panelling and brown leather chesterfield sofas. It was a cosy room, with a log fire burning in the large grate, but unmistakably the room of a gentleman who'd received little, if any, of a lady's opinion on its decoration.

Alice took a deep breath when they entered the room. Emily, she noted, was already talking nineteen to the dozen with Frankie by the huge panelled fireplace. He had his arm resting on the mantelshelf, a protective gesture that framed Emily and gave him the chance to lean more closely towards her. They were very familiar with each other, as if they'd been courting forever, and looked to be sharing confidences as he whispered in her ear. He didn't even look up when they walked in, but Alice wasn't sure she wanted to see what he thought of her. She wasn't ready for any scrutiny or cold regard that might reveal his true feelings.

Jonathan greeted them in his usual warm manner before introducing his new guests, Kit and Camilla Branwell, and their friend, Fergus Dauncey.

'Dauncey?' interrupted Lady Milton before Jonathan had a chance to speak further. 'This cannot be a coincidence. You *must* be related to our Lieutenant Dauncey. Well, I'm sure he'll be here in a moment, and you can see him for yourself.'

At precisely the same time Beth guessed the connection between them, she wondered if Gilbert had suddenly dashed off because he realised his brother was about to turn up, though why *he* felt he ought to be out of the way didn't seem fair.

'I'm afraid I received a letter this morning from him,' Jonathan went on to explain, 'Lieutenant Dauncey has had to return to London on some urgent business. Unfortunately, he won't be coming this evening.'

'No, it's a great pity,' added Fergus Dauncey speaking up in a cultured voice. 'As soon as we met, Jonathan enquired as to whether there was a connection, and we soon realised he was talking about my very own brother. Sadly, I haven't seen him for some time, and we've lost touch. Jonathan was telling me how he's become a part of your circle here in Stoke Pomeroy. I should have loved to see him.'

Jane and Beth exchanged glances. Whatever Gilbert might think of his brother and he'd made it clear there was no love lost on his part, Fergus seemed to be declaring the opposite, though he could hardly have denied all knowledge of him.

Fergus Dauncey was a very handsome man, Beth decided, though he looked rather haughty and pleased with himself. He was dressed expensively, the cut of his jacket tailored to show off his broad shoulders, but she wasn't convinced one little bit by his apparent sincerity, and didn't trust his appearance of goodness. Gilbert was so kind, funny, and always trying to please. That anyone could have treated him the way his so-called brother had was simply awful, but she was intrigued, deciding that if she ever got the opportunity she'd see just what Fergus had to say for himself. She couldn't help noticing that now the introductions were over and everyone was sipping a pre-dinner drink, he was not making much of an attempt to socialise. He was talking to Kit and Camilla the whole time, as if nobody else existed. Of course she couldn't expect that he'd look like Gilbert, as they weren't actually related, but she decided that although Fergus was good-looking in his own right, he wasn't a patch on his brother. He wore an impassive expression, and looked slightly bored, as if he didn't really want to be there.

Emily was in a skittish mood. Decidedly pleased with the way things were going between her and Frankie, she cast around to see if there was anyone else who needed a helping hand with their love lives. She thought of herself as a sort of cupid's helper, bringing together people who were simply meant for one another. Having felt assured that she was entirely responsible for the vicar and his wife tying the marital knot, she'd been wondering who might need her help next, and after seeing Jessie Beales and Captain Bartlett at the last event dancing together she thought it was high time they were helped along to connubial bliss. All it required was a word in the captain's ear, telling him how much Jessie was always talking about him, and how much she admired him.

'I shan't be long, Frankie,' she said, 'I've just remembered I haven't given the captain the details about the picnic next week. I'll just be a minute.'

Of course, Emily knew it would never do to share her plans with anyone. They might easily misconstrue her carefully considered schemes. She made a beeline over to the captain, and when she could, extracted him from Cora's side.

Frankie looked round the room for the first time. He recognised most of the people there, and apart from the newcomers thought there were one or two he couldn't place who must be friends of Jonathan's he hadn't met before. There were two girls he didn't recognise standing with their backs to him, talking to Lady Milton. The slightly shorter girl was wearing a pink dress just a shade darker than her skin, and the scooped back of her dress showed the most tantalising glimpse of fine shoulder blades. He couldn't help admiring the lines of her neck, and the way her hair curled into the nape. He felt intrigued and curious to find out more.

A voice brought him out of his reverie. 'You look lost in thought, Frankie ... a penny for them.'

It was Will, and Frankie looked at him with a smile. 'Oh, I was just thinking that I know everybody here, but for those two girls standing with Lady Milton. Who are they?'

Will laughed. 'You *do* know them, Frankie, they're just looking a little different this evening.'

Alice chose that moment to turn round and glance in their direction, almost as if she'd felt their eyes burning into her back. On any other occasion she might have turned back timidly, but she immediately saw a look of shock turn quickly to one of gasping appreciation, and so she gave Frankie the benefit of her most winning smile before turning her graceful head once more. Jane turned seconds later, and this time she saw something of Will's expression. It was obvious pride in his sister's appearance, and she could see Frankie saying something that was obviously highly complimentary. Will fixed on her face momentarily, and she felt his dark eyes fuse with her soul, tugging on her heart with a stream of delicious consciousness between them, before she told herself that this sort of thinking was romantic folly and complete stupidity.

Good heavens, what is the matter with me, she thought. Next, I'll be imagining that he likes what he sees, and that he is falling in love with me, when it's perfectly plain he's just a good-looking man who enjoys eyeing up young ladies. It must be something to do with my newfound youth, I suppose, and all these strange feelings that I'd absolutely forgotten about, and don't quite know how to manage. If only my heart would stop skipping like a spring lamb, I'd be perfectly fine. I shall not look at him again this evening … it's just not good for me.

Mae and Julius were sitting in their usual style on a sofa, and were indulging in a favourite topic, that of secretly discussing everyone else in the room whilst openly laughing about them.

'What *is* Jessie Beales wearing?' commented Julius. 'I've never seen such a hideous sack, and it must be at least five years out of date.'

'Julius, you are too awful for words, you know that's not very nice, even if it is absolutely spot on. She's got a very good figure though, even you must admit that, and she can't help being so poor you know, though heaven help me, I don't have as much money to spend on my clothes these days, and I seem to manage.'

'But, you have good taste, and that can't be bought. She looks a fright, and as for her hair, I never saw such a bird's nest. Someone really ought to recommend a good hairdresser to the poor girl. It's far too long for one thing, she ought to get it cut.'

'Do you think I should get mine cut, Julius?'

Suddenly Mae felt concerned that he might not like her long hair.

'Oh no, it looks just right on you, my dear, but the more I look at Jessie, the more I want to laugh.'

Mae watched him studying Jessie earnestly, and felt a little uncomfortable, especially when she turned to catch them both staring, which made her redden instantly. Julius could be wickedly behaved at times, but Mae loved his outspoken sense of humour and his unpredictable streak, as well as the fact that he made her howl with laughter.

'When can we go to your house, Julius? You promised we could go as soon as I was better, and I'm only hobbling the smallest bit now,' she said, wanting to change the subject and have all his attention back on her again.

'Oh, Mae, I wish we could go this week, but my aunt has taken up residence, and I'm not sure how long she's going to be with me.'

'Your aunt? I thought you always lived alone?'

'Well, I do, most of the time, but it has to be said, Aunt Dolores is just the smallest problem. The trouble is I am wholly dependent on her for a little while longer. The house and an inheritance are mine all right, but not quite in my name until she "pops off", so to speak.'

'Oh dear, I did hope we might be able to spend some time alone together.'

'Don't despair, Mae, I'm sure I'll think of something. In any case, she loves visitors; perhaps you'd like to come and meet her.'

'Really, Julius ... you'd introduce me to your aunt?'

'She'd just adore you, I know. I wouldn't put you in a compromising situation, we don't have to be engaged or anything like that ... she's not that old-fashioned. Dolly's met a lot of my friends, and she loves a chat. I hate to say it, but she's a bit of a snob, and I should just love to see her face when I tell her you are Lord Milton's daughter. She'll be all over you like a rash.'

Mae screamed with laughter. 'Julius, you have an incorrigible streak, but I can't help liking you.'

'I'm so glad, Mae, and it's good to hear you know exactly what I'm like!'

Dinner was being announced, and for the first time since arriving in Stoke Pomeroy Jane could honestly say she was looking forward to a meal she'd heard much about. The others were pairing up, and she saw Jonathan Keeling leading Lady Milton off to the dining room with the others trailing behind. Will took Mae's arm, and Jane could see him talking quite earnestly. It hadn't escaped many people's notice, she didn't think, that she and Julius were behaving very rudely. It would be timely advice if Will were telling her off. The captain was just a little way in front with Emily, and there seemed to be a lot of whispering from her, much of it rather loud. She seemed to be telling the captain to make his move before the end of the evening, and she urged him to make sure Jessie understood his interest. Jane could only feel sorry for Captain Bartlett, and decided that she would have a word with Emily before the evening was over. It wasn't fair to make him one of her experiments, and she thought if the captain had any idea he wouldn't want to be any part of it.

The dinner was every bit as good as expected, and after potted shrimps with melba toast, a hearty fish soup, a side of beef with all the trimmings, and a rich trifle washed down with glasses of wine, the conversation flowed.

Once, Alice overheard Frankie talking about the time he'd started off on his career as an actor, when he hadn't a penny to his name. He didn't look once in her direction as he spoke, but she wondered if he'd made the association of their last time together in his mind, as she had.

'When I first got to America I lived on the streets, and was so hungry for the first weeks, I didn't think I'd get through the night.'

'So what happened to change it?' asked Lady Milton. 'Did someone take pity on you?'

'I managed to persuade a lady to give me a job as a waiter, and then I had the biggest stroke of luck. Cecil B DeMille came in one day, and I was working his table. I got a bit part in one of the greatest films ever made, and that set me off on the path to other directors and many more films. I was a very lucky guy.'

'But, I'm sure it was more than luck,' said Emily fervently, 'he could see talent and good looks just oozing out of every pore, I think.'

Everyone laughed, even Lord Milton. Alice could see how impressed her father was by him, but it was as if the past had been completely eradicated and none of it had ever happened.

There was no communication between Alice and Frankie, not even when they happened to walk alongside one another back to the drawing room where everyone urged her to play the piano for some dancing. Even in the hallway surrounded by people he failed to acknowledge her. She began to think that the look of plain admiration on his face earlier had been nothing but a trick of her own imagination. He was only interested in Emily, she could see. Yet, that didn't stop her remembering how, in a large party during their former days together, they'd been drawn to the other, unsatisfied with anyone else's company, gravitating to their own corner to be alone as soon as possible. They'd been as one person, their thoughts and feelings in complete harmony, and utterly in love. Alice despaired of her thoughts. She'd been so determined to move on with her life, but seeing Frankie, and hearing his voice was just so hard.

Alice's eyes filled with tears, but she kept her head down in the pretence of flicking through the music sheets, as she sat at the piano trying to find something suitable. At least she didn't have to dance and started to play a cheerful tune as soon as she could in an attempt to brighten her mood.

Emily and Frankie danced right past her, their heads as close to the other as possible.

'No, Alice never dances,' she heard Emily say, and for a moment she caught his gaze. He looked so penetratingly into her eyes that she missed the next note, but Alice thought she recognised that look of pity once more. Perhaps he was trying to see some vestige of the beautiful girl he'd once known, she thought, instead of the sham substitute she'd become.

Emily and Beth took turns to play a few songs on the piano, and with everyone gathered round to sing there was a festive air. Lady Milton heaped praise upon her girls though Jane noticed their playing was shockingly bad. No one seemed to notice Alice's excellent playing, so Jane remedied that by declaring how brilliant she was in a loud voice, which encouraged Jonathan Keeling and Captain Bartlett to applaud extra hard when she sat down to play again, and say that Alice was a marvel. Even Jessie took her turn eventually after much persuasion, and Julius who was rather worse for wear insisted on accompanying her, turning the pages, whilst staring into Mae's eyes so much that she bit her lip with embarrassment.

Kit and Camilla played a duet, an amusing song that had everyone falling about with laughter.

'I must apologise for my playing,' he said, 'I admit when it comes to the piano, you ladies beat us for flair and virtuosity. You're all so talented, and can sing like angels.'

'But, we adored your playing, and you're being far too modest,' said Lady Milton. 'Cora is very good, you know, I should love to see you both perform a duet for us.'

Cora slunk down in her chair, and Kit who thought she looked a sweet girl said he would love to hear her play another time.

The evening seemed to pass very quickly and all too soon they were thanking Jonathan for a wonderful evening and heading off into the cool night air. It was very quiet on the way home, each person seemed lost in their own thoughts. Though Alice was trying her best, she felt she'd failed to turn over the new leaf she'd promised to do, and try as she might she couldn't help feeling that she had a long way to go.

Jane felt the oppressive atmosphere. Will hadn't spoken a word to her all evening, and when she glanced at him sideways, he looked as if he might growl if she started a conversation. She knew Alice was upset, but it wasn't possible to talk to her with everyone able to listen, and so the journey home was quiet and strained. Alice practically ran to the house when they arrived, and though Jane wanted to rush after her, she felt someone else restrain her, catching hold of her arm.

'I think it's best if you leave her be, Miss Austen,' said Will, hanging on to her sleeve. 'If I know my sister she'll want some time alone, though

I know how much she appreciates talking to you, and I'm sure she'll want to discuss everything in the morning.'

'You're right,' said Jane, unable to meet his eyes. 'Thank you, I should have realised that now would not be a good idea.'

'You just wanted to help ... you're very kind.'

There was a further silence, he let go of her arm, and Jane was about to wish him goodnight when Will spoke again.

'I didn't have a chance to say it earlier, but you looked absolutely beautiful tonight. Forgive me for saying so, it probably isn't polite or appropriate, but there it is ... my thoughts couldn't help just popping out of my head.'

Jane stammered something, probably thank you, but later couldn't recall exactly what, and when he offered his arm to escort her back into the house she could only think it would be rude to reject it.

Chapter Thirteen

Sunday passed in the usual way with Jane accompanying the girls to church whilst Lord and Lady Milton were left behind. The whole family seemed even more at odds than ever, arguing with one another and having little dramas about the slightest complaints. Jane was sure this was due to a combination of too many late nights and an over consumption of cocktails, and yet they all continued to pour gin into glasses as if it was medicinal and would make them all feel better. Alice looked sadder than ever, and Jane was sorry there wasn't a single opportunity to be alone to talk. Even when they had a few minutes before dinner, people kept coming in, or a maid would appear with a question, which was very frustrating. When they sat down to eat the roast dinner they were all expecting, the meagre rations were smaller than ever, the beef cold and the Yorkshire puddings burnt to a crisp. Lord Milton was in a foul mood, made worse by the fact that Will disappeared down to the village, and Jane could only think he'd gone to the Tolleywicks Inn for his dinner. It was with some relief that she went to bed.

In the morning she spent the first five minutes thinking over some of the events of the dinner at Buckland Priors. She hadn't allowed herself to think about what Will had said that evening, but she was pleased they were friends again. Jane couldn't help repeating the flattering words he'd spoken in her head. She didn't want to acknowledge the tingling pleasure the thought of their exchange gave her, even if she allowed herself to revel in it for a further ten minutes. After that, she wore her sensible "hat" and decided that it was best not to believe anything he said, carefully considering she should remain suitably guarded against such teasing and pretty speeches.

She began to think, instead, about some of the other events of the evening, of how everything seemed to be going so badly between Alice and Frankie, and how little she seemed to have accomplished since coming to Manberley. Her writing book was lying on the desk sadly neglected, without a word written beyond the title of *The Brothers*, and she began to think perhaps the book would never be started, let alone finished. There wasn't much point in dwelling on it now; the day was about to start, and she'd be required to spend it with the Milton girls. But, despite spending a lot of time with them, Jane still felt she hardly knew them. Apart from Alice and Cora who shared a love of books, the great interests of the rest seemed to be in dancing and young men, though she'd overheard Mae saying she loved to paint. Whilst Jane understood the desires of young girls' hearts, she thought that every one must have interests she didn't yet know about, and if they didn't she ought to set about changing that in some way. It was all very well dressing up and having fun at parties, but there ought to be more to life, and none of them seemed particularly prepared for any existence beyond the house where their every need was catered for. Jane was determined she should take more time to get to know them, and besides that, she had an idea to get them all engaged in something to both educate and yet be an enjoyable experience that might also serve to solve another particular set of problems.

It was Jane's idea that to help the sisters become closer they should enjoy a variety of shared activities, something where pulling together in a common cause for the greater good would encourage them to work as a team. Quite what or how that would be accomplished was a small detail, though she knew it would require all the tact and diplomacy she possessed.

When she walked into the breakfast room she found herself alone, and remembering that she'd passed three of the maids laden down with trays, she was not surprised. The dining room table was laid as if the family were to eat together, and enough food for an army was laid out on the side, shockingly wasteful to anyone's thinking, Jane thought. She knew the maids would be in to clear in another half hour, and wondered what they thought about the time they wasted clearing up and laying tables for people who couldn't be bothered to get out of bed. No wonder they didn't have time to clean the house, which looked in a filthier state than the day she'd arrived. And how disheartening it must be for the cook, she thought, who never knew how much food to prepare from one day to the next. It was no wonder her evening meals were so uninspiring, even if she didn't have as much as she'd like to spend on food, Mrs Wickens had probably given up long ago.

Jane ate her egg on toast in the peace and quiet, savouring her morning cup of tea, then picked up her plate, deciding to return it herself to the kitchen. She'd not been downstairs since she arrived at the castle, and she thought it was high time she went and introduced herself to Mrs Wickens whom she'd heard much about.

The smell of bacon and sausage permeated the dark corridors below stairs. All she had to do was follow her nose to find the cook's domain. Jane could hear Mrs Naseby in the distance remonstrating with one of the maids before she appeared, bustling past in the corridor with a nod of her head.

'Oh, Miss Austen, I am sorry I cannot stop, I shall never catch my tail this morning if I do,' she cried, and with a wave of her hand she was gone.

Jane was very slightly tempted to make her pause for a minute, and as she watched her retreating figure she could imagine a sleek black tail waving from the folds of her gown, rather like the one that belonged to Quince, Mr Quance's cat. She sauntered on to the kitchen and stood in the doorway poised to knock at the door, noting the large figure of Mrs Wickens, her hands on her hips, as she sadly contemplated a vast pile of vegetables and a lump of meat not much bigger than Jane's fist. She looked up as Jane knocked on the door, and all hope seemed to drain from Mrs Wickens's red face which was mired with sweat and plastered round with greasy grey hairs escaping from a grubby mob cap.

'If you've come to tell me that Mr William Milton has changed his mind and wants his breakfast now, you're too late,' she said, wielding a wooden spoon in a sturdy arm. 'There's nothing but cold left, and if he wants it warmed up, I've nobody here to fetch it.'

'No, Mrs Wickens, please don't worry, I just came to introduce myself. I'm sorry, you're clearly very busy, but I've been here for nearly a month and I haven't even said hello.'

Mrs Wickens saw Jane's plate, and took it from her, then wiped her hands on her apron. 'You must be the new lady's companion I've heard about, Miss Austen. I'm sorry to be so gruff; I've forgotten my manners I'm that worn out. Well, I hope you're comfortable here with those youngsters, though they're enough to drive anyone mad. They eat us out of house and home, though it's to be expected, I suppose. And there's never enough to go round with the price of meat going up. I don't suppose you've put any weight on since you got here ... you look as if you could do with a bit of feeding up.'

Jane didn't know quite how to answer, or tell her that feeling near starved was a constant sensation apart from when they dined out, but when Mrs Wickens laughed out loud she relaxed a little.

'Come and sit down, I've got a bit of seed cake left over that I made for King Zoot. He loves his cake, and I can't resist his smile any more than her ladyship! I know he won't mind if we share a slice over a cup of tea.'

Jane laughed too, and sat in the Windsor chair next to the grange. One or two of the maids came in then, grumbling about the weight and state of their dirty breakfast trays before dumping them on the side. The kitchen maid appeared to fill the sink with steaming water, and stood sullenly in silence, her chapped hands plunging in and out of the grimy depths to bring up a seemingly endless supply of shiny wet teapots, plates, and cups.

'I don't know what I'm going to do with those scrawny scraps, I'm sure,' Mrs Wickens said jerking her head towards the meat and vegetables on the kitchen table. 'I'm not afraid to tell you, Miss Austen, I'm at the end of my tether. I used to love cooking, but now it's just a job, and a poorly paid one at that.'

'It must be very hard trying to think of meals to make with such little produce, especially if you've lost that spark of inspiration.'

'That's just it, and I can't see it getting any better. I'm sorry to moan when we've only just met, but no one could do better on my budget. There's no help, except Becky the kitchen maid. The others have enough to do without having to help me with the cooking.'

'It's a pity the maids have to serve breakfast upstairs,' said Jane thinking out loud. 'If everyone ate downstairs, their time would be much better employed.'

'My thoughts exactly. And, I shouldn't like to talk out of turn, but if Lady Milton refrained from buying just one less dress a month, we'd all have fuller stomachs. But, I'm not one to gossip.'

Jane felt rather guilty that she, herself, was benefitting from Lady Milton's extravagance. She took a bite out of the seed cake which was delicious.

'And now I've embarrassed you,' said Mrs Wickens. 'I don't mean to be disloyal, but the truth is I haven't had a proper day off for more than six months now, and I should warn you, Miss Austen, the same will happen to you, if you let it.'

'Oh, how dreadful,' Jane exclaimed, thinking that she'd not yet had her first day off, which had been and gone without acknowledgement. 'That's not acceptable, Mrs Wickens, I hope you've complained.'

'Not yet, but I'm just biding my time. What I'd really like is a few days off to go and visit my sister Flossie in Paignton. I haven't seen her for a year, and we love to spend time together. It's not much to ask, is it, just a few days with your sister.'

Jane thought how much she would love to see Cassandra, and almost at the same time another idea formed in her mind. It would have to be a three-pronged attack, she decided. Alice, she knew, would present no difficulty in seeing the wisdom of her plans, and Beth, Emily and Cora might be persuaded if the scheme was introduced in the right way. Lady Milton might not immediately see the advantages and benefits to her daughters' education, but Jane was determined that if she were to fulfil her role as chief advisor to the household, she would persevere. As for Mae, Jane knew there lay the sticking point. She was not hopeful that she could bring Mae round, though a little psychology might be helpful.

'Would you trust me, Mrs Wickens? I'm a good plain cook, and with a bit of help I could take over for a few days so you could go away with a clear conscience. I'm sure Lady Milton will listen to me.'

'But, Miss Austen, even if you were the best cook in the land, you'll not have the experience, and I've told you there's no help to be had. It can't be done, but you're a sweet girl for thinking of me.'

'I don't want to sound as if I'm trying to teach my grandmother to suck eggs, but let me prove to you that I know what I'm doing. I used to cook often at home for a large family so I'm well practised. I've got an idea for a couple of recipes, and a plan for help, which might just work.'

Mrs Wickens wiped her eyes with her apron, as the tears pricked her eyelids. 'Can you really mean it? I don't know what to say I'm that grateful. I've stood looking at that lump of meat until I can't look a minute longer.'

'My friend, Martha Lloyd who cooked for my family for many years was testament to the fact that the right name can add a dash of excitement to any dish. Plain soup with vegetables and herbs was always known as Swiss soup, and a few boiled turnips in a dish with a dash of cream were called a fricassee. Well, I'm sure I don't need to tell you, Mrs Wickens, but I think if we draw up a menu we might get away with it, and help whet their appetite into the bargain.'

'I haven't got time for writing menus, Miss Austen, though I agree, there's a lot to be said for not calling a turnip a neep! And we've plenty of turnip babies in the garden just now, sweet enough for eating.'

'Leave the menus to me,' Jane insisted. 'We'll have a curry for the main course, if we use enough onion and potatoes the meat will go further.'

'Oh, I don't know that I hold with the likes of curry. Lord Milton has terrible trouble with his digestion, and besides, I've no Indian spices ... haven't cooked with them for years.'

Jane folded her arms and looked business-like. 'Lord Milton will be perfectly fine with a fricassee of turnips to settle his stomach first. I assure you, Martha's curry was a favourite with my family, and I've heard went a long way to persuade my brother Francis to marry her. And do not worry, I've an idea who will oblige us with the turmeric, galangal, and cayenne pepper.'

Jane had been so pleased when she'd learned from Dr Lyford that her sailor brother Francis had married her lifelong friend in 1828. She knew Martha would have been very happy with him and his children in Portsmouth, and she couldn't think of anyone more deserving.

'Well, you certainly sound as if you know what you're doing, but I can't just turn up in Paignton like that, I'll have to give Flossie notice.'

Jane searched the air for inspiration. 'You must write to her immediately, and with luck and the last post, you'll get your answer later. I'm sure Flossie is as keen to see you as you are to visit her. Now, if my plan is to work, you will have to feign illness for the rest of the day. Go to your room, and lie down on the bed. Please don't worry, this is most important if Lady Milton is to realise you need a holiday.'

Jane couldn't help congratulating herself later when her ideas were put into action. Lady Milton was horrified that Mrs Wickens was ill, and hadn't had a holiday for a year, and Jane managed to leave her with such feelings of guilt that the cook was given a fortnight off complete. At the same time she persuaded her ladyship that even if the girls were to marry lords, they needed to know how the kitchen operated, and that a girl marrying into the best houses in the land ought to know the rudiments of cookery. She was willing to teach them all that her friend had taught her, and pointed out that the daughters of aristocrats even attended cookery schools these days. It was all the vogue, and Flora Milton, not wishing to be unfashionable, gave her blessing.

Jane consulted Alice first, and after hearing all that she had to say about still feeling impossibly in love with Frankie, but determined to forget him, she seemed very pleased with Jane's scheme, and said it would give her something else to think about.

'I do feel I can meet him now without much alarm,' said Alice. 'It's been difficult watching him with Emily, but I am resigned. And now I shall have plenty to occupy my mind, and being active will stop me dwelling on gloomy thoughts. I am looking forward to learning to do a little more cooking, and it will be most useful if I ever get a job in London.'

Alice's nursing spirit came to the fore, and she was very helpful when telling the other girls of the new cookery lessons. The combination of Jane's way with words, and Alice's quiet persuasion meant that all the girls with the exception of Mae were down in the kitchen just half an hour later. Jane managed to be business-like with Will, and was especially careful to avoid his beautiful eyes which were looking at her with admiration. He was despatched to Sherford Park to see George Bartlett about some Indian spices, and Jane hoped, knowing the captain's generous nature, that Will might return not only with the spices, but with a little extra something for the pot.

Jane chose her moment to involve Mae in her schemes very carefully. Whilst everyone else was left happily peeling and chopping turnips for the fricassee, and cabbages, asparagus, and herbs for the soup, Jane went back upstairs as soon as she was sure Mr Weatherfield had arrived.

Mae and Julius were sitting in the drawing room with Lord Milton, though the latter had a newspaper over his head, accompanied by the gentle sounds of snoring as he slumbered. Every now and then a louder whiffle disturbed the paper, lifting a corner high into the air, much to the amusement of the two on the sofa.

Jane decided she would get straight to the point and ignore Mae's look of scorn as she walked into the room. 'Mr Weatherfield, I wondered if I might trouble you with a request from downstairs, only Miss Alice Milton has heard you are an excellent artist, and requires a little help with something decorative.'

'Well, I've been known to dabble slightly,' he added uncertainly. 'What can I do?'

'Well, the point is Mrs Wickens has been struck down and taken to her bed with fatigue. She's very poorly, and is about to be packed off to Paignton. Miss Milton has taken over the kitchen with wartime spirit, and as tonight is her very first dinner, she requests some help with the menus. It's just writing them out, but she thought a little artistic embellishment would be the very thing. She is hoping someone of your splendid talents will bring a certain extraordinary flair to the whole project.'

'Well, I'm very flattered,' he began.

'I don't know, Julius, if this is quite your thing,' Mae began, clearly put out that she'd not been consulted. 'You're more of a fine artist, I believe, very good at landscapes and that sort of thing, but this sounds just perfect for me. It's often been remarked upon that I have a fine calligraphic hand, and I can paint notepaper in a Florentine style so you'd never know the difference.'

Jane bided her time. She didn't speak for fear of setting Mae against her own decision to help.

'I rather like the idea of a painting challenge, and I have a neat hand, if I say so myself,' said Julius. 'We could do it together, I'm sure, Mae, I daresay you'll be requiring more than one menu, Miss Austen.'

'Yes, two or three at least, thank you very much,' said Jane. 'Miss Milton has the paper, pens and paint laid out in the kitchen. She thought you'd be most comfortable there; the table is an enormous one. It's rather a party atmosphere down there, everyone is helping to cook for the dinner.'

Mae looked as if she might change her mind for a moment and say no, but then Julius pulled her to her feet, saying it did sound very amusing, and besides, he was just dying to prove that his calligraphic skills were just as good as Mae's.

Will duly returned within the half hour, not only with the spices, but with the captain who brought some shoulder of lamb to add to the pot. He was very excited about the cooking of curry, his favourite food, and when he offered to take over that part of the teaching Jane couldn't have been more pleased. He proved to be a very good cook, and peppered his talk with many anecdotes about his adventures in India. Even Mae couldn't help listening, and once, laughed out loud when he described the first time he tried a chilli pepper and thought his mouth was on fire.

It was all going rather well, Jane thought. There was a busy hum of activity, and everyone was co-operating wonderfully. There hadn't been a cross word all morning. Julius and Mae were busy outdoing one another on the menus, but everyone praised their efforts, and when Jane remarked on Mae's beautiful painting she was rewarded with a half smile, which was progress, indeed. Beth and Cora were entrusted with the soup, Alice and Emily were making the fricassee, and Jane was making a trifle with some leftover Madeira cake, eggs for a custard on top, and finished with a cream syllabub laced with sherry. Will loitered by her side, offering to stir the custard, and sticking his finger into the cream. He insisted on whisking the eggs and sugar as she poured the hot milk mixture from the saucepan into the bowl, before returning it all to the hot pan.

'We make a good team, don't you think?' said Will taking over to stir the custard.

'Everyone is pulling together quite wonderfully, I have to agree,' answered Jane; looking round the kitchen knowing full well that wasn't what he meant.

He leaned towards her, his hair flopping forward over one dark brow, and gently whispered in a low voice. 'You know the way to a man's heart is through his stomach?'

Jane heard the humour in his voice, and to stop herself smiling she moved away to busy herself lining a glass dish with the slices of cake. She was determined to put him in his place. 'And the way to a woman's is to avoid all witticisms and old proverbs.'

Will laughed and pushed back his hair as he straightened. 'You have a way with words, Miss Austen.'

'I like to think so.'

'Alice tells me you like to write.'

'I do when I have the time. Sadly, that's not been the case of late.'

'Haven't you a day off coming up?'

It was now or never and she didn't hesitate. 'That was precisely eleven days ago, and it didn't happen.'

Jane knew she sounded cross, but she had a right to be.

Will looked genuinely mortified. 'Oh, my dear Jane, you should have said something ... can you possibly forgive us? We must do something about that immediately! I will inform Flora that you're to have the rest of the day and tomorrow off to do as you like.'

He sounded so apologetic that she forgave him at once, and though she protested at first, she agreed that she'd spend some time upstairs after dinner. Thinking she shouldn't have spoken out so vehemently Jane went on to say there'd be no one to supervise the kitchen in her absence if she had a day off, but Alice who was horrified that no one had remembered it, assured her they would manage. The captain added that he'd be delighted to help out once more, and went so far as to say he'd bring his own cook over for a day or two to help out.

Jane couldn't help feeling excited, even though she felt guilty that her plans were now being put on hold. But, it was so long since she'd had any time to herself, and now a whole evening and the day beyond stretched luxuriously ahead.

Chapter Fourteen

Jane's walk down into the village the next day was a most enjoyable experience. For one thing, she couldn't stop smiling at the sense of freedom she was feeling, and the sheer excitement at the thought of all the preparations she'd made for the day. For another, yesterday had turned out to be a tremendous success, and the dinner had proved to be not only delicious, but had gone a long way to achieve what she'd set out to do. Jane had witnessed definite proof that when employed in a positive activity, the Miltons were all capable of getting along as a family, and even of being kind to one another.

Last night, after Alice and Will had made sure Jane was excused once dinner was over, she'd actually started writing out a plan for her novel, and having the time to do as she wished in the evening had been wonderful. She'd decided to save the first sentence of her new novel for when she was sitting on the beach with her notebook in hand looking at the view. There was nowhere as inspiring as the sea, and she couldn't wait to get started. Her notebook and pen were tucked safely in her basket and Alice had made sure Jane had a bottle of lemonade too, though added she must be sure to treat herself to a crab sandwich and a pot of tea for her lunch from the lady who looked after the tea hut on the sands.

Jane reached the village in good time and thought she'd stop off at Mrs Foxworthy's tearooms to buy herself an iced cake for a treat before making her way down to the beach. As she passed Miss Beales' milliner's shop, she happened to look in the window, and saw the array of summer hats on display. She couldn't help admiring the cloche hats, which were designed especially to show off a bobbed haircut, and now she'd been paid for her first month's work she wondered if she dared buy one. As she gazed intently through the bow window trying to decide between cream linen, or a straw trimmed with sage green, she noticed a familiar face inside. Julius Weatherfield was in deep discussion with Jessie Beales who was behind the counter looking rather flustered. Jane sensed Jessie's unease, and in pretence of examining the grosgrain ribbon on a garden hat, observed them an instant longer. Julius leaned forward to whisper something in her ear before he took Jessie's hand to his lips and kissed it, a moment so intimate that Jane felt she ought not to have witnessed it. Jessie instantly snatched her hand away, turning scarlet in the process, and Jane turned away feeling very troubled by what she'd seen and wished she hadn't lingered. Though she was sure he might dismiss the gesture as one of mild flirtation, Jane could see Jessie was very upset by it. Yet there was something more, and it was the way Jessie had recoiled from him that Jane found not only perturbing, but also puzzling. She decided to go in with the object of buying a hat, and see if she could discover what was going on.

'Miss Austen, what a pleasure,' said Mr Weatherfield, raising a very smart panama from his head as she entered. 'Jessie has persuaded me to buy this spiffing new hat, and I am certain she'll do the same for you.'

'Good morning, Miss Austen,' said Jessie ignoring him. 'How can I help you?'

Jane pointed out the hats she'd liked to try on, and Jessie, still flaming red in her cheeks, turned to the window, stretching over with one leg in the air to reach them.

Mr Weatherfield was making a great study of Jessie's figure from the rear, Jane noticed, by his approving eyes. He seemed to have forgotten she was there, and felt embarrassed by his obvious appreciation.

'I was just asking Jessie if she was coming to the picnic at Ashcombe Falls a week on Saturday,' said Julius snapping back to the conversation and turning to smile at Jane. 'Did you know of the change of plan, Miss Austen?'

'I heard something about it yesterday from Emily,' said Jane who'd heard all the discussion in the kitchen, 'but not all the details.'

'It seems Jonathan Keeling suggested the walk to the waterfalls instead of having a picnic on the beach. I think he wishes his friends to see something of Devon's beauty spots, and he thought Fergus Dauncey might be interested because there used to be a working silver mine nearby.'

'It sounds quite delightful, I must admit,' said Jane. 'I am looking forward to seeing the waterfall and the fern gardens very much.'

'Yes, it's a pity we can't go sooner,' said Julius, 'but apparently Jonathan is very busy with his guests. I daresay they're a lot more important than the rest of us.'

Jessie set the hats down on the counter and asked which she'd like to try first, which spared Jane having to reply.

'Is there anything else I can do for you, Mr Weatherfield?' Jessie asked rather pointedly.

'I know when I'm not wanted, ladies,' Julius said with a grin. He tipped his hat once more. 'I'm just off to the castle, I hope you both have a lovely day.'

Jane couldn't help wondering why Jessie looked so upset, and as she tried the hats on and examined her reflection she could see Jessie through the looking glass following Julius's progress down the road. There was something going on there, she decided, but couldn't make up her mind quite what, and as she also proved to be just as indecisive about the cloche hats, which would match her summer dresses to perfection, she purchased them both. If Jane had any misgivings on certain aspects of Mr Weatherfield's character it was that he wore his passions too openly, that he was altogether too enthusiastic, too ready to please, and gave his opinions far too readily. And besides all that he was a great flirt as she'd just witnessed. Where Mae needed checking, he indulged and laughed at her, and the more Jane saw both of them together the more convinced she was that it was not a good pairing. But, she hesitated to think badly of him, putting it down to youthful exuberance, and decided she must take more pains to get to know him in case she'd read him wrongly.

Jessie didn't say very much as she started to wrap the hats in tissue, though she did look pleased when Jane said they were exactly what she was looking for, and that she would wear the straw hat for going down to the beach, and pick up the other later on her way home. Whilst Jessie was finishing packing the hat box Miss Beales came into the shop from upstairs and the atmosphere immediately lightened, though Jane knew that meant she wouldn't be able to escape for at least another fifteen minutes, as Miss Beales wouldn't stop talking. But, at last she was free, and she stepped out with a light heart feeling wonderfully smart in her new hat, and with the purchase of an iced bun accomplished just two minutes later, Jane started off for the road down to the beach.

It was sheer bliss to sit in a deck chair on the sands, a wonderful invention, Jane thought, as she gazed out to sea under the shade of the Japanese parasol Alice had insisted she take to keep cool. Tints of paper flowers dappled her arms in tones of jade and pink, whilst everywhere else sunshine gilded the rocks, and shallow pools, glittering the calm waters with shards of gold like darting fish.

It was the strangest feeling to be alone when she'd been unused to being solitary for such a long time, but she loved being lost with her thoughts. Opening her notebook and seeing the virgin paper held such promise, and a sense of thrilling anticipation quickened her senses. It was impossible to see the title and the sea without thinking of her brave sailor brothers, Frank and Charles, and she couldn't help wondering how different the lives of all her brothers might have been if they'd been born in a later time or sacrificed to the war she'd learned so much about. She'd never doubted that her brothers wouldn't return from fighting on the seas, but this last so-called Great War had claimed so many lives, that she was glad she'd been spared the kind of heartache other families had endured. Though heartache she'd suffered, none the less, on learning of their deaths. Still serving his country at the grand age of seventy three, Charles had died from cholera, and Frank had survived even Martha, surrounded by the family he loved but succumbing at last to old age at ninety one. Jane struggled to imagine them as old men, and pictured all of them together in her mind, James, Edward, Henry, Frank and Charles, as she liked to think of them. She recalled learning sign language so she could communicate with George, her poor deaf brother whom she'd visited whenever she could, and remembered his dear face and innocent nature. But, of course none of them were perfect, and like other families there'd been times when they'd squabbled and had their fallings out.

Jane smiled to remember the time when Henry and James had both fallen head over heels in love with their cousin Eliza, and how they'd almost come to blows one Christmas. Henry had persuaded their father to have the barn fitted up as a theatre. Lengths of green baize were ordered for curtains and scenery was painted on old sheets stretched over batons and fixed into place by Frank who was the carpenter of the family. Cassy had drawn the designs and the chief of the painting, and Jane had helped to fill in the carefully drawn trees, hills and flowers, feeling very proud of her efforts. The makeshift stage was fashioned from hay bales disguised with wooden planks, and when the candle footlights were lit, the brass reflectors had glowed just like those in a real theatre.

There'd been much discussion and argument about which play would be most suitable. Jane closed her eyes and pictured them all in her head. Eliza was such a strong image for one so small and delicate, but with a personality that filled the barn.

'For my part, we cannot do better than perform *Which is the Man*? or *Bon Ton*,' said Eliza, who was a great theatregoer. 'I saw both performed in Tunbridge Wells in September and I know you would love them.'

'But will there be parts enough for everyone? James asked, ever practical. 'Though, I should be disinclined to act myself. I am a man of the cloth, after all.'

James, recently ordained, was laughed at for becoming overly serious.

'But, Jemmy, you must act!' Eliza could be very forthright when she wished to be. 'A talent like yours cannot be hidden because you are now ordained. Come, say it is not so.'

James blushed to the roots of his powdered hair. 'Put like that, I can hardly object, though I feel uneasy. I will have quite enough to do in directing the players. And what of the theme of the play? It must be suitable for our neighbours or mother will have a fit.'

'The theme of both plays is wonderfully droll,' said Eliza, casting her eyes round at her rapt audience. 'They are both comedies, about conflict in love, between the laissez-faire attitude of the darling French against the rather more cautious and sober one of her English cousins.'

There'd been a general murmur of approval and before anyone could object, Eliza went on. 'Good! It is settled ... how I shall love playing Lady Bell Bloomer in *Which is the Man*? Every role is so amusing, but do not worry, we shall find a dashing part for you, dear Jemmy, ... and Henry, the part of Beauchamp was simply written for you. He is a soldier and I am sure you would dazzle us all in scarlet.'

In the end the play chosen was *The Wonder! A Woman Keeps a Secret*, though Eliza pulled a face at first, until she learned that her part was that of Violante, an independent woman of great spirit, and then she was happy. Set in Lisbon, *The Wonder* was about two lively and vivacious young women plotting to get their own way and the men they desire, against the wishes of their fathers.

'Cassy, would you be comfortable playing the part of Isabella?' Jemmy asked.

Eliza squeezed Cassy's hand when she nodded her assent. 'We will set the stage on fire, my dear cousin. Now, little Jane must also have a part. Which is it to be?'

Jane remembered playing the part of a maid, glad that with little to say she knew the fun would be in watching everyone else.

'I think Felix is best suited to my character,' Jemmy offered, which would mean he'd play Eliza's love interest. Henry was not at all happy about that.

'But, if you are also to direct us, should you not consider a smaller role for yourself?' said Henry. 'I am just as happy to play Felix.'

Eliza was ten years older than Henry, but the chemistry between them was plain for all to see. They shared a book as they read the play, their fingers so close they were almost touching.

'You're not old enough to play Felix,' Jemmy answered, unable to keep the frustration from his voice, 'the part requires a certain sophistication.'

'But, I am far too young to play the part of either the father or Captain Britton.'

'Perhaps Madame should choose for herself,' said cousin Egerton, who'd come to join the troupe, intent on making mischief and being thoroughly outrageous. 'Whom would you rather have make love to you, Eliza?'

Cassy nudged Jane under the table when they heard that – it was all they could do not to laugh.

Eliza laughed it off prettily, flicking out her fan to examine the landscape painted on its silk for a moment, before flicking it shut again. Looking up she wore her most bewitching expression. 'Gentlemen, I blush at your remarks. I will put it to the public vote for I will be happy with any Don Felix that is chosen for me.'

'Why not toss for it?' Egerton produced a penny from his pocket. 'Heads for Jemmy as the elder, and tails for Henry.'

Tossing the coin into the air, they watched it spin, Jane crossing her fingers hoping Henry would have his heart's desire.

'Well, Madame, which is the man?' Egerton laughed at his own joke, the coin trapped between his hands.

Eliza looked as if she really would not mind the outcome. Her attitude was girlish, as she waited, her eyes sparkling in the candlelight, soft curls falling upon her powdered skin.

'Tails it is!' Egerton called, revealing the penny underneath. Jemmy's face fell, whilst Henry and Eliza tried their hardest not to appear too pleased with themselves.

The actors split off into groups or pairs to rehearse and Jane watched Henry and Eliza deep in conversation. The fifth act brought a scene between them which interested her most particularly, and which she was longing and dreading to see how they would perform. Jane recalled how they would disappear to rehearse in private, and on stage they embraced and touched one another. Henry kissed Eliza's hand very convincingly with many protestations of love, and when their eyes met the sparks flew. The old parsonage was awash with romance, inspiring Jane's writing. The ongoing tussle of hearts and minds between Henry and Eliza, made her think about what she believed was right and wrong in the world. Five years passed by after that during which time Eliza and Henry's attraction grew and diminished. Henry distanced himself for a while, as if he was no longer content to be Eliza's plaything. Going to Oxford helped, but Jane always had the feeling that neither of them would be content to put the past to rest.

There were times when Jane had felt outraged about the way Eliza twisted Henry's heart. He was like her pet pug, a plaything for her to discard whenever she felt like it, and she'd hated to see him upset, although he never admitted that Eliza's behaviour hurt him. He vented his feelings in his own writing. Jane doubted anyone was fooled by his stories about the anguish of being in love with an older woman published in the magazine, *The Loiterer*, that he produced with James. At the last, she was happy he'd won her heart for his sake, but a part of her thought Eliza had been responsible for setting him on a path that led to his eventual ruin. Persuading him to wear a scarlet coat and join the army, and then later to start his own bank, which failed in the end was under Eliza's influence, Jane thought. But she was not one to dwell on what should have or might have been, or to apportion blame.

Jane supposed seeing Julius and Jessie that morning had triggered something off in her memory to remember those days with such vivid clarity. She didn't want to spend any more time thinking about the past, and as she was determined to enjoy the day, she put those thoughts to the back of her mind to be examined another time.

The morning passed swiftly, and Jane wrote page after page, letting the words flow onto the paper. Writing in a contemporary style didn't come easily, and she found a tendency to keep drifting back to the language she'd known and which had flowed seamlessly over a hundred years ago, but on the whole she was happy. It felt so good to be writing again, and she was pleased that she'd accomplished the bones of a first chapter before she started to feel peckish and the thoughts of tea and crab sandwiches kept halting her concentration. She folded the parasol, tidied away her notebook, and was just looking for her purse, when a shadow fell over the basket, blocking out the sun. A silhouette of a man blackened the white sand, and when she looked up she cried out in surprise.

Chapter Fifteen

It was Doctor Lyford! Jane felt shocked, yet delighted to see him, and scrambled out of the deck chair to take his hand. He was looking rested, she thought, and very dapper in cream linen with a smart straw boater. He had the kind of eyes that crinkled into laughter lines when he smiled, and he seemed as glad to see her, as she was to see him.

They both spoke at once, and then Jane waited for him to speak.

'I've only just discovered it's your day off, and I'm so sorry to intrude,' he said, 'but I'm visiting a friend in the area, and I couldn't come without saying hello, and seeing how you are. But, I can tell from your face you must be happy, you're looking so wonderfully well. And I do love your hair.'

'Oh, Doctor Lyford, what a lovely surprise,' said Jane knowing his remarks were causing her to blush, 'and it's the most welcome intrusion, I assure you. Come, let us find you a deckchair. I was just about to have some tea and a spot of lunch. Would you care to join me?'

'I would love to if you're sure I'm not interrupting,' he said pulling a stray deckchair over to place it next to Jane's. 'I went up to the castle first, and a chap called Will told me you were writing and wouldn't like to be disturbed.'

Jane took Dr Lyford's arm as they walked over the sands.

'Will Milton, he's the heir to Manberley,' said Jane. 'And he's right in a way. No, I wouldn't want to be disturbed by most people, but you are the one exception. And I've finished writing for the day. All work and no play … if you know what I mean.'

'Quite! Well, I'm very pleased to hear you're taking the afternoon off, I will feel much better about taking up some of your time before I visit my friend.'

They stood in the queue at the tea place, a ramshackle wooden hut with a most delightful array of sandwiches and fruit cake on display under glass domes.

'Is it Mr Quance, by any chance?'

'It is indeed, Miss Austen, and now I feel you must think I've put out my spies to keep an eye on you.'

'Not at all, it is good to know someone cares enough about me to do that. And Mr Quance hasn't been in the way, he just wanted me to know he was there should I need him.'

'He wouldn't overstep the mark, he's a big fan of yours.'

'So I gathered,' said Jane with a smile, 'and he's very sweet and kind.'

'And how are you finding the children?'

Dr Lyford's eyes were twinkling, and he was smiling broadly.

'Did you have any idea of there being no small children before you sent me here?' Jane asked.

'I'm afraid I had the slightest hint from Mrs Naseby, but I felt sure you'd never agree to the job if you knew the truth so she agreed not to mention it in a letter or even until Lady Milton had informed you. I also thought you'd be happier in the long run if they were older and wouldn't require so much looking after. Will you ever forgive me?'

'Of course I will, and you are right, I should have run a mile, yet although the Miltons are an odd bunch, I must admit to be enjoying my time at the castle in a strange way. Alice is a particularly kind young woman, and I value her friendship. The most challenging pair are Mae and Emily, but lately I've seen the slightest hint of promise there too, though I think if I were to live there a lifetime it might not be long enough to make a sufficient dent in their sensibilities.'

Dr Lyford gave the order and waited whilst the lady filled a tray with a selection of crab sandwiches and fruit cake on crocus patterned plates. A big brown betty teapot was heaped with several spoons of tea and held under the hissing urn.

'They sound most entertaining.'

'Oh, they are in their own way, and they do all love to be in the thick of a drama. I cannot understand it myself, I much prefer a quiet life. If I ran the castle I'd spend my mornings sitting by a fire writing endless novels, and my afternoons walking about the estate, or taking a swim in the moat.'

'And how are you truly feeling, in yourself?'

'I've never felt better. I can truthfully say I feel healthier than at any time in my life before.'

'There have been no symptoms of a return to your old problem?'

'No, should there be?'

'Not at all, but you would let me know, wouldn't you, at the first sign of illness?'

'What, even a trifling cold? Dr Lyford, I am made of sterner stuff, I assure you.'

'I don't doubt your mettle, Miss Austen, but it is extremely important. If there is any change at all, you must let me know.'

Dr Lyford carried the heavy tray and set it down on the sands, whilst they settled back into their deckchairs.

Jane turned to look into his hazel eyes. 'I promise. Thank you for taking such good care of me. It's been very difficult in many ways, I will admit. Not about being young again, obviously, I've really taken that in my stride. How I delight in being able to walk a mile without feeling any fatigue, and how I love looking in the glass again, I am vain enough to tell you.'

'But, you must miss the old times ... your family, and your sister most particularly.'

Jane picked up the teapot and started to pour hot tea into the cups. His voice was so tender she thought she might crumple and cry. 'I confess I do, and everything is just so different, and yet the same. I keep thinking I shall wake up and find this has all been a dream. That's how it feels, as if my past life was just an illusion, or that I've come back from a trance.'

'And if you could, would you go back?'

Putting the teapot down, she clasped her hands together. 'To see my sister, to hear her voice once again, and feel her arms around me, I would be prepared to do anything. If I could have a moment to be the age I am now and walk back into Steventon rectory to see my beloved father or hear my mother telling me all will be well, I would return if I could. But to go back in order to face such illness again; no, I couldn't do that. To endure such pain, and lack of hope … in any case, I prefer to look forward, not back, though my memories intrude on my thoughts occasionally.'

Dr Lyford put out his hand to pat Jane's reassuringly. 'It is only natural.'

It was wonderful to be able to talk to someone freely who understood what she was feeling, and who knew her story. Realising she'd been keeping most of her feelings buried, it felt so good to let them out and talk to one who truly had her best interests at heart. Suddenly, she was overwhelmed by her emotions, and the tears spilled over her cheeks. Brushing them away hastily, she saw Dr Lyford leaning towards her once again. Jane felt the grip of his strong fingers as he held her chin steadily, and with a cotton handkerchief in his other hand he softly wiped away her tears.

Looking into his eyes Jane saw that look of intense caring that she'd seen before. His eyes were twinkling with the reflection of the sea in their depths. One minute they shone with a hazel light, the next with moss agate, but his eyes sparkled mostly with pure compassion. He made her feel safe and secure, and her trust in him grew further.

'It was so kind of you to come, I'm so very grateful,' she started to say, as she took his proffered handkerchief, but something just out of the corner of her eye made her turn her head. She'd known who it was before she'd really registered the fact. Will Milton was standing a little way to one side watching them. Jane saw him nod in their direction, before he looked as if he might walk on, but she called out in an attempt to stop him.

'Mr Milton, come and join us.'

Will hesitated for a moment, then strode towards them, and shook Dr Lyford's hand vigorously.

'Will Milton, this is Doctor John Lyford,' said Jane, 'he lives in Winchester.'

Jane couldn't decide whether to go into more detail than that, but then thought that might lead into a whole set of questions she wouldn't know how to answer, so she added nothing.

'How do you do,' said Will. 'I saw you up at the castle ... I see you had no trouble finding your way.'

'No, thank you, Mr Milton, your directions were very concise.'

Will waved the basket in his hand, and looked down at their crab sandwiches. 'I was just going to have a little picnic. As a matter of fact, Miss Austen, I was coming to see if you wished to share it, I thought you might be on your own. Dr Lyford told me he was visiting a friend.'

'Oh, I am visiting him later for afternoon tea,' said the doctor, 'but please join us. We've only just got ourselves settled.'

'Yes,' said Jane, 'I can pop back and get another cup and saucer in no time.'

Will was looking handsome with a straw boater set at a jaunty angle on his head, his tanned face in contrast to the white summer suit he was wearing. She felt his eyes bore through her.

'I don't want to intrude,' he said. 'No, you carry on as you were. I've just seen some friends further along the beach ... I'll go and join them.'

'But you wouldn't be intruding,' said Jane thinking how it would all look to Will, feeling quite mortified that he must have seen John Lyford holding her face in his hands, whilst simultaneously wondering why she cared so much what he thought. 'Do sit down.'

Will ignored her, turning to wave at his friends who were all young girls.

'It's good to see you having some fun, Miss Austen,' he said turning back again, 'but I will leave you now. Will you be joining us for dinner, Dr Lyford?'

'No, it's very kind of you to offer, Mr Milton, but I must catch the six thirty train back to Dawlish.'

'In that case, I wish you a speedy journey. Enjoy the crab, Miss Austen ... will you be back for dinner or do you have another assignation?'

Jane glared at him. How dare he make fun of her in front of Dr Lyford, and even if she had several assignations, as he called them, it wasn't any of his business. 'I will be taking a light supper in my room. It is my day off to do with as I choose, if you remember.'

'I do indeed, dear lady. I suppose you'll be wishing to write more of your romantic novel in that gothic tower of yours. That touching scene I just witnessed here on the beach ... the hero comforting the heroine with a handkerchief ... you really should find a place for its inclusion in one of the early chapters. Women love that sort of sentimental nonsense.'

Jane behaved as if he didn't exist, insisting the doctor sit down again. Picking up the plate of crab sandwiches, she offered it to her companion who took one without hesitation. He could see just how cross Jane was feeling, and he sat back quietly in his deckchair to munch silently, afraid to speak again until she recovered.

One of the girls barely dressed in a swimsuit and a towel robe dashed over to take Will's hand.

'Come on Will, we've got something for you,' she said, pulling at his arm, and giggling affectedly.

'Goodbye Mr Milton,' said Jane, picking up her tea, 'I think your friends are very keen for your company.'

Will hadn't quite spoiled what proved to be a lovely afternoon, even if Jane was always aware of him sitting a few yards away with the presence of several girls who seemed to shriek with laughter at everything he said. Never before had she been so attentive to a partner, but she wanted Will to see her enjoying the company of another man and really put him in his place.

Dr Lyford stayed with Jane until four o'clock, when he said he really must go and meet Mr Quance. Jane took his arm companionably to walk with him up to the village, but made sure she didn't once look back to see if their progress was being monitored. Let Will think what he likes, she thought, he'd really embarrassed her, no doubt because he thought he'd guessed all about her relationship with the doctor. She wasn't going to let him ruin her day, and as she said goodbye at the bookshop door, Jane realised just how glad she'd been to see John Lyford.

'You will come again soon, I hope,' she said, shaking his outstretched hand.

'You may depend on it,' he answered. 'Are you quite sure you won't come in and see Mr Quance, I know he would love to see you.'

'No thank you, it's most kind, but I am anxious to get back to the castle. It's silly, but I've quite missed them all today in an odd way.'

'And I daresay you'd like to get back to your writing. You must wish to make the most of a day like this, I'm sure.'

'Oh, Dr Lyford, I cannot tell you how much it means to me to have the chance to write again.'

He gave her hand one last squeeze, and tipped his hat. 'Do take good care of yourself, Miss Austen.'

'I will, I promise … and thank you again … for everything.'

Chapter Sixteen

With Mrs Wickens away and the new system in place the castle became almost unrecognisable. Lady Milton cunningly invited Captain Bartlett to stay, which meant his valet, Mr Sullens, two extra maids, and most importantly of all, his cook, Mrs Muckle, came too. A formidable creature, thin as a lathe, and with a no nonsense approach, she would not have her kitchen maids put upon, and as the family were all frightened of the fearful combination that she and Mrs Naseby made as a joint force of nature, they observed the correct hours for meals, even coming down to breakfast on time. Flora started a new habit of appearing for breakfast well before noon, but she put her foot down at being dressed for the day, and floated into the dining room every morning in a different silk peignoir in various hues of apricot, powder blue, and tea rose, much to the discomfort of George Bartlett who blushed like a girl at a debutante's ball, and didn't know quite where to rest his eyes. Whilst early mornings didn't suit them all, they seemed to be civil at least, and with Alice in charge of the housekeeping under Mrs Naseby's watchful eye, even the younger members seemed willing to help when called on for ideas.

Jane, keen to get on with her plan for improvements suggested to Alice that Mae, with her eye for fashion and decoration, should be put in charge of brightening up the hall and supervising the maids with any help they could get from Mr Bell, Mr Sullens, and the footmen in moving furniture and cleaning the stairs. Alice put the proposal in place with much flattery, as if it were her idea, and armed with a stack of Vogue magazines begged Mae for her consultation.

'There's nothing for it, those sagging armchairs must go,' said Mae, as if seeing them for the first time, 'though we've nothing to replace them with, certainly nothing modern enough to feature in a magazine.'

She was beginning to believe she had some talent artistically, and it was rather lovely to have one's opinion asked.

'I thought you might take a look in the attics,' said Alice, 'there must be all sorts of things up there that we don't know about.'

Mae was about to protest when she realised that if Julius were to help her they might get some time alone together. 'Yes, I think that's an idea, there's a definite nod to the past being featured in some of these pictures,' she said, 'Julius must help me investigate and see if we can't find some quirky antique pieces that have been long forgotten.'

'Cora, you'll help too, won't you?' said Alice, keen not to put Jane in a confrontational situation with her sister, by saying she would accompany them upstairs.

'Yes, Cora, do come and help,' said Julius immediately, ignoring the widened eyes and heavy sighs from Mae.

Cora looked very excited to be noticed and needed, and went skipping off behind them. Jane, though surprised at the intervention was glad Julius was being so kind to Cora, and certain they'd be well chaperoned if she was with them. She noticed how well Mae was moving now, with not a sign of her injured knee giving any trouble. Dressed in a bohemian style in a flowing romantic dress of cerulean blue, with a long cherry amber necklace contrasting in colour, Mae seemed to be giving vent to her artistic sensibilities, no doubt, as a result of reading lately about the artist Vanessa Bell in the newspaper. She'd loved her work ever since she'd been taken to see an exhibition of paintings in London a couple of years ago. A carnelian silk scarf wound through her curls that fell to her shoulders in lustrous waves to match the teardrop earrings that dangled and swung with every turn of her head. It was observed that George Bartlett had been unable to take his eyes off her at breakfast, and without Jessie Beales to distract him it seemed he was a lost cause. Jane saw that with Mae being so much happier her attraction for any men who turned up at the castle seemed to have increased tenfold now she was not being so sulky and was joining in a lot more often. Mae was even talking about painting some murals with Julius's help, until it was pointed out that some of the panelling was Grinling Gibbons, but some sketches of the peacocks in the gardens were drawn out, nevertheless, in preparation of a painting on canvas.

By the end of the week everyone was drafted in to help. The maids feather-dusted and polished, cleaned and swept until all was gleaming. Bell and Sullens directed the footmen who dragged down the furniture from the attic rooms with much complaining, and Emily, Beth and Cora helped to sort through a mound of textiles for curtains, before choosing lengths of chartreuse brocade which, when hung, reflected pools of apple and jonquil sunbeams on the whitened stone floor. The final preparations took all day, but when they were finished everyone thought it had all been worth it. Light poured through the long polished windows on the stairs shimmering in silver chevrons through a glass vase of ostrich feathers, to sparkle on boxes of enamel and mother of pearl arranged on a central table. In place of the sagging armchairs an elegant pair of Edwardian tub chairs with clean lines, as close to a modernist style as could be found in the castle attics, were placed either side of the great fireplace. Above it, in pride of place hung Mae's peacock painting, an abstract triumph in shades of turquoise, aquamarine and viridian, the perfect foil for the warm tones of the wooden panelling. Terracotta urns with majestic palms completed the transformation, and as Mae called them all in to see what had been accomplished everyone was astounded.

Lady Milton, coming down from her room paused on the stairs to take in the view through the window, one she'd not seen for quite some time.

'Oh, it's quite beautiful,' she said, moved to describe the sea bay in the distance as a plate of sapphire blue under a flamingo sky as the sun lowered to the horizon.

Even Lord Milton was impressed though not so poetically effusive. 'I've never seen the place so clean or looking so loved since I was a boy. There'll be an extra shilling for the maids and footmen, and a bottle of something to share for Mr Bell and Mr Sullens. Mind you don't spend and drink it all at once!'

The maids curtsied and beamed, the footmen cheered up considerably, whilst Mr Bell and Mr Sullens tried not to look too disappointed at the lack of a cash reward.

'Mae, Miss Austen tells me this was all your idea,' Lord Milton went on. 'I think you've done a marvellous job, and that painting isn't half bad.'

Mae glanced over at Jane, and smiled. It was a real, genuine, up to the corners of her eyes smile, which Jane did her best to return. Alice must have spilled the beans, she realised.

Lady Milton descended the remaining steps knowing all eyes watched her progress waiting to see if she would add anything more. She crossed the hall to take Mae's hand and kiss her cheek. For once, Mae didn't flinch or pull away.

'Mae, you have a real talent as an artist, and I've no doubt would make a remarkably fine interior decorator. Thank you, my dear, it looks absolutely heavenly.'

'It was nothing, Flora,' said Mae who was looking quite overwhelmed. 'The truth is Miss Austen had the idea, and Alice helped enormously … all I did was pull a few pieces out of storage.'

'Credit where it's due, my dear,' said Flora. 'I meant every word, and I know one day you'll go out into the world and become a great artist. Alice, you are a treasure, as ever, and you too, Miss Austen, I thank you both from the bottom of my heart.'

'Hear, hear!' called Will who'd been very quiet until that moment. 'Let us drink to the Milton girls of Manberley Castle, and their governess, Miss Austen.'

Jane couldn't decide whether he was serious or not, but when he winked at her she couldn't help but forgive him for his silliness on the beach. It occurred to her that as the heir to Manberley he wasn't used to people snubbing his offers of anything, least of all a prepared picnic, even if she was sure he'd had nothing to do with its provision. But, she could not wink back at him or even smile, and the usual awkwardness she felt around him seemed to rise even greater, like the waves crashing on the rocks and foaming into pearls.

Chapter Seventeen

The day of the walk to Ashcombe Falls was heralded in by a blaze of sunshine and a blast of heat, which announced that July had well and truly arrived. Jane was woken early by the light, spangling her room with beams of gold, and she jumped out of bed feeling excited about the day. For once there was steaming hot water coming from the taps in the bathroom and she luxuriated in the warmth, taking her time to bathe with a bar of scented soap and washing her hair with the shampoo that Marcel had given her. She had to admit a bath was a wonderful indulgence, and she could have stayed immersed in the water for a lot longer, but she didn't want to be late. Hopping out, she dried herself on one of the fluffy towels that had been bought especially for her, and choosing a cream linen dress, and a cardigan in case the weather chilled, she took her new straw hat and pulled it on. Jane had the biggest surprise of all when she found a pair of walking boots outside her door with a note from Mae saying she was sure they were the same size. They fitted perfectly so Jane dashed downstairs feeling quite the part, to join the breakfast party and to give Mae her thanks. Whilst they were not exactly best friends and Mae still barely exchanged a word with her, Jane felt much progress was being made. At breakfast Alice managed to whisper she'd had nothing to do with her sister's thoughtfulness and generosity, insisting it was all Mae's own effort. Jane felt quite touched, for not only was she receiving the occasional smile from Mae, but she also no longer dreaded walking into a room where the latter was the only occupant.

Before breakfast was quite over, Nora and Jessie Beales arrived half an hour earlier than the expected time, which George Bartlett fortunately anticipated. Fearful of being left behind, they always turned up before being needed, and today was no exception. George was waiting in the hall, and now it was such a congenial space they stayed there to chat whilst waiting for the others to join them. Jessie Beales looked particularly fetching this morning, George thought, dressed in forest green linens, which set off her auburn hair, and for the first time he thought she looked quite pretty.

Jonathan Keeling's party arrived on time from the Priors and were astonished to see the other Miltons appear at the same moment. Not known for their punctuality, Jonathan was sure they'd be kept waiting as usual, but there the Miltons were, suitably dressed for the occasion in country clothes and stout walking boots. Lord and Lady Milton welcomed their friends but declined the invitation pressed on them once more, her ladyship declaring that too much walking didn't agree with her. Lord Milton did his usual disappearing act as soon as he could but his wife remained, as gracious, Jane thought, as any lady to the manor born, waiting to wave them all off at the door.

The Wallis brothers were ten minutes late, and Emily quickly detached herself from Jonathan's side as soon as Frankie walked through the door, but at last the assembled walking party left in high spirits. They set off over the fields to the west of the house and took the coastal path, heading towards Salcombe Magna, which was the nearest village to their destination. Nora Beales kept up a stream of chatter as she declared how divine it all looked.

'Jessie, my dear, did you ever see such a beautiful tree in all your life? Just look at that sweet cow lying under it in such an attitude of sheer languor. How I should love to spend my day with such a panorama. A cow has a rather good life, I think.'

'Yes, it must be wonderful being milked night and day, and having your carcass melted down for candles and glue in your old age,' said Emily, none too quietly, looping her arm through Frankie's and grinning at him.

Jane saw Jonathan Keeling observing Emily disapprovingly, but so intent was she on trying to impress Frankie with what she imagined were witty observations she was completely unaware of it. Frankie, looking suitably embarrassed changed the subject immediately and started talking about some of the trees he'd climbed nearby as a boy.

The party fell into straggling groups, Frankie, Emily, Eddie and Will led the way in front, followed by Jonathan and his friends, with Beth and

Cora closely behind. A bit of a gap opened up as Nora Beales struggled to keep up with the younger set, though the captain gallantly kept by her side entertaining both she and Jessie with tales of India. Jane and Alice came next, whilst Julius and Mae brought up the rear, dawdling along making no effort to keep up the smart pace.

The route was circuitous and difficult in parts, but the views over the silver sea were breathtaking. They could still see the rooftops of the village tumbling down to the water, and the line of the shore shimmering in a ribbon of mother of pearl. An ancient stone marked the miles yet to go, and Miss Beales who was already starting to flag looked, for a moment, as if she might just turn around and head back home.

Frankie stopped, as the terrain altered, to warn them of the dangers up ahead, cupping his hands to his mouth and shouting to the others. 'The path is very narrow here, and rather steep. I suggest the ladies take an arm of the nearest gentleman.'

As if he'd predicted a fall, Beth suddenly felt herself slipping on the dry sand path, slithering down the gulley worn by generations of feet, but just as she thought she might tumble, was caught at the last moment by Fergus Dauncey who turned to grab her arm, and set her back on her feet.

'Hold onto me, Miss Milton,' he said rather gravely, and Jane saw Beth hesitate, as she knew she would.

'Come, I insist, the path is treacherous.'

He didn't look as if he would take no for an answer. Beth took his arm reluctantly, and without another word spoken the pair continued along the path in awkward silence.

There wasn't a cloud in the sky, and the sea glowed mysteriously in bands of cobalt, violet and periwinkle, making Jane wonder what secrets lay in its depths. The path turned away inland, and the sea disappeared behind gorse bushes and pine trees before descending steeply once more into thicker woodland. The gaps between the groups were growing bigger, and Jane could see that even Alice was finding it hard to keep up. She linked her arm into her friend's and was grateful when the land seemed to flatten out once more through the twisting path where the forest trees provided cool shelter from the searing sun. Dappled sunlight lit up the earth and the banks of high ferns that lined the path, scenting the air as the vegetation warmed, bringing forth so many recollections of past times that Jane struggled to keep them at bay.

She'd fallen deeply in love at the seaside many years ago, and taken a walk with the young man in scenes so similar she recalled every word as if they'd just been spoken, and every feeling with poignant recall. The hopes and dreams they'd shared came flooding back with every step amongst the pines, and every mournful cry of the seagulls overhead.

Cassy who'd meant to be chaperoning them had fallen behind on the path until she could no longer be seen. A glimpse of Sidmouth was caught in fractured pictures through the trees, but they'd left the town far below them, and the ordered streets and houses far behind.

Jane saw it all again, fresh in her mind. She heard his voice, saw the auburn curls dance on his forehead in the summer breeze. She tasted the tang of the sea and felt the briny salt carried in the wind on her lips. But most of all she felt the thrill of knowing that her feelings were returned, recognising that she'd found the one who seemed above all others to have been made just for her.

Jane had sworn she would never love a clergyman until it happened. Most men of the cloth were ridiculous in her eyes, and unworthy of the job they were entrusted to do. She'd encompassed all her derisive and mocking ideas into the character of Mr Collins in *Pride and Prejudice*, a melding of all the clergymen she'd ever known, with the exception of her father whom she believed was the epitome of all that a rector should be.

Now, in her mind's eye, as she walked with Alice clinging onto her arm, she remembered her very own clergyman, the most handsome gentleman she had ever known, and the only one who had ever truly been the world to her. He'd been the love of her life, an unexpected late flowering passion that had burned brightly, but fleetingly.

They'd first met down on the beach at Sidmouth against a backdrop of soaring red cliffs, as they scoured the pebbles looking for fossils, and she'd been attracted to him immediately. He was on holiday himself, and dressed, as anyone else might be, more for the country than the town, and without a clergyman's collar or hat. She'd often wondered if the attraction would have been quite so immediate or there at all if he'd been recognisable as a man of the cloth, but because the discovery was made later as they came to know one another better, in the end, its importance had seemed hardly significant. Jane was lost in reverie, brought back to the life she'd lived by the fragrance of pine needles, and the smell of the sea.

He straightened, and halted in his pursuit of ammonites and fossilised bones on seeing the Miss Austens, and his smile lit up his face as a cheery wave animated his whole body.

'Good morning!' His voice rang out clearly, echoing back from the towering cliffs behind him. A tall man with the same wavy hair as her brothers, curling back from an open face, he exuded such an air of ease and confidence she felt she knew him on sight. 'You must come and look at this, I'd love your opinion.'

Jane and Cassy scrambled over the pebbles slipping under their feet, still damp with the sea and sparkling in the early morning light. He held out a horn of palest blue, displaying the tiniest set of teeth, and insisting she examine it further, put it into Jane's hand.

'I've found a wonderful fossil, the like of which I've never seen before except in books. I believe it's an example of bone turquoise,' he said.

Jane turned over the strange piece in her hand, fascinated by the tiny teeth protruding on one edge. 'I couldn't say, I'm not an expert, though it's a beautiful colour. I cannot imagine what processes it must have undergone and over how many years.'

'Many thousands I shouldn't wonder, but I can't think what kind of creature it might have been.'

'It is strange indeed, yet most fascinating. Perhaps Mr Anning at Lyme Regis might know. I'm sure he would take a look at it for you.'

'Yes, that's an excellent idea. I daresay he'd want to add it to his collection of snake-stones and devil's fingers, as the locals call them.'

And, so began a friendship which rapidly turned into something more, and much greater than either of them could have imagined. Jane had never known anyone quite like him. They found ways to meet every day, along the beach in the mornings, above on the cliff tops in the afternoons, and at the assembly rooms to dance together in the evenings. They rapidly and deeply fell in love like Anne Elliot and Captain Wentworth, and her family loved him quite as much. It was a meeting of minds, of hearts, and of their souls.

Jane didn't want to remember any more, that when he left them, he was not to return, struck down a short while later by a tragic illness from which he was never to recover. Their walk through the woods at Pinny was the last she'd seen of him. It had been impossible to believe that such a strong, vital man was no more, but she'd been soberly informed of the fact in a letter written from his brother, whose heart was also torn in two.

Enclosed in the package was a gift, the saddest and most heart-rending token she ever received. A ring of polished turquoise set in gold, which his brother explained had been made especially to secure their engagement winked back at her from a leather box. Jane knew she'd seen the stone before in a slightly different form, and slipping it on her finger had given in at last to the racking sobs that she'd been trying so hard to suppress.

If she closed her eyes she could bring his beloved face into view, still feel the connection between them, those feelings of never quite having enough, of never being physically close enough, and of not being able to fully express every emotion. But they'd shared the anticipation that one day they might be everything to each other: to have and to hold, to kiss and caress, to love as man and wife. But it was never meant to be, and now there were only memories left, and the sharp pangs of empty longing which still occasionally crept into her dreams or took her unawares when she found herself, like now, in a place where his spirit visited her once more.

The path took a turn again, forcing them to climb ever higher. Jane saw Fergus Dauncey ahead turn and offer his arm once more. Beth refused it this time and struggled valiantly on, determined not to rely on him a second time. There were banks of steps cut into the earth, and clearly hewn by a man, Beth thought, made for a man's stride. It was tough going, and she could see Miss Beales hanging on to the captain's arm not wishing to let the party down. They'd gone too far to be able to turn back now.

Will's voice came down from on high amplified by a gust of wind. 'Not far now, this is the worst of it, but I promise, it will be worth the struggle!'

Beth decided it was now or never. She wasn't sure she'd be presented with such an opportunity again. Making her legs work harder she soon caught up with Fergus's loping stride. Never one to mince words she came straight to the point.

'Why did you disinherit your brother?' she demanded.

Fergus turned to look straight into her eyes. He was frowning, Beth saw, and looked really cross. 'I beg your pardon?'

'I think you heard me the first time. Why would a man who has the riches of a fine home and vast inheritance deny his own brother his share of the spoils? Gilbert told me everything. Do you know how much he has suffered?'

Beth watched Fergus rake his fingers through his dark hair before sighing loudly. He seemed to be searching for the right words. 'I don't know what on earth you're talking about, and quite frankly, I'm not sure it's any of your business. But if Gilbert's been making up stories again, which I have to tell you is a particular forte of his, then I'm afraid I have no compunction in telling you the truth. The house, Rosamorna, is mine by birthright certainly, and a share of the inheritance will be Gilbert's one day when he has proved he can handle money in a sensible way.'

'He told me there will be no money. And even if there were, who are you to judge what is the right and wrong way to spend it? Gilbert not only lost his beloved parents but any means of looking after himself. Luckily for him he possessed the wherewithal to find his way into the army.'

'And it seems he is much improved for keeping down a steady job. Jonathan Keeling says he's been greatly impressed by him. I hope he *is* changed for the better, though I doubt it. He always had a talent for charming people ... even duping my family.'

'How could you say such things about your own brother?' Beth said with more passion in her voice. 'How could you be so cold-hearted about one who shared your life from such a young age? Gilbert told me how he always looked up to you, how much he loved and adored you when he was little.'

'Yes, I think he did,' said Fergus without hesitation, and for a moment the mask of hardness Beth had witnessed seemed to slip away. 'And I've always tried to help him. I hope he is as recovered as you say. He knows what the terms of the will are, though I doubt he will act on them.'

'I don't understand,' said Beth.

Fergus Dauncey's face clouded, and his mouth was set in a firm line. 'No, I don't expect you would, and as it's a case of his word against mine and you've already decided where the truth lies, I shall say no more.'

Fergus walked quickly away to catch up with Kit and Camilla. He could see his friend chatting happily away to Cora as if he'd known her for years, but then he'd always had that talent for making friends easily. Fergus's efforts at getting to know Beth better had gone so horribly wrong, and she wasn't quite the girl he'd thought. Beautiful with expressive eyes and a lively spirit he'd been attracted to her almost straight away, but if anything she was a little too opinionated, and clearly thought the very worst of him. Well, he wasn't looking for love right now, he considered, and he'd certainly give Miss Beth Milton a wide berth from now on, though he'd be damned if he couldn't find a way to change her mind about him.

As they climbed higher nearing the source of the waterfalls the sound of rushing water grew louder, and a vast cloud of mist permeated the air. A great roar of water greeted them and as they climbed the last steps the sight of the tumbling water cascading over rocks, dropping away to crash on the river bed far below them was an awesome sight. They could see the path turning downward again with a multitude of steps and signs to the fern gardens and lake. At last everyone caught up, finding one another again, and with lots of excited chatter about the beauty of the falls they were all anxious to get moving to see more.

'Shall we meet in an hour for lunch?' said Will to the assembled party. 'There are too many of us to keep together without endless stopping on route. If we meet by the lake a little later we can have our picnic and it's such a lovely spot for exploring.'

'Where are Mae and Julius?' asked Beth who quickly noticed the pair was missing.

'They were behind us not long ago,' said Alice. 'Though they were dawdling, I'm sure they'll soon catch up. Julius was saying he knows the area well yesterday, it's a stone's throw from his house, I believe.'

'I'm sure they'll be here in a minute,' said Will who wasn't the only one to wonder if they'd turn up at all, thinking they'd probably veered from the path altogether and gone to Salcombe Magna. 'This place isn't so big you can get lost too easily, I'm sure we'll bump into them in time.'

The group set off down the steps following the course of the falls, Will waiting at the top watching everyone pass by him, until at last Alice and Jane caught him up.

'I'll walk with you for a while if you'll have me,' he said.

Jane and Alice exchanged smiles.

'I think we'll allow it,' said his sister.

'In any case,' said Jane, 'you're carrying one of the picnic baskets. It's in our best interests not to lose you.'

Will and Alice laughed and the three of them followed the party snaking their way down the rocky steps lined with ferns. It was a little bit like being in heaven, thought Jane. The landscape on either side was breathtaking with the sun slanting through the trees above their heads, and the ferns waist high. Fading rhododendrons tumbled in mauve cushions down to the water's edge, all accompanied by the music of the water as it gushed and trickled, surged and flowed in a never-ending cycle.

Captain Bartlett who was still looking after the Misses Beales stopped a little way in front. He'd bought paper, paint and paintbrushes and was setting up all three in order to paint their surroundings. Jane and Alice heard Nora saying how much she'd always enjoyed painting.

'Though I've no talent for it, I do think it's one of the nicest ways to spend some time,' she said. 'I can sit for hours painting, though it has to be said I'm always disappointed with the finished product. Now Jessie has a real bent for anything artistic, have you noticed, Captain Bartlett? She's so good at everything she tries, and I always say what a pity it is that her dear mother isn't alive to witness the fact. Do you remember, Jessie, when you went to stay with friends on the Isle of Wight in April? I think it was that time, anyway, and not when you went last summer. You did that lovely painting of Osborne House, looked like a professional had done it.'

Jessie looked a little embarrassed by her aunt's praise, and she grinned nervously at George who said he'd love to see the painting.

'It's hanging in the hall above the shop,' said Nora. 'You must come in and see it next time you're in the village, Captain. I've hung it opposite the door so it's the first thing you see when you come through it. Oh, ever so many people have commented on it. I don't know why Jessie doesn't take up painting more. She could do it for a living I think, but then I daresay she could do all sorts. You've heard her sing, haven't you, Captain? She could be on the stage with that voice … voice of an angel, that's what everybody says.'

George Bartlett must be the kindest man in the world, Jane thought, to put up with the constant stream of chatter from Nora Beales, but she knew Jessie would be enjoying his company too. She didn't seem to spend much time away from her aunt though it was good to hear she occasionally had a holiday on her own. They passed them sitting on squares of Mackintosh which Miss Beales had produced from her bag, saying it was well to be prepared to deal with the damp in any situation.

The group was splitting up again, and Jane saw Emily leading Frankie away down a fern-filled path until they were quickly out of sight.

Jane and Will exchanged glances. 'I think it's fine,' he said in a low voice so Alice couldn't hear. 'I trust him to behave himself, and I'm not about to let you go off anywhere, least of all to chaperone them. Emily may make a fool of herself, but she has to learn sometime.'

Jonathan's party struck out for the lake with Eddie, Beth and Cora joining them. Jane watched Cora and Kit walking side by side and decided they made a very sweet couple, and she was clearly getting along well with his sister Camilla who also seemed to be hanging on Fergus's every word, if looks were anything to go by. Beth and Fergus were studiously ignoring each other. He seemed a rather angry young man, Jane thought, whose moods were displayed candidly on his features.

Will, Alice and Jane all agreed to go off on their own to explore the fern gardens first before going on to the lake. There were so many varieties of fern, planted by the Victorian collectors who'd chosen to develop the gardens and lake, Will told them. It was done so naturally that it was hard to imagine that it had ever looked any other way. The paths twisted between high rocks where the ferns cascaded alongside banks of trailing ivy, and Jane couldn't help being reminded of her ideas about how Dovedale might have looked when she was writing *Pride and Prejudice*.

'I'm feeling a little tired,' said Alice. 'There's a grassy spot just over there where I might sit down for a minute. Don't mind me, I'll soon get my breath back.'

'We'll come with you,' said Will. 'I'm sure we could all do with a sit down.'

'Please, I shall be quite fine for five minutes. You and Jane go and explore on your own. I've brought my book with me and I shall enjoy a little quiet reading. If you will just leave me with a blanket to sit on I shall be perfectly happy, and I can look after the picnic things.'

Alice was most insistent and shooed them away, ignoring every attempt to include her in their plans.

Jane felt suddenly self-conscious being alone with Will, as they walked along in the cool shade, and neither of them seemed to know what to say at first. The gardens were quiet save for the sound of distant water and a bird calling every now and again high above their heads. It seemed words were unnecessary and the companionable stillness made Jane feel completely at peace. It didn't feel awkward or strained, the quiet calm seemed to unite them in a way Jane was sure he could feel too, as if the absence of words brought them closer together in spirit. Occasionally, Will stopped to point out something of interest, and likewise, Jane would comment on her own observations. It felt so easy and natural, as if they'd known one another forever.

'Did you enjoy your day off, Miss Austen? He seems a good sort of chap, your doctor,' Will said.

Jane could tell that he really thought Dr Lyford must be her sweetheart. Though in one way she wanted to keep up the pretence, in another she really wanted him to know the truth.

'Dr Lyford is very kind and he's been a good friend to me. I owe him my life, Mr Milton.'

'The best relationships are often those that start in friendship,' he said.

'It is a friendship, but nothing more, whatever you might think,' answered Jane. 'I know how it must have looked ...'

She trailed off thinking the conversation couldn't get more awkward if she tried, and was cross with herself for feeling she ought to explain. They were walking side by side, and his nearness and the intimacy of the situation was making her feel increasingly nervous.

'I think you underestimate the gentleman's feelings. You should be careful there, he's clearly in love with you.'

'That's nonsense. You couldn't possibly understand.'

'I understand a lot more than you think. Men are always attracted to beautiful women. And why were you crying?' he blurted out. 'Is life at the castle so awful? I couldn't bear it if you were miserable. You've made us all so happy and yet I know something is troubling you. I saw it that day, and I've seen it on other occasions when you have a far away look in your eyes. Please tell me the truth.'

Jane knew she should say something to allay his fears. He was looking at her intensely, and she could see genuine concern in his eyes. And besides all that he'd hinted that he thought she was beautiful. Had he really meant it?

'I'm not unhappy, and I am enjoying life at the castle. I was ill a while ago, and I suppose I worry from time to time that I might be unwell again. That's all ... it's just a silly fear.'

'I would like you to see my doctor in London; he is the very best that Harley Street has to offer. Jane, we will make certain you can never be ill again.'

'Oh no, I couldn't allow that. Dr Lyford's work is pioneering, and I'm afraid I couldn't trust anyone else with my health the way I do him,' said Jane insistently. 'But thank you, it means a great deal to me that you care so much.'

'Jane, I do care, if only you knew how much,' Will said quietly, as they came to a standstill and he turned to face her. 'And I know exactly how your doctor felt when he was looking into your eyes that day. I envied him, if I am to tell you the truth. I wished it were me that was comforting you, stroking your cheek and brushing away the tears.'

'Please don't say anything else,' Jane said unable to meet his gaze.

He stretched out his hand towards hers and when he took it she didn't resist. She felt the warmth of his fingers enclosing hers, and it felt so natural, reminding her again of another moment in time when she'd felt everything was right in the world.

In that moment Jane realised the hopelessness of her situation. She would never be able to allow herself the luxury of falling in love or having any relationships, knowing that she'd never be able to share the truth about herself. Jane couldn't feel anything but moved by his words though couldn't bring herself to look at him.

'I know you will tell me I'm wrong to feel this way, but I'm falling in love with you,' said Will looking deeply into the eyes that met his own.

Jane recognised the connection, felt again all that she'd known deep in her soul, whilst telling her mind and body to deny it. 'But you hardly know me.'

Will took a step towards her and she saw him raise his other hand, felt the soft touch of his fingers running down her cheek and along her jaw, a single finger tracing the line of her neck until it found the curving hollow at the base. She stared back into the dark serious eyes that glanced at her mouth, and as his head moved closer her eyes closed in response. Tilting her head back she felt his fingers caress her neck, pulling her closer, and his lips linger on hers with a tender touch before he pulled instantly away.

'I'm so sorry, I shouldn't have done that,' he said, unable to look at her, casting his eyes to the brown forest floor. He let go her hand. 'What on earth must you think of me. I promised I wouldn't let my feelings get in the way.'

Jane couldn't speak. She knew she'd wanted him to kiss her as much as he'd clearly been unable to stop himself. Her throat constricted, every sense in her body and every emotion in her mind was telling her what she knew already. She was in love with Will Milton and there was nothing she could do about it.

Will took her silence for anger and outrage. 'Believe me, Jane I won't let it happen again. Can you please forgive me?'

'Will, there is nothing to be sorry for.'

'I'm a complete cad, you were right.'

'Please, don't say that. Truly, there is nothing to forgive, it is all forgotten,' Jane answered, 'but I think we must get back to Alice. She will be wondering where we've got to.'

Jane didn't know what to say. More than anything she wanted to tell him that she felt herself falling in love too, that the realisation of it had been creeping up on her with an inevitability that seemed pre-destined. And yet, it was all so hopeless, as dispiriting as any love affair she'd ever enjoyed. Perhaps she was not meant to find happiness like other people, she decided. Every time she'd ever come close to finding happiness it had been snatched away. The words Jane wanted to say wouldn't come, as she considered the sorrow of her situation, and they both became awkward with the other. They meandered along the water's edge where the falls burbled along at a slower pace. Will seemed cross, kicking at twigs in his path, throwing pebbles like a small boy into the water to skim and bounce, rippling the water in circles, and ringing off the stones in the bottom of the river bed.

Chapter Eighteen

Alice was sitting quite comfortably reading her book, glad that she'd managed to persuade Jane and Will to go off on a little walk together. She had already decided that her brother and her friend were just right for one another, and was prepared to do anything to encourage and promote a courtship. Alice opened her book; one of her favourite summer reads that she returned to again and again. *Emma* by Jane Austen was a complex tale of mistaken romances, misunderstandings and riddles. In fact, that was the fun of the book; it was a huge riddle and though, once solved, it was never quite the same after the first reading, Alice still found the tale thrilling, and wondered again at the genius of Jane Austen. There was so much to discover in the book, and every time she read it she found something new. She'd just got to the part where they were all to picnic at Box Hill, and Alice couldn't wait to read the next chapter.

It was a delightful spot she'd found with the most wonderful views around her. The stillness and beauty of the place felt sacred, as if the goodness of the earth was distilled in this one area. Nature was in full riot, everywhere green and verdant, with the birds singing in the trees as if they knew their special luck in finding such heaven on earth. Her only slight complaint was that she felt a little chilled in the dense woodland where the sun's rays hardly touched the earth's floor, but she blamed herself for not remembering to take her cardigan from the canvas bag Will carried on his back.

Alice put her book down, and shivering in her thin lawn blouse, she wrapped her arms round to hug her knees. It was then that she heard the soft thud of footsteps coming up behind her, but before she had a chance to turn, she felt the warmth of a man's jacket being placed around her shoulders. It was a second or two before she registered the fact that it wasn't Will's, but she didn't need to look to realise whose jacket was flooding her with warmth, the scent emanating from the soft tweed told her all she needed to know. Frankie - no one else smelled so divine in all the world. It was Frankie's jacket - and then she heard his voice behind her, soft and gentle, close to her ear.

'You must be cold. Here; you'll soon warm up.'

Before she could turn her head, she felt the nearness of him, crouched on his knees behind her, his fingers touching the nape of her neck. He was fiddling with the collar, pulling it up to give more protection against the cool air, and rearranging the jacket to fit more snugly on her shoulders. But, his touch was like lightning bolts entering the very essence of her being, and she almost jumped out of her skin. His fingers, like sweet caresses on her skin, heightened every sensation she'd ever felt in his presence like never before. She couldn't speak; all Alice could feel were burning firecrackers scorching their way to the core of her heart.

'I thought Will might be here,' he said eventually, sitting down beside her on the blanket.

'I'm sure he'll be back in a moment,' she said, hardly able to get the words out. She touched the jacket, pulled it firmly round her arms so she was completely enveloped by it, and his fragrance. It was all she could do not to bury her face in the cloth. 'Thank you.'

The words trailed away, silence reigning again, and Alice was so overcome by her emotions that she couldn't think how to carry on the conversation.

Moments later the quiet tranquillity was broken by the sounds of running footsteps from behind them, and howls of laughter, which rang out echoing back from the rocks. Emily ran round and stood before them, her hands on her hips.

'Oh, there you are, Frankie,' she shouted in a mocking voice. 'I knew I'd find you easily. That's a pretty poor hiding place.'

Frankie looked up, but didn't say anything. He looked lost in thought.

Emily tried again 'We were playing hide and seek, Alice. Do you want to join us?'

'Oh, no thank you,' Alice managed to answer. 'I'm just waiting for Will and Jane. They've gone exploring, and I wanted to read my book.'

'I've had enough now, Emily,' said Frankie wearily. 'It must be nearly time for lunch. Come and sit down, we'll wait until Will comes back.'

Alice watched Emily flop down on the blanket next to Frankie, and saw her lean against him. Frankie immediately jumped up, saying he would just go and see if Will was coming, and Alice and Emily were left on their own.

Luckily, Alice didn't have long to wait for Will and Jane, and she suggested immediately that they go to the lake and get the picnic ready for the others. Jane observed Alice take the jacket from her shoulders, giving it back to Frankie with a wan smile, and heard her thank him, saying she'd be quite warm enough now they were walking. Emily hung on to Frankie's arm, but though he did nothing to either encourage or dissuade her, Jane sensed that he didn't want to be so manhandled.

The lake, adorned with water lilies breaking up the silvered mirror surface drew sighs of wonder from them all, as a pair of black swans swam into view. It looked like a scene from a fairy tale, and as they ventured round the first curving edge to emerge from a belt of silver birch trees like pillars rising from the bracken, they found the perfect spot set back from the water. There was a lot of laughter and excited chatter as they all set about picking the sunniest spot with parasols for those who wanted shade or dappled light under the silver grey leaves of the trees. Picnic hampers were opened, and the feast spread on blankets. Captain Bartlett's cook had done them proud. There were dainty sandwiches with cucumber and prawns, a pink ham, and a side of sliced beef with bread rolls and butter, so yellow it looked as it had been made with the help of the buttercups scattered on the grass at their feet. There were lavish fruit cakes, iced sponges, and a selection of home baked biscuits, all to be washed down with glasses of wine, beer or cordial.

'We will miss Mrs Muckle when Mrs Wickens comes back,' said Emily. 'We've never eaten so well at the castle.'

'It's not her fault, Emily, said Alice, 'she does her best. Poor Mrs Wickens, I hope she's enjoying her hard-earned holiday. I think we ought to be prepared to help out more often, though now father has agreed to raise the food budget it should all work out much better.'

'When I marry, I shan't be helping anyone in the kitchen,' said Emily. 'Do you have servants in America, Frankie?'

For the first time Jane saw a look of shock and astonishment on Frankie's face. Those two sentences uttered so closely together had made them all start a little. It was quite clear what Emily had in mind.

The arrival of Jonathan Keeling, Kit and Camilla Branwell, Fergus Dauncey and Eddie Warren broke the flow of the conversation, much to the relief of them all, Jane was sure. Beth and Cora joined them moments later, and soon the captain was there with Nora and Jessie. The group spread out to add more blankets and settled themselves on the ground. There were too many of them to make general conversation easy, but every now and again someone spoke up loud enough so that they could all hear what was going on. More baskets with delicacies and dainty finger sandwiches were heaped on plates, and as they started to eat they realised just how hungry they were.

Emily was feeling very fed up with Frankie. Despite all her efforts to get him on her own nothing seemed to be working. He'd been distracted all morning, and was in a very dull mood. Nothing seemed to please him, and now it seemed he wasn't even speaking to her. It hadn't escaped her notice that he'd gone looking for Alice, nor that he'd given her his jacket to keep her warm. Yet, it wasn't just Frankie who was getting on her nerves. When she looked round at them all, she found much to criticise. Nora Beales was talking incessantly about how wonderful Jessie's painting was and where she might hang it. There was no talent for painting that Emily could see, and Jessie was such an insipid character who never had a word to say for herself. As for Jonathan, who'd always been her friend since time began, all he kept doing was scowling at her as if he disapproved of her very breathing. He'd been chatting up Camilla ever since they sat down.

'My word, I'm famished,' said Will tucking into a cucumber sandwich. 'There's nothing like a good walk to make an excellent appetite.'

'I always say so,' said Nora Beales. 'That's the furthest I've walked in a long time, and I'm as hungry as a horse.'

'Perhaps you'd prefer sugar lumps like our pony, Valentino,' said Emily, laughing at her own joke. There was a little laughter amongst the scattered groups, but it was more of the embarrassed sort than anything else.

'I confess, I'm rather partial to a sugar lump,' said Nora. 'I like them in my tea, and crushed on the top of an iced bun. In fact, I'm rather fond of food full stop. There's so much to choose from here I hardly know where to start, and it all looks so delicious I'm sure I won't know when to stop.'

'We'll find you a nosebag, Nora, then you can save yourself some trouble and stuff it all in one go,' said Emily getting carried away whilst staring pointedly at Miss Beales's food. 'Besides, it doesn't look as if one plateful will be enough.'

Nora went very quiet, and the entire colour drained out of her cheeks. 'Oh dear, Miss Milton, I must appear rather greedy. I've too much cake on my plate, haven't I?'

'Well, I'm sure if you just put back one or two of those with cream, and if you had two sandwiches instead of six, it might be better for your health apart from anything else. For one thing, you'd be able to walk a lot faster, if you lost a little weight.'

The shocked silence permeated to the very edges of the furthest group. Emily had gone too far this time, but she did her best to laugh it off.

'Let's go for a swim in the lake,' she shouted, leaping to her feet and grabbing her bag. 'Come on Frankie, I'll race you. Whoever gets in the water first can choose where we go for our next outing.'

Emily who was sure that Frankie would follow her disappeared round the curve of the path to find somewhere to change, and as an awkward hush descended, all eyes were turned on Frankie. He immediately offered Nora Beales an extra cushion, and commented that she might like to sit further round, next to him in the shade where the sunlight wasn't so dazzling. He made a huge fuss of her, and slowly she looked as if the feelings of mortification were subsiding under his care.

Eddie, Beth and Cora jumped up, more from embarrassment than a desire to go swimming saying they'd like to take a dip, and then Will was talked into joining them too. Jane watched them all disappear, the girls and the men dividing at different points along the lake.

When everyone was talking once again and Emily seemed forgotten, Jonathan sat fuming trying to think what he should do. He couldn't think why she was behaving so badly, and he felt she'd really let herself down in front of all the people she loved, as well as his friends. Emily had always listened to him in the past, and if he did nothing else he would make her hear sense again. Since Frankie had come on the scene she'd reverted to behaving like a child who was suffering from want of attention. It was a pity; he liked Frankie even if he wasn't sure they were that well suited. Prior to him arriving Jonathan had thought how well Emily was starting to grow up, maturing into someone he enjoyed spending time with, and who seemed to think of others apart from herself.

Jonathan slipped away to see if he could find her. It didn't take long. Emily was sitting wrapped in a bathing robe at the side of the lake, all ready to go for a swim. She was brushing her long golden tresses and coiling them up into a chignon on top of her head before fixing it with combs and pins, as if she hadn't a care in the world. He marched straight up to her and launched into his subject.

'Emily, I cannot watch you behaving so badly without saying something. How could you be so spiteful and unfeeling to Miss Beales? I am utterly and completely shocked; I'd never have thought you capable of such unkindness.'

Emily immediately blushed, but then tried to laugh it off.

'Oh, she knew I didn't really mean it. I only said what everyone else was thinking ... it wasn't that bad. I don't think she took offence.'

'I assure you she did, and I can tell you we none of us were thinking the same. She felt your full meaning. I wish you'd heard Nora talk about how she values your advice in all things, and I wish you could have heard her saying how much she wished to be more like you.'

'Oh, heavens,' cried Emily, 'but you must admit, she's never taken any advice on that score. I'm only trying to prevent her from having a heart attack.'

'It's not your place to lecture Nora on how she lives her life, and it is the cruellest unkindness to point out such things in front of others. You were born with many privileges, and enjoy the status of a woman who comes from a class she can only admire from a distance. Her lot will always be to struggle in life. She'll never be your equal, she'll always be poor; and her situation should guarantee your compassion. It was badly done, Emily, very badly done! You, whom she's known since you were a baby, and who has been a dear friend to the family, to have you now humiliate her, in front of her niece, too … and before other people, is the most shameful act. I'm not enjoying telling you this, and I'm sure you do not wish to hear it, Emily, but I will tell you the truth as I see it, because I must. I've always been your friend, and I always will be, but I wouldn't be your true friend if I didn't say it. All I can hope and trust is that you will some time or other turn out to be a better credit to me than you are right now.'

While he talked Emily turned her face away, and didn't speak. She felt only anger with herself, deep embarrassment, and the most awful shame. Every word he spoke struck like an arrow causing physical pain to her heart, and she wondered if she'd ever be the object of affection to him she'd once been, the replacement for the sister he'd lost. He was the man she admired most in the world, even more than Frankie, she realised at that moment, and with hot tears threatening to course down her cheeks she buried her head in her knees clasped close to her chest.

Jonathan thought she should say sorry, at least, but when it was clear that no apology was forthcoming, he simply got up and walked away before he said something he'd truly regret. Emily looked back at the last minute, determined to call him but it was too late. She was beyond every feeling. Never had she felt so upset and anxious or so desperate at any time in her life. She recognised the truth in all he'd said. How could she have been so brutal, so spiteful to Miss Beales? Emily was mortified to know she'd let others see her cruel nature and she felt more ashamed than at any other stage of her life. The fact that she'd let Jonathan go without saying how she would listen to him more often, and how grateful she was to know he cared was the worst thing of all.

Time didn't help. As the afternoon wore on, and she could hear them all splashing about in the water having fun, she reflected on all that had happened with increasing sorrow. It was impossible to join them; she couldn't face any of them. She'd never been so depressed, and as Emily felt the tears running down her cheeks she simply couldn't stop them. When Jane came to find her there was no need for any words though she said over and over again how sorry she felt. It wasn't necessary to add to her sorrows, Jane could see she felt all the weight of her shameful behaviour, and when Emily threw herself into her arms all she could do was hold her until her shuddering sobs came to a halt.

Mae and Julius appeared at five o'clock, just as the others were thinking about heading home. They both looked rather pleased with themselves, and Mae was finding it difficult not to gush about everything she'd been doing.

'Salcombe House is simply wonderful! It's the most elegant house I've ever seen with the most wonderful walks down to a private beach. And we had lunch with Julius's Aunt Dolly,' she said. 'What an entertaining lady ... and she made me so welcome.'

'It might have been an idea to let us know where you were going,' said Will. 'We were concerned.'

Mae ignored him. 'I've had an invite to join her and Julius any time I like at her house on the Isle of Wight near East Cowes. She showed me a photograph ... it's utterly beautiful.'

'East Cowes?' chirped Miss Beales. 'Jessie stayed near East Cowes last summer, didn't you, dear?'

Jessie turned her customary shade of scarlet, which tinged her ears in the sunlight to a deeper shade of cherry. With her eyes downcast it was fairly obvious that she didn't want to speak on the subject.

'Does your aunt live near Osborne House, Mr Weatherfield?' asked

Nora Beales.

'It is in the vicinity, I believe,' said Julius not giving much away. 'The area is quite remote, and the house stands in its own grounds.'

'What were the name of the people you were staying with, Jessie? Your old school friend, now what is her name?'

'I do not think Mr Weatherfield will know my friends, Aunt Nora.'

'I'm sure he will if he travels there a lot. The Isle of Wight is not a big place, and I'm sure everybody knows one another. Now, don't be shy, Jessie.'

'Wilcox,' said Jessie at last, looking up and meeting Julius's gaze.

'No, I can't say I know it,' he said. 'Sorry, but I'm not awfully good at remembering names. I never forget a face, but ...'

The others were beginning to pack away the picnic things, and Julius and Mae were soon forgotten. As Jane folded the blankets and stacked plates, she was lost in thought. Parts of the puzzle were fitting together in her mind, and although there were pieces that just would not match, she was determined to solve the rest yet.

Chapter Nineteen

The weather broke just a day later, and the sunny days they'd come to expect on a daily basis soon became just a memory. It wasn't just dull, rain lashed down from the kind of grey skies Jane had seen when she'd first arrived in Stoke Pomeroy. Everyone was out of sorts and as gloomy as the storms that drenched the landscape. Plans for taking boats out around the headland, day trips to Totnes and visiting Stoke Pomeroy Castle were all postponed much to the disappointment of them all.

Mrs Wickens came home looking much refreshed and very happy to find she had a little more money to spend in the butcher's shop in the village, and some willing helpers in the kitchen from time to time, though now the days were so much better organised, she found she could mange quite well enough without their interference.

'I like my kitchen to myself, by and large,' she said to Mrs Naseby, 'we'll get on quite well enough without the Miss Miltons, though I'm very grateful to them all for taking up the slack whilst I was away.'

'I never thought I'd see the day,' remarked Mrs Naseby, 'but should you fall ill again, at least the Milton girls won't let us starve. You won't believe me, I'm sure, but if they ever found themselves on very hard times I think they'd make the grade as cooks if needed.'

It was good to see Mrs Wickens so cheerful again, and even Mrs Naseby said how much she'd missed her old friend. Mrs Muckle was all well and good, but she'd found her rather dour, to say the least.

'It just wasn't the same with you gone, Edie,' she said, using Mrs Wickens's Christian name as she did on rare occasions. 'I'm that glad to see you in the old Windsor chair!'

Jane tried to forget what had happened on the day of the picnic, and she was more resolved than ever to make sure she didn't come into contact with Will. He seemed to be absorbed in his work, and even disappeared off for a week to attend an agricultural show in Exeter. Though she often didn't see him when he was working, after he left it was as if the place was mourning him, and the very air seemed to vibrate differently without his energy and life. It was important to keep herself occupied, and what with becoming a closer confidant to all the girls, and writing her book in the evenings, she was kept very busy indeed.

Mae was feeling bitterly disappointed with the way her relationship was going with Julius. Whilst initially feeling pleased at the success of her meeting with his aunt, and Julius's reaction to that, she reflected on the fact that although they'd often been given the chance to be alone, nothing had ever really happened between them. Julius had clearly delighted in showing her off to his aunt, but not once had he tried to be alone with her or kiss her, even when they'd taken a stroll, hand in hand, down to the beach.

'I'm sure he's just being a gentleman,' said Alice when Mae complained of his conduct. 'Julius knows that Will wouldn't like you to be taken advantage of, and it's clear he respects you.'

Mae, Jane and Alice were sitting in the library before a roaring fire. Rain lashed against the long windows overlooking the garden, as the cold air seeped through the glass, making them sit as close as they could to the roaring flames. It was quickly becoming the favourite meeting point for all the girls. On cold days there was always a fire laid, and apart from the wonderful shelves of books to read, there were the squashiest sofas and comfiest cushions, and a table bearing the latest copies of Vogue magazine.

'Of course I want him to respect me, but I've never known a single gentleman not try and give me a peck on the cheek … he hasn't even kissed my hand more than once.'

Jane remembered the time when she saw Julius doing just that to Jessie Beales's hand, and couldn't help wondering if his behaviour had something to do with wielding power over the two young women. Jessie hadn't wanted his attentions, but perhaps Mae was giving off such yearning emotions to be adored, he already felt he'd conquered her soul.

'I've often found that being cool and off-hand with a man that I liked has done the trick,' said Alice with a grin.

'Yes, men can't stand to be ignored,' agreed Jane. 'I don't think it hurts to tease them mercilessly, either, or abuse them to their faces at all times.'

Mae and Alice both laughed at that.

'I know you're both right,' said Mae, 'but I'm finding it so difficult to be like that with Julius. Every man I've ever known has doted on me, and he is the first one I don't feel is completely under my command. He says all the right things, but he doesn't act. It's very frustrating.'

'Are you in love with him?' asked Alice. 'I think perhaps you are, and if you're truly honest you'll admit that none of the others mattered.'

'Being in love is so hard,' added Jane. 'All that hoping something will happen so you'll know it's quite real, and not knowing whether your feelings are being returned in quite the same way. Oh, the awful waiting … longing for a look, a touch or a sign.'

All three were silent for a moment, as they watched the flames licking up the chimney. Mae pulled her feet up under her on the sofa, and sighed.

'Yes, I think I am in love for the first time, and I can't bear it. Whatever shall I do?'

Alice and Jane didn't reply. They were both lost in thought of the men they loved and of their own particular hopelessness.

Manberley Castle seemed quiet without a constant stream of visitors. Even Julius Weatherfeld stayed away, and Jonathan was particularly quiet. They hadn't seen him or his friends for two weeks, and though Emily was sure that was largely down to her and what had happened at Ashcombe Falls, she was also secretly pleased. She couldn't face him, not yet, and besides that she wanted to think of a way to make it up to Nora Beales. Unfortunately, she was not to be given the chance. When she braved the weather to walk down to the village armed with a large umbrella, she found a notice pinned to the shop window. The Misses Beales were gone to Worthing for their annual holiday and would not be back for a month. They were staying with relatives, Emily knew, and it was a holiday destination they enjoyed every year. Well, she'd just have to wait until they came home, she thought, and in the meantime conjure up a plan of action to make sure Nora might forgive her.

July disappeared in a torrent of rain and August came in with a whimper. Jane could see the lack of occupation wasn't a good thing for the Milton family who quickly descended into languor if not kept busy, and she was racking her brains to think of a new scheme to cheer them all up. When she heard Beth and Cora reminiscing about the Manberley balls of the past, Jane showed her interest, and brought up the conversation with Lady Milton. A few timely inquiries, one or two flattering observations and suggestions from Jane were enough to make Lady Milton announce that she was to revive the summer ball, which had been a tradition as long as Miltons had reigned at the castle. Flora was completely convinced it was all her own idea, and though there hadn't been a ball due to a lack of funds for some years, she persuaded her husband it was the very least they should do for their girls. If a season in London was not to be had then the opportunity for dancing with the most eligible men in Devonshire was an absolute necessity.

Jane heaved a sigh of relief, as a frenzy of activity soon followed. The invitations were sent out, and plans were made. The kitchen buzzed with excitement, as sets of dinnerware were dusted off and polished, along with the best silver cutlery and glassware. Recipes were pored over by Mrs Wickens, and Mrs Naseby consulted on supper dishes for the party.

There was much discussion and remonstration with Lord Milton about new gowns, new curtains and much besides, but at the last he put his foot down and declared they would all have to make do, even Lady Milton.

'You must have a dozen dresses or more you can make use of or have altered,' he said, his moustache bristling with fervour. 'I am laying out quite enough without frocks as well ... I will not be cowed!'

Lady Milton said nothing, but made sure even if new dresses could not be had they would not be short on accessories. Beaded headdresses and caps, satin shoes and bags arrived by the caseload, ordered from London. Lady Milton knew exactly how to get round her husband, and even he seemed pleased to see the fripperies by the time she'd finished attending to his every need.

There was just over a week to get everything ready. Extra food was ordered, and Mrs Wickens prepared to face the challenge of catering for an event they hadn't seen the like of for several years. They would make the most of the local fish and their own pigs, which could be had in plentiful and cheap supply, she decided, knowing that Captain Bartlett and Jonathan Keeling might also add generously to the fare with offerings from their own estates. She and Mrs Naseby were quite excited by it all, and even Bell, the butler said he looked forward to twirling them round in a dance in the servant's hall.

As if a magic wand had been waved the day of the ball dawned bright and fair, and by the afternoon Bell and the footmen were out in the gardens hanging lanterns and setting out chairs in anticipation of their guests drifting out beyond the French windows leading from the ballroom. Flowers were cut, the best vases found, and soon the heat was warming scented petals to fill the rooms with fragrance. Preparations were at fever pitch, and the house a hive of activity.

In the afternoon, Mae and Alice put Jane through her dancing steps.

'If you're going to make *me* dance again, then the very least you can do is join in too,' said Alice who was in charge of the gramophone. They were in the library again, and had moved the table and chairs back to the walls in order to practise the Tango, the Foxtrot and the Charleston.

'I think I've got the hang of most of the dances, but I admit, I don't much enjoy the Charleston,' Jane answered. 'I feel quite self-conscious ... I am trying, but it just doesn't feel natural.'

'No, it doesn't,' agreed Mae, 'but you must let yourself go of any inhibitions, Jane. Come along, you wouldn't give up on me when I needed you, now you must listen to me.'

Jane felt quite emotional at those words. She couldn't believe what a long way Mae had come, and could see the young girl blossoming into a lovely woman. She knew she still had a way to go with Emily, but it was so good to observe Mae becoming more confident in her own skin. She'd even seemed less intense on the subject of Julius, and the fact that he'd not been around much seemed to be helping. Jane loved watching the sisters interacting with each other again, closer than ever. She couldn't help thinking about her own beloved sister, and remembered Cassandra with a pang of sadness that pierced her heart.

Lady Milton had presented Jane with a ball gown the day before, the most delightful cast-off she'd ever owned and now Jane slipped it on over her head, as she dressed with greater care than usual. In tones of bronze and copper, the silk chiffon felt like a dream next to her skin and she felt utterly different wearing it. The colours set off her hazel eyes, and with a matching scarf to bind her curls she was thrilled with the vision she saw in her looking glass. Though quite whom she was expecting to impress she couldn't say. More determined than ever not to engage with any men, let alone Will, Jane decided her vanity was all for herself. She couldn't help wondering about the unfamiliar young woman she saw in the glass, hardly recognising the sophisticated creature that glanced back at her as if she were ready to take on the world. The floor-length silk dazzled on her slender frame, the colours highlighting the warm tones of her skin. Possessed of a confidence she'd never experienced before, she remembered as she'd grown older in her past life how she'd hated being in the spotlight, but since coming to Manberley Castle all that had changed. Jane couldn't help feeling that despite the fact that they were a raggle-taggle bunch, all with problems of their own, they'd been largely responsible for her own transformation. She'd become more self-assured, just as dependent on them as they were on her, and with feelings she could only describe as love, Jane knew she adored every one of them for all their faults. Of course one particular Milton really had her heart, but she wouldn't think about him.

Chapter Twenty

The guests were arriving when Jane reached the hallway where the Milton family were waiting to greet them. Jane was pulled into line between Alice and Mae, and she tried not to look further down at Will who looked so devastatingly handsome he made her heart turn over.

'I don't think this is my place,' said Jane. 'I can wait for you all in the ballroom.'

'Nonsense,' said Alice, 'you're one of the family, and I won't hear of you standing there on your own. You need to be introduced formally to our neighbours. I know Flora would want nothing else.'

There were so many people to meet as hundreds streamed past that after a while it became a blur of faces and names. Jane was glad when it was all over and they headed off to the ballroom where King Zoot's band were playing some old-fashioned tunes to set the tone, and the room buzzed with chatter and the clinking of glasses. Sparkling chandeliers, gilded mirrors and the reflections of hundreds of white wax candles guttering in the soft breeze from the open doors, showed off the ballroom's splendour and had everyone commenting on Manberley's wonderful renovations. The ancient candelabra and beautiful pier glasses were buffed and polished to a glittering finish, and everyone said how much they'd forgotten the glorious magnificence of the ballroom.

Captain Bartlett looked a little lost without the Misses Beales who'd taken up so much of his time lately, but when he saw Jane he didn't hesitate to ask her for the first dance. When she'd first heard about the ball Jane had intended not to dance with anyone, but having finally persuaded Alice she should dance, the deal struck between them was if that Alice would, then so would Jane. She couldn't refuse him, and he asked so particularly kindly, it would have been impossible to say no even if she hadn't learned the waltz.

They headed out onto the dance floor, and as the music started he took her in his arms. Jane was nervous for a moment, but she was soon stepping out as if she'd waltzed all her life.

'I must congratulate you, Miss Austen,' he began. 'The castle is quite transformed, as are all the people in it.'

'I'm sure that has nothing to do with me,' said Jane, 'but I agree, the castle is a different place from when I first arrived.'

'It's happiness, Miss Austen. You've a gift for spreading joy, and making people around you feel valued. I can see the difference you've made to Alice and Mae's lives, and even Lord and Lady Milton seem changed since you came.'

'Well, that's very kind of you to say so, but perhaps they were just ready to make some changes. And if not for you and your marvellous help in the kitchen we'd never have made those first steps.'

'What a lovely time I had with everyone. I've felt quite lonely at home after being with so many people. But one thing has become clear.' Captain Bartlett looked a little sad as he reflected on what he was going to say. 'I've decided that if I can't be with the one I wish, I'd rather remain as I am.'

Jane understood straight away. He still wanted Mae; he was in love with her and despite how things might look with Jessie, knew he didn't want to settle for second best.

'I do understand,' said Jane. 'Even with the best efforts we cannot deny our true feelings. It's impossible to make ourselves fall in love with other people.'

'Quite ... I've had a lot of time to think about it all, put my feelings for Mae in their proper place. I wondered if my emotions were misplaced, that because she reminded me so much of my wife I saw her through rose-coloured spectacles. But, she's like an injured bird to me, Miss Austen, someone who needs nursing. I fell in love with Mae knowing life had been unfair and that being so sensitive she'd found the only way to arm herself against disappointment and lack of love was by growing a hard shell. Over time I saw all her creative pursuits left behind, she stopped painting and singing, as if she'd died inside. I tried to get her interested in art again, but failed miserably. It's so wonderful to see you succeed where I failed, to have her finally coming back, and I find I am just as in love with her as ever. And if she will not be my wife I don't want anyone.'

'At least you are at peace with the decision you've made.'

George stared at her closely and raised a quizzical brow. 'You sound as if you've regrets of your own, Miss Austen.'

'Oh no, Captain,' Jane lied, 'I suppose I have had my regrets, but I'm fortunate enough to say I have no more.'

Beth and Cora were having a lovely time, having both enjoyed their first dance. Eddie Warren had stepped up to take Beth's hand and Kit had been there from the very first to take Cora's. They moved together so well, and Cora thought he really was such a good-looking man and the best dancer in the room.

'You and Kit make a lovely couple,' ventured Beth, as they stood watching Kit dance with his sister.

'Do you really think so?' Cora replied, darting round in her excitement. 'I do think he's the loveliest man I ever met.'

Beth laughed. 'He seems very kind-hearted, and he's certainly handsome, which is more than I can say for his grumpy friend.'

Both girls looked over to Fergus Dauncey who wasn't dancing with anyone, and was wearing a scowl on his handsome face.

'Perhaps he doesn't know anyone or is a bit shy,' said Cora. 'Kit's so good with people but Fergus doesn't strike me as being at ease in company.'

'Well, that's a poor excuse for grumpiness,' said Beth. 'I suppose he's had his usual one dance with Camilla and that will be it.'

'I expect he's more at home in a Cornish landscape where his rugged good looks and scowling features suit the wilds of the terrain. He's always looking at you, Beth. I'm sure he's trying to pluck up the courage to ask you to dance. You ought to walk over there, help him out a little.'

'He likes to stare, certainly, but I am not going to encourage him. I can't stand him. When I challenged him over the way he's treated his brother at Ashcombe Falls he could hardly answer me. No, Cora, even if he begged me I wouldn't dance with him. And now I'm all hot and bothered at the very thought. Would you like a drink, I feel as if I need one!'

Beth went off to find some cocktails, skirting round the edge of the dance floor in the opposite direction to where Fergus was standing, keen to avoid him at all costs. She could see another dance starting, and Kit rushing across the room to persuade her sister to dance again. Not that she needed any coercion. Lord and Lady Milton were taking to the floor again, and Beth was thrilled to see her parents looking so happy. She couldn't remember the last time they'd spent so much time together. Mae and Julius were dancing, but neither looked particularly happy, though Beth suspected that might have something to do with Mae pretending she didn't know who he was when he'd first arrived, saying he'd been gone away so long she thought he must be a stranger. Frankie and Emily were dancing, but Frankie seemed a bit distracted. It didn't escape Beth's notice that he was watching Alice who was standing with Jane at the side of the room surrounded by young men. They both looked to be having a wonderful time, and Beth thought she'd never seen Alice looking quite as beautiful.

Emily was aware that she wasn't holding her partner's attention as well as she might. In fact, ever since that day at Ashcombe Falls she'd known Frankie seemed rather withdrawn and absent, almost as if he were somewhere else entirely. She'd tried every trick to get his notice, but nothing was working, and at the back of her mind she was sure that his lack of interest in anything she said or did was everything to do with the way she'd behaved that day. It was dawning on her that everyone had been a witness to the fact that she'd treated Nora Beales very badly. Emily had behaved like a brat, she knew it and felt sorry. How she wished she could change the past and have the chance to start the day at Ashcombe all over again, completely fresh. That wasn't a possibility, however much she replayed it in her head, but she could try and show Jonathan and the others that she really was a nice person, though quite how she was going to do that she didn't know.

When they came off the dance floor, Frankie said he'd seen an old friend he wanted to catch up with, and Emily was left on her own. She really was beginning to feel miserable, and deciding she'd be much better out of the way she set off for her room, holding back the tears as she went. How horrible to have made such a mess of things. Even her beloved Jonathan hadn't a good word or a kind look for her any more. He hadn't spoken a word to her all evening, let alone asked her to dance.

As she reached the top of the landing on the first floor, her tears were flowing, and she paused for a moment to dry her eyes. Looking down from the gallery she could see all the comings and goings below, and felt glad she'd escaped. The strains of music for a Charleston could be heard floating upwards, and she saw a group of flapper girls scream in excitement in their haste to dash to the ballroom, followed in hot pursuit by a group of eager young men keen to grab a partner. Everyone else seemed so blissfully happy when she'd never felt so miserable in her life. As she dabbed her handkerchief over her cheeks and tried to stop crying she couldn't help thinking what a contrast she made with all the revellers who were laughing and chatting. She was equally sure no one had even realised she was missing and even if they had she didn't think they would care. Emily was feeling very sorry for herself and turned to go to her room, but she was too late. Someone was coming, looming out of the darkness and running up the stairs two at a time. When the lamplight shone on his features she couldn't believe who was striding up the steps, and she stood like a frightened rabbit, unable to move one way or the other. Not knowing which way to go, she was determined he wouldn't see her and decided to duck into the shadows.

'Emily, I know you're up there,' Jonathan was calling. 'Please wait for me.'

Emily felt embarrassed to be crying and wallowing in self-pity, and thought she must look an awful mess. In the seconds it took her to decide she must go Jonathan reached her side and then there only seemed one thing to do. As he stood with his arms open she flung herself against him, sobbing her heart out. And as he gently kissed the top of her head, enfolding her in his arms as he stroked her back with affection, the tears started to subside at last.

Beth was feeling very pleased that she'd managed to persuade Will to fetch her some drinks, but he'd dashed off after getting them in record time. Returning through the crush of people in the drawing room where the refreshments were being handed round, she was just bringing back two champagne cocktails for her and Cora when she saw Kit's sister Camilla coming into the room.

Beth offered a beaming smile, and was intent on passing quickly by when Camilla stopped her by placing a beautifully manicured hand on her arm. It was clear she had something to say and wasn't going to let Beth go.

'This is such a super party, Beth, it's so kind of your parents to invite us.'

'It's an absolute pleasure; I do hope you and Kit are having a lovely time here in Devon,' said Beth, thinking she might be able to leave quicker if she made a little small talk. 'I must admit, we've all quite fallen in love with your brother, and it's so good to have another girl along to keep those bossy boys in their place.'

'We are having a splendid time, thank you, Beth,' said Camilla. 'Kit is a special person, you are quite right. You may imagine my brother breaks hearts wherever he goes, and I'm almost ashamed to say he has a string of girls hanging on his every word back in Cornwall. But, he doesn't like to be tied down … Well, I don't suppose many young men do.'

Was she imagining it, thought Beth, or was Camilla trying to warn Beth that there could be nothing serious going on between Kit and Cora. And yet, Beth didn't see a mild flirtation between them. Perhaps, at first, but then any relationship took time before the possibilities showed, she considered, and even then not all blossomed in the end. But she was sure this one was different, and wondered why anyone wouldn't be delighted to have their brother linked with her lovely sister. Cora was a perfect complement to Kit; surely anyone could see that.

'Cora is very fond of Kit, they seem to like spending time together,' said Beth, wondering what Camilla would say to that.

'Yes, your sister clearly likes him, though I do hope she isn't entertaining any hopes of something more,' said Camilla bluntly. 'He's practically engaged to a girl in Cornwall. The family is terribly rich, and I know both sides would love to see them married.'

'I see,' said Beth, who felt outraged on Cora's behalf.

'I wouldn't have said anything, but I shouldn't like Cora to be hurt. It might be an idea to say something, warn her against becoming too much in love with my brother.'

Beth was sure she was wrong. She couldn't believe that Kit could be almost engaged to someone else, and yet be behaving as he was to Cora. Everything he did and said showed how much he liked her. They were spending time together more and more.

'And whilst we're on the subject of home truths, I think it's important that you know the truth about Gilbert, Fergus's brother,' Camilla went on. 'He cost his family dearly when he invested unwisely in some mines in Yorkshire, far from the family business where his brother could keep an eye on him. It was touch and go whether they'd lose the lot.'

'Money, that's all you people care about. Gilbert is his brother and he's cast him off like an old shoe,' said Beth feeling crosser than ever. 'Do you know Gilbert was homeless for a while?'

Camilla laughed. 'Believe me, Beth, Fergus isn't your villain, however much you might want him to be. Gilbert lied about everything, even swindling Fergus out of much of his inheritance before it was all spent, frittered away on a lavish lifestyle that was impossible for him to keep up without his brother. That's why Fergus had to cut him off. If you don't believe me, you should ask Kit. He'll tell you. Our father found Fergus's solicitor, and Kit knows all the details of the case.'

Beth didn't want to ask Kit. If the story was true then Gilbert must be the worst of men, and if Camilla was right about Gilbert then perhaps she was right about Kit, and Cora was in danger.

'And why should I believe your brother?'

'That's something only you can decide, Beth, I was just trying to be helpful … I'd hate to see you waste your time hoping for something with Gilbert which will only end in disaster.'

Camilla turned, and Beth watched her walk away.

The happy reunion Mae had wished for with Julius was turning out to be far from all she'd dreamed. They'd danced twice, but she'd enjoyed neither. Julius had practically held her at arm's length, and not only that but he seemed totally distracted. He'd had to answer two telephone calls since they'd sat down, and now he was saying he'd received some very bad news.

'I'm sorry, Mae, I'm going to have to leave the party early,' said Julius. 'It's Aunt Dolly, she's had a bit of a turn.'

'Oh no, how awful. Is there anything I can do?' Mae asked, feeling so sorry that the vivacious lady she'd just met a couple of weeks ago could be poorly.'

'No, I'm afraid not. It's rather worse than I feared too. She's declared that nothing makes her better than being in London, and she's asked me to take her down to her house in Portman Square. Dolly always was a party girl; she says Devon's air is too clean and is making her cough. She's incorrigible ... but there's nothing I can do.'

'I do understand, but couldn't I come too? I'm sure I could come up to London with Alice and Jane as chaperones.'

'Mae, I don't think that's a good idea. I'm sorry to be so blunt, dearest, but I will have many things to sort out, and if she has one of her proper turns it will mean hospitalisation. I simply won't have time to be sociable. I'm sorry, I do hope you understand, but it can't be helped.'

Mae's disappointment instantly showed on her face. She tried to think of a reason to change his mind and opened her mouth to protest but she saw immediately it was useless.

'Look here, I really must dash,' he said, as he shook hands with her. 'Please send my apologies to your parents ... I don't want to disturb them ... I'll call soon!'

Mae lifted her hand to wave, but he didn't look back as he rushed away, weaving his way through the crowds, and she was left all alone feeling very sorry for herself.

'Oh, you silly goose, don't cry,' said Jonathan, stepping back to look at Emily. He took his handkerchief from his pocket and handed it over, and as she blew her nose and wiped her eyes he listened to her pour out her heart.

'I'm so sorry, Jonathan. I know I behaved terribly on the day of the picnic, and I can't apologise to you enough. I didn't have a chance to say sorry to Nora before she left for Worthing. And everyone must think I'm horrid ... I'm sure they all hate me, and I don't know what to do about any of it. I can just about bear them all thinking awful things, but not you. I can't cope with my best friend being so cross with me.'

A fresh bout of crying ensued and Jonathan pulled her closer again. 'Come on, Emily, I'm not cross with you, and I know you're sorry. It's all over, and you'll get your chance to apologise to Nora. We all make mistakes when we're young. I did too, once upon a time.'

Emily stepped back to look into his kind eyes, and sniffed back the tears. 'I bet you didn't do anything half so bad.'

'You'd be surprised. But, I'm not going into all that, and we're not going to waste any more time on such negative thoughts. It's time to forge ahead, and forget it all. Have you thought about writing to Nora? You can say a lot in a letter that might be more difficult face to face.'

'I knew you'd know what to do. Of course, I'll write straight away.'

'I'm sure it can wait until the morning now. Stop worrying ... let's get back to the ball and we'll say no more about it.'

'Yes, I'd like that ... if I don't look too red round the eyes.'

'You look perfectly lovely. There'll be a queue of young men wanting to dance with you. Now let's decide before we go back ... whom do you think you'll dance with next?'

Emily looked thoughtful for a second or two, and then answered hesitantly, 'With you, if you'll ask me.'

'Will you dance with me, Miss Milton?' Jonathan requested with a bow, offering his hand.

'Yes, I will,' she said taking it. 'And you can stop acting like my big brother now or it will seem completely strange.'

Jonathan seemed to find that amusing and laughed. 'Absolutely, I quite agree, though I have to assure you I certainly do not look on you as a little sister!'

She wasn't quite sure exactly what he meant by that but with his hand clasping hers they walked back downstairs together, Emily happy again that the world felt just as it should.

Beth found Cora just coming off the dance floor with Kit. They were both laughing and she looked so happy, that when Beth was reminded of Camilla's warning she felt very uneasy. Kit was such a lovely man Beth decided, as she saw him tend to every whim of her sister's, finding her a chair, making sure she wasn't sitting in a draught, and generally looking like a man falling in love.

'Let me relieve you of those drinks, Beth,' he said, taking them and putting them down on one of the little tables at the side. 'I haven't seen you dancing very much. It's about time we got you up on the dance floor.'

Beth laughed at that, and was just about to say she'd be delighted to dance when Fergus Dauncey came off the floor with Camilla on his arm.

'Miss Milton, will you dance?' he said immediately, which left Camilla looking quite put out.

Beth was so surprised and taken aback that she couldn't think of a way to refuse him, and in the next second he'd taken her arm and was leading her off. The dance was a foxtrot in which Beth knew she excelled. Fergus was a good dancer, she had to admit, and it wasn't long before she felt completely at ease in his arms. He didn't speak, which wasn't unusual, but if she had to dance with him she was determined to make him talk to her.

'I'm very honoured,' said Beth as sarcastically as she felt able. 'I've never seen you dance with anyone apart from Camilla.'

'Well, I am a gentleman, and I like to behave in the correct manner. It would have been rude to leave you standing there without a partner much longer. You've been left at the side on so many occasions, I felt rather sorry for you.'

Beth fumed with indignation. 'I was just accepting a dance with Kit, as a matter of fact, and far from being left unattended, I have chosen exactly when and with whom I wanted to dance tonight. I accepted you because I was shocked that you asked me, quite frankly, and I can assure you that if I'd had any time to think about it I'd have said no.'

'Well, we're dancing now. You're not a bad dancer, and I'm very good. I think half the room is watching us, but I suspect you know that already. You're the type that likes to make an exhibition, have everyone think how wonderful you are.'

Beth gasped with outrage. 'And you're clearly the very worst example of narcissism with a grandiose view of your own talents and a craving for attention. I wouldn't notice whether anyone was watching or not. You seem to think the whole room is admiring *you*.'

'You must admit, Beth, you're not averse to admiration. You craved my brother's affections, I've heard.'

'You're not to talk of Gilbert, and my relationship with him is none of your business.'

'Not even now Camilla has informed you of the truth about him. Do you still doubt her word?'

Beth didn't want to confess that she'd been slightly taken aback by what Camilla had told her. She didn't want to believe her, the more so because of what Camilla had said about Kit.

'I don't know what to think,' said Beth, 'apart from the fact that you've clearly told her what to say. Anyway, I've had enough discussion on that topic and I don't want to talk about it any more.'

Beth was glad the dance was coming to an end. Fergus didn't speak another word, and didn't take her hand to escort her back to her sister, which left her trotting behind him feeling very foolish. As soon as she could she excused herself and went off to look for Alice. She didn't know what to think about Jonathan's friends, but she knew she couldn't spend any more time with them. Perhaps Alice and Jane might know what to do for the best about Cora. If she was honest, Gilbert's memory was becoming a bit of a blur. She hadn't heard a word from him since he left for London, and she decided she'd probably been fooling herself where he was concerned. And yet, that didn't excuse Fergus or his despicable behaviour. Beth couldn't wait to talk to Alice and Jane, and hurried off to find them.

Jane was beginning to enjoy herself, and glad to see Alice at the centre of so much attention. They'd both had several dances with some of the local young men, and Jane had even managed a passable Charleston, much to her delight, but her greatest pleasure was seeing just how much Alice was coming out of her shell. She could see someone else had also noticed. Frankie hadn't been able to take his eyes off Alice, and Jane noticed how much he was observing her with huge admiration. She wasn't sure if Alice was aware of it, and hoped in a way that she didn't know just how jealous Frankie looked. Keep him at arm's length, a little bit longer, Jane thought. Show him you don't care even if every beat of your heart is for him alone. Stay aloof as long as you can - you'll soon have him eating out of your hand. She didn't think Emily would be hurt if Frankie came to his senses, and had already decided it would be a very good thing if he did. It was clear that Emily was simply infatuated with Frankie, impressed by his celebrity status, and riches. And she was quite sure that after Ashcombe Falls Frankie had witnessed quite how much Emily still needed to grow up. If he wanted a wife, she was sure he hadn't the time to wait for Emily, and in any case, she would have put money on the fact that he was still completely in love with Alice. Jane could see him looking longingly, and no man's expression ever got past Miss Jane Austen in whatever century it was witnessed.

As for herself, she'd hardly given Will a thought, she decided, though she had noticed he'd not danced at all, preferring to talk to the locals, circulating amongst the guests being his usual affable self. She'd enjoyed the company of other young men, and was resolved on light chat and as many partners as asked her to dance. Perhaps spending time alone with Will had been a mistake, one she would be sure not to repeat. Until he asked her to dance, of course.

How could she have refused him? He came to her looking like a god amongst men, with his beautiful hand outstretched, and the words softly spoken. She saw a myriad of detail as her heart beat faster: his fine shoulders, a flash of silk lapels, a snowy white shirt-front with its stiff starched collar and white tie. When she allowed herself to look up she traced the lines of the firm jaw, and the curve of his mouth. His lips, those lips that had kissed hers briefly but unforgettably, were begging her to dance, and his eyes, soulful in the candlelight would not allow her to say no.

Jane was glad it was a slow waltz, and melted into his arms and against his body in complete surrender, as if she'd always belonged there. The dance floor was so crowded there was hardly room to move, and they swayed together, shifting from foot to foot. Words seemed unnecessary, they had their arms round one another and she let herself enjoy every step, as they moved together as one. His cheek was next to hers, and every now and then she felt him press closer, his breath like a whisper on her face.

When he took her hand to lead her through the doors of the French windows into the warm scented evening, she still didn't utter a word, and even as they gazed at the sky stained with pink as the sun said goodbye it seemed wrong to break the silence. However, at last, it came.

'I'm going away for a while, Jane,' said Will looking into her eyes. 'Frankie's asked me to go to Bath with him for a few weeks.'

'Oh, I see,' said Jane with the sudden realisation that she didn't want him to go.

'Well, he seems in a bit of a spot, and said he needs to get away.'

Jane wanted to protest, to ask him how he could possibly leave her without knowing when he'd be back, but she just thought about what a lovely man he was instead. 'You're a very good friend, Will.'

'Perhaps, though I have my own selfish reasons for wanting to go too.'

He didn't explain further and something about the way he said it made Jane feel she couldn't enquire.

'I think Frankie is still in love with Alice,' Jane ventured. 'He hasn't taken his eyes off her all evening.'

'I suspected as much. Perhaps he's having second thoughts about being too serious with Emily.'

'Well, going away and having some time to think may prove valuable, and he'll be able to decide what to do.'

She watched Will rake his fingers through his hair. 'Let's hope that's the case for us all. Anyway, I just wanted to say goodbye, Jane.'

No one had ever spoken her name quite as he did. She wanted to hear him say it over and over again. 'Goodbye, Will. Thank you for dancing with me.'

Not knowing what else to say, she just managed to stop herself from begging him to hold her once again. Jane couldn't watch him walk away, and chose instead to flee down the stone steps leading from the terrace into the fragrant night.

Chapter Twenty One

Lady Milton thought the ball had been a huge success, and for some it had been a joy. Cora was dancing on air, and walked about in a dream-like trance, Kit on her mind most of the time. Emily was feeling much better now that Jonathan had forgiven her, and if they were friends then everything was right with the world. The fact that Frankie had been out of sorts at the ball didn't seem to matter so much. If he wanted to behave like a grouchy schoolboy she'd let him get on with it, though when he told her he was going to Bath with her brother and Eddie, Emily felt more put out than ever. But her pride prevented her from appealing to him to stay, and their last evening together was punctuated by long sulky silences that she did nothing to prevent.

Alice felt she'd made huge strides in being able to participate in the ball fully, even though she nursed a secret disappointment that Frankie hadn't asked her to dance and coming on top of the news that he was leaving was a real blow. Jane, likewise, was hiding her own feelings about the prospect of Will leaving for Bath with Frankie and Eddie. He hadn't said how long they'd be gone, and she knew even if she wished it otherwise, his absence was going to leave a big hole, most of all in her heart.

Beth was still in two minds about Fergus though she convinced herself that was more to do with his arrogance than anything she might have learned. She was cross that he'd managed to make her dance with him, though sometimes she caught herself picturing him in her mind. It was undeniable. He really was a marvellous dancer even if she couldn't stand the sight of his handsome face.

A kind of flatness descended on the house, and despite the continuing warm weather most of the Miltons felt they didn't quite know what to do with themselves. Will was gone in a day, off to the West Country with Frankie and Eddie, and then came the unexpected news shortly after, that Jonathan and his party of friends were also going away. Camilla sent a note round to Cora to inform her of the fact.

Dear Cora,

I'm just dashing off this note because I'm in rather a hurry and have so much to do! The whole party at Buckland Priors are off to Fergus's townhouse in Berkeley Square - he has some matters of business that can't be attended to in the depths of sleepy Devon, but I must admit I'm excited at the prospect of going up to town even if a lot of the first families will be in the country. I've just heard that my dear friend, Diana Hooper will also be in town. She's from our part of the world, is an heiress with a vast fortune just waiting to be joined in matrimony to another. I know you will not mind me confiding in you, dearest Cora of my hopes for my brother and dearest Diana. Jonathan is looking forward to a change of scene, and Fergus will be quite glad to get away.

Kit wanted me to pass on a message for your sister Beth whom, it appears, has quite decided against Fergus's good character. He went so far as to say he'd lay down his life for his friend Fergus, who is a gentleman of the first order with an impeccable character. I don't suppose she'll take much notice, and I'm not sure why Fergus is so bothered about what Beth thinks of him. I'm sure I wouldn't care about the opinion of anyone so stubborn who'd taken such an obvious dislike to me.

I fear we may not have time to return to Devon on our way back from London to Cornwall. I am sorry for I have enjoyed the time I spent with you. Please pass on my very best regards to your parents.

Yours sincerely,
Camilla Branwell.

Cora was naturally upset at the news, and found Beth as soon as she could.

'I hope you've not taken any notice of this, Cora,' said Beth as soon as she read it, thoroughly tempted to screw up the piece of paper in her hand. 'I wasn't going to tell you, but Camilla said something about this Diana girl at the ball. If you ask me she knows Kit is falling in love with you, and she's trying to put you off.'

'She'd never do that, but how on earth can I do anything about the situation. We know we cannot go to London, and Kit will just forget all about me. They'll be going back to Cornwall and I'll never see him again.'

'I don't know, Cora darling, but we'll think of something. And I just have a feeling he won't be able to stay away for long.'

'How do you feel about what Kit said on the subject of Fergus?'

'I must admit, I am surprised, but far more ready to believe Kit than Camilla.'

'She's not so bad, Beth, and she's been very kind to me.'

'Well, if that's kindness I'd hate to see her when she's being cruel. Say what you like, I shall not change my opinion on Kit's scheming sister, even if I might bend a little on my opinion of their friend.'

Cora smiled. She'd seen Beth and Fergus dancing together, and was quite sure there was a growing attraction between them even if neither of them wanted to admit it.

Lady Milton's initial feelings of elation were quickly giving way to those of despondency and she was feeling cross that all her plans to have her daughters married off were all going awry. She'd felt sure the ball might prompt one or two engagements, and the fact that so many young men were taking off for different parts of the country was causing her no end of anguish.

She chose to bring up the subject for discussion at dinner when her husband was feeling contented after a particularly good meal washed down with a bottle of claret.

'We simply must go to London, Albert,' Lady Milton said. 'If we don't I will not answer for what devastation may result.'

'Will the earth stop revolving, Flora? Will the sun refuse to rise? I do not share your view. London means one thing to me ... money. We have none to spare, and besides all that, we've had this discussion before and I will not have it again.'

'But the girls do not need a season, exactly. You do not need to lay out money for new gowns, and I'm sure their friends in town will entertain them. Jonathan Keeling is there with those nice friends of his, and I'm sure they'd love nothing more than to see our girls.'

'Oh, yes please, Father,' said Cora trying not to show her desperation. 'I should love to go to London and see the sights.'

'I'd like to go to Bath,' said Emily, thinking of Frankie at once, and Jane who was observing them all couldn't help thinking about Will, and wondering what he might be doing. Was he missing her as she was missing him?

'And we wouldn't spend any more money than necessary,' said Beth.

'Which is precisely what I'm worried about,' said Lord Milton. 'No, I'm putting my foot down. There'll be no jaunts to London or anywhere else. We're staying put, so get used to it. If you start saving now, perhaps you can go on a visit next year.'

There were audible groans all round, as Lord Milton pushed back his chair, taking his glass and a newly lighted cigar off to his study where he could be left in peace.

The days passed into weeks, and before they knew it August was almost over. Their time had been spent as well as it could be for five girls who were all missing someone they thought of fondly. As for Jane, she tried not to think too much about Will, though he had a habit of creeping into her dreams which made her feel restless on waking and filled with a desire to see him and hear his voice once more. In her dreams he was always about to kiss her but then he'd evaporate into nothingness or tell her he had to go. She concentrated on the girls in the daytime, thinking up lots of activities to stop them all from brooding too much. Without Will they didn't have a driver, which made Jane all the more determined she would learn to drive as soon as she could. In the meantime they took a few trips on the bus and the train, visiting Exeter, which Jane thought hadn't changed too much in a hundred years, and to other seaside places along the coast.

Jane taught them all to sew and embroider one wet afternoon, and even Lady Milton joined in much to Jane's great amusement. It was lovely to see them all getting along and admiring each other's handiwork. There was a pattern of busy employment to the days, and in the evenings which were spent quietly at home, Jane's love of books and reading aloud was transforming the sitting room. No longer were quarrels the inevitable ending to the day, and every one of the girls seemed eager to have their turn to read the next chapter. Lord Milton didn't seem quite so keen to leave after dinner and joined them to hear the latest book offering, complaining if he missed a single episode. More often than not, he and Flora were seen sitting together on the sofa holding hands and sharing looks between them, which made the girls nudge one another in quiet approval.

As for writing, Jane couldn't be happier. Whenever she could escape she would rush to her room to sit at the desk and write. She'd reached the halfway stage of the first draft of her new novel, and it was going well. If only Cassy were there to read it through and give her opinion she would be content, but the thought that her sister had arranged everything so she could now be in the wonderful position to continue her work spurred her on. Cassy would not have wanted her to spend time mourning the past, and she sent up another silent prayer thanking her for all that she'd done.

Sometimes Alice came up to see her, bringing her own writing or a piece of sewing and the two would sit in companionable silence, neither needing to talk. Occasionally one of them would stop, perhaps fetch tea and biscuits, and then they'd chat.

'It'll be September in another week,' said Alice. 'Frankie is due to go back to America to make a new film. There wasn't any mention of it in Will's letter, but I feel sure he will go.'

'Has Will written recently?' Jane asked, trying not to show her excitement at the thought of a letter.

'Yes, it came this morning. I didn't have a chance to show you earlier. You might like to know you get a warm mention.'

'Oh, really? What does he say?'

Alice took out the letter and read.

Dear Alice,

We're all well here in Bath, and I hope you are too. Frankie and Eddie make great companions - I'd quite forgotten what fun we've always had together - it feels as if we're all twelve years old again. We've visited all the tourist spots like the Pump Rooms, and the Roman Baths, and we've walked up to Beechen Cliff. In fact, we've done a lot of walking whilst we've been here, and even took a couple of tents out with us up to the countryside near Combe Hay. We camped out for a couple of nights, and fried bacon in a pan over a fire - like boy scouts.

Frankie was a bit quiet when we first got here, but he seems to have come out of his shell quite a lot. He told me he was worried about the impression his friendship with Emily had made on her and everyone else. When she'd started talking about getting married, he realised he'd given her the idea that he was seriously courting her, that it all might lead to something else or that he was about to propose. He feels quite awful about it, and says though he's very fond of her he never meant to give her the notion that marriage was on the cards. Frankie wanted to say something before he left, but told me he's going to write to her very soon. I wondered if you'd mind looking out for the letter, not that you have to do anything, but just so you know in case she's terribly upset. Also, I don't know if Jane could be on hand when the inevitable happens, but I can't think of anyone else who will know exactly how to handle both Emily and this whole awkward situation.

I'm sorry to send a letter with such disquieting news, but I thought forewarned would be forearmed. Send Jane my best regards.

Yours ever,
Will.

Jane felt herself blush as Alice finished reading the letter. His best regards were not exactly a declaration of love but Jane was glad she'd been remembered, and what was most thrilling of all was the fact that he entrusted her above everyone else with looking after Emily. The thought made her glow with pleasure.

'My brother holds you in high estimation, quite rightly. I don't know what to think about it all, really, I was convinced Frankie was in love with Emily.'

'I suppose it might have looked that way to a lot of people.'

'What do you mean?'

'I wasn't convinced that Frankie shared the same feelings. There was always a certain reserve about him.'

Alice was not to be drawn. 'What do you think … can you be on hand to help Emily?'

'Yes, of course I can. I'd be delighted to help in any way.'

Alice folded the letter, and put it back in the pocket of her dress. 'I expect he doesn't want to leave her with any expectations, especially as he will be going back to America soon.'

Jane was thoughtful. She didn't see the situation in quite the same way. 'At least he's come to his senses; anyone could see that relationship wasn't going to work.'

'I didn't … I thought he was as besotted with her, as she was with him.'

'That's because you couldn't see how much he is in love with someone else.'

Alice looked stricken. 'Who can you mean?'

'You, of course. It's as plain as the nose on my face.'

'I think you have a rather fine nose, but you're wrong, in any case. Frankie isn't in love with me.'

'Well, have it your own way, but if we don't see him before he goes back to Hollywood, I shall eat my best hat.'

Alice laughed. 'I hope you have the stomach for cream linen,' she said, 'because it's my bet that won't happen.'

Chapter Twenty Two

They were all sitting at breakfast on the very first day of September when the post came in. As the first autumn leaves fluttered past the window like copper pennies, Mr Bell flourished the silver salver which held two letters, firstly towards her ladyship, and secondly, in front of Emily. Jane and Alice exchanged glances as soon as they saw them, having a good idea from whom the letter for Emily might be, and when she rushed from the room in great excitement it was confirmed.

'I'd better not go up to her just yet,' said Jane in a low voice to avoid being overheard. 'I'll bide my time.'

'Quite right,' said Alice, 'and if you need me to come with you just say the word. It's a bit rotten for you on your own.'

'I'll be fine, don't you worry. I've a feeling Emily might fear the worst as far as your concerned, however unfounded you think her worries might be.'

Jane finished the last spoonful of her egg with the last neat square of toast she'd saved in order to relish it. One couldn't do anything on an empty stomach, she thought, and felt fortified, ready to face the worst.

Lady Milton opened her letter declaring it was from Lady Celia by the look of the scrawl on the envelope.

'Good Lord, Celia's back in London, Albert,' she said. 'I thought she'd gone to Paris for good.'

'Beats me,' said his lordship. 'Celia's never been one for staying in the same place, and she always liked London. I suppose when she hotfooted off to Paris she needed a change after bringing up Will, Alice and Mae, but I really thought she'd gone forever this time.'

'Well, she's answered all our prayers into the bargain,' said Lady Milton looking round the table triumphantly.

'How so?' asked her husband, putting down his knife and fork with a clatter onto his plate.

'The girls can go to London. I'll write immediately and with a bit of luck they'll have an invitation by return of post.'

'Oh, Flora, must we?' Mae spoke up. 'I'm not just speaking for myself, but for all my sisters. Aunt Celia means well, but she holds the dullest parties, and we won't be allowed any freedoms.'

'Mae, it's very unkind of you to talk about my sister in that way,' said Lord Milton. 'She looked after you from the goodness of her heart. Besides, when you were young, you needed a firm hand.'

'Believe me, Beth, Emily and Cora will hate staying in that great mausoleum. It's like a shrine to the dead,' added Mae. 'The only good thing about it is its being in the heart of Bloomsbury. There are artists to be bumped into every day simply by stepping out of the door.'

'Your Aunt Celia was bereft when your Uncle Peregrine died,' her father replied. 'There are a few statues too many of him, I will admit, and perhaps it's not in the best taste to have his false wig feature so prominently on one of them or his false teeth on another. Even so, Mae, sometimes you need to watch your tongue.'

Everyone started laughing, and soon even Beth and Cora were swapping stories about the eccentricities of their aunt. Jane was enormously amused and couldn't help wishing that Lady Flora's idea for them all to be invited to London would come true. She certainly sounded like a character she could use in a book, though if a little too unconventional Lady Celia might prove difficult to be used convincingly.

'Now you will be able to have a season of sorts,' said Lady Milton, 'Celia knows some of the best families in London.'

'I suppose it would mean I might get to see Julius again,' said Mae. 'I do hope his aunt is recovering, but I haven't heard a word from him, and I can't help thinking the worst.'

'There, that's more or less settled. We will all go, and Albert, you needn't look like that. Think of the money we shall save on hotel bills. Why, there might be some shopping to be had based on what will be set aside. I can't go to London and not buy a new season's hat from Lucile. What would she think if she found out I was in London and had not been to her salon?'

'That you must have better things to spend your money on, I shouldn't wonder. There'll be no hats, no frocks and no Lucile! All I can hope is that

Celia has a house full of guests already.'

When Jane went up to see Emily she had the latest film magazine in her hand, her excuse for knocking on the door. Jane took a deep breath and waited for the sounds of distress she was expecting. Nothing could have quite prepared her for the cheerful voice she heard or the self-composed young woman who invited her in. Emily was sitting at her dressing table putting the final touches to her appearance.

'Oh, Jane, come in,' she said. 'It's lovely to see you. I haven't had a chance to see you on your own or say thank you again for being so kind on that day when I behaved so badly. I really am awfully sorry about the whole episode. I've written to Nora and I hope to visit her as soon as she comes home.'

'I know you didn't really mean to be unkind, and I'm sure you didn't mean to behave as you did. Let's put it behind us … I know you'll do all you can to make it up to Nora when you have the opportunity.' Jane held out the magazine. 'Here, take this, I saw it in the Newsagent's and thought you might like it.'

'What did I do before you came to Manberley, Jane? Thank you so much for bringing me such a treat. I'm sure I don't deserve it.'

'Well, I know how much you enjoy the films and the stars of the silver screen … I wondered if there'd be a picture of Frankie in it.'

Emily tossed the magazine down on the bed as if to dismiss it. 'I expect so, there are not many issues which don't have a feature on him, but frankly, if you'll excuse the pun, I'm not quite in the mood for him today.'

'Is everything all right, Emily?'

'I don't know. I think so, yet it ought not to be. I can't really explain the way I'm feeling. By rights, when you knocked on my door you should have found me lying prostrate, face down on the bed bawling my eyes out, but I must admit I feel absolutely fine.'

Jane didn't like telling lies, but she knew there were exceptions to the rule, and surely this was one of them. 'What do you mean, what's happened?'

'Frankie's finished with me. It was all over before it really began, I suppose. Any other time I might have been tremendously upset, but though it was unexpected and I'd started thinking something may come of it, at the back of my mind I knew it would never work. Film stars don't really court ordinary girls like me, and I've been racked with guilt about Alice, never thinking for one minute about how she must feel.'

'Perhaps you were in love with the idea of being with Frankie, rather than with Frankie himself. It wouldn't be unusual to feel that way, he's very glamorous and cuts a dashing figure.'

Emily laughed. Oh, Jane, sometimes you sound like a heroine from one of Georgette Heyer's novels. You do make me chuckle.'

'And what sort of books does Miss Heyer write?'

'Romance in the Regency ... heavily influenced by Jane Austen, I'm told. Alice lent me a couple, and I quite enjoyed them, but I haven't had time to read very much lately. Anyway, I can't quite see Frankie as a Regency hero though I must admit I'd like to see him in a pair of breeches.'

'He's not broken your heart then?'

Emily hesitated, before shaking her head. 'No, I can't say he's done that, and though I'd love nothing more than mooning around for a couple of days feeling sorry for myself listening to songs we loved on the gramophone, I have to admit to feelings of relief. I really don't think I could have been truly in love if I feel like this.'

'Well, I am glad to hear you're not suffering,' said Jane standing up. 'I'm sure sooner or later you'd have worked it out for yourself, but perhaps having the situation forced on you is better in the long run. I don't mean to sound unsympathetic, but there's nothing worse than going on with something if your heart is not really in it. It wouldn't be fair on either you or Frankie in the end.'

'You're right, Jane. I was feeling a little guilty about not feeling devastated, but you always make sense of a situation. I will miss going round and about the place with him, of course, but I wouldn't be telling the truth if I didn't say that was because I enjoyed all the attention I was getting as Frankie's girlfriend.'

'You felt very flattered, didn't you?' said Jane, 'He is a very charming gentleman, but I'm not convinced he's the only man who will ever make you happy or the sole person who will make you feel special in their company.'

'There haven't been many,' Emily began before she stopped.

Jane could see she was thinking, and she'd have made a bet there and then that she knew exactly whom she was thinking about. She stood up to leave, and advanced towards the door. 'Sometimes the very people under our noses turn out to be the most surprising, and often the ones we ultimately love best.'

Emily looked at her quizzically. She might not yet be prepared to listen to her heart, Jane decided, but she didn't think it would be much longer before Emily realised what her heart had known all along.

Before the end of the week Lady Milton's plans were falling into place. Much to her jubilation the invitation from Lady Celia arrived, and there was a flurry of activity in the house, the like of which had not been seen since the preparations for the summer ball. Trunks and cases were fetched down from the attics, and the maids ran round purposefully packing huge quantities of clothing, quite aware that they, themselves, might not be needed in London, and could look forward to a little holiday of their own. Lady Celia had a full complement of staff, and they knew Lady Milton would enjoy taking full advantage of that.

Before leaving Jane knew she must divulge the Miltons' plans to Dr Lyford who was back in Winchester and give him a forwarding address, and after the letter was written and posted she decided she really ought to visit Mr Quance down in the village, for not only did she wish to say goodbye to him but there was also a special request she wanted to ask of him.

There was no one in the shop when she got there, and the bookseller was so pleased she'd come to see him, especially when she said his help was very much needed. He ushered her through to the back room, dimly lit by a single latticed window where a pot of geraniums gave a splash of colour and a delicious scent. There was a dresser full of blue and white china against one wall, and a round table covered with a chenille cloth. A fire burned in the grate and two armchairs on either side looked inviting with cushions in periwinkle and marigold. No sooner had she sat down than Mr Quance's cat, Quince, jumped up onto her lap, and settled himself down to purr loudly as Jane stroked his sleek black fur.

'Miss Austen, I am beyond words, and truly honoured that you should seek my opinion,' said Mr Quance after Jane asked him if he'd read her manuscript.

'Well, it's not completed, of course, but I was always so used to having my sister look over chapters for me, and though I know Alice would be happy to take her place, I rather think someone a little outside will give me a far more impartial view. I am not seeking praise, you understand, Mr Quance, but an editorial critique, and I hope you will let me hire you in that capacity.'

Mr Quance set down a tray of tea things. 'My dear Miss Austen, I could not take a single penny for an exercise which will be a great pleasure and privilege. Please allow me to assist you in any way I can.'

Jane opened her mouth to say she could not possibly accept his kind offer.

'No, my dear, I insist,' he continued, pouring her a cup of tea and placing it on a side table. 'I will not hear any more against it. Now, do tell me all about this new novel.'

To have the chance to discuss her book with someone who understood and admired her writing was something Jane hadn't done for a long time. She settled back in her chair and began to speak watching Mr Quance's eyes grow wider in wonder. And when she'd finished he wanted to know all about what she thought about going to London.

'I am very curious to see London again, Mr Quance. Whilst I've never wanted to live there, my visits to see my brother Henry and his wife were always highlights of the past, and of course it was where my books were published and sent out into the world. It was the most wonderful time of my life, and seeing my very first book published was the most exciting of all.'

'That was *Sense and Sensibility*, wasn't it?'

Jane nodded. 'I remember the overwhelming excitement of being in Sloane Street when I was editing *Sense and Sensibility* for publication, and how Henry's house was always chock full of visitors. I will never forget that April of 1811, the sights and smells of spring lilac in Kensington Gardens, the visits to art galleries and the theatre ... it was all very thrilling.'

'History in the making,' said Mr Quance, 'Oh, do tell me more, Miss Austen.'

Jane recalled a party at Henry's when she was still editing her final draft, and her brother was dealing with the publisher on her behalf. She only had to close her eyes to see it all again, and Mr Quance hung on her every word.

'The party went off extremely well,' she went on. 'There were many anxieties and a crisis or two beforehand, of course, but at last everything was quite right. The rooms were dressed up with armfuls of flowers, and pink chimney lights set either side of the looking glass above the mantelpiece sparkled prettily. Mr Egerton and Mr Walter arrived at half-past five for dinner, at half-past seven the musicians arrived in two hackney coaches, and by eight the lordly company began to appear. I spent the greater part of the evening chatting pleasantly with my friends George and Mary Cooke ... the drawing room soon became hotter than we liked, and so we placed ourselves in the cooler connecting passage, which gave us all the advantage of the music at a distance, which I preferred, as well as giving us the first view of every newcomer.'

'What wonderful memories, Miss Austen, I can picture it all.'

Jane privately remembered wearing a dress trimmed with bugle beads, and a headband to match threaded through her curls, a flower tucked into her décolletage. If not in the first flush of youth she'd been quite surrounded by gentlemen; and what with Mr Hampson, Mr Seymour, Mr Knatchbull, Mr Guillemarde, Mr Cure, a Captain Simpson, Mr Walter and Mr Egerton, in addition to the Cookes, and the ladies, Miss Beckford, and Miss Middleton, she'd had her work cut out with entertaining them all.

Later on, she'd heard Mr Knatchbull had described her as a "pleasant-looking young woman", which she'd decided was as much as she could hope for at her grand age of thirty-five.

'Sixty-six people attended, considerably more than Eliza had expected ... the house was full,' Jane continued. 'The music was delightful, and between the songs were lessons on the harp and pianoforte together. There was one female singer, a short Miss Davis, all in blue, whose voice was said to be very fine indeed; and all the performers gave great satisfaction by doing what they were paid for, and giving themselves no airs. No amateur could be persuaded to do anything. I remember it all fondly, along with the growing thrill of knowing that at last my little bound notebooks were being made into three volumes, and my dream of becoming a published author was to be accomplished at last.'

'And so you are to return to the place of their birth.'

'Yes, silly of me, I know, but every one is like a child to me. And, going back to London presents so many different emotions. How strange it will seem to travel through streets and pass houses where those vital beings no longer draw breath,' she said, unable to say very much more to Mr Quance for the moment.

'My dear, Miss Austen, if I could but spare you the pain.'

To think she would not be seeing her beloved Henry who would have been the first person to meet her in London on any other occasion, she could hardly contemplate. All she could hope was that London was so changed she would not be constantly reminded of all that had been and of those happy memories which were so very much a part of her entire being.

Jane managed to smile. 'One does not love a place the less for enduring some painful thoughts and recollections, and my memories are such that I only feel happiness for those lost times. New memories will be made, I am certain, and I must look to the future and give thanks for my extraordinary good fortune. Thank you, Mr Quance for reminding me of the past and helping me to look forward to the future.'

Chapter Twenty Three

'Lord, just look at it,' said Mae as the car drew up before Lady Celia Broughton's townhouse. 'Why is it that my aunt's house looks the dreariest in the row?'

Jane, Alice and Cora were sitting in the back of the car looking out at the row of Georgian houses that appeared to be considerably shabbier, Jane thought, than they would have done in her day. Beyond the road that divided them was a square of green lawn enclosed by black railings, a rectangle of formality lined with plane trees already losing their leaves. It was very odd seeing such buildings with an appearance of antiquity, partly blackened by London soot produced by the constant belching chimneys. It had taken all day to be driven up to London in a hired car with stops on the way, and it was already growing dark. The nights were drawing in earlier than ever, and there was a definite change in the weather, and a chill felt in the air.

Just pulling up in front were Lord and Lady Milton, Emily and Beth, and they were the first to get out and stretch their legs.

'Oh dear, it does bring back some rather gloomy recollections,' said Alice. 'But, let us not be down-hearted, we'll be back in Devon in three week's time, at least, if I don't happen to find myself a job.'

'Are you really going to find a job?' said Mae. 'I really couldn't spend longer than three weeks with Aunt Celia even if I had the best occupation in the world.'

'I am seriously thinking of it. What else awaits me in Devon, but a life of idleness and decreasing poor spirits? Besides, just lately, the thought of being an independent woman with my own income is one that excites me very much. And, even if I do stay in London, I shouldn't like to impose on Aunt Celia. No, I shall have a flat all to myself, and my own front door key.'

'Oh, Alice, I must admit that sounds so exciting, and very tempting,' said Mae. 'Could we share, do you think?'

'I'd like nothing better,' said Alice, 'though you'd have to help with the rent, perhaps get a job yourself or find a way to sell your paintings. I couldn't really manage on my own, places are so expensive in London.'

Jane was silent. Suddenly aware of her own position, she was beginning to realise she might not have a job for very much longer. Then what would she do? None of the girls really needed a companion, much less a governess. The truth was that they never had, and now they were all beginning to find their feet Lady Milton was sure to start seeing her as an unnecessary expense.

'We could find a three bedroom flat and Jane could come too,' said Mae sensing the latter's mood. 'There must be so many jobs you could do, and yet still have time to write in the evenings. I'm not suggesting being a governess again; I know you could do so much more. We'll help you, won't we, Alice?'

Jane was overwhelmed by Mae's kindness. Alice agreed it was a splendid idea, and it was with a light heart that Jane stepped out of the car and into the cool of the autumnal night.

As the butler let them in to a grand hallway decorated in a very heavy Victorian style, Lady Celia appeared out of the gloom along the dark passage. She was not a woman of fashion, and struck Jane as rather an eccentric character in a dress which would not have looked out of place in her own time. It looked hand-made, and was full-length, embroidered around the hem with hollyhocks, a peasant style Jane had seen worn by the writers and artists of the day. Jane couldn't help wondering if she'd have been drawn into wearing such garb if she'd been a contemporary writer, but thought not in conclusion. She much preferred her short haircut, the modern styles, and the freedom of movement they gave her.

'Come along in, you'll catch your death standing on the front step. I am very susceptible to colds and cannot abide draughts. Dinner will be served in half an hour, though you're extremely lucky that the cook is so obliging. You are very late, Albert, and eating at such an hour will play havoc with my digestion. Still, you won't find a finer dinner anywhere in London. I always keep the best cooks, if I say so myself.'

Alice put her arm through Jane's as they strolled behind Lady Celia's formidable figure. 'I always forget quite how acerbic Aunt Celia can be,' said Alice. 'You mustn't take any notice; her bark is much worse than her bite.'

Jane couldn't help smiling. Here was food for thought and possibly a great inspiration for her writing.

They were shown to their rooms, and Jane found much pleasure in discovering that hers was next to Alice and one step away from Mae. They were all becoming so close, and to have their friendship was the greatest happiness. Jane's room looked over the square, and the road surrounding it still saw the occasional car, circling round, headlamps on full beam. It was such a different scene than any she remembered and passing through the streets had been like visiting the moon, let alone somewhere she'd once known. But London was a much bigger place these days, and she'd heard Alice talk about the shops at Sloane Square. In Jane's day, the area had been a village and she'd walked into London to go shopping. Thankful that she wouldn't be reminded too much of the past, she still felt a certain trepidation at the thought of visiting places like Kensington Gardens which she felt might provoke more memories than she'd like.

The dining room was opulent, in the same dark Victorian style as the rest of the house. Deep purple curtains were draped at the windows in funereal style and a black marble clock on the mantelpiece ticked loudly, the only distinguishable sound apart from the sputter of lit candles dropping wax softly onto the tablecloth. There was no fire in the grate, the room felt damp, as if hardly used, and apart from the smell of mould seeping through the cold air, Jane could detect the unmistakable odour of mice. It was clearly a room not used much for entertaining, and she couldn't help thinking about poor Alice, Mae and Will growing up in such a comfortless home.

Lady Celia stared at them one by one through a lorgnette, which dangled from a gold chain round her neck. When she spotted Jane, she stopped and stared.

'So, you're the lady's companion I'm expected to house, though why a family of five girls need any companions but themselves is absolutely beyond me. A terrible waste of money, to my way of thinking.'

Jane was shocked by her rudeness but looked steadily back at the lady who was squinting sideways at her. 'My name is Jane Austen, your ladyship, it's so very kind of you to accommodate me.'

'Mmm ... you're not exactly what I expected. I was told you were the daughter of a clergyman, but I don't recall ever having met one of that class who were dressed in the first style of fashion.'

'We are indebted to Jane,' Lady Milton spoke up immediately before Jane felt she ought to answer. 'She's been such a pleasure to have at Manberley, and she's become one of the family.'

'Well, if she is useful to you I expect it was my recommendation to find her in the pages of *The Lady* that found you the most suitable person. I have discovered it is quite the best place to find decent hard-working companions and governesses who do not encourage idle and lazy habits. It is marvellous how many families I have been the means of supplying in that way. I am always glad to get a young woman well placed in a household. Four nieces of my housekeeper, Mrs Buttle, are most delightfully situated through my influence; and it was only the other day that I recommended another young gel who was merely accidentally mentioned to me, and the family are quite delighted with her. Albert, did I tell you of Lady Palfrey's calling yesterday to thank me? She finds Miss Green a treasure. "Lady Celia," she said, "you have given me an angel from heaven itself." So, I am not surprised in the least. Good advice is always worth having ... and my friends tell me I am indispensable to them in that way.'

Jane saw Lady Milton roll her eyes at her husband who promptly turned his head, pretending not to have seen it.

When the dinner came in Jane could see that although there seemed numerous footmen to serve it, the food itself was on a par with that once served at Manberley Castle with mean portions. The thought of being starved for three weeks and insulted into the bargain was not very cheering, and as she looked round the silent table she could see they were all thinking the same thing.

'So, I thought tomorrow morning we'd call on Lady Soames first thing,' continued Lady Celia, 'and if there is time I'd like you to meet Lady Calthorpe. Her son is unmarried, and as yet, seems unable to find someone to suit. I feel sure Alice would do for him.'

'But *he* would not do for Alice,' Jane spoke up immediately in the firm tones of a practised governess. 'Besides, we have other plans for the morning.'

There was a great sound of breath being sucked in at an alarming rate, and when Jane looked, Lady Celia wasn't the only one to have her mouth open in horror. She took no notice. Recognising a bully when she saw one Jane knew the only way to tackle her was head on.

'I am taking the girls to the British Museum in the morning,' said Jane, picking up her wine glass, 'and then onto an exhibition in the afternoon at the Royal Academy. We would not like to disrupt your usual habits, Lady Celia, and I do think regular instruction of young ladies is most vital if they are not to become idle.'

Mae stifled a snigger down the table. She couldn't help it, knowing that Jane had promised to take them to Hyde Park, and a boat on the Serpentine if it was fine, before going on to have afternoon tea.

Lady Celia sniffed and looked most put out. 'You are very outspoken for a lady's companion, I am not at all used to being spoken to in such a manner.' She looked as if she might demand obedience for a moment but then backed down. 'Very well, Miss Austen, but I require everyone here in the evening. We have been invited to a musical soirée with Lady Calthorpe, followed by a séance with the Bloomsbury Spiritual Society, and I do not wish to miss it. We came so close to speaking to Peregrine last session that I feel sure it will be within our grasp, and I am certain you should not wish to miss it.'

'Oh, we wouldn't miss it for the world, Celia,' said Flora Milton. 'I can't think of anything more exciting than an evening spent talking to the dead.'

Mae's spluttering was quickly disguised as a cough, as the others stared wide-eyed, and winked surreptitiously whenever they caught another's glance, conspirators united as one.

The day went off exactly as planned. Lady Milton said she preferred to do some shopping on her own and see her friend Lucile, the fashion designer, and as Lord Milton was heading for his club in St James, it was agreed that they would meet up later before dinner and the inevitable dreary evening. Jane and the girls set off in high spirits, glad to have escaped the confines of the house. Firstly, they spent some time in the British Museum looking at the antiquities from Egypt, which they were all fascinated to see, before stopping for lunch in a Lyon's Corner House, which Alice said would not be too expensive. The overwhelming fragrance of flowers and chocolates as they walked in was such a delicious smell Jane thought they'd found heaven on earth and after a hearty meal, followed by rum babas for pudding, they felt fit for anything. The exhibition at the Royal Academy was showing some Impressionist paintings, which they all admired, and then they walked off their lunch on their way to Hyde Park. London roared on all sides with trams, carts, horses, and omnibuses. Jane had never heard such a noise in her life before, but there was an energy and excitement in the hustle and bustle, which she liked very much. It was all very exciting.

Hyde Park was a rural idyll in contrast to the busy streets, with sheep scattered everywhere munching on the grass to keep it down. It was peaceful and quiet in many places, but there were still large numbers of people to observe, chatting and smiling, or thoughtful and reflective as they walked. The girls dawdled through the park, and stopped to feed the swans at the side of the lake, watching the uniformed nannies out with their charges trying to wear them out before bedtime. Strolling lovers sauntered by, hand in hand, oblivious to all but themselves.

Jane and the girls split into two groups to take rowing boats out on the Serpentine. Jane, Mae and Cora took the first one, and Alice, Beth and Emily the second, taking it in turns at the oars. They were all laughing so much as they tried unsuccessfully to manoeuvre the boats and race one another, that soon they'd had enough of competing, and were content to let their fingers trail in the cool water, lying back to contemplate the sky feeling the warm September sun on their faces. The boats glided through the water, side by side, as they dozed.

'This is such fun,' said Mae tilting her head to the sun. 'Thank you, Jane, I can't begin to think what an awful day we'd have had if not for you.'

'Hear, hear,' called Emily from the other boat. 'Three cheers for Jane.'

'It has been fun,' said Jane sitting up and shading her eyes as she looked across the water. 'I can't remember laughing so much for a very long time. Thank you for spending such a perfect day with me.'

It was true. Jane spoke from the heart, and she felt, once more, a pang of uncertainty and what she could only describe as cold fear. Sometimes she felt so very alone in the world. Without realising it she'd become very attached to the Milton girls, she knew it would be an awful wrench to have to leave them, and whatever Alice might say about helping her to find another job, she wasn't so sure she'd get one. She would have to start thinking very seriously about her future, and try to remember that the Milton girls, however lovely, would never belong to her, and could not be a part of a real family for her.

But after the pleasure comes the pain,' groaned Mae. 'I am not looking forward to Lady Calthorpe's party in the evening.'

There was a chorus of noises in agreement and Beth burst out, 'I cannot think of anything more morbid than a séance.'

'Well, it might be fun to try and work out how they do it,' said Cora. 'I remember reading a case in the paper not long ago where they discovered that the 'medium' was moving the table with her foot, and that the ectoplasm emanating from her was merely a sheet of muslin.'

They all laughed at that. 'I shall never be able to keep a straight face,' said Mae. 'It will be just like when we had that governess all those years ago. You remember, Alice, Aunt Celia thought she was wonderful, but she didn't have a clue how to make me behave. She smelled of mothballs, pear drops and barley water in that order, and she had whiskers protruding from her chin. Whenever I got the giggles one stern look was sure to make me worse.'

'And then you'd set me off too,' said Alice, 'and the more we tried to stop the worse it got. Oh dear, she really was a tyrant, though you were a very naughty little sister.'

'I was, I can't deny it,' said Mae, 'but look at me now, I'm as good as gold.'

Though everyone was laughing Jane thought what a difference she'd seen take place in Mae's personality. She seemed so much happier, though sometimes she had a bit of a pensive expression and a faraway look to make Jane wonder if something was troubling her. She suspected Mae was pining for Julius though doing her best to hide her feelings. As far as Jane knew there'd been no further communication from him.

As if Beth read her mind she said, 'Have you any plans to see Julius now we're in London?'

Mae shrugged, but didn't shift or open her eyes. 'No, though I've an idea where he lives. I could go to his aunt's house and surprise him.'

'Do you think that's wise?' asked Jane. 'Perhaps you'd be better off sending a postcard to let him know you're here. Just a casual note, as if you're not really bothered one way or the other might do the trick.'

'Yes, I'll see,' Mae answered. 'Anyway, he's not the only man in London. What about you, Beth; is your handsome lieutenant still here? And Cora, wasn't Jonathan bringing Kit down to the city?'

Both Beth and Cora didn't seem to want to reply, but at last Beth spoke. 'I'm not sure what I think about Lieutenant Dauncey any more. By all accounts and I've had a few now, he isn't the man I thought at first.'

'I'm sorry, Beth,' said Alice, 'you looked so well together and he seemed such a nice man.'

'Well, apparently he's a swindler and a crook according to Fergus, Kit and Camilla, and I have to say that he's pretty well left me in the lurch. I'm not even sure he liked me that much, and if it's money he was after he's obviously realised I'm as poor as a church mouse.'

'And I was so looking forward to a wedding this year,' said Cora. 'Goodness knows we could do with a bit of glamour in our lives.'

'Marriage isn't necessarily glamorous, Cora,' said Emily. 'I'm not sure I'll ever get married. One thing I've discovered is that falling in love with the right person isn't easy or obvious. You think you've found the right person and then you discover he wasn't right after all.'

'However, I do think one of us has found the right one,' said Alice. 'I've no doubt it's Cora who will be the first to hear wedding bells.'

'But I'm sure if Camilla has anything to do with stopping her brother making such an unsatisfactory match, she'll do it,' added Cora. 'I don't know. I thought Kit liked me but he left me with no idea of coming back. Why are men such a problem?'

'What about you, Jane?' asked Mae. 'Has anyone stolen your heart?'

'Oh no,' Jane smiled bravely, 'I'm not interested in anyone like that.'

As if to contradict her words a gust of breeze snatched her hat from her head, and it landed in the water. She couldn't help thinking of Henry immediately; it had always been a favourite trick of his, to snatch her bonnet and throw it up into the air if he caught her telling tales. If she'd been a superstitious person she might have believed it was his ghost who'd visited her, and pierced through the ether for a moment in time to let her know that he was aware she wasn't telling the truth.

Chapter Twenty Four

In the end, the evening at Lady Calthorpe's had been a weird mixture of tediousness and hilarity. Lady Celia's friends were an odd bunch with artistic pretensions. All claimed to be writers, poets and artists, though Mae assured Jane she'd only ever seen the ghastliest work produced by any of them. The séance had been hilarious, and though all the Miltons and Jane had tried their very best to be serious about the whole affair, when their dead Uncle Peregrine's 'voice' boomed out from behind a door in a ghostly wail, it was all any of them could do not to laugh.

After such an evening, the girls were keen to go out again the next day, and Jane planned trips with them to visit the science museum, and the Victoria and Albert in the Cromwell road. Looking at the costume collection proved to be very entertaining. Jane loved seeing the Elizabethan dresses, but was amused when the other girls described the Georgian and Regency dresses as ancient, though after a hundred years the gowns had certainly lost a look of freshness. It seemed bizarre to be exhibiting clothes she'd worn just a short while ago behind glass cases, and she was aware, once more, of how dream-like the past was becoming, almost as if she'd never lived another life.

The days passed by filled with busy nothings, and though the girls were enjoying seeing the sights of London Jane knew each one still harboured a longing for the men they missed. Jane thought about Will often, especially as walking through the London parks was becoming a favourite habit. On her day off, when the late sunny weather reminded her of their time together at Ashcombe Falls with the sun filtering through the branches above her head, she'd close her eyes and remember. Jane felt the touch of his hand on hers, his fingers tracing her cheek, and that swift but sweet kiss that made her long for more. Jane hoped Will was enjoying himself, but she wished he'd come back, though she knew he had no plans to come to London.

Mae wrote several letters to Julius at his aunt's address, but she received no answer to any of them, and in desperation for any sign of him she slipped out one afternoon to make her way to Portman Square. After staring up at the blank windows of the imposing house where the blinds and curtains appeared to be drawn, she didn't have the courage to knock and she left soon after. The house looked empty, as if they'd gone away. It was all so strange and Mae was beginning to lose hope that she'd ever see Julius again. If she couldn't get in touch with him, how would he know that she was so near to him? She remembered their conversations about living in London, and she clung on to the hope that they might find one another still, and that all their plans might be put into place.

Three weeks went quickly by and autumn blazed across the parks in flaming orange, burnt umber and sienna. Leaves were piled high on the ground, and though the sun shone, it was colder and seemed to have a wintry paleness to its glinting rays, which lit up the landscape in rosy hues.

Alice had only received one more letter from Will since the last one, and this time he mentioned that Frankie was getting ready to go back to America. Her heart felt heavy at the thought, but she knew she should let go of his memory however hard that might prove to do. She suffered bouts of feeling despondent, a recurring state of being at this time of year when everything about the season reminded her of those feelings of so long ago. In her mind's eye she remembered seeing Frankie on the day he left Devon for good. Quite by chance on that fateful day she'd been down to the village and bumped into him on his way to the station. His look of reproach she would never forget, his unsmiling face and his refusal to speak had cut her heart in two. His expression was forever etched in her mind, a haunting face that appeared to mock her in dreams. Would she ever recover, she wondered? How long might it be before she could get on with her life?

One thing she'd started to do was to scan the newspaper columns for job vacancies. Most of the advertisements wanted women who could type, which was a bit of a problem. On the other hand there were plenty of courses for those wishing to learn, but Alice felt she would be too nervous to go to classes on her own. She had some savings put by, and an incredible idea began to form in her mind. Feeling so much braver about putting her new schemes into action she felt might be able to look forward to the future in many ways. But, she also had another secret, one she was dying to share with Mae and Jane, but which she was nursing to herself for just a little while longer. Alice didn't think for one moment she could pull it off, whilst able to indulge in the fantasy of exactly what might happen if she did.

Cora wrote to Camilla saying she was in London, but anxious about receiving any correspondence in front of her aunt or the rest of the family, she made a habit of sitting on the stairs waiting for the post, and would dash to examine the letters before the butler had a chance to get to them. She became most excited when a note in her friend's handwriting hit the doormat, but Camilla's note was short and to the point, saying that although she would have loved to see Cora she was unfortunately committed to many social engagements and her diary was full. Cora didn't know what she could do, it was hopeless, and she gave up dreaming about dancing with Kit at a London party or even seeing him. Camilla was not the friend she thought, after all, and there was nothing she could do about it.

They were all sitting at breakfast one morning discussing their plans for the day when Lord Milton, who rarely spoke to any of his family before ten o'clock, put his newspaper down to speak.

'What was the name of your Mr Weatherfield's aunt, Mae?'

'Dolly ... Dolores Weatherfield,' said Mae, looking puzzled. 'Why do you ask?'

'Well, I'm sorry to tell you, my dear, but she passed away last week, it says here. There's something about her nephew inheriting everything ... it takes up a good quarter page.'

'Does it say how much?' Lady Milton was suddenly animated, insisting that Albert give her the paper at once.

'Oh, how sad,' said Mae. 'That might explain it, why the house looked so shut up. Julius's aunt must have been very ill, and the curtains drawn to keep out the harsh light.'

'You went over there?' said Lady Milton. 'When was that? Didn't you call?'

Mae reddened, as tears sprang to her eyes. 'I didn't like to, I lost courage. It felt like I'd be intruding, and I didn't want to be in the way.'

'Well, I'm sure that won't be the case now, you must get over there and console poor Julius at once,' said Flora patting Mae's hand and offering a handkerchief. 'There'll be so much to sort out, and I'm sure he could do with a helping hand.'

'I wrote ages ago to tell him I was here in London. I'm sure I don't know why he hasn't got in touch.'

'He's clearly been nursing his aunt, and it's a pity you weren't doing so, too. Still, there's nothing wrong in going over there now and offering your condolences. I should think he'd be glad to see a friendly face. Goodness, it says here that Dolores Weatherfield is worth two million, and that's not including her property.'

'Oh yes, I knew Dolly very well,' said Lady Celia. 'I had not realised you were friends with her nephew, Mae.'

'They are very good friends,' said Lady Milton, 'Julius has spent practically the whole summer with us.'

'Well, I expect Dolly was very pleased about that connection,' said Celia. 'From all accounts Julius is a bit of a wild young man, and has made some very unsuitable friends in the past. I believe he has a penchant for girls from the lower orders. I'm sure Dolly hinted at some scandal with a housemaid … she must have been ecstatic when he met Mae.'

Jane could see Mae looked extremely uncomfortable as Lady Milton and her sister-in-law continued to discuss both Julius and poor Dolly Weatherfield's wealth, even going on to talk of wedding plans as if Mae wasn't there. They obviously thought it was going to be a matter of time before Mae and Julius were married.

All the girls left the house as soon as they could escape. It was a dreary day to match their mood, and as they stepped outside they realised they'd need to take umbrellas from the stand in the hall. None of them had any particular plans, but when Alice suggested a visit to Hatchard's on Piccadilly to choose a new book, they all thought that was a wonderful idea.

'We need cheering up,' said Alice, 'and I will treat you all to a new book. Besides, I've had some good news this morning and I feel like celebrating.'

They all turned expectantly, wondering what it could be that was making Alice smile so much.

'Come on, Alice, stop looking so secretive and mischievous,' said Mae. 'I always know when you're up to something.'

'I sold some of my poems to a magazine,' Alice said unable to stop smiling. 'I didn't want to say anything before I knew it was really happening, but I got the letter confirming it this morning. I'm going to the publisher's office tomorrow, and I'm so excited I think I might just burst.'

'Alice, how wonderful, I am so happy for you,' Jane was the first to exclaim as they all threw their arms around her in turn and offered their congratulations.

'So, I will not hear any nonsense about us not having any money for treats. I am quite rich this morning, and the money I've not yet received is burning a hole in my pocket. We will buy books, and then have lunch out again at Lyons'. I'm afraid I can't quite run to a splendid restaurant yet, but give me time.'

'You're a dark horse,' said Mae. 'How many poems did you sell?'

'Half a dozen, but they do want more, and that's why I'm going to see them tomorrow. Some of them may be published in a book.'

'A published poet, how perfectly wonderful,' said Jane. 'When will you give your first reading, do you think?'

'Now, you're teasing me, though I have to say the thought of public performance is terrifying.'

'I'm not teasing, and I think you'd be an excellent orator,' said Jane. 'We'll start practising, and then you'll be ready to meet your public.'

The girls' spirits were lifted with Alice's news, and Jane always made them feel better. Alice began to believe that anything was possible, and Mae, who hadn't wanted to come out at all, started to enjoy the day. There wasn't much she could do about Julius, she decided, even if her heart was breaking. Perhaps he just needed time before he made contact, but she hated the thought of him grieving alone, and wished she could make him feel better.

A whole morning was spent in Hatchard's bookshop. Having such a treat as a new book always took so much time in the choosing, and every one of the girls relished perusing the shelves, and poring over the books.

'There's such a magical fragrance in a bookshop,' Cora said with a pile of books by her side. 'I'd love to distil it into a scent bottle so I could sniff it any time I like.'

'And every bookshop is slightly different,' added Alice. 'It would be lovely to have phials of every one.'

'Do you think poetry smells different to fiction?' asked Jane.

'Without a doubt,' Alice agreed, 'though I'm not sure which is my preference. Both are equally delicious.'

In the end, Jane chose *Mrs Dalloway* by Virginia Woolf. She was curious to read the work of contemporary writers, and had read about the experimental work that was going on in new works of fiction. Fascinated to hear that the author printed her own books, Jane thought what a marvellous satisfaction that must be to produce a book, and have one's own publishing house.

Cora changed her book several times, and was the most indecisive, but in the end everyone was ready and took their purchases to be paid for and wrapped up at the till. As they stepped out into Piccadilly, they were glad a short walk would take them to their lunch, and before they'd got too far, the heavens opened and the rain came down. Everyone out on the streets dashed for the cover of hotels and shops, or ran for shelter with umbrellas held high.

The corner house was full when they got there, and they were lucky to get a table by a window where the glass was so steamed up they couldn't see out. They didn't have to wait too long before a cheerful waitress in a black dress and white apron came with the menus, saying she'd be back in a minute to take their order. The orchestra struck up a tune on one side of the room, and the girls turned to watch the musicians.

'It's a wonderful place for people watching, don't you think?' said Emily, unbuttoning her coat, and taking off her gloves. 'And there are so many people in here today. I suppose they've come in out of the rain, but even so, it seems particularly busy.'

'Have you ever sat and wondered about everybody's lives when you're sitting in a restaurant?' said Cora. 'All these people have come from all over London and the suburbs, not to mention further afield, and all have places where they live, houses and families of their own.'

'Oh, yes, it's absolutely fascinating,' Mae agreed. 'Look at those two to our left, though don't all look at once. They must be secret lovers, don't you think? He looks far too old for her, for one thing, and she's certainly not his daughter. I bet she's his secretary, but I don't think he's got work on his mind from the way he's looking at her.'

'Mae, you're very wicked,' scolded Alice, 'but in this particular instance I think you're absolutely right. Gosh, how terribly shocking.'

'And what about that beautifully dressed lady over there on our right?' said Beth. 'She has so many parcels and bags, and looks a bit out of place in here.'

'Yes, I think I know what's happened,' said Jane with a mischievous grin on her face, 'she's spent far more than her usual allowance and is feeling very guilty. In an attempt to make herself feel better, she's opted not to go to the expensive Throckmorton restaurant for lunch and is thinking how she can tell her husband about all the money she's saved him by having a quick bite in a Lyons' Corner House. Look, she's only ordered Welsh rarebit and a pot of tea, the cheapest items on the menu.'

There were giggles all round, and then Cora said, 'Goodness me, isn't that Julius Weatherfield over there?'

Mae had to ease up out of her seat to look across the crowds, but they could all see she wasn't prepared for the shock of seeing him. And neither was anybody else. For what Cora had failed to see, having her view marred by a vast decorative pillar complete with modernist palm leaves, was that Julius wasn't alone.

'Good Lord,' said Mae standing up, ashen-faced and trembling with quiet anger, 'that's Julius all right, but what I'd like to know is why he's here with Jessie Beales, and why he's also holding both of her hands.'

Chapter Twenty Five

It was fairly obvious to them all that Julius and Jessie were a couple by their very body language, and the fact that they were totally unaware of anyone else in the room. But, it didn't take long before the two of them became conscious of the girls who were all on their feet and craning their necks to see. Jane saw Julius suddenly aware of their presence, and caught his expression of horror, and when Jessie saw them she looked positively frightened. Even so, neither Jessie nor Julius made any attempt to immediately let go of the hands they were holding across the table, though they clearly looked embarrassed and didn't know quite what to do.

Mae's anger subsided as quickly as it erupted and she flopped back down in her chair to dissolve into racking sobs almost instantly. As every table around them turned curiously to see what was going on, Jane urged them all to gather their things together.

'Let's get Mae home,' she said standing up and helping Alice assist her sister with her coat.

'Make him speak to me, Alice,' Mae began through her tears, calling out far too loudly. 'Make him come over and explain exactly what he's doing.'

'It's time to leave, Mae,' said Alice quietly. 'Come on, we'll talk about what's best to do when we get home.'

With apologies to the waitress who'd rushed over to see if she could help, they managed to weave their way through the crowds, knowing that every eye was turned in their direction as Mae's crying showed no signs of stopping.

'There might be an explanation we don't know about,' said Cora, trying to be helpful. 'It may just be an innocent meeting.'

'I think it's fairly clear exactly what's going on,' said Mae crossly between sobs, 'he's playing a double game and I won't have it. How could he do this to me? It's utterly unbelievable! I can't stop thinking about how he kept telling me how unattractive Jessie was, and how he didn't like her, when he must have been thinking the complete opposite the whole time.'

'I thought Jessie was in Worthing with her aunt,' said Beth, 'it's all rather mysterious. I've never even seen her talking to him.'

The only person who wasn't completely surprised by the turn of events was Jane, but even so, she felt there were many questions left unanswered. Poor Mae was in a hopeless state, and Jane couldn't help feeling sorry for her.

When they got back to Aunt Celia's townhouse Mae rushed upstairs. She wanted to be alone, she said, and the other girls reluctantly let her go. They went into the sitting room where the long windows looked over the square. The rain was ceaseless, dripping down the windows and blurring the view like Mae's tears, and they all felt very helpless.

'Poor Mae,' said Alice, 'what an awful thing to have happened. I wish I could help her. I have to say I didn't see this coming.'

'No, nor did I, though I must admit to having some reservations about Mr Weatherfield,' said Jane. 'We'll go and check on her in half an hour, she might want someone to talk to by then.'

The girls didn't know what to do with themselves and wandered restlessly round the room unable to settle to anything, and even their new books couldn't help. They picked them up and put them down unopened, and the only topic of conversation revolved on how such a thing could have happened when they'd all been so sure that Julius had loved Mae as much as she'd loved him. Jane didn't mention the time she'd seen Julius kissing Jessie's hand in the hat shop. There didn't seem any point now.

Lady Milton and Lady Celia came home ten minutes later and found them all looking very upset.

'I can see from your expressions you've heard the news,' said Lady Celia.

'I cannot believe it,' said Flora, 'I'm sure there must be some great mistake.'

'What news is that?' said Alice not wishing to give anything away.

'I had a letter after you left this morning from Lady Calthorpe who was a great friend of Dolly Weatherfield. She told me Julius is engaged.'

'Julius Weatherfield is engaged?' Alice said incredulously.

'To a milliner, she said,' Lady Celia announced. 'Apparently they've been secretly engaged since last summer because Dolly didn't look on the pairing very favourably. It's all come out ... I shudder to think, she must be turning in her grave, poor dear. It's all exactly as she feared.'

'Of course, they must have met in the Isle of Wight,' said Jane. 'I'm sure the Wilcox's that Jessie mentioned must have been mutual friends.'

'Well, that's despicable,' said Emily, 'I'm surprised at Jessie, and as for him, Mae is better off without such a scoundrel.'

'Yes, I completely agree,' said Alice echoing the thoughts of all the girls.

'I feel rather sorry for Jessie in a way,' said Jane. 'I don't expect she really wanted to be a part of such a plan. In fact, I'm sure of it. I saw them together in the shop once, and it was clear she was extremely cross with him. I sensed something was going on, but I didn't know what. But Julius needs his ears boxed playing with Mae's heart like that. He made us all think he was in love with Mae, when it's clear he carried on with Jessie and lied to his aunt so he wouldn't lose the inheritance.'

'And he made Mae fall in love with him for his own ends,' said Alice, 'how could he have done such a thing?'

'Oh dear, how is poor Mae?' asked Lady Milton. 'I would go to her, but I'm not sure if she'll want to see me.'

Alice smiled. 'I'll tell her you're asking after her, but I think I'd better go and check on her. Jane, will you come with me?'

Telling Mae what had happened was the hardest job Alice and Jane thought they'd ever had. It brought on a fresh bout of tears, but after a while, Mae became quieter and more thoughtful.

'I really did believe that he loved me in the beginning,' she said. 'I can't believe how someone could behave like that when they're engaged to someone else. How Jessie must have hated me. Can you imagine how she must have felt?'

Alice and Jane were quite surprised by Mae's reaction. The fact that she was empathising with Jessie gave them some hope.

'No one could help falling in love with you, however horrible their intentions,' said Alice. 'I believe he was genuinely torn, and I know you don't want to hear this, but you're better off without him.'

'Mae, I am so sorry this has happened, but I promise you will get over it in time, and one day you'll be able to say you're glad that things turned out the right way for you,' added Jane.

'Where would I be without the two best girls anyone could have in their life?' said Mae trying to smile. 'I know you're both right, and though my heart is hurting I have to say the only feelings I have left for Julius are not very charitable ones. I will get over him, I am determined I will.'

Though clearly putting on a brave face both Alice and Jane thought it might not be too long before Mae would start to feel better and be thankful that she wasn't in Jessie's shoes after all.

It wasn't easy for Mae in the end. Her initial determination to get on with her life came to a halt when she heard the news that Julius and Jessie were to marry at the end of October in London. Mae wouldn't eat and started to miss out meals much to Alice's consternation. It was very difficult to get her interested in anything or even to engage her in conversation. She didn't want to leave the house and became obsessed with the idea that she was being talked about by the circle of friends that her aunt saw every day. Gradually, she became so unwell that she wouldn't leave her room. Another fortnight passed by before they began to see any improvements, but it was clear that Mae had been changed forever by the episode. She was quieter and sadder; a state of being that made all who had known her happy personality despair that there'd ever be any change for the better.

Strangely, one of the few people who seemed able to get through to her first was Captain Bartlett. He came to London at the beginning of October, having heard the news, and though he didn't want to be in the way, he did what he knew best. His kind and thoughtful ways made an impression on everyone. He didn't call round at first, but sent gifts of fruit baskets and boxes of flowers, which Mae couldn't help but be impressed by. He didn't send letters, just a note with each gift saying he'd heard she was unwell or that he hoped she was feeling a little better. There was something every day, books on art, and books on painters Mae admired, or sheet music with the latest songs, and then at the end of a fortnight he sent an invitation to them all with tickets for a new exhibition at the Royal Academy.

Mae, though delighted with the attention, wanted to make sure that no one was getting any ideas about she and the captain becoming an item.

'I'm only coming to the exhibition because George Bartlett is so kind,' she said. 'And I'm relying on you all to talk for me. I don't want him getting ideas of any partiality or interest in him, just because I've accepted his invitation I hope you all understand. He was always rather sweet on me, and I don't want to look as if I'm encouraging him.'

'I don't know why you're so worried,' said Emily. 'It isn't as if he's asked you to go on your own. He may be interested in *me* for all you know, or Cora. And I think he's always had a soft spot for Jane.'

'Perhaps he intends to propose to us all,' said Jane, which prompted gales of laughter. 'You'd better be careful, Mae, I might just say yes.'

The afternoon was a success. Captain Bartlett, though polite on seeing her showed no interest in Mae whatsoever, which really made her cross. In fact, Jane could see he was ignoring her beautifully, which was exactly the advice she'd given him when they'd met in Hyde Park just the day before. Jane had told him that where Mae was concerned a little psychology might help his case along, and she was gratified to see it working so quickly. Before the afternoon was over, Mae and George were discussing the paintings, though he was always careful not to spend too much time with her alone. He was an excellent pupil, thought Jane, and she had hopes of splendid things to come.

When Lady Milton heard about the success of the afternoon she was so pleased she said they ought to celebrate Mae's good health. Lady Celia offered to throw a little party, which Flora declined firmly, but politely, saying that on this occasion she wanted to treat her daughters to an evening out. What she had in mind would have shocked Lady Celia, but Flora had been thinking for quite some time that if she were not to go completely mad they needed some fun. And as far as she was concerned that would involve dancing, cocktails and the best nightclub in town.

Fortunately Lady Celia was otherwise engaged on the evening that Flora made her plans. Albert, who'd actually managed to save a little money whilst they'd been in London by putting his foot down on Flora's expenses, actually yielded when she pleaded with him for a little extra to make sure the evening was a success. He was as relieved as anybody else that Mae seemed to be making a recovery at last, and was now able to have a conversation without venting about Jessie or Julius. There were only three days to go, and Flora was as giddy as the rest of them about the prospect of an evening out. Jane was intrigued by the idea of going to a nightclub and couldn't help feeling more than a little excited. It would make fascinating research for her writing, apart from the natural curiosity she felt about such a place. And, she had to admit; it felt most daring and more than a little wicked to think that she, a clergyman's daughter, was intent on such a night out.

Alice was feeling very happy now that Mae was recovering, albeit slowly. She'd felt very guilty about her own personal happiness, and the great strides she was taking in her own life. The meeting with the publisher had gone very well, and not only had she been asked to produce more poems for the magazine, but she'd been given a book contract. Feeling excited about the future and the possibility of becoming an independent woman, she tried not to think about how much she would have loved to tell Frankie all about it. She'd been paid an amount for her poems, and an advance for her book, but there was only one thing she wanted to buy with her money and she couldn't wait to see Jane's face when she'd present her with a gift to say thank you for all she'd done to help her. Alice kept her plans secret though she thought she might burst with excitement before she was able to put them into place.

Even Mae began to look forward to the evening out though there'd been another blow when she'd heard Julius and Jessie were honeymooning in the south of France. She was so cross with herself for not realising how much she was to blame over the whole mess. When Mae really examined the relationship she'd had with him, it was painful to realise that he'd never declared any love for her or taken advantage by trying to kiss her, and most of what she'd thought was a growing passion had been on her side alone. Fooling herself that he'd felt the same way had been part of the problem though when she voiced her opinions out loud Alice and Jane quickly scolded her, saying he'd convinced them all that he was falling in love with her. Whatever the case, Mae vowed never to let herself be fooled in the same way again.

Chapter Twenty Six

Once more Jane was forced to reflect on the changes that were taking place in her life as she dressed for their evening out at the nightclub. The very word was enough to make her laugh out loud, and she couldn't help thinking what her mother would have said if she'd had any idea. No doubt she'd have been scandalised to think of her daughter contemplating such an outing, though surely being escorted by Lord and Lady Milton made the whole experience far more respectable. It took her an age to decide which of the wonderful dresses Lady Milton had given her would be given its first airing in such a place, but in the end she opted for the Nile green chiffon with spangles of copper. She was feeling very nervous about the evening, and even though her reflection showed someone looking quite poised she felt anxious about how she'd fit in with such a glamorous crowd. She told herself not to be so silly; it wasn't anything she was ever going to have to get used to, she decided, and thought how she should try to enjoy it and use the evening as a chance for observation.

Just as she was putting the finishing touches to her appearance there was a knock at the door, and there was Flora Milton saying she must complete her outfit with a fur-trimmed cape of midnight velvet, embroidered with the most exquisite peacock in shades of emerald and turquoise.

'I've never been able to thank you properly for all you've done for my girls, Jane,' Lady Milton began, 'and, indeed, the whole family, but I want to do so now, and hope you'll accept this small token of my gratitude.'

Jane thought she must be referring to the wonderful cloak, but Lady Milton had a small box in her hand, which she pressed into Jane's. As she opened the box a pair of diamond earrings twinkled back at her like stars in a night sky, and Jane was so overcome she couldn't find the words to speak at first.

'Thank you, Lady Milton,' she said at last, 'but this is beyond generosity.'

'Call me Flora, dear,' came the command, 'Lady Milton makes me sound like one of those fusty old dowagers and I will not have my friends using the title, though it has its uses, I should say. Now come along, Celia has promised us taxis to the Blue Angel, and we mustn't be late.'

'Is Lady Celia coming with us?' Jane asked in all innocence.

'Not on your life, my dear. Good lord, heaven preserve us from that miserable fate!'

Jane wanted to laugh. Flora Milton was a one-off, and as she followed her out of the room with her ears sparkling in diamonds, and the glorious cape flowing behind her she knew whatever happened, she was sure to have a good time.

The Milton girls and their very nervous companion were soon tripping down the steps in their Louis heels and dancing on their toes in the frosty night air as they waited for the butler to hail their taxis. Lord and Lady Milton made an appearance at the last minute, arm in arm, and looking for all the world like a pair of young lovers, as they all piled into two taxis that screeched off into the night, roaring down the glittering streets at top speed. London was lit up like a Christmas tree, Piccadilly a blaze of illuminations. The streets were full of people in evening wear, young men stopping to buy a buttonhole or a corsage for their lady from a flower seller in a black straw boater, her basket filled to the brim with bouquets and nosegays. Jane wondered where so many people could all be going, the crowds looked as numerous as they did in the daytime, but most exciting of all was the fact that she felt a part of the whole picture. No longer was she the outsider, the girl who lived on the edge of life watching everyone else take part, and even if she was fooling herself a little because she felt really nervous, she was almost ready to take on the world.

They drew up before the curved frontage of the building, lit with hidden bulbs casting a shimmering glow onto the damp pavement where a blue carpet was unfurled down the steps and a liveried commissionaire rushed forward to open their doors and usher them in.

'Lord and Lady Milton,' he said, removing his peaked hat and bowing before them, 'what a pleasure it is to see you both after all this time. We were so excited to hear you were coming back to the Blue Angel.'

'And we're delighted to see you too, Harry,' said Flora, 'you haven't changed a bit.'

Harry looked bashful, and went red to the tips of his ears as they all followed him through the double doors into the blaze of glistening light, entering the foyer alive with the crush of bodies who were queuing for the cloakroom, greeting their friends or heading off to the nearest cocktail bar. Jane stared with wonder. There were so many people all in one place, the ladies perfumed and beautiful in diaphanous chiffons and lustrous silk with boyish hair gleaming, the men dapper and handsome in black tie and suits. The crescendo of voices rose to the ceiling and up the wide central staircase where Jane followed the rest of her party who were all chattering at once. The music was growing louder, throbbing with life and making the blood pound in her ears, and when they reached the inner sanctum, doors held open on sight as they passed, Jane tried very hard not to feel overwhelmed. Such a sparkling sight met her eyes. The vast circular room was lined with tables across the polished floor, each with its own rosy lamp blooming with pinkish light on a snowy cloth, and it seemed as if everyone gathered there turned to stare as they made their entrance. Jane felt very self-conscious, but after seeing one or two appreciative nods in her direction, and hearing a couple of comments from the ladies on the exquisite colour of her gown she began to feel much better. When she caught her reflection in one of the huge gilt mirrors surrounding the room she did a double take, and began to feel more confident. Was that sophisticated woman really *her*; she wondered as Alice caught her eye at the same moment and grinned.

People applauded as Lady Milton walked through the room, the gentlemen standing to bow in her direction, the women clapping and pointing out to their friends that Flora was back. King Zoot, standing on the podium against a backdrop of a golden sunburst, halted his jazz band for a moment before breaking the silence with Flora's favourite tune, *She's the Gal we all Adore*, and the place erupted. She was inundated with people all wishing to say hello, and to remind her of an old acquaintance. Waiters dashed along with trays of cocktails held high before presenting them in offering to their goddess with the compliments of the management. Their table was surrounded, and Lady Milton did her best to wave, nod and smile to old friends and admirers. Then everyone was curious to know everyone else and introductions were made all round. The Milton girls were introduced to the crushing throng with much fascination, and then Lady Milton spoke again.

'And last, but not least, is my dear friend, Miss Jane Austen of Hampshire.'

Jane was very touched that Flora had called her a dear friend, and tried to smile at the crowd who swarmed on every side. It was all very overwhelming, but then she saw a familiar face and felt very much better.

'Miss Austen, how very pleased I am to see you here,' said Captain Bartlett dropping a kiss on her gloved hand.

'I'm sure not as pleased as I am to see you,' she said. 'What a positively terrifying experience.'

'But no one would suspect as much,' he said with a smile, 'you are the epitome of sophistication and composure, as always.'

'Thank you, all I can say is that I'm glad you can't see what's going on inside; I'm a bag of nerves. But, enough of me, how are you?'

'Trying very hard not to show pure elation at the prospect of dancing with Mae. She accepted without any hesitation, and though I want to skip around the room I'm trying to follow all your instructions to the letter. I've not even had a conversation or asked her for the *first* dance. I'm rather hoping you'll do me that great honour.'

'Captain Bartlett, you will make me the happiest woman. I can't think of anything nicer than dancing with a friend.'

'And if I am your friend then it's George from now on, none of this standing on ceremony. I don't know how to thank you enough, Jane, but without your advice I know Mae would still be running in the opposite direction every time she saw me.'

Jane couldn't help but smile. 'I've done nothing. I know Mae, and if she didn't like you it wouldn't matter what I said to you. It's been all on your own merit, and I think she's beginning to realise that men are more than just a handsome face. You are lucky because you have good looks, charm and a fascinating personality, and besides all this, you're one of the kindest men I know.'

'You're making me blush, dear Jane, but I won't have another word said on the matter. This place may be named after an angel, but I think I met a real one the day I met you.'

Suddenly, they heard loud cheers go up from the others and were surprised to see the unexpected appearance of three gentlemen who loomed out of the dim light, all extremely delighted to have found their friends.

'Jonathan!' screamed Emily as soon as she saw him, running over and throwing her arms around his neck. 'Where have you been?'

Jonathan hugged her back, simultaneously stretching out his hand to shake those of Lord and Lady Milton, whilst trying unsuccessfully to say hello to everyone else. Eventually, Emily let him go, choosing instead to thread her arm through his and look up at him with an adoring expression. Kit and Fergus came up behind him, and for a moment Jane thought Cora might faint with shock.

'Hello everyone,' said Jonathan, shouting slightly over the noisy background, 'I'm so sorry we haven't been able to come and see you before now, but the truth is we've not been in London the whole time, but on something of a mission. Fergus wanted some help in tracking down his brother, and I'm glad to say we were finally successful in reuniting the pair of them.'

'Yes, we eventually found Gilbert in Cornwall,' Fergus spoke up, his gaze directed at them all, but more particularly at Beth who looked back at him as if she were holding her breath. 'But, he's back at Rosamorna now where he belongs, and he sends you all his fond regards.'

'Well, that is good news,' said Lady Milton, 'even if it is a pity he couldn't come back to London with you. I'm sure Beth would have particularly liked to see him. Still, perhaps she will in time if she's ever invited to Cornwall. And, in the meantime, Jonathan, I do hope you and your friends are going to join us.'

Jane could see Fergus was still watching Beth's face intently, and when she smiled at him he walked over to speak to her. In a matter of moments he was explaining everything to Beth who listened eagerly with much nodding of her head and a continuous smile on her lips. Extra gilt chairs were brought over and joined together with yet another large table so that they could all chat comfortably. The band struck up playing a foxtrot and Flora waved over at them saying they must all have a dance as she pulled her husband to his feet and led him out to the floor, his pride at accompanying the most celebrated woman in the room, etched on his face. Kit immediately walked over to Cora who was pretending that her heart wasn't racing at the very sight of him, and tried to look as if she was in deep conversation with Alice. When he asked for a dance her face lit up with joy, and Jane wanted to hug him for making her sweet friend happy again. It hadn't escaped her notice that Camilla was nowhere to be seen, and she was dying to know what had happened. She didn't think Kit's sister would have passed up on the opportunity to be in London with them if she could have been.

Jane enjoyed her first dance with George, and didn't even have to think about the steps since she'd become such an expert, which gave her a chance to watch everybody else. Cora and Kit were dancing cheek to cheek. Neither of them seemed to be saying very much, but Jane guessed words were totally unnecessary, and she knew the words would come later. They were in the moment and treasuring every second being back in each other's arms. Alice was dancing with one of the young men who'd been hanging on Flora's every word, a type Jane had seen made fun of in the newspapers as a "stage-door Johnnie", an admirer from Lady Milton's colourful past. It was lovely to see Alice laughing and brimming with confidence as she danced gracefully around the room. Emily and Jonathan were inseparable, as if they were only just realising all that they meant to each other and Jane thought it wouldn't be long before their relationship might take a turn. Beth was the most surprising of all. Fergus was holding her closely and she wasn't resisting him in the least. Her body was curving into his as they moved so beautifully together; anyone looking might have thought they'd been an item forever. She was gazing up at him, and being amused by everything he said.

Mae was sitting out the first dance, content to watch everyone else, but the person she seemed to be observing the most was George, and he was still doing an excellent job of ignoring her. He was looking particularly handsome this evening, and Jane thought she might have been very tempted to flirt with him if not for the fact that more than ever she felt the loss of Will. Life just wasn't the same without him, and as she danced she couldn't help wondering if he was out dancing in Bath too. He'd been away for so long, time enough to have moved on and met someone else. Such a wonderful man - kind, good-looking, eligible, and just about perfect in her eyes, he was bound to attract attention from all the young ladies who must still flock to Bath in search of a husband, she thought. He wouldn't remain single for long and when the dance came to a halt, she tried not to think about the fact that she must forget about him. It was possible, she told herself, and if she were to concentrate on her writing career and find another job to pay her a good salary she would have to erase him from her mind completely.

George took her back to the table and she sat down, glad to see him taking Mae's hand to lead her out onto the dance floor. They were soon lost in the sea of couples moving round the floor, and so Jane turned her attention to Beth who was coming over, looking especially radiant with a beaming smile.

'Fergus is just ordering some champagne,' she said sitting down next to Jane. 'He feels like celebrating, and I don't blame him. He explained that he always wanted to find Gilbert again, and once he had, they managed to put the past behind them and everything is forgiven. Fergus said he has me to thank for helping him to see that we only have one family and that we must learn to love and cherish them whatever their faults. But I told him that was a lesson I'd learned from you. So, I've just come to say thank you, Jane, I know without you I'd never have been able to appreciate my own madcap family with all their weird foibles or come to know my sisters as I have.'

'You've no need to thank me,' said Jane, 'it wasn't my doing, I'm sure. Anyway, I want to change the subject before your handsome partner returns to take you away with him again. I just have to say how lovely you and Fergus look together … though I was surprised to see you dancing, I thought you didn't like him very much.'

Beth could see Jane was teasing her. 'I didn't at first, I must admit, but I have to say I've been gradually changing my mind, though I would never have admitted it, not even to myself. I misjudged him in so many ways. I wasn't prepared to listen to his friend or try and see any merit in anything he did. Besides, I didn't know he owned a house in Berkeley Square.'

Jane chuckled. 'I'm sure that's shed an altogether different light on the matter.'

'Seriously,' Beth replied, 'I was blind and prejudiced, and couldn't see beyond believing everything I'd been told. Considering what Gilbert did, Fergus has been wonderful to take him back under his wing.'

'Forgiveness is a difficult matter, and so often our pride and prejudice prevent us from behaving as we should or from reaching the right conclusions sooner,' said Jane. 'But it seems in this case you and Fergus have found the path, and come together at last. You might even be very good friends, I think.'

'I hope so,' said Beth, her face lighting up as Fergus wandered back into view. 'Jane, I really hope you're right.'

Jonathan and Emily chose to sit together after their first dance and she was bursting to catch up with all his news. They'd never been separated for so long before and Emily was beginning to realise just how much she'd missed him and how important a person he was in her life.

'I'm so glad to hear that everything has worked out with Gilbert and Fergus,' Emily said. 'But I'm surprised Camilla isn't here. I'd have thought she wouldn't want to miss a night like this one.'

'She's in London, but seeing a friend of hers this evening. The truth is that I think she really thought Fergus liked her friend enough to propose marriage but he made it very plain that he just wasn't interested. Still, for all her meddling, I have to say Camilla's a fabulous girl. She's got everything: stunning looks, a striking personality, and a share in an inheritance ... she'll make someone very happy.'

'I'm sure she will,' said Emily, and without knowing quite why she was struck forcibly by such feelings of jealousy she couldn't speak again.

'We spent a lot of time together,' said Jonathan. 'I must admit, I wasn't too sure about Camilla when I first met her, but I've completely changed my mind.'

'It certainly seems as if you have,' said Emily trying to sound as if her feelings weren't gnawing her in two.

'Well, having fun is one thing, but I seem to have missed so much, Em, and I'm only just catching up on all the news. I heard about Julius and felt so sorry for Mae. I couldn't really believe he and Jessie were engaged at first.'

Emily told him all about the day they'd seen Julius at the corner house, and how awful it had been. It hadn't escaped her notice that Jonathan was calling her "Em" again, an affectionate name he'd used since she was a little girl. The truth was, she decided, she really didn't want him to think of her as a younger sister any more, and though they chatted away as they always had, she was consumed by the idea that he was in love with someone. He kept throwing Camilla's name into the conversation, and for the first time in her life Emily felt real panic. The prospect that Jonathan might like Camilla enough to want to settle down with her was a distinct possibility. Suddenly, she saw them in her mind's eye; Camilla in a white dress and veil gazing into Jonathan's eyes as he carried her over the threshold into Buckland Priors.

'And how about you, Emily, have you been enjoying yourself?' asked Jonathan. 'I was sorry to hear from Will that Frankie was going back to America. This summer has gone so quickly ... I expect you'll really miss him, won't you?'

'Frankie can stay there as far as I'm concerned,' said Emily, 'You might as well know that he finished with me, but I have to say that far from being upset I was actually quite relieved.'

'I thought you were in love with him.'

Emily ran her fingers through her hair. 'I thought I was for a while until I realised that I simply liked being seen with him, and acting the part of a film star's girlfriend. I am ashamed to say it was all for vanity's sake, but when I really looked into my heart I knew I wasn't in love however appearances may have looked.'

Jonathan was nodding, and looked very serious. 'Sometimes it takes time to realise the true feelings of your heart.'

They sat in silence for a moment. Emily felt his eyes on her face, and knew he was thinking. It seemed clear he had something on his mind, and she had a good idea what that might be. He was going to tell her he was in love with Camilla; she knew it. He'd been building up to telling her, going round the houses in his usual way. She couldn't bear it, she thought.

'I've been coming to some conclusions of my own about life and love,' he continued.

'Don't say any more,' urged Emily, suddenly feeling sure she didn't want to learn the truth. 'Let's have another dance for old time's sake.'

'You don't want to hear what I have to say?'

Emily thought about how he'd always been there to listen to her and share in everything; her joys, her upsets, her trials and triumphs. If he wanted to talk to her about his love for Camilla the very least she could do was listen.

'Of course I love to hear everything you have to say to me,' she started. 'I have always been your friend, and if you want to talk to me about how you've fallen in love, then I am glad to hear it. I sincerely hope you and Camilla will be very happy.'

'Is that it then? You think I am in love with her?'

Emily slowly nodded hardly able to look up into his eyes.

'And you wish to be a friend to me. Emily, is that the only way you would ever see me?'

'I will always be here for you, as a friend, even when you're married.'

'Then I've no hope, it seems, though I've come this far and I find I cannot go back. Dearest, Emily, tell me if I have no chance of success.'

Jonathan hesitated and his expression changed. He picked up her tiny hand and clasped it between his long fingers, gazing again into her eyes with a look that made Emily reel with the feelings of love she felt for him.

'Beloved Emily, for dear and loved you are to me; I do not know quite where to begin. I've spent your entire life scolding you, lecturing you, as well as telling you how to behave, and no one could have borne it all as you have.'

'But, I'm sure I deserved it all, every last telling off,' Emily said, looking back into the eyes that she loved so much. 'I know I've been so much trouble to you.'

'Emily, what I'm trying to say so very badly is that I'm in love with you, and wish to spend the rest of my life with you if you'll have me. Oh, I'm hopeless with words, and I've been utterly useless as a lover, I'm well aware, but if you'll give me a chance I'll show you how much you mean to me.'

Emily was lost for words, and was in such a state of shock that she wondered if she'd ever find her voice again. She stared at him, her eyes wide and disbelieving.

Jonathan swallowed and carried on. 'My dearest wish is for us to be married one day if you can find it in your heart to love me. But if your answer is no, as I fear it must be, I promise I will never mention the subject again.'

The agony in his eyes and the intensity in his voice could only mean he was sincere. Emily didn't wait to put him out of his misery.

'Yes! The answer is yes, my darling ... can it really be true? Are you sure that you love me as much as I love you?'

'Let's be married in the new year,' Jonathan said drawing her closer and tracing a finger down her cheek. 'Do you think that will give us long enough to be sure and time to plan for it all?'

'Oh, Jonathan,' she cried, throwing her arms round his neck. 'You've made me the happiest girl alive!'

It really was turning out to be the most wonderful evening, thought

Jane. Watching Jonathan with Emily, and then seeing him privately address Lord and Lady Milton before the latter threw her arms round him in an expression of joy, she was sure could only mean one thing. Jonathan and Emily's engagement was announced moments later, and the whole room buzzed with the news.

After several bottles of champagne to celebrate, and several more dances everything stopped for the cabaret. Jane watched it all with great fascination, as so many different kinds of performers got up to entertain them. There were a couple of gentlemen tap dancers, followed by a funny man accompanied on the piano, who soon had them all laughing out loud at his jokes and antics. Then there was a dance troupe all performing a very exaggerated form of the Charleston with high kicking legs that displayed the ladies underclothes to such an extent that Jane felt she didn't quite know where to look. Finally, a beautiful lady singer came to the microphone and sang. It was a love song, which made Jane think of Will, and she was sure there wasn't a dry eye in the house. The young lady, Miss Sylvia Vane sang two more songs to rousing applause and then stopped to make an announcement.

'Thank you, Ladies and Gentlemen, it's always a pleasure to sing at the Blue Angel. Over the years we've seen lots of singers come and go, and I'm sure I don't need to tell you we have one highly distinguished performer with us here this evening who has been missed more than any of those who have ever graced this stage. Please put your hands together for the wonderful Lady Milton, who I've managed to persuade to thrill us once more with one of our favourite songs.'

There was a drum roll and spotlights roamed the room until they came to rest on Flora's bowed head. As she rose to her feet the crowd were frenzied and applause rippled round the room like a succession of crashing waves upon the beach. Bowing and smiling Flora stood like a queen before her subjects and with a nod to Zoot, the band struck up as the voice of an angel rang out across the room. It was just one song, but it was heavenly, Jane thought, and she couldn't help taking great pleasure from watching Flora's daughters watching her with pride on their faces as the performance came to an end all too soon.

Everyone rose to their feet, and Flora was surrounded by her admirers once more as she was escorted back to her seat. King Zoot's band struck up again and the room rose as one to take their partners to the floor.

'Come along,' called Lady Milton holding onto Albert's hand. 'The night is almost over, and we'll have to leave soon. It would be a pity to miss the last two dances.'

Jane and Alice watched them all from the side, glad to have a moment to sit together, but feeling a little left out, knowing they couldn't really be a part of the final slow dances that were taking place. The whole room was awash with love, and every couple looked so happy. Jane was sure Alice was thinking about Frankie just as much as she was about Will, but it was no good dwelling on what couldn't be. She must put him out of her mind.

'I had no idea that Flora could sing like that,' Alice said breaking their thoughts.

'Wasn't she simply wonderful?' said Jane. 'I can quite see how your father came to fall in love with her.'

'Yes, I don't suppose I ever really thought about it before, but I know he was desperately lonely when mother died. I'm so glad he met Flora, and though I don't think it's been plain sailing, you can see how much they're still very much in love.'

Lord and Lady Milton were gazing into each other's eyes like a pair of love struck youngsters, and it was quite a sight to behold.

'People are so lucky if they find real love in their lives,' said Alice. 'At least I've known what it is to be in love, and even if I never experience it again I shall treasure the memory of it forever.'

'Yes, memories can be a wonderful thing,' agreed Jane, 'if bitter sweet in the remembrance.'

Alice and Jane fell silent for a moment, and as they watched the couples twirling round the room, they both became lost in their own thoughts and memories, which simply wouldn't let them go.

There was a constant flow of people coming through the large doors at the back of the room, even at this late hour. The huge clock on the wall was saying it was well past midnight, and Jane thought it very amusing to be up so late. Dances in her day were over by eleven o'clock except at private parties, but even then they were usually tucked up in their beds by twelve. Every now and again as she looked across the throng she saw a figure or the shape of a head silhouetted against the bright lights to remind her of Will. She knew that her mind was working overtime and that her wish to see him was so great that every time she thought he must be there, she could only be disappointed. He was in Bath and probably making his way home from a similar night out. Jane pictured him in her mind's eye, a young lady on his arm, and she tried to banish the thought as quickly as she could.

With these thoughts in mind, she was watching the progress of two young men who'd just walked into the room. There was something so familiar about them, though it was hard to see across the dimly lit room, but then her heart began to beat wildly with recognition, and she grabbed Alice's sleeve in astonishment. It was Frankie she saw first, with his golden head and impeccable clothes, and Eddie walking by his side talking avidly. Jane scanned the room, her heart hammering so loudly she was sure the whole place must think it was an extra accompaniment for the drummer, and then she saw him. There was Will, no figment of her imagination, looking more handsome and divine than she'd ever seen him. He was there in all his beautiful manly state, walking across the room and waving at her. She didn't know what to do. Jane stood up one moment and sat down the next, then stood up again with feelings she couldn't describe at seeing him, and made an attempt to wave.

Alice was in shock. When she saw Frankie she became such a mess of emotions she couldn't move, talk or even think. She was aware of Jane waving at them all, and then before she knew what was happening Frankie was there. But, where he might have pretended he was unaware of her existence in the past, now he was standing right in front of her, and she couldn't believe the words that were coming from his lips.

'Alice, will you do the honour of dancing with me?'

She met his green eyes that were looking with such intensity into her own and could only put her hand into his. Alice felt she was dancing on air, floating above the ground as he led her out onto the floor. There was no hesitation as he took her in his arms and it felt so wonderfully right. She felt his cheek on hers, and his hand pressed into the small of her back, and when he pulled her closer she thought she might faint altogether. They didn't speak, but held onto one another like two shipwrecked lovers who'd been cast in an open sea. Alice wanted the dance to last forever but the music came to a halt, over far too quickly, and she knew there was only one dance left.

'Is there somewhere we can talk, Alice,' he began. 'I've so much to say to you.'

But the music was starting again, and Frankie wanted to hold her again. He was pulling her into his arms, and murmuring in her ear. 'God knows I've waited long enough, my love. I can be patient no longer and will say what I have to right here and now. Please tell me I'm not too late, that the precious feelings we had for one another are still as strong with you, as they are with me. I've loved only you, though I was stupidly blind to the fact for a while. Alice, dearest Alice, I thought I could forget you, but I find I am in love with you as much as ever, and all I can hope is that you'll find it in your heart to forgive me.'

They stopped in the middle of the dance floor, unaware of the others pressing on all sides, dancing into them.

'There's nothing to forgive,' she said, looking into Frankie's eyes to see the love she'd known before. 'If anyone is to blame, it's me ... I should be the one seeking your forgiveness. I allowed myself to be persuaded against you instead of listening to my heart, and to my deep regret I thought you were lost to me forever. The truth is I never stopped loving you, Frankie, and I never will.'

Will didn't wait to ask Jane to dance. He simply took hold of her hand and led her onto the floor. It felt so right to be in his arms again, and Jane rejoiced in the feelings. She didn't care what the future might bring, she decided, or how wrong it was for her to be enjoying such emotions, a mixture of love of the deepest kind and the purest passion. All she knew was she couldn't deny her feelings any longer.

'I've missed you so much, and I don't care if you don't love me,' he said, 'I just have to tell you that I love you with every breath in my body, and that I will never love anyone else. I've just spent the last few miserable weeks thinking only of you, and I don't know what else I can do but to tell you how I feel. You alone have brought me to London and whether you like it or not, I am going to do everything in my power to make you fall in love with me, and prove to you that I am the only man you'll ever need.'

Jane's heart turned over as she listened to his heartfelt words. She couldn't doubt her feelings any longer.

'I've lied to you, Will, and I'm sorry, but I know I can do so no longer. I love you too, that's all I can say. It's the truth and I can't deny it another second.'

Will stopped, and looked down at the sweet face he'd come to love so much. 'Do you really love me, as I love you, Jane?'

Jane gazed back at him; hardly able to believe the words she was hearing. She was overwhelmed once more by the emotions that washed over her in waves making her feel light-headed, almost dizzy. Opening her mouth to speak again, words were forming on her lips, but she couldn't give her answer. Aware that the room was spinning far too fast, a fug of velvet blackness was clouding her vision. Had she drunk too much champagne, she wondered, as she tried hard to stay on her feet. Clinging onto Will she felt herself falling into a dark pit of nothingness, as all sounds and scents, the touch of his hands and the sight of his lovely face faded before her eyes and were sucked away, disappearing into a hole of empty nothingness.

Chapter Twenty Seven

Jane's eyes flickered open. She was aware of soft pillows under her head, the fragrance of fresh linen tucked about her, the sputter of a crackling fire and the ticking of a clock. It was a moment before her eyes could focus and other senses quickened into life, but there was her beloved sister sitting at her side. Lying on a chaise longue, a blanket wrapped over her slight form, Jane stretched her cramped toes and winced with the pain that threatened to overwhelm her. Cassy wrung out the soft cloth in cool water once more and applied it to her sister's forehead, pressing it lightly over her temples. 'Don't worry, Jane, Dr Lyford will know what to do.'

'Thank you, Cassy; I cannot think how I'd manage without you. Will he be here soon?'

'I sent a note just ten minutes ago. He won't be long, I promise. You fainted, but I think it's most likely your old problem come back. Just try and rest, Dr Lyford's medicine will soon cure you.'

As if Cassy had summoned him by enchanted means Jane heard the horse's hooves clattering to a standstill in the street outside, the doctor rapping on the door downstairs and in moments he was shown up by the maid. The pain came in spasms once again making Jane reel and retch in response.

'Oh, thank you for coming so quickly. Please hurry, Doctor Lyford, she's just been getting worse and worse,' said Cassy, wiping Jane's mouth, and sponging her hair.

Jane tried not to show the agony on her face as she watched him quietly and efficiently take the phials from his bag, grinding the ingredients to a powder with a pestle. Cassy fetched a glass of water and they both encouraged her to swallow her medicine and take a drink. The taste of the powders was foul, but the water was as pure as if drawn from a Steventon spring from a time long ago. Jane saw her childhood home in that moment, and felt the comfort of the memories that came flooding back. Chawton had been a wonderful home, but the binding childhood ties to the place of her birth would never be broken, and a thousand memories of Steventon filled her mind, giving rise to bittersweet feelings.

'Little Jenny's going to be a fine writer some day,' said her father to the group of young boys assembled there. They were all sitting at the large table in the dining parlour with their books, a makeshift schoolroom for the boys that the rector took in to teach.

Jane gazed up at her father with love and affection. He'd let her join in their lessons for the day, and she was finding out that she could keep up quite well enough with the young boys who were older than her by at least two years. She'd written a composition, and she loved nothing more than writing stories, thinking about the characters and what they might do. She heard the great grandfather clock ticking in the corner, whirring away the passage of time, and the burning logs shift and sputter in the grate, sending up a flutter of sparks up the chimney. The comforting smells from the kitchen where her mother was helping out told her there'd be a shoulder of pork for dinner and her tummy rumbled in anticipation.

'Shall we hear Jenny's composition first,' said Mr Austen proudly. 'I know how reluctant you boys are to read aloud.'

Jane got up, and opened her book at the correct page. Reading to an audience was one of her favourite things to do, and if it was a story of her own making she had to admit she loved the praise that came afterwards. She knew her mother would scold her for such thoughts, but there was nothing like an appreciative audience, and she'd written this tale with the boys in mind. Ghostly stories, like the ones her father read out loud in the evening just before she had to go to bed were her favourite, though going upstairs with a flickering candle making ghoulish shapes on the whitewashed walls was always a frightening experience afterwards. And there was always a brother, not to mention a scholar willing to leap around under a sheet and scare her witless.

'Jane, can you hear me?' Dr Lyford's voice sounded urgent. She could hear his voice but it was so far away, and she couldn't answer him. Every time she opened her mouth to speak, the overwhelming darkness took hold once more, and she felt as if she were being sent back down through the tunnels of time. She could smell pine needles, and the scent of yew, and whether it was the association in her mind, Jane didn't know, but she was sure it must be Christmas in the old rectory.

Cassy and Henry were laughing, and she could see them in her mind's eye hauling the pine boughs into place on the mantelpiece, threading scarlet ribbons through the luscious greenery.

'We are going to church in a moment,' Cassy said. 'There's nothing so exciting as Christmas Eve and singing all the old songs.'

The church was full of people, and they all rose as the strains of a simple pipe organ started to play. Their voices floated up to the roof, young and old singing an ancient hymn together. There were wreaths and garlands of winter greenery, holly and ivy, glistening in candlelight, glossy leaves and scarlet berries dark against the white walls. Jane squeezed Cassy's hand, and looked at her sister with great admiration. Dressed for warmth in her Sunday scarlet cloak, Cassy's lovely face peered out from under the hood, her dark chestnut curls swept back, save for one or two tendrils dancing upon her forehead. At thirteen, Cassandra was turning into a young woman before her eyes and compared to Jane, two years seemed a great distance. She could not imagine herself so composed or so sophisticated.

Sitting next to them were their cousins, Jane and Edward Cooper, who were spending the Christmas holidays with them, and further along sat her mother with little Charles, Frank on the other side keeping his brother amused. Jane had missed him so much. Darling 'Fly', who always found it hard to sit still had surprised them all when he'd said he wanted to be a sailor, though they should have known that he'd want to seek his fortune by adventurous means, and how better than to do it on the high seas? Frank was home from Naval training at Portsmouth for the time being, and with her beloved Henry, Jane was happy to have any brothers at home that she could. To her left sat her glamorous cousin, Eliza, an exotic bird who'd swept in on a cloud of perfume, rather like the jasmine scent of some colourful Indian bazaar. With her elegant ways and sweet disposition she was breaking the hearts of dozens.

As soon as the service was over, the entire congregation moved as one, all hurrying to the door and out into the snow with goodnight wishes on their lips. This time of year held certain magic, the church and the rectory seemed under a spell, and with thoughts of the Christ child soon to be born, they ventured back down the hill between the hedgerows with thoughts of supper on their mind. Henry held the lantern, which cast beams of golden light upon the snowy landscape, and every so often, his long legs would run with it into the distance and he'd disappear into the dark before a snowball would come pelting through the air to hit Frank or Charles squarely on the chest. Mrs Austen scolded, but nothing could spoil the high jinks and when Jane's father joined in too, the whole party capitulated and the air was thick with flying snow.

'Jane, can you hear me? Please wake up.'

The voice she heard was soft and tender, a sound to make her feel safe and secure. No, more than that, the very music of it made her feel loved, inspiring such incredible feelings inside her that she felt she was being pulled towards a light. Warmth, and golden light, the scents of Christmas joy and a spicy fragrance of something else she couldn't put a name to at first. She breathed it in, the deliciousness of sandalwood and ginger, before the wonderful voice called to her again.

'I love you, Jane ..., please come back to me. I can't spend the rest of my life alone without you.'

Jane's eyes flickered open. The first thing she saw was a Christmas tree blazing with coloured lights in a corner, its boughs heavy with sparkling ornaments. The lights ran into one another and dazed her vision, but then as she started to focus, she saw a familiar face. It was Dr Lyford, the young doctor she'd come to know and love.

'Oh, Doctor Lyford,' she said at last, 'I don't know where I've been or where I am, but I've been having the strangest dreams. Is my sister here?'

'No, Jane, I'm afraid not. I expect you've been dreaming; the unfortunate side effects of the drugs I've been giving you. I'm so sorry, but this happened before if you remember. Take your time; I'm sure everything will come back soon.'

Jane closed her eyes wearily and tried to remember. She heard the sound of the sea and felt the sun on her cheeks. 'I was in Devon, at least, I think so.'

Jane concentrated as hard as she could, and the images came tumbling into her mind. She saw a house on the cliff tops, the valley and the sea stretching into the distance. There was Flora Milton and all her girls, and then Alice was holding Jane's arm and smiling in a wooded landscape before someone else, a man with the kindest eyes and the widest smile stepped up to take her hand. Her eyes flashed open.

Dr Lyford spoke again. 'When you're ready there is someone here who is anxious to see you.'

Jane turned her head, and saw the man she loved best in the whole world. Sitting right by her side looking on, with all the love he possessed in his eyes and a very worried expression sat Will Milton and she felt her heart might burst with love.

'I was so worried you wouldn't come back to me, Jane. I've been praying that you would.'

Jane smiled. 'And it must have worked because I heard your lovely voice, and you brought me back, and I'm so glad that you did.'

'I've a few telephone calls to make,' said Dr Lyford getting up and making for the door. 'I promised Lady Milton I'd ring as soon as you came round.'

When he'd gone, Will took Jane's hand and dropped a kiss in the palm of her hand. 'I thought I'd lost you forever, dearest Jane. Promise me you'll never leave me again.'

'I don't know that I can promise you that,' said Jane thinking it was now or never. The very least she should do was attempt an explanation. 'I don't know where to begin to tell you my story.'

'You don't have to say anything else on that score,' said Will, squeezing her hand, 'Dr Lyford has explained everything. I will admit, it was a tremendous shock to learn I'd fallen in love with the greatest writer of our times, but I've had a couple of months to get used to the fact.'

'Is that how long I've been ill?'

'Yes, it's nearly Christmas, Jane. It'll be Christmas Eve in a couple of days.'

'I expect it was the tree in the corner that made me dream as I did,' said Jane, 'I was dreaming about Christmases long ago.'

'All happy memories, I hope.'

Jane nodded. 'Yes, I have wonderful memories of another lifetime … I daresay they will always be a part of me. But tell me, Will, how is everyone? Gosh, I'd love to see them all,' said Jane thinking of the family she'd come to love like no other.

'They're all very well, and longing to see you at home.'

'At home … that sounds so wonderful,' she said, feeling the delicious pressure of his hand, his fingers stroking her own.

'It's your home now … at least …' Will paused, and looked intently into her eyes. 'I was asking you a question just before you blacked out. I'm not sure if you remember but …'

Jane hadn't forgotten; all the glorious memories of that evening were flooding back into her mind as if they'd just happened. 'Oh, Will, I remember it all, every word.'

There was no need to say any more. Will had been waiting for too long to hesitate further and Jane's lips were just begging to be kissed.

Jane saw Will's eyes filled with love, and felt his hand on her cheek. 'My beautiful Jane, how long I have waited for this moment.'

Then he pulled her into his arms and he kissed her so gently and tenderly, but with such sweet passion she wished it would never end. The thrill of his kiss would live in her mind forever more, as he buried his face in her hair and whispered words of love, his hands wrapped around her slender body, her quickening heart beating in rhythm next to his own.

Chapter Twenty Eight

Lady Milton thought all her Christmases had come at once. To hear that Jane was well on the road to recovery, and was coming home with Will for Christmas was the icing on the cake. As if that wasn't enough Will's news that for the first time in ten years the estate was turning over a profit, was more than enough to complete her happiness. If she didn't manage to spend all the profits by the New Year, she'd be doing well, and she and Albert were both looking forward to having a wonderful Christmas with their family.

Jane was still feeling ill before making the journey to Devon, but she'd been determined to accomplish it. She was feeling quite tired by the time they reached Manberley Castle so when Will insisted on carrying Jane in over the threshold, she didn't protest too much, and a resounding cheer went up as they made their entrance through the door into the hall where the whole family was gathered to welcome them. Alice had kindly prepared one of the sofas in the drawing room with blankets and cushions so Jane could lie down and yet feel a part of everything that was going on, and she'd also made up one of the guest bedrooms for her on the first floor so Jane wouldn't have to struggle up to the top of the tower. Alice had arranged for all Jane's things to be brought down to the room, and though Jane was cross she'd caused such a fuss for her friend, she had to admit it was good not having to climb so many stairs or have Will trying to carry her up such a long way.

Alice looked very happy, and Jane couldn't wait to hear about all that had happened. Will had refused to tell her anything, and said she must wait or Alice would never forgive him. When they had a moment on their own together in the afternoon, Alice told her all about it. Jane might have guessed by the expression on her face, but she and Frankie were officially engaged, she said. He'd proposed just a day after the magical evening, and Alice now wore a beautiful diamond ring on her finger.

'He asked father for permission to marry me, though I said I would marry him no matter what he said. We knew he wouldn't be refused this time, and Frankie handled everything so beautifully.'

'I'm so sorry I missed it, and all the final pleasures of the evening at the Blue Angel,' said Jane.

'Yes, I think Will thought he'd finished you off for good, and we were so worried about you. We were all for sending you to hospital, but Will said there was only one doctor you'd want to see, and he just put you in his car and drove you to Winchester.'

Jane wondered how much Alice knew, if anything. 'I have so much to be grateful for, and Will has been marvellous,' said Jane.

'Will told me everything, but don't worry, I'm the only other person who knows the full story, and your secret is safe with me,' said Alice. 'I always knew you were a special person, and in a way finding out who you were just confirmed it. I know it sounds silly, but it didn't seem such a great surprise or in the least fantastical when he explained everything. I'm so very honoured to know you, and I know I could never replace the sister you lost, but I hope I can be all that you'd wish for in a friend.'

Jane felt the tears prick behind her eyelids. Reaching out to squeeze Alice's hand she thought she must be the luckiest woman in the world.

'Alice, you are the dearest friend, as much like a sister to me as I could ever ask. I've had time to realise just how much I've fallen in love with you all, not only with your brother. I just wish you weren't going off to America. I realise Frankie has to work, but I will miss you so much.'

'You won't have a chance to miss me at all. We're staying put for the time being,' said Alice. 'I think Frankie's decided he wants to start his own film company here in England, and I'm so relieved. Of course, he'll make the odd film over there, and I'd follow him to the ends of the earth, but I love Devon and can't imagine being far away. We're looking at houses between here and Moorford. I think we've found the very thing, and I'm just so excited.'

'That's the most wonderful news I could have, though I feel very put out that I've missed all the excitement. I just knew as soon as I saw Frankie that evening at the nightclub that he was determined to put things right, he had such a look of determination about him.'

'Oh, wasn't it thrilling when we saw them looming out of the darkness, that first glimpse of seeing Frankie again was enough to overwhelm me,' said Alice. 'I couldn't believe he was there, especially as I was sure he'd gone back to America.'

'Yes, I thought my heart might stop beating,' said Jane. 'I saw Frankie and Eddie first and then when I saw Will it was all too much.'

'I suspected you two had fallen in love,' said Alice. 'I knew as much long before that day at Ashcombe, though it was most obvious then.'

'And I thought I was doing such a good job of hiding it,' said Jane with a laugh. 'I always hoped you'd find your happy ending, but I was absolutely certain I wasn't going to find mine.'

On Christmas Eve the snow started falling, shaken from the skies like feathers from a pillow, settling on the cold December earth and piling in drifts across the fields. Even the most cynical of them were excited to see it, and there were plans made to go sledging as soon as it stopped.

Jane, propped up in her makeshift bed in the sitting room by the fire watched the snowflakes twirling through the air and was glad she was tucked up in the warmth. Will, Frankie and Eddie were out chopping down Christmas trees with some of the footmen, a job which they'd performed as young boys round the estate, and one which they all took very seriously. There were trees to be chosen for the church and vicarage in the village, as well as for Eddie's church at Moorford, and it was bound to take them a long time. Jane worried about Will in the downpour of snow and hoped they'd return home soon, no worse for the experience.

It was lovely to be back at Manberley, though she wished she could feel better a lot quicker. It was so tedious being ill, and she couldn't wait to improve. Every day she felt a little stronger, and she looked forward to making a good recovery. Dr Lyford had been very frank with her when she'd finally asked him about her chances. Jane knew that she had every possibility of making a full return to health, and he thought it was very likely she'd live to be a very old lady. Knowing that life was so precious she was determined to live it to the full. And now she had Will to live for, she knew nothing was going to stand in her way.

As if her thoughts had conjured him into being, she saw him standing in the doorway looking over with such an expression of love she felt bashful as he stared, a great big smile lighting up his dark eyes.

'I've got a surprise for you,' he said. 'Are you up for a short trip to the hall?'

'I can come by foot if you'll let me,' Jane answered, knowing that he wouldn't let her stand for two minutes, let alone walk.

'Dr Lyford insisted on bed rest until Boxing Day at least, and I'm not about to let you do anything to jeopardise a full recovery,' he answered crossing the room at speed and taking her up in his arms.

Jane hooked her arms round his neck and kissed him on the nose feeling deliciously safe in his strong arms. 'You make me feel very special,' she said.

'I haven't even started,' Will replied, 'just you wait and see.'

Before they reached the hall the smell of pine, Christmas greenery, and oranges was overwhelming, fragrances that inspired fond memories of the past and new ones soon to come. Jane gasped when she saw the enormous tree, its branches touching the ceiling and spreading wide as if it might be about to drop a curtsey. A couple of the maids and one of the footmen were helping to hang the glass decorations that Alice took lovingly from a large box, and Frankie was high up on a tall ladder tying an angel to the very top. Mr Bell was fixing white candles into gilt holders before passing them up to be secured and evenly spaced throughout the branches. Will set Jane down on a chair and tucked a blanket round her knees. She watched them all working on the wondrous tree that winked and blinked in the fading light with precious treasures: glass angels, silver balls, Chinese lanterns and golden birds, slices of dried orange and bundles of cinnamon sticks tied with bows of scarlet ribbon. She'd never seen anything like it, and when it was finished and they lit the candles in the darkening space, everyone came to admire the glittering tree shining like a beacon of hope.

Jane looked round to see everyone she loved gathered all together. There was Mae sitting next to Captain Bartlett who was whispering something in her ear and making her laugh, and Jonathan who'd come over through the snow had arrived with a brace of pheasants from his estate, a hearty hand shake for Lord Milton and kisses for all the ladies. Emily was given an especially warm one, and Jane noticed how she twiddled her new emerald engagement ring on her finger in response. Fergus was sitting next to Beth, so closely there could be no mistaking how they felt about one another, and Cora sat next to Kit as they gazed at one another with sheer adoration in their eyes. Best of all, Alice and Frankie were standing hand in hand, a couple perfectly matched in every way.

Lord and Lady Milton made their entrance, and after sighing with admiration over the tree stood arm in arm at its foot.

'This is always my favourite time of year,' said Lord Milton, 'when special friends and family are gathered together. It's been an extraordinary few months for the Miltons and we shall be celebrating in style, have no doubt about that. But before the festivities begin, there is one special person we want to particularly address. Alice, I think you should take over now as the best person to talk on everyone's behalf.'

Alice let go of Frankie's hand to take her place in front of the tree. 'Jane, I know you will not like it if I spend too much time singing your praises because you're the most modest person I know. But, everyone here has something to thank you for, whether you like it or not, and we're all indebted to you for making us feel like a family again, not to mention making us a bigger family than we've ever been before. In gratitude we have a small token which we hope will be very useful to you.'

Alice's words made Jane blush, and when all the praise was over she hoped there would be no more. When Alice presented her with a parcel beautifully wrapped in Christmas paper she was completely overcome. Peeling back the layers of paper she wasn't prepared for the shock when she opened the box with a bit of help from Will and saw what was inside. It was the typewriter Alice had wanted to buy all that time ago, with a card to say how much they loved her and hoping she'd finish writing her best-selling novel very soon.

'Thank you, there are no words ...' Jane began, completely at a loss to know what to say.

'And none are expected,' said Alice. 'I've booked us both on a typing course, Jane, which I think we'll both find beneficial. If I'm to help Frankie with the new company, he's going to need a typist, naturally, though I've a funny feeling I shall be doing a whole lot more.'

Everyone laughed, and Jane looked round once again at the happy faces, all looking so different from when she'd arrived all those months ago. It was very gratifying to see how everything was turning out, and she was sure if they were all very patient there'd be a few more announcements yet.

Just as she thought it was all over, and there could be no more surprises there was a great knocking at the front door, and when Mr Bell returned she couldn't believe her eyes. Swept in from the outside with a flurry of snowflakes came Dr Lyford, his sister Elsie, and Mr Quance who kissed both her cheeks and squeezed her hands.

'I've just come to keep an eye on you,' said the doctor, 'make sure you don't overdo it.'

'Lady Milton suggested it,' said Elsie, 'John couldn't rest until he knew you were making good progress.'

Jane thanked him again for everything he'd done for her, and said there was no chance that she'd be allowed to do anything but behave herself. 'I'm being looked after so wonderfully well, and feel very cherished.'

Mr Quance whispered how much he'd enjoyed reading her manuscript and looked forward to spending some time discussing it with her. 'It's the most wonderful writing,' he said, 'and I can't wait to read more.'

Jane was feeling very close to tears, but she managed to say a few words before her feelings got the better of her.

'I'm so thrilled you could all come for Christmas, and I feel so spoiled. Thank you, Lord and Lady Milton, for arranging such lovely surprises, and to you all. Your kindness means so much to me.'

There was a round of applause and then when the deafening cheers were dying down, Will stepped forward to speak.

'I cannot let the day go any further without adding something I'd like to say about the wonderful woman you see before you. I fell in love with Jane from the very second I saw her, and though she resisted me extraordinarily well for an awfully long time, in the end she succumbed to my charms ... well, to be perfectly honest, I don't think she could resist me.'

There was a ripple of laughter and Jane saw Will look deeply into her eyes with an impish smile playing at the corners of his mouth. 'Jane, only you have the power to make me the happiest of men, and all I ask is that you will allow me to love you for the rest of our lives together.' Will paused to kneel down at her side. 'Please say you will do the honour of marrying me.'

Jane felt her heart leap with sheer joy. She didn't hesitate, answering with a resounding 'I will,' and allowed him to take her in his arms once more.

'Welcome home, Jane,' he said, as they later watched the snowflakes spinning like the lost feathers of winged angels beyond the windows in the glimmering blue light of evening. Curled up together on the library sofa Jane nestled her head on his shoulder, and caught hold of the arm wrapped protectively round her. She couldn't help glancing again at the new ring on her finger; the blue sapphire surrounded by white diamonds twinkling in the firelight, and knew she'd never been so happy.

'I am home,' she said, 'I knew it the first time I saw you, and the first time I set eyes on this crumbling castle. You both needed the love of a good woman.'

'I suppose you thought you were just the person for the job.'

'I suppose I did.'

'And I guess you were absolutely right.'

Jane knew her life would never be the same again, but she had no fears for the future, and as he took her in his arms to tell her he loved her again, she knew everything she'd been looking for was finally found. Now she possessed all that she'd ever dreamed of and everything her heroines sought; the most handsome of men, the truest love and a wonderful home to call her very own. Not to mention her very own typewriter and the gift of time to write as many novels as she'd like.

'I love you,' she said in return, as the silver moon appeared and the stars glimmered mysteriously under the heavenly dome.

About the Author

Jane Odiwe is a British author with a special interest in writing novels inspired by Jane Austen's works. Her books continue the stories of beloved characters like Elizabeth Bennet and Mr Darcy in *Mr Darcy's Secret*, or tell Jane Austen's own story, as in the novels, *Searching for Captain Wentworth*, *Project Darcy*, and *Jane Austen Lives Again*. Other works include the novels *Willoughby's Return*, *Lydia Bennet's Story* and the novellas, *Mr Darcy's Christmas Calendar*, and *Mrs Darcy's Diamonds*.

Jane is an ambassador for the Jane Austen Literacy Foundation, established by Jane Austen's 5th great niece, Caroline Jane Knight. She is also a member of the Jane Austen Society, and the Romantic Novelist's Association. When she's not writing she enjoys painting and trying to capture the spirit of Jane Austen's world. Her illustrations feature in a short biographical film of Jane Austen's life, and in the picture book, *Effusions of Fancy*.

Born in Sutton Coldfield, England, Jane gained an arts degree in Birmingham where she indulged her great loves of Fine Art, Literature, and History. After teaching in the Midlands and London for some years, writing novels took over her life. Jane lives in London with her husband, children and two cats, but escapes to "Fairyland", Bath, whenever she can.

Jane Odiwe comes to it steeped in Austen, in all her renditions; Odiwe's sentences often glint with reflections of the great Jane ...
Historical Novel Society

Odiwe certainly writes a page-turning romantic mystery - her characters are intriguing and her narrative full of surprises and suspense. She blends historical fact and fiction with great style, and the settings are spot on in what the writer describes as her "love letter to Bath."
Jane Austen's Regency World Magazine

Twitter: @JaneOdiwe
Website: http://austeneffusions.com
Blog: http://janeaustensequels.blogspot.co.uk
Facebook: http//facebook.com/JaneOdiwe

Other Books by Jane Odiwe

Mr Darcy's Christmas Calendar

Lizzy Benson visits Jane Austen's house in Chawton, and buys a special Advent calendar in the gift shop, but strange things start to happen when she opens up the first door and finds herself back in time with all the beloved characters from her favourite book, *Pride and Prejudice*. As she finds herself increasingly drawn into an alternate reality, Lizzy discovers not only is Mr Darcy missing from the plot, but also that Jane Austen has never heard of him. All Lizzy can hope is that she can help to get the story and her own complicated love life back on track before Christmas is over, and bring everything to a happy resolution in Jane Austen's imaginary world!

Searching for Captain Wentworth

When aspiring writer Sophie Elliot receives the keys to the family townhouse in Bath, it's an invitation she can't turn down, especially when she learns that she will be living next door to the house where Jane Austen lived. On discovering that an ancient glove belonging to her mysterious neighbour, Josh Strafford, will transport her back in time to Regency Bath, she questions her sanity, but Sophie is soon caught up in two dimensions, each reality as certain as the other. Torn between her life in the modern world and that of her ancestor who befriends Jane Austen and her fascinating brother Charles, Sophie's story travels two hundred years across time and back again, to unite this modern heroine with her own Captain Wentworth. Blending fact and fiction together, the tale of Jane Austen's own quest for happiness weaves alongside, creating a believable world of new possibilities for the inspiration behind *Persuasion*.

Project Darcy

It is high summer when Ellie Bentley joins an archaeological dig at Jane Austen's childhood home. She's always had a talent for 'seeing' into the past and is not easily disturbed by her encounters with Mr Darcy's ghost at the house where she's staying.

When Ellie travels into the past she discovers exactly what happened whilst Jane danced her way through the snowy winter of 1796 with her dashing Irish friend. As Steventon Rectory and all its characters come to life, Ellie discovers the true love story lost in *Pride and Prejudice* – a tale which has its own consequences for her future destiny, changing her life beyond imagination.

Mr Darcy's Secret

After capturing the heart of the most eligible bachelor in England, Elizabeth Bennet believes her happiness is complete-until the day she unearths a stash of anonymous, passionate love letters that may be Darcy's, and she realizes just how little she knows about the guarded, mysterious man she married... Mr Darcy's Secret is a story about love and misunderstandings; of overcoming doubt and trusting to the real feelings of the heart - Elizabeth and the powerful, compelling figure of Mr Darcy take centre stage in this romantic tale set in Regency Derbyshire and the Lakes, alongside the beloved characters from *Pride and Prejudice*.

Willoughby's Return

In Jane Austen's *Sense and Sensibility*, when Marianne Dashwood marries Colonel Brandon, she puts her heartbreak over dashing scoundrel John Willoughby in the past. Three years later, Willoughby's return throws Marianne into a tizzy of painful memories and exquisite feelings of uncertainty Willoughby is as charming, as roguish, and as much in love with her as ever. And the timing couldn't be worse—with Colonel Brandon away and Willoughby determined to win her back, will Marianne find the strength to save her marriage, or will the temptation of a previous love be too powerful to resist?

Lydia Bennet's Story

In *Lydia Bennet's Story* we are taken back to Jane Austen's most beloved novel, *Pride and Prejudice*, to a Regency world seen through

Lydia's eyes where pleasure and marriage are the only pursuits. But the road to matrimony is fraught with difficulties and even when she is convinced that she has met the man of her dreams, complications arise. When Lydia is reunited with the Bennets, Bingleys, and Darcys for a grand ball at Netherfield Park, the shocking truth about her husband may just cause the greatest scandal of all ...

Mrs Darcy's Diamonds

Elizabeth is newly married to Fitzwilliam Darcy, the richest man in Derbyshire, landowner of a vast estate, and master of Pemberley House. Elizabeth's new role is daunting at first, and having to deal with Mr Darcy's aunt, Lady Catherine de Bourgh, is a daily challenge. But, Elizabeth is deeply in love and determined to rise to every test and trial she is forced to endure. When her husband presents her with a diamond ring, part of the precious and irreplaceable Darcy suite of jewels, she feels not only honoured and secure in her husband's love, but also ready to accept her new responsibilities and position.

Elizabeth knows she will face exacting scrutiny at the approaching Christmas Ball, but it will be her chance to prove that she is a worthy mistress, and she is excited to be playing hostess to the Bennets, the Bingleys, and the gentry families of Derbyshire, as well as Mr Darcy's French cousins. Antoine de Valois and his sister Louise have arrived at the invitation of Lady Catherine de Bourgh and Elizabeth is delighted that this young and lively couple are helping to bring Miss Georgiana Darcy out of her shell. However, when her ring goes missing before the ball, Elizabeth is distraught, and her dilemma further increased by the threat of a scandal that appears to involve the French cousins.

Reviews

Mr Darcy's Christmas Calendar
Mr Darcy's Christmas Calendar is a feel-good Christmas read, perfect for those who wish to travel back to Austen's day or those who enjoy seeing the magic of Christmas bring about true love. - LEATHERBOUND REVIEWS

Project Darcy
Odiwe writes with great charm and assurance: her contemporary characters are engaging, her historical protagonists convincing. In *Project Darcy* she takes a slice of literary history and turns it into a thoroughly entertaining, often very funny, and frequently touching piece of modern romantic fiction. - JANE AUSTEN'S REGENCY WORLD MAGAZINE

Searching for Captain Wentworth
Searching for Captain Wentworth will send you on a magical journey through time, and your heart, that you will not soon forget - AUSTENPROSE

Mr Darcy's Secret
Jane Odiwe comes to it steeped in Austen, in all her renditions; Odiwe's sentences often glint with reflections of the great Jane ... - HISTORICAL NOVEL SOCIETY

Willoughby's Return
Odiwe's elegantly stylish writing is seasoned with just the right dash of tart humour, and her latest literary endeavour is certain to delight both Austen devotees and Regency romance readers - BOOKLIST

Lydia Bennet's Story
Odiwe pays nice homage to Austen's stylings and endears the reader to the formerly secondary character, spoiled and impulsive Lydia Bennet ... devotees will enjoy - PUBLISHER'S WEEKLY

Acknowledgements

Firstly, I'd like to say an enormous thank you to every reader of my books for keeping me going, for inspiring me to write, and for all your fabulous emails and letters. Thank you very much to my family and friends, in particular, Olivia Odiwe and Gaynor Eldon who have worked tirelessly and helped enormously during the writing of this book, Caroline Turner for finding wonderful research books, teashops and excursions when I needed a break, and Jenny Murison for fabulous tea, lunches and sympathy in her cosy kitchen. Grateful thanks are due to my amazing husband who cooks, cleans and generally runs around as deadlines approach, and helps give birth to all my books - I couldn't do it without you. Huge thanks also to Daniel Thomas for his motorcycle expertise. You can view his beautiful bikes here: http://www.lionsdencustoms.com.

Printed in Great Britain
by Amazon.co.uk, Ltd.,
Marston Gate.